TodHunter Moon
~ Book Three ~
StarChaser

TodHunter Moon
~ Book Three ~

StarChaser

Angie Sage

Illustrations by Mark Zug

KATHERINE TEGEN BOOKS
An Imprint of HarperCollins Publishers

Katherine Tegen Books is an imprint of HarperCollins Publishers.
Septimus Heap is a registered trademark of HarperCollins Publishers.

TodHunter Moon, Book Three: StarChaser

www.harpercollinschildrens.com

ISBN 978-0-06-227251-5

Typography by Joel Tippie
16 17 18 19 20   CG/RRDH   10 9 8 7 6 5 4 3 2 1
❖
First Edition

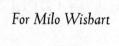

For Milo Wishart

↦ CONTENTS ↤

TODHUNTER MOON

~ BOOK THREE ~

STARCHASER

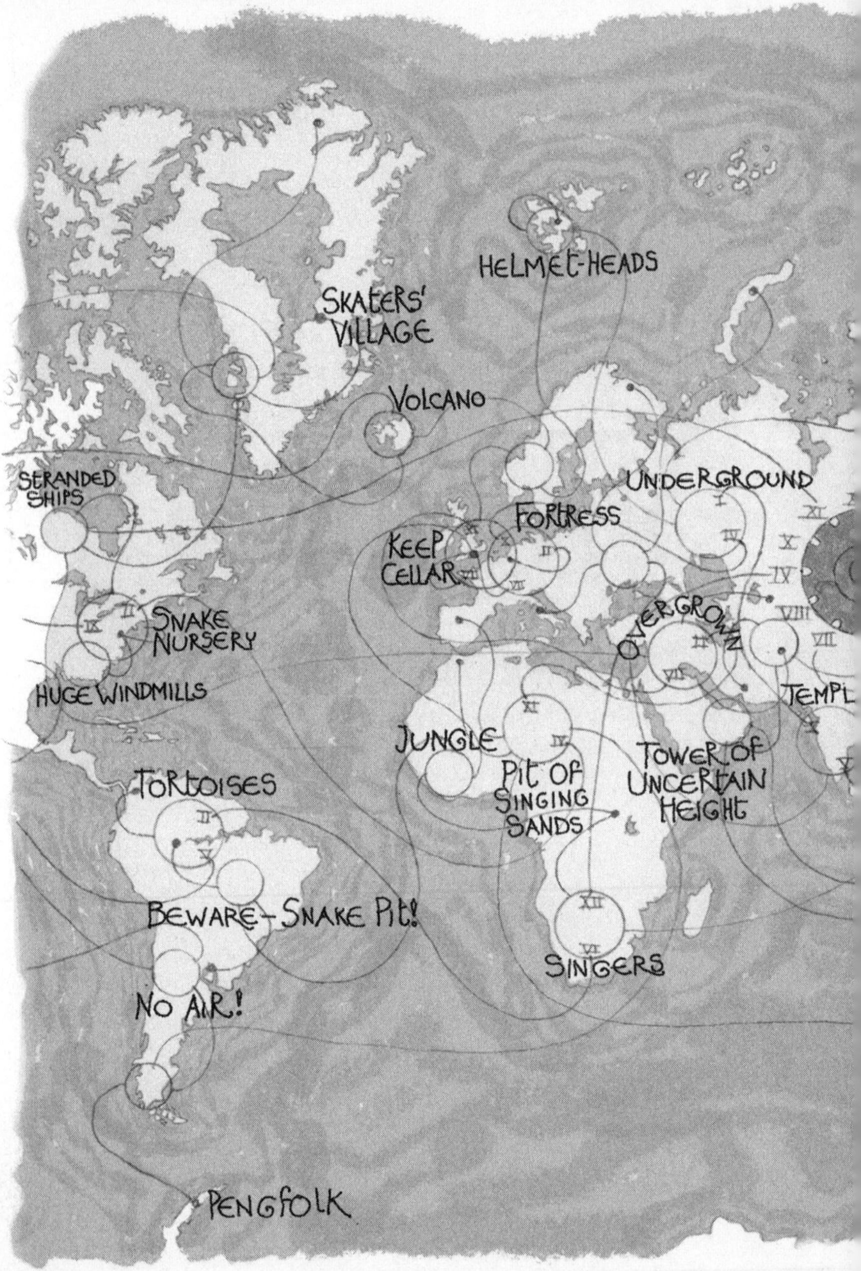
HELMET-HEADS
SKATERS' VILLAGE
VOLCANO
STRANDED SHIPS
UNDERGROUND
FORTRESS
KEEP CELLAR
SNAKE NURSERY
OVERGROWN
HUGE WINDMILLS
TEMPL
JUNGLE
TORTOISES
PIT OF SINGING SANDS
TOWER OF UNCERTAIN HEIGHT
BEWARE-SNAKE PIT!
SINGERS
NO AIR!
PENGFOLK

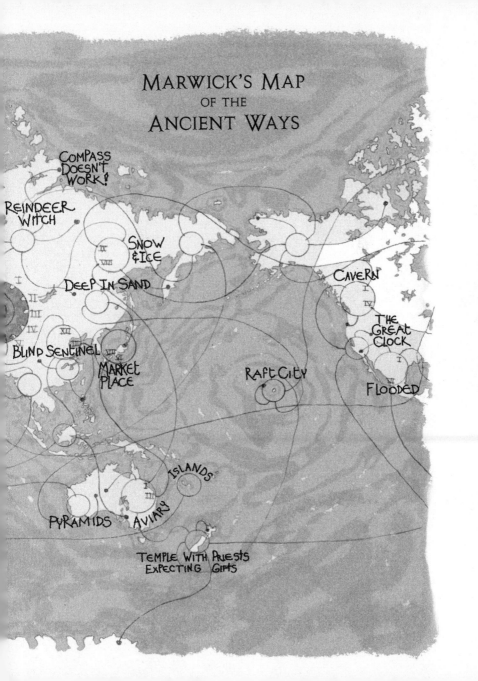

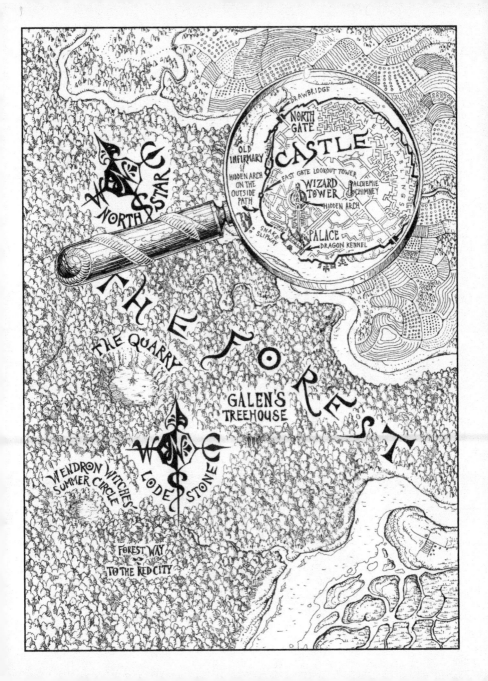

PART
I

THE QUEEN'S CHAMBER

The last echoes of the midday bells faded away. In a secret chamber deep in the heart of the Red Palace, three dusty women stood trembling before the Red Queen. The room, at the very heart of the palace, was hexagonal and dimly lit by one slit window high in the only wall that faced the central gardens. Despite its opulence, it felt like a prison.

From her golden throne on a dais, the Queen glared at the women. "And where," she demanded, "*where* is the sorcerer I sent for?"

The women did not respond. This was not because they had no answer, but because the guard at the door had told them that if they valued their lives they must wait five seconds before replying. The Red Queen was offended by those who did not appear to think carefully about their answers.

Conscious of the Queen's pale blue eyes upon them, two of the women were pretending an interest in the red and gold tiles of the floor. The third, the youngest, stared ahead beneath lowered eyelashes.

The Red Queen sized up the women. There was a large blowsy one wrapped like an untidy parcel in blue silks, who was known as the Lady and was the sister of the sorcerer the Queen required. To the left of the Lady stood her sidekick, Mitza Draddenmora Draa: a square, hatchet-faced woman with hair scraped back and a mouth like the edge of a knife. In Mitza the Red Queen recognized a kindred spirit.

The third woman was little more than a girl. The Queen regarded her with narrowed eyes. This one she knew only by the name Marissa. She had an insolent stare and was dressed in what the Queen considered to be a most peculiar style: she wore beads woven though her hair, a leather headband, a dusty green cloak and heavy boots. She was scruffy and pretty and the Queen did not take to her at all. The Marissa girl had, she thought, the look of a witch about her.

Marissa felt the gaze of the Red Queen upon her and risked an upward glance. Their eyes met. The Queen saw something dark and shifting beneath a layer of carefully constructed innocence. Just as the Queen was wondering whether it might be wise to chop this witch's head off before she caused any trouble, the five-second pause was over and the Lady stammered out her answer.

"Y-your Majesty. My brother is ill . . ." Her voice faded away under the steel-blue stare of the Red Queen.

The Queen said nothing. She moved her gaze to a point just above the women's heads, and once again an uncomfortable silence fell. The Queen was thinking out her strategy. She knew that she appeared to have all the advantages and those before her thought they had none, but this was not so. The women held the key to something she had been promised. The Queen wanted it—and she wanted it *now*. With a great feeling of longing she thought about the distant Castle the sorcerer had promised her. His descriptions of its beautiful old buildings and its biddable inhabitants longing for a strong ruler replayed in her head. Not to mention its rich surroundings that would also be hers for the taking: the verdant farmlands, the nearby forest, a wide river running to the sea and a wealthy Port. The Red Queen wanted to have that Castle so much it hurt. She was sick of the dry red dust and the heat of her city, the press of the people, the beggars crowded outside the city walls. Her subjects were surly fools who did not obey her as they should—it would be wonderful to have a new start. The Queen glanced down at the sharp dagger of sunlight that stabbed through the window slit and cast a white strip upon the red floor. She longed for the gentle green of what she now thought of as *her* Castle.

However, the Red Queen was not going to admit to any longings. No one had ever given her anything just because she longed for it, and she did not expect that to begin now. She must play this game carefully to get what she wanted. Her low voice flowed menacingly around the chamber. "I did not ask about the state of the sorcerer's health," the Queen said. "I asked for his whereabouts. I repeat: *Where is the sorcerer?*"

The sorcerer's sister just about managed to speak. "Y-your Majesty. M-my brother is at Hospitable Gard, for which we thank you. It is only your immense kindness and hospitality that—"

The Queen cut her short. "That is not where he is meant to be," she snapped. "I summoned him to my presence for the midday bell. *Why* is he not here?"

The woman in blue hardly dared to repeat what she had already said, but she could think of no alternative. A small, frightened voice emerged from the bundle of blue silks. "Because, Your Majesty, he . . . he is ill."

"No one is too ill to refuse my summons. *No one.*"

The Lady glanced helplessly at her companions but they would not meet her gaze. She became flustered. "Your Majesty. I *beg* you. My brother cannot move. He has the most terrible . . ." Her voice failed her.

"Terrible *what?*" demanded the Queen.

"Headache." As soon as she said the word the Lady knew she had a made a mistake. It sounded like such a pathetic excuse. There was a silence that seemed to go on forever. The Lady heard the trickle of water from the fountains in the gardens beyond and she felt as though her life were dripping away with it.

"Headache," the Red Queen finally repeated, as if the word was a piece of dog dirt she had found upon her shoe. "The powerful sorcerer Oraton-Marr has a . . . *headache.*"

"Yes, Your Majesty," said his miserable sister. And then added, "It's really bad. Really, *really* bad. It's—"

"Silence!" the Queen barked. She continued in a low, menacing voice. "I have a way of curing headaches." The Queen's hand went across to her sword, which hung down from a scabbard attached to the left side of her throne. "If your brother does not respond to my next summons I will assist him with his little problem. I will make sure that he has no *head* to *ache*. Understand?"

"Y-yes, Your Majesty," the Lady stuttered.

"Now—*go!*"

Behind them the doors swung open and the women backed out, amazed at their reprieve. But they knew it would not last.

THE SUMMONS

Oraton-Marr lay prone on his bed as he had done for many weeks. Beside him sat his sister, still trembling from her audience with the Queen. "Orrie," she whispered anxiously. "Are you feeling any better?"

"Gerrrr . . ." was the only reply.

His sister persisted. "Orrie, the thing is, the Queen is getting impatient. She wants her Castle. You know, the one those kids and that dragon came from. The one you promised her." She refrained from saying *the one you so stupidly promised her, which was not yours to promise anyway.* The Lady had learned not to upset her brother in his present state.

His reply was another groan.

"She's going to summon you again, Orrie. And if you don't go to her I think something very bad will happen. I think . . ." The Lady paused. She hardly dared put into words what she thought would happen, but she was desperate. She had to somehow get her brother up from his sickbed. "I think she might cut off your head."

Oraton-Marr thought the Queen would be doing him a favor if she cut off his head. It was no use to him in its present state. It felt as though someone were driving a red-hot spike through it and nailing it to the bed. He could no more go to see the Queen than he could fly to the moon. "Good," he said.

It was four in the morning, in the deep, dark hours before dawn when a fearsome knocking on the door of Hospitable Gard woke the entire household. The Lady sat up in bed, her eyes wide with fear as she listened to the pounding echoing up the stairs. She got out of bed, wrapped her silk coat around her and crept down to the ground-floor atrium. There she found a wild-eyed Mitza clutching a hammer and Marissa looking artfully disheveled in a long nightdress, beneath which the

Lady spotted a pair of sturdy boots, ready to flee. The three women stared at the heavy front door, which shivered under the onslaught of the pounding.

"What shall we do?" the Lady whispered.

Mitza tightened her grip upon her hammer. "We must answer it, my Lady," she said. "And see what they want."

"But we *know* what they want," said the Lady. "They want Orrie."

"Then they will have to have him," Mitza said coldly.

Suddenly the pounding ceased and a shout of "Open up in the name of the Red Queen!" came from the other side of the door.

"We should open the door," Marissa said. "They'll break it down otherwise. It's best to look helpful."

The Lady knew Marissa was right, but even so she had hoped for a little more resistance. "You open it, then," she said sulkily.

Trilling out in her most girly voice, "Hang on a mo'! It's a bit heavy for us girls!" Marissa made a lot of noise pulling back the long bolt, then she heaved the door open, flicked back her hair and leaned languorously against the door breathing heavily, as though exhausted by her efforts.

The three guards outside were speechless for some moments until one of them managed to mumble, "Sorry, miss."

The Captain of the Guard recovered his senses. Steadfastly avoiding looking at Marissa, he stepped forward brandishing a scroll with a large red seal. "I have a Royal Summons for the sorcerer Oraton-Marr," he said.

The Lady held out a chubby, shaking hand. "I'm his sister. I'll give it to him," she said.

The Captain kept hold of the scroll. "Madam, I am ordered to deliver it to the sorcerer personally. Take me to him. At once!"

The Lady knew there was no point in arguing. The two remaining guards watched the Lady lead the Captain up the stairs, then they turned their attention to Marissa.

"What's a nice girl like you doing in a place like this?" the youngest one asked.

Marissa giggled. "Same as you. Doing what I'm told."

"Are you some kind of maid or something?"

"Something," Marissa said, casually letting the top few buttons of her nightdress fall open. "What are you looking at?" she suddenly demanded.

"Um . . . your, um . . . *key*," the young guard stammered. "It looks . . . um . . . very nice," he finished lamely.

"Oh, *this* key," Marissa said, sounding bored. She lifted up the plain iron key that she wore around her neck on a piece of green ribbon. "This is the key to the Castle. Now that is something the Queen would *love* to get her hands on."

It was all too much for the young guard, who turned bright red. "Ha! I'm sure I would too," he said with a nervous snort.

"Quiet!" the older guard said, cross at being left out of Marissa's game.

"So," Marissa asked, "are you taking the sorcerer away?"

"It's not for us to say, miss," the other guard said grumpily.

"If he doesn't come now, we'll be back later," the young guard said. "To surprise him."

"What a good idea." Marissa giggled. "You are *so* clever. So . . . what time is best for surprising sorcerers, then?"

The older guard stepped between them and roughly pushed the younger to one side. "Cut it out, Number Three—or there'll be trouble."

The young guard cut it out. Silence fell in the atrium and they listened to the footfalls above. Soon footsteps were heard on the stairs and the Captain appeared without the summons, closely followed by the distressed Lady. "Please," she begged, "please, surely you can see how impossible it is for him to even move from his pillow, let alone come to the Palace."

"I merely deliver the summons," the Captain said gruffly. "It is not my job to comment upon the capabilities of those receiving it." With that he strode over to the door and the two guards fell in behind him. Marissa arranged herself so that she was leaning dreamily against a pillar, and as the young one went by he whispered, "See you again at three bells tomorrow morning." He winked. "The best time for collecting sorcerers."

Marissa smiled. "Can't wait," she said.

And then the Queen's Guards were gone, leaving behind a wide-open door, the rush of cold night and a long wail of despair from the Lady as she fell to the floor.

While the Lady was being inexpertly comforted by a kneeling Mitza (gripping a hammer in one hand while with the other at arm's length she warily patted the Lady like one would a small, snappy dog), Marissa shut the door and bolted it. Then she turned to the huddle on the floor and said, "I have a plan."

The Lady looked up with an expression of despair. How could Marissa possibly have a plan? She was just a silly, empty-headed girl.

Marissa knew exactly what the Lady was thinking. That was fine by her. Let her think it. She would find out soon enough that she was wrong.

TEA AND PLOTS

Marissa shepherded the Lady and Mitza to the divans arranged around the edge of the atrium. She sat them down, found soft blankets to wrap around them—the Lady was shivering from shock—and told them to wait while she fetched some mint tea. Then she tiptoed away to the servants' kitchen, hoping they did not notice her boots.

Marissa lit the small spirit burner to heat the water, and as she snipped off the tender top leaves from the peppermint plant, she considered her course of action. Marissa had far more to gain from the sorcerer's recovery than she would ever admit to her two companions. Before Oraton-Marr had been poisoned with a **HeadBanger** potion, when he was convinced he was about to become the world's most powerful sorcerer and take over the fabled Wizard Tower, he had been rather free with his promises. Not only had he promised the Red

Queen the Queenship of the Castle, he had also promised
Marissa that he would help her become Witch Mother of the
Wendron Witches, the coven that inhabited the Forest just
outside the Castle. Marissa had also extracted a promise that
the coven would, for the very first time, be given a base inside
the Castle. She had her eye on a nice row of houses near the
Moat.

Like the Red Queen, Marissa was reluctant to let go of the
dream that Oraton-Marr had dangled before her. There was,
she thought, still much to play for. Marissa enjoyed a game,
and this was an exciting one with a good prize at the end of it.
But she must play it carefully.

Marissa walked softly into the atrium carrying a tray
of sweet peppermint tea and saffron wafers. Trying to look
humble—but not entirely succeeding—she placed the tray
upon the low table in front of the divan, dropped to her knees
and poured the tea. Marissa waited until both the Lady and
Mitza had settled comfortably back against the cushions
and then, still kneeling, she began to speak. Careful to refer
to Oraton-Marr in the way he had insisted upon before the
HeadBanger potion, she said, "We must do our very best to
save His Highness."

"But what can we possibly do?" said the Lady. "There are guards on the gate."

"We could smuggle him out," Mitza suggested. "Put him in a sack. They might think he was turnips."

The Lady looked horrified. "Orrie? *Turnips?* In a *sack?*"

Marissa supressed a smile. She would love to put the sorcerer in a sack—and hurl him off the top of Hospitable Gard while he was in it—but she had her career to consider. "It's simple," Marissa said. "We must get His Highness well enough to answer the Queen's summons—and, more important, well enough to take over the Wizard Tower."

"But *how?*" the Lady wailed.

"I will go and get the antidote from the Apothecary—"

But the Lady was not listening. All her pent-up grievances and petty annoyances with her brother were tumbling out. "He's hopeless! I told him he shouldn't count his Orms before they were hatched, but he wouldn't listen. And then he promised that awful Queen something that there was no way he could give her. And even if he gets better now, what use is the Wizard Tower to him without the Orm? He's never going to be powerful enough to run a place like that. *Never.*"

Marissa saw Mitza looking at the Lady, shocked.

"Well, he's *not*," the Lady said defiantly. "I know my brother. He needs all the lapis lazuli he can get to be even a half-decent Wizard. He knows a few **Darke** tricks and he can **Conjure** up some nasty creatures, but he's not properly trained."

Marissa busied herself pouring out more peppermint tea, listening with great interest as the Lady continued to pour out her frustrations about her brother. At last the Lady subsided, exhausted by her rant.

"Actually," Marissa said, "the Orm is already where His Highness wants it: in the Castle. I hear they are going to set it burrowing under the Wizard Tower so there'll be plenty of lapis lazuli for him. It already sits on a load of the stuff anyway. In fact there will soon be so much lapis underneath it that anyone could run it." Marissa affected a giggle. "Even little old me."

"Huh!" Mitza burst out. "A silly, empty-headed little thing like you? That, girl, is taking things too far."

Marissa felt like kicking Mitza, but she merely said, "Miss Mitza, do have a drop more tea." Marissa poured the tea and then hurried upstairs to get her witch cloak. She took a wad of money and a few trinkets from the Lady's bedroom in case a bribe was needed, then ran back down and headed for the door.

"Marissa," the Lady called querulously. "Where are you going?

Marissa stopped halfway out the door. "To the Apothecary. To get the **HeadBanger** antidote. Must go. Got a camel train to catch."

"But *Marissa* . . ." the Lady called as the door was closing.

"What now?" Marissa demanded.

"You won't be back until nearly midnight. What shall I do if they come for Orrie before then?" The Lady's voice rose into a wail.

What Marissa wanted to say was, *Who cares what you do, you stupid old bat?* But she restrained herself. "They won't," she said, and slammed the door.

Mitza waddled over to the door and pushed the bolt across. "She'll never get it. There is no way that nasty Apothecary woman is going to give that silly witch the antidote to the **HeadBanger**. No way *at all*." Mitza shook her head with a grim enjoyment.

The Lady sighed. "Well, if anyone can persuade that ghastly Karamander Draa woman to hand it over, Marissa can. She seems very determined, don't you think? I find her rather scary, to tell you the truth."

Mitza tried not to look surprised at the Lady's confidential way of speaking to her. She had noticed that since Oraton-Marr had been rendered incapable, the Lady had relaxed and begun to take her into her confidence. Mitza realized that she was metamorphosing from a servant to a companion—maybe even, she thought, a friend. Although Mitza was not entirely sure what a friend actually was, she liked the idea. It would give her much greater influence over events. And probably better food, too.

Mitza considered her answer carefully. "There is indeed something about that witch, my Lady," she said. "But even so, I do not think the Apothecary will give her the potion. She will not forget that His Highness stole her children from her."

"But it's not as though he kept them," the Lady protested a little petulantly. "She got them back in the end, didn't she?"

Mitza nodded. "She did indeed. And why she wanted them back I cannot imagine. That small one was a noisy little brat. And the big one was plain rude." Mitza sighed. "But children are precious to their parents, so they say. And that can come in useful at times." She smiled, showing her sharp little white teeth, so closely packed together. "Very useful in all kinds of ways. Ha-ha."

The Lady flashed Mitza a puzzled glance. Sometimes the woman worried her.

Mitza warmed to her theme. "Perhaps Marissa is planning to do something unpleasant to one of them and use it as a bargaining tool. I imagine that would work."

"I imagine it would," the Lady replied, a little uncomfortably. Then she brightened up. "Well, as long as she comes back with the antidote I won't be asking how she got it."

Mitza was silent. The talk of children and their parents had turned Mitza's thoughts to Alice TodHunter Moon and the Castle, where the girl now lived. If there was any chance of going there soon, then Mitza must make her own visit to an Apothecary. She would hate to be unprepared for a meeting with young Alice. It would be a wasted opportunity, and Mitza hated waste.

FISHFACE

Dawn was breaking as Marissa hurried out through Beggars' Gate, the only unguarded entrance to the Red City, and joined the queue for the camel train. As Marissa waited, she took in the scene. Spread before her was a sprawling encampment of tents of all shapes and sizes and conditions, ranging from a ragged blanket thrown over a few sticks to some large circular

structures of richly embroidered cloth, which were quite beautiful. Their inhabitants were a mixture of beggars, free spirits,
criminals, conjurers, mavericks and misfits—anyone who
preferred to live outside the harsh regime of the Red Queen.
Many there felt that the sacrifice of a house with stone walls
was worth the peace of mind it brought. It was, with some
justification, known as the City of the Free.

As Marissa shuffled forward, getting ever closer to the
steaming, harrumphing camels, she gazed down at the sea
of tents, many of which glimmered from within with candlelight, and in the dull light of the dawn they looked far more
enticing than the camel train ahead. Marissa watched the
early-morning activity; she saw fires being coaxed into life,
listened to the gentle murmur of conversation and smelled the
coffee being brewed. Then she looked out to the empty desert
beyond and up to the lightening sky, where a few stars were
still visible. Marissa was used to the confines of the Forest and
the city, and the great emptiness of the desert sent a feeling of
panic rushing through her.

To overcome the panic, Marissa concentrated on the camels
ahead. She saw hot camel breath steaming in the air, heard the
phlegmy snorts, felt the ground shake with the thud of their
stamping feet and watched their ungainly lurching lope as

they set off with their passengers. Which made her feel even worse.

So Marissa turned her thoughts to the earlier hours of the morning. What stuck in her mind was her comment to Mitza about the Wizard Tower: *Anyone could run it. Even little old me.* Mitza's scathing response rang in her ears, and Marissa thought how fed-up she was with people treating her with no respect. If she ran the Wizard Tower, that would show them. No one would dare belittle her then. Marissa allowed herself to savor the idea: Witch Mother in charge of the Wizard Tower. Why shouldn't a witch run the Wizard Tower? With all that new lapis soon to be made by the Orm, it was true that pretty much anyone with a little bit of **Magyk** could run it. All they needed was the nerve to walk in and do it. And *she*, Marissa thought with a smile, had more nerve than anyone else she knew.

The queue shuffled forward one place and the person behind stepped on Marissa's cloak. Fired up with her newly imagined status, Marissa turned around and glared imperiously at the man, who, to her immense satisfaction, shrank back with a hasty apology. Marissa turned away nursing a smile. She could get used to this.

Suddenly, Marissa found herself at the head of the camel

queue. Her smile changed to an expression of distaste as she eyed "her" camel. It was a large, ragged beast. Its hair was coming off in clumps, half its ear was missing, and its yellow eyes regarded Marissa with undisguised malevolence. It did not smell too good either.

"Where to, missy?" the camel driver asked.

A sudden realization came over Marissa: *she did not want Oraton-Marr to recover.* She didn't want him bossing her around again and making snide remarks—and more to the point, she did not want *him* in the Wizard Tower—she wanted it for herself.

Marissa looked at the camel driver: small, wrinkled and burnished like a nut from the desert sun. She saw his one-toothed smile and his calculating leer, and it was with great pleasure that she told him, "Nowhere, Fishface," then turned on her heel and walked away.

A LOZENGE FOR A BAG OF KRAAN

Marissa took the path down into the encampment and wandered slowly through the tents. She stopped a few people to ask for what she sought, and after ten minutes she found herself outside a beautiful tent with faded red and blue stripes. A small handbell sat on a low stool; Marissa rang the bell and waited. Some minutes later—just as Marissa was thinking of giving up—a tiny woman with piercing blue eyes looked out suspiciously.

"Yes?" she asked.

"Are you an Apothecary?" Marissa asked.

"What if I am?" the woman demanded angrily.

Marissa took out the money that she had intended for Karamander Draa and held the notes out flat on her palm, as though she were offering sugar lumps to a horse.

The woman looked at the notes; it was more than she would earn in months. "Come in, my darling," she told Marissa. "You are lucky. You have found the most skilled Apothecary in the City of the Free. I can supply anything you wish." The woman cast her shrewd gaze over Marissa. "And no questions asked, my lovely, no questions at all."

Marissa handed over the notes and stepped into the dimness of the tent, redolent with the tang of bitter powders, fragrant with the oily musk of suspensions.

An hour later, Marissa slipped unnoticed into Hospitable Gard. To the sound of snores drifting down the stairs, she quietly made Oraton-Marr's favorite sherbet drink and laid it on a tray with a small bowl of sugared almonds—the only food he could bear to eat. Beside the bowl she placed the green lozenge for which she had exchanged her handful of notes. Treading softly on the stone stairs in her bare feet, Marissa took the tray up to Oraton-Marr's room on the upper floor. As she pushed open the door the long white muslin drapes in front of the window moved gently in the cool morning breeze.

The sorcerer lay prone on a simple, low bed covered with a linen sheet. His green eyes, dark with pain, watched Marissa as she walked lightly across the room. As Marissa knelt down beside him with the tray, Oraton-Marr attempted a smile. It was, Marissa noted, very weak. She did not give him much longer in this world. "Good morning, Your Highness," she whispered. "I have brought you something to ease the headache."

Oraton-Marr groaned. "Nothing . . . will ease it," he whispered. "Only . . . only the Apothecary . . ."

"I have been to the Apothecary," Marissa said, well aware that there was only one Apothecary who Oraton-Marr would think she meant.

His eyes lit up with hope. "She gave you something?" he whispered.

"She gave me this." Marissa showed him the green lozenge.

"For *me*?" he asked.

Oraton-Marr's expression reminded Marisa of a dog begging. It revolted her, but she hid her revulsion well. "It is indeed for you, Your Highness," Marissa replied. "And here is a sherbet to help you swallow it."

With a wheeze of pain, the sorcerer struggled to raise his head.

Marissa closed her fingers over the lozenge, trapping it inside her fist. "But first," she said softly, "first, there is something I want."

Oraton-Marr let his head fall and gave a cry of pain. "A price . . ." he murmured as his head hit the pillow. "But of course . . ." He looked Marissa in the eye. "Name it. I will pay."

"I need a bodyguard," Marissa said. "Something really scary."

"How scary?" asked Oraton-Marr.

Marissa leaned forward. Oraton-Marr smelled her breath, sweet with one of his sugared almonds. "*Extremely* scary," she whispered. Marissa had given some thought to how she was going to clear the Wizard Tower of its current occupants. "And it must particularly prey on Wizards. Oh, and Apprentices too, of course."

Oraton-Marr opened his eyes wide in amazement. But he felt too ill to question Marissa. All he wanted was the lozenge. "I have . . . something," he croaked.

"I knew you would," Marissa said.

Oraton-Marr said nothing. Marissa was extremely lucky that he had what she wanted. He was an itinerant sorcerer and traveled light, with little **Magykal** hardware—as it was known in the Wizarding trade. He kept what he had in a wooden trunk recently painted purple in honor of the position he had hoped to occupy in the Wizard Tower. The contents of the trunk were a mixture of stolen **Charms**, **Engenders** and **Talismans**—none of which were of any use to him in his present state. "Kraan," he whispered. "In the trunk. They kill . . . anyone with . . . green eyes."

Marissa rifled through the contents of the trunk, gritty with sand. She had no idea what she was looking for. She held up each object in turn until she showed him a soft black leather drawstring bag. "Yes," he grunted.

Marissa weighed the bag in her hand. It was very heavy for its size. She pulled open the cords and peered inside to see it was full of shining red beads. "So how do they work, then?" she asked.

"Instructions in . . . bag," Oraton-Marr whispered. "Take

six beads. Only six. Makes one Kraan."

"I'll take the whole bag," Marissa said, jiggling it up and down, listening to the glassy clinking of the beads, as though it were a toy.

Oraton-Marr groaned. The noise felt like needles stabbing his eardrums. He looked regretfully at the soft black leather bag. He would miss those little red beads. He had been planning to use the Kraan to help him take over the Wizard Tower—once he had acquired a pair of dark glasses, of course. But Oraton-Marr would pay anything the witch asked if she would only give him the green lozenge to cure his headache.

It was only after he had swallowed the lozenge and was falling headlong into a deep pit of sleep that Oraton-Marr realized that Marissa had never actually said that it *would* cure his headache.

With the bag of Kraan weighing heavy in her pocket, Marissa let herself into a deserted courtyard, which contained nothing more than a channel of cool, clear water running around the edge of its high walls and a single palm tree in the middle. She walked into the small patch of shade beneath the tree and disappeared.

PART
II

DUST IN HIS EYE

In the Castle, in the cool of the early morning, Septimus Heap and his young Apprentice, Alice TodHunter Moon—known to most people as Tod—were setting off to visit Septimus's eldest brother, Simon Heap.

They hurried down Wizard Way, the broad avenue that led from the Wizard Tower to the Palace, keeping to the middle to avoid the early-morning bustle that accompanied the opening of the various shops and businesses that lined the Way. The rays of the sun, still low in the sky, skimmed across the low roofs and sent shafts of light glinting off tall silver torch posts, eclipsing the light of their still-burning flames. At the far end of Wizard Way, Septimus and his Apprentice took a sharp right turn into Snake Slipway. This was a much narrower, winding street that led down to the Moat. On either side were houses, the more impressively tall ones on the right-hand side, but it was to the smaller houses on the left that Septimus and Tod were heading. The waters of the Moat were in sight, flowing sluggishly by the end of the slipway, when Septimus took a turn into a pretty front garden, walked up a short path and knocked on a bright red front door.

A young woman opened the door. Lines of worry etched her face, and her brown hair was hastily braided and tied in a knot, lacking her usual ribbons. She wore a long white tunic covered with intricate colorful embroidery, and some serious brown boots. "Hello, Lucy," Septimus said. "I just got your message."

"Oh, Septimus. Thank you for coming," Lucy Heap said with a strained smile.

"Tod's with me; hope that's okay?"

"Tod is welcome here anytime," Lucy said. She looked at Tod, who was hanging back behind Septimus. "You know that, Tod, don't you? Anytime, night or day. After what you did for our William, this is your home too. Anyway, come in, both of you. Simon's upstairs."

Septimus and Tod followed Lucy along the narrow corridor to the stairs. "Your message said that Simon has dust in his eye?" Septimus asked.

"Yes. *Dust*," Lucy said.

Septimus thought she sounded somewhat overwrought about such a little thing. "I was wondering," he said carefully, for Lucy was clearly on a short fuse, "whether Simon should see a physician. Have you asked Marcellus to look at it?"

Lucy wheeled around to face her visitors. "It's not that kind of dust," she said desperately, and she turned and ran up the stairs. Septimus and Tod hurried after her.

Lucy led Septimus and Tod into the large room at the front of the house. Simon was lying on the bed, which was made up for the day and covered with a patchwork quilt. He was half propped up on a nest of pillows with his head tilted back and his eyes closed. "Si," Lucy said quietly, "there's someone to see you."

Simon covered his right eye with his hand and pushed against it hard as if to keep it in place. Warily, he opened his left eye. "Oh," he said. "Sep. Tod. Sorry, can't sit up. Afraid of it all . . . falling out."

"Falling out?" asked Septimus. "What . . . you mean your eye?"

"Yeah. What's left of it," Simon answered quietly.

Lucy slipped her arm around Tod's shoulders and they drew

back while Septimus went over to his brother. "It's your lapis eye?" Septimus asked, knowing full well it was, but needing time to think. The iris in Simon's right eye, already injured, had turned to lapis lazuli after he had used **Darke Magyk** to travel through solid lapis in order to rescue his son, William. This had, of course, blinded him in that eye, but apart from that had given Simon no trouble—until now.

"When did it happen?" asked Septimus.

"Been coming on for some time, I think," Simon said. "It's been feeling very scratchy, like there was grit in it or something."

"And the color changed too," Lucy chimed in. "It used to be so bright, such a brilliant blue with a little streak of gold in it, but for a few weeks now I've thought it was getting duller, and then last night I thought it looked quite gray. But this morning it was . . ." Her voice trailed off and she put her hand over her mouth to stifle a sob.

"Could I take a look?" Septimus asked Simon. "Just so I know what we're dealing with."

"Yeah. I warn you, it's not a pretty sight," Simon said.

Gingerly Simon took his hand away from his eye and opened it. Septimus leaned over and was shocked to see a damp clump of gray dust filling the eye socket. He had never thought of Simon as blind in one eye before, for the lapis had had a sparkle to it and had suited him. But the grayish-white dust looked dead and blank.

Septimus straightened up and tried to think of something positive to say. "It looks like it's still in one piece. I don't think it's going to fall out."

"Doesn't feel that way," Simon said.

Suddenly Lucy burst out with, "But *why*? Why has it done that? Don't you have any idea, Septimus?"

Septimus shook his head. "I suppose the **Magyk** that transformed the living eye to lapis has faded." He shook his head. "But it is very odd. The lapis seemed so stable."

"Can't you put the **Magyk** back somehow?" Lucy asked. "Make it turn to lapis again?"

Septimus was not at all sure that he could, but he didn't want to upset Lucy any more than she was already. "I'll do my best to try, Lucy," he said. "I'll go straight to the library and look it up. I'll ask Marcia, too. I'll do everything I can. I promise."

"Thanks, little bro," Simon said. He put his hand firmly over his eye once again and leaned back on the pillows.

Lucy showed them out. "Promise you won't tell anyone?"

she said. "You know how gossip gets around, and I don't want William to hear it. I don't want him scared." She lowered her voice. "Simon thinks that it's going to spread. Because it was only the iris that was lapis, but now his whole *eye* is dust. He's afraid his brain will be next."

"No!" Septimus was shocked. "That won't happen. Surely. It's just the eye, that's all."

Lucy shook her head. "I don't know, Septimus," she said. "I think Simon might be right, and I can't bear—"

A sudden thud from the attic made Lucy stop midsentence. "That's William," she said. "I must stop him running in to bounce on our bed. And . . . oh gosh, he'll be late for school if I don't hurry."

Tod and Septimus walked back to the Wizard Tower. "Did Simon's eye look bad?" Tod asked.

"It did," Septimus admitted. "It looked horrible."

"Do you think you can you find some **Magyk** to turn it back to lapis?" Tod asked.

Septimus shook his head. "I shall turn the library upside down to look," he said. "But what happened to Simon's eye is some kind of ancient Earth **Magyk**, and very little is written about such things."

Tod was silent for a while. As they walked beneath the

Great Arch into the Wizard Tower courtyard, she said, "So . . . could it spread into Simon's head?"

Septimus sighed. "Maybe if I understood what has caused this, I would know the answer. But right now, I don't."

"So we have to find out," Tod said.

"Yes, we do," Septimus agreed. But he did not sound very hopeful.

GROUNDWORK

Some miles away in the depths of the Forest, Marissa was stepping out of what looked like a small ramshackle hut built of logs and festooned with twigs. No stranger to the Forest, Marissa then made her way confidently through an avenue of immensely tall trees and set off along the dark and narrow Forest paths. She walked alone, but her plans for the future kept her company, whirling around her head, growing ever wilder and more exciting. Marissa longed to take the first step with her plans and **Engender** a bodyguard Kraan, but before she did that, there was something she had to fix.

Before Marissa had left the Forest for the Red City, she had asked a select band of the younger witches loyal to her—known to the other witches as the Toadies—to kidnap the baby Orm from the Castle. This had been part of Marissa's old deal with Oraton-Marr. Her new plans called for something quite different. She now needed the Ormlet to take up residence in the Wizard Tower and start producing precious lapis lazuli beneath it as soon as possible. There must be no stealing of the Ormlet—or Ormnapping, as the witches called it. Marissa hoped they had not already done it; the last thing she wanted was to turn up at the Summer Circle to find that vicious little creature waiting inside her tent.

Marissa hurried along the path that led up to the coven's Summer Circle, and as she rounded a bend she was pleased to see two young witches, Ariel and Star. They were wandering along deep in conversation, but at the sight of Marissa they became silent and looked, Marissa thought, a little guilty. Anxious to get on with her plans, Marissa ignored her niggle of doubt. "Hey, guys!" she said brightly.

"Hi there," Ariel said.

"How's it going?" asked Star.

"Oh, really well. Fantastic, in fact," Marissa said. "How's Morwenna?" Morwenna Mould was the ailing Witch Mother of the coven.

"Not great," Star replied. "It's sad, really. She keeps falling over. And she's going a bit . . . you know . . . strange. Obsessed with searching for some kind of key."

"We've found all sorts of keys for her, but they're never the right ones," Ariel added.

Marissa knew perfectly well what kind of key the Witch Mother was searching for: the Universal Castle Key. Many hundreds of years in the past it had been lost by a careless ExtraOrdinary Wizard and picked up by a passing witch, who had soon become Witch Mother of the coven. Since then the key had been passed down as a secret symbol of office from one Witch Mother to the next. Marissa—and the young guard—knew exactly where the key was: hanging around her neck on a green ribbon. "Oh, that's so *sad*," she said, trying to sound sympathetic but failing utterly.

"Yes, it is," Star said crossly.

Ariel hurriedly changed the subject. It would not be good to alienate the person who was clearly going to be the next Witch Mother. "Marissa, it's good to see you," she said. "We've not seen so much of you recently."

"We're all up in the Summer Circle now," Star chipped in, understanding what Ariel was doing and trying to be friendly herself. "It's great after that gloomy quarry."

"Yeah," Marissa said. "I hate that place. So dark."

"Mind you, you look like you've been in the sun," Star said.

"Really?" Marissa laughed. "It must be all that fresh air down in the Port. I've had a bit of business. With You-Know-Who."

Ariel and Star gasped. "Not the Port Witch Coven?"

Marissa put her finger to her lips. "*Shh*. I'm saying nothing. Hey, guys, listen. There's something important I need you to do. Okay?"

"Okay," said Star.

"You know the plan to get the Ormlet? Well, it's canceled."

"Oh! But why?" Ariel asked.

"I'll explain later," said Marissa. "No one's got it yet, then?"

"Not after it bit Selina's little finger off, no," Star said a little sourly.

"Oh, did it?" Marissa thought how glad she was not to have to deal with the Ormlet anymore. "Well, pass the word, will you? Ormnapping is off. Okay?"

"Okay," Ariel said.

"Quick as you can." With that Marissa turned on her heel and hurried off with the air of important things to do.

Ariel and Star—personal spies of the Castle Queen, Jenna—watched Marissa stride away into the leafy shadows.

"I hate the way she calls us 'guys,'" said Ariel.

"And then treats us like servants," added Star.

"So do we report this?"

"Yeah, you know what Queen Jenna said: Report *everything*. And besides, I fancy lunch at Wizard Sandwiches, don't you?"

"You bet I do," said Ariel. "And supper."

It was late afternoon when Marissa finally had her destination in sight: the old Castle Infirmary. A dilapidated wooden building set away from the Castle on the far side of the Moat, the Infirmary languished in the shade of the outlying trees of the Forest and had a dank, musty air to it. Recently it had been the subject of a little more attention than it had been used to, for it had become the venue for wild parties thrown by the older Castle Apprentices, scribes and the younger witches. This had done little to enhance its looks.

Marissa took the Universal Castle Key from around her neck and turned the lock of the battered Infirmary door. It swung creakily open and Marissa stepped into the musty gloom. She locked the door behind her and crept stealthily through an eerie ward of empty beds with bare mattresses. Spooked by the dimness of the ward, the festoons of cobwebs and its gloomy shadows, Marissa stopped at the nurses' desk

and found her supply of candles. With the help of a lighting
flint she managed to get a candle lit, but a sudden gust of
wind blew through a broken window and snuffed the flame
out. With shaking hands, she grabbed all the candles and lit
the lot.

Marissa sat for a few minutes watching the candle flames
burn bright. She took a deep breath to steady her nerves and
then opened the bag of Kraan and looked at the little red beads
inside. They shone in the candlelight like hundreds of knowing little eyes staring at her. Fear stole over Marissa like a dark
cloud. She felt as though the beads were ganging up on her,
whispering to one another, laughing, plotting . . . She shoved
the bag of Kraan into a drawer and slammed it shut.

A wave of exhaustion engulfed Marissa. She lay down on
the nearest bed, pulled its blanket around her and fell asleep,
leaving the forest of candles burning merrily.

Charm School

That afternoon, when Tod came into the Charm Library on
the tenth floor of the Wizard Tower, she found Jo-Jo Heap
leafing through the Global Charm Index. That was strange,

she thought. Jo-Jo was not a frequent visitor to the Wizard Tower.

Jo-Jo looked up and saw a girl, tall for her age, with brilliant green eyes and her dark hair cut short except for a long, neatly plaited elflock. She wore leggings and a short jacket in regulation Apprentice green, and around her waist was a battered but impressive thick silver belt. "Oh, hi, Tod," Jo-Jo said.

"Hello, Jo-Jo," Tod replied coolly. She found Jo-Jo the least likable of the six brothers of her tutor, Septimus Heap. Although Jo-Jo was almost four years older than Septimus, he did not seem very grown-up. He hung out with the more unpleasant Apprentices in the Wizard Tower, and Tod knew he was friendly with Newt Makken and his brother, Drammer, another first year Apprentice. Drammer was no friend to Tod. He blamed her for taking away his chance to be in the prestigious Apprentice Sled Race and never missed an opportunity to taunt her for not finishing the race.

But the Makken brothers were nothing compared to Jo-Jo's ex-girlfriend: a witch named Marissa. Marissa had recently put the lives of Tod and her two friends, Ferdie and Oskar Sarn, in great danger, and the Wizard Tower gossip was that Marissa and Jo-Jo were back together. Tod had no wish to be in the same space with someone who had anything to do with Marissa. If she had not had a tutorial with the **Charm** Wizard, Rose, she would have walked straight out and not come back until Jo-Jo had gone.

But Rose was already coming out of the inner **Charm** Chamber. A fairly new Ordinary Wizard, Rose still wore her blue robes with a sense of pride. As **Charm** Wizard she had her specialist's symbols embroidered on the sleeves, which were edged with a darker blue ribbon. Tall, with her long brown hair neatly plaited into a braid that hung down to her waist, Rose brought a sense of calm wherever she went. Her light green eyes lit up with pleasure at seeing Tod. "Hello, Tod. I've been looking forward to this all morning."

Rose held open the beautifully painted door to the **Charm** Chamber and a waft of chilly air came out. Tod stepped inside the icy chamber—but not before she had caught a sidelong scowl from Jo-Jo. Rose closed the door behind them and quietly slid the lock across. "Good, he's out of the way. Now, Tod, are you wearing your **Charm** bracelets?"

Tod held up both wrists to show Rose two broad pink bands. These helped counteract the low temperature needed to keep the older **Charms** stable.

"Well remembered," Rose replied. "Would you like a FizzFroot?"

"Oh, yes, please."

Tod loved the Charm Chamber. It made her feel as if she had been wrapped up in a huge, multicolored patchwork quilt; although in reality it was a highly organized twelve-sided room in which resided every known example of Charms. The quilt effect was the result of the hundreds of tiny lockers that lined the walls. They were stacked from floor to ceiling, each one painted with different patterns and colors. Tod had a breathless feeling of excitement when she thought about all the Magykal possibilities they contained.

Tod followed Rose past the Charm desk—twelve-sided, rich with complex wooden inlays in which all the keys to the Charm lockers were kept—and headed through a door set within the wall of cupboards. The door was painted to look as though it too were made of cupboards. The very first time that Tod had visited the Charm Chamber Rose had gone through the door without her noticing. Tod had looked up to find that Rose had apparently vanished.

The trompe l'oeil door led to Rose's private office—a small room with a window looking out over the Forest. It contained a writing desk, two chairs, a tiny sink and a Magykal FlickFyre burner on which sat a neat little copper kettle.

"Sit yourself down, Tod," Rose said. She clicked her fingers

at the burner and told it: "**Light!**" and then perused the jars
set above the sink, each containing small cubes of various
colors. "I've got blue banana, pink grape, red pineapple and,
er . . . something green with orange spots."

"Green with orange spots, please," said Tod. She watched
Rose take the **FizzBom** cube from its jar, place it in a jug and
pour hot water over it. The water fizzed up into a dark brown
froth, and Rose carefully poured it into two glasses. They
waited for the bubbles to settle and then drank the ice-cold
fizz.

"That is weird," Rose said. "It tastes of . . . um . . ."

"Chocolate orange," said Tod. "With a tang of mint."

"So it does," Rose said. She put her glass down and leaned
closer to Tod. "I'd like your opinion about Jo-Jo. He's up to
something, I know he is. Every time I try to see what he's
reading, he covers it with his arm. If I ask him if he needs
help finding anything, he just grunts. He's cross because I
won't let him in the **Charm** Cupboard without a permit." Rose
sighed. "He seems to think that because he's Sep's—I mean
the ExtraOrdinary Wizard's—brother he can go anywhere he
wants in the Wizard Tower. But he's only got basic clearance,
and he's lucky to have that if you ask me, given the people he

associates with." Rose took a gulp of FizzFroot. "I'm sorry, Tod. This is *your* time, for you to learn about **Charms**, not for me to dump my work worries on you."

"I don't mind at all," Tod said. And she didn't. She liked Rose very much and was flattered to be taken into her confidence.

Rose stood up. "Enough of Jo-Jo Heap," she said. "We've got far more important things to think about. Now, Tod, one of the most interesting—and tricky—things about **Charms** is the choosing of them. Of course if you only have one **Charm** available, then there is no choice, but if you find yourself in a **Charm** library—and there are many around the world—you will discover that there are hundreds of different **Charms** for the same thing. The skill is in choosing the right one. You have to learn to **Listen** to what they tell you. Let's have a go, shall we?"

Intrigued, Tod followed Rose back into the **Charm** Chamber. Rose opened the central panel of the desktop to reveal a series of concentric circles of tiny keys lying on faded blue felt—one for each **Charm** Locker. Tod was amazed that Rose knew precisely which locker each key fit.

Despite there being so many keys, not one had a twin.

Some were gold, some silver, some battered, some shiny and new. The bows were an array of all possible shapes and designs—bejeweled, incised, filigreed, enameled or just plain—and they all lay beneath Tod's gaze as she wondered what possibilities they held.

After some minutes Rose said, "So, Tod, are you drawn to any particular key?"

There was indeed one key to which Tod's gaze had repeatedly returned. She had tried to ignore it, for it was by no means the most interesting and certainly not the most beautiful. But the key seemed to be jumping out at her. Tod pointed to a simple blackened key made of pitted metal, its bow an uneven five-pointed star. It lay in the innermost circle. "That one."

"Then you must take it," Rose said.

Tod lifted the key from its bed and put it carefully in the flat of her palm just as Rose had shown her on her first visit.

"Very nicely handled," Rose remarked. "It's so sad to see some of the keys with the finer work snapped off. Now I shall leave it to you to figure out which locker this opens." Rose saw Tod's look of dismay. "But I'll give you a clue first," she said. "It is in the inner ring; therefore it is an ancient **Charm**. Do you remember where their section is?"

"Up there." Tod pointed to the top circle of lockers that ran all the way around the chamber just below the ceiling.

"Well done. Use the ladder and make notes on each one. Then you can decide which cupboard the key fits. If you get it right, you can use the **Charm**."

"I can actually *use* it?" Tod asked.

"Why not?" Rose smiled. "I know you're careful. But the deal is you'll have to get the locker right the first time. Okay?"

"Wow. Yes, totally okay!"

Rose took the key and placed it on a red velvet pad in the center of the table. Then she sat quietly updating the **Charm** index while Tod methodically trundled the ladder around the circle of lockers, running up and down, making notes and drawing sketches of all the lockers. At last she was finished. She had a shortlist of three, which she showed to Rose.

"They've all got stars on them," Tod explained.

"They do," Rose agreed.

"So . . . I think I need to know a bit about what the **Charm** does before I can choose the right locker," Tod said.

"You do indeed," Rose said, sounding pleased. "That is one of the most important things to understand about how to use a **Charm**. Always make sure you know exactly what it will do. Don't rely on what people tell you—make sure that you know." From beneath the **Charm** desk, Rose took a leather-bound book titled *Ancient Charm Index* and handed it to Tod.

"This lists all one hundred and sixty-nine Ancient **Charms**," Rose said. "They are indexed in three ways: design of key, name of **Charm**, effects of **Charm**. Many of the effects sections will be blank, as for some we have no information at all. You will also find the **Charm Chant** by most of them, but again, not all."

Ten minutes later, Tod had matched her sketches of the lockers with the entries in the index. She showed Rose the one she thought referred to her key. It was named StarChaser.

Rose put on a tiny pair of pink-glass spectacles and peered at the minute faded writing in the book. "StarChaser," she murmured. "Well, you've chosen an odd one there, I must say. We've got no information about it at all."

"Oh." Tod felt disappointed.

"However," Rose said cheerily, "I have a feeling that you're going to find it out for us. But first let's see if you've picked the right locker."

Tod had a strange feeling as she climbed the ladder, and it wasn't because of its teetering height. She felt as though she were climbing toward something really important in her life. At the top of the ladder, she looked closely at the locker. Like the key, it was a dull silver color—pure silver leaf—and etched into it was a scattering of tiny dark blue stars. It looked very mysterious. Tod began to feel excited.

The key turned easily and the locker's little door swung open. Tod glanced down at Rose, who was looking up with a broad smile. "Well done!" she called. "Right the first time! Not one Apprentice has ever done that. Now see what's inside."

A little nervously, Tod put her hand into the darkness of the locker. She was surprised to find how deep it was—her whole arm had disappeared into it before the tips of her fingers at last managed to touch the back wall. At first Tod thought that the locker was empty: all she could feel were its polished smooth sides. But as her fingers fluttered like trapped butterflies against the silvery back of the locker, a small box made itself known beneath them.

With the key back in its place inside the Charm desk, Tod and Rose sat gazing at the box. Like the locker, it was covered in battered silver leaf with the dark ghosts of stars scattered across it. Just looking at it made Tod shiver.

"Are you going to open it?" Rose prompted.

Tod hesitated. She felt strangely nervous.

Rose smiled encouragingly. "Why don't you see what the Charm Chant says?" she suggested. "It's not here in the *Index* and I'd really like to add it."

Tod lifted the lid to the box. Inside lay a five-pointed star made of a thick, coppery metal with shifting blue patterns that moved over its surface like oil on water. The star had a random pattern of small holes strewn across it and was pierced with a central hexagonal hole. It lay on a scrap of grubby turquoise wool that smelled of oil.

"It won't bite," Rose said with a smile. "You can pick it up."

Nervously, Tod held the StarChaser in her palm. It was heavy and covered most of her hand—just a battered piece of metal that looked as though it had once been part of a machine. There was no sign of a Charm Chant inscribed on the uppermost side of the star, so Tod turned it over. That too was blank.

"No Chant?" Rose inquired.

"No. It must be in the box, I suppose," Tod said.

But it wasn't. Tod and Rose even rolled back the wool lining of the box to see if the Chant was hidden beneath, but all they saw was plain silver, as smooth and unmarked as the day the box had been made. Rose fetched an **Enlarging Glass** and ran it slowly over both the box and the **Charm**, but she found nothing.

"Most peculiar," Rose said. "It's not marked as an orphan."

"An orphan?" asked Tod.

"That's what we call **Charms** that have lost their **Chants**. They're marked in the *Index*." Rose checked the *Ancient Index* once again. "And this one isn't. I shall have to correct it." Rose sighed. "I'm so sorry, Tod. This StarChaser is pretty useless; Ancient **Charms** always have to be started with a **Chant**. But you were clearly drawn to it for some reason. Why don't you keep it for a while?"

"*Keep* it?"

"I'll check it out as a long loan. You can get to know it. See if it tells you anything." Rose smiled. "I've learned with **Charms** that you have to **Listen** to them sometimes. And not everyone can **Hear**. But I think if this **Charm** wants to tell anyone anything, you will be the one it chooses."

Tod looked at the heavy metal star lying quiet and warm on her hand. It felt to her as though it belonged somewhere she knew, but had not yet found. "Thank you," she said.

"On one condition," Rose said. "If you find out what the

Charm is for, you will tell me. Okay?"

"You'll be the first to know," Tod said.

For the rest of the afternoon Tod sat making notes on the *Ancient* **Charm** *Index*, aware of the great weight of the StarChaser **Charm** snug in its box and sitting deep in her pocket. By the time Tod had finished her notes, the StarChaser had begun to feel as if it were part of her.

Before she left, Tod helped Rose wash up the FizzFroot mugs. Twilight was falling and through the sparkling window—Rose kept a clean kitchen—Tod could see candles flickering in the attic windows of the houses that lined the Moat. She folded up the drying cloth and looked out the window.

"I love this time of the day," Rose commented. "All the candles being lit. And the torches blazing up along Wizard Way."

"And the Forest looking so dark and scary." Tod shivered. "I'm so glad I'm here and not out there. I never want to be in the Forest at night again. Ever. Oh . . . Isn't there a light in the old Infirmary?"

Rose peered over Tod's shoulder. "So there is. Candlelight."

"I suppose they're getting ready for the party," Tod said.

Rose clicked her tongue disapprovingly. "I don't know why Septimus allows those parties," she said. "It's a big mistake."

"He says it keeps trouble out of the Castle," Tod replied loyally.

"Those parties bring trouble right up to our doorstep," Rose said. "Which is too close for my liking."

Tod did not disagree.

A few minutes later, Tod and Rose emerged from the **Charm** Chamber into the lobby. They were both pleased to see that Jo-Jo Heap had gone.

"I wonder if he found what he was looking for?" Tod said.

"Hmm," Rose replied. "I rather hope he didn't."

Tod rather hoped so too.

WIZARD SANDWICHES

Dusk was falling by the time Tod said good-bye to Rose. With her hand in her pocket clutching the warm metal of the StarChaser, Tod walked dreamily out of the door and along the wood-paneled passageway that led to the silver spiral stairs. These were, like much of the Wizard Tower, powered

by the ancient **Magyk** that took its energy from the great
block of lapis lazuli that formed the bedrock of the tower. The
stairs moved constantly, turning like a massive corkscrew. At
this time of day they were busy with Wizards returning to
their rooms. Tod stood in the soft light of the corridor, waiting for three empty steps—it was considered bad manners for
anyone, especially an Apprentice, to crowd someone out by
occupying the immediate step above or below.

While she waited, Tod drew the StarChaser from her
pocket and let it sit heavy in her palm. She gazed at it intently,
convinced that now she was alone with it she would be able
to see the **Chant**, which it was keeping only for her eyes. The
StarChaser remained as unmarked as ever, but as she looked,
Tod thought she caught ancient echoes of a mechanical
thrum. She was so entranced that when there was a space on
the stairs she automatically stepped on, only to realize some
four floors up that she was going the wrong way. She leaped
off and found herself on the eighteenth floor.

Bother, Tod thought. *I really do not want to be here.*

The eighteenth floor of the Wizard Tower was a strange
place. Like most of the floors it consisted of a central corridor
with rooms leading off, but it differed from the others in that

it still had its original decoration: slate walls with thousands of silver-leaf pictograms in vertical columns that ran from ceiling to floor, the translation of which was kept locked in the safe at the end of the corridor. Like Tod's StarChaser, this place too was full of ancient echoes, but unlike the StarChaser they were more than a little disturbing, for it was here that Septimus held the new **Darke** course for final year Apprentices.

Tod knew that only those in their final year were allowed to set foot on the eighteenth floor, and the echoes of lingering **Darke** spells spooked her. As soon as the stairs reversed direction, she jumped back on and with a feeling of great relief, headed down into brighter spaces.

The **Darke** echoes had unsettled Tod and she felt afraid for her StarChaser. Remembering that Rose had told her the best way to keep a **Charm** safe was to wear it close, she got off the stairs at the seventh floor and hurried along to the Junior Girls' Apprentice Dorm. The dorm was set out with twelve tented spaces; Tod's had recently acquired a new design—silver stars on dark blue in honor of a certain tent in a distant desert. Tod carried her much more substantial star into her tent and from her desk beside the bed she took a spare leather bootlace. She threaded it through the center of the StarChaser and put it around her neck. Tod already wore her **PathFinder** around her neck, and the two sat well together, as if they were old acquaintances. She put the StarChaser's empty silver box into her pocket and hurried off. She was looking forward to spending the evening with her best friends from her home village, Oskar and Ferdie Sarn.

On Wizard Way the torches atop their tall silver posts were being lit, and the smell of spices from the curry cart made Tod hungry for supper. She wandered along, enjoying the relaxed evening slowness. She was heading for Wizard Sandwiches—a café frequented by Apprentices, scribes and the occasional witch—where they had planned to meet.

Tod spotted Ferdie and Oskar hanging around outside, their red curly hair shining in the twilight with the typical **PathFinder** sheen. She waved and the Sarn twins hurried to join her. Quickly Ferdie took one arm and Oskar the other.

"We had to wait outside," Oskar said.

"You'll see why when we go past the window," Ferdie added.

The twins walked Tod toward Wizard Sandwiches and as they went by, Tod glanced into the café window. "Oh!" she said.

"See?" said Ferdie.

"There's no way we're going in there to sit with *witches*," Oskar said.

"But aren't those the nice ones?" Tod asked.

Ferdie pulled a face. "There is no such thing as a nice witch," she declared.

Tod felt much the same. They had all suffered a terrifying time at the hands of the Wendron Witch coven. Tod willingly allowed Ferdie and Oskar to sweep her away, off to Snake Slipway, where Ferdie lodged with Lucy, Simon and William Heap.

"We'll have to be quiet," Ferdie warned. "Simon's not well. Something horrible has happened to his eye."

"What kind of horrible?" Oskar asked, sounding interested.

Ferdie lowered her voice. "I don't know. But don't say anything. Lucy is really scared, and she doesn't want William to know."

Tod said nothing. Her visit to Simon that morning had been Wizard Tower business, which was not for her to talk about.

"I bet William *does* know," Oskar said.

Ferdie was inclined to agree. "I think he does. He was very quiet when he got home from school."

"So why don't we take him out in a paddleboat?" Oskar suggested. "That should cheer him up."

And so the three friends—known to one another as the Tribe of Three—set off to extract William Heap from the sadness of a frightened household and hire one of his uncle Rupert's paddleboats.

From the other side of the window, Ariel and Star watched them go. "That's those kids," Ariel said. "You know, those snow sprites that Morwenna nearly threw in the fire."

"Yeah, they had a lucky escape," Star said.

"Thanks to us," said Ariel.

"Not that they bothered to actually *say* thank you," said Star. "Ungrateful little tykes."

Ariel shrugged. "No one ever thanks witches. It's a fact of life."

"Queen Jenna's all right, though," said Star.

"Yeah, she's okay. While she has a use for us, at least," said Ariel. "Are you finishing that Tank or shall I?"

One of the perks of their job for the Queen was free food at Wizard Sandwiches, and the witches were making the most of it. Between them was a large plate on which lay the remains of the biggest sandwich that the café produced: the Tank. The Tank was two loaves of bread, hollowed out and filled with a savory bean mixture then stuck together with thick gravy. The two witches had personalized the mix with extra chili and chunks of fried squirrel—which was, Star thought, a mistake. She had a squirrel bone stuck between her teeth. "You have it," she said.

While Ariel chewed her way through the last of the Tank, the remaining member of staff, the washing-up boy, began to close up. The witches had been there the whole afternoon keeping customers away; all the staff had gone except for him, and he wanted to go home. He had already wiped the tables, cleared away the menus and counted the takings. He now set about noisily putting the unoccupied chairs up on the tables and then in desperation started mopping the floor, spraying water everywhere.

Ariel and Star watched him impassively as they very slowly finished their pudding: sweet banana rolls topped with chocolate sprinkles. Then they wiped their fingers on the tablecloth and sauntered out through the puddles.

"So," said Ariel, as the boy hastily locked the door behind them, "I suppose we had better go and deliver Marissa's message to the Ormnap team."

Star looked at the lights of Wizard Way; she saw the happy pottering of people wandering along, taking in the evening air, gazing in the lighted shop windows. The thought of returning to the darkness of the nighttime Forest was not attractive. "Why bother?" she said.

"Yeah," Ariel agreed. "Rude cow. She can tell them herself."

Ariel and Star linked arms and set off for Gothyk Grotto, a shop selling what was known in the Castle as Witchery-Fakery. At night Gothyk Grotto—or the Grot as it was affectionately known—became a meeting place for the more goth-minded teens. It was a place where witches were always welcome. As the evening gave way to night, in a cobwebby corner at the back of the Grot, Ariel and Star began the **Darke** card game of Hangman Jack.

THREE IN THE MORNING

In the Junior Girls' Apprentice Dorm in the Wizard Tower, Tod was asleep with the StarChaser under her pillow. In her dreams she moved slowly through a dark space dotted with tiny lights that guided her toward something familiar, but as yet unknown. Just before three in the morning Tod woke with a start, convinced she was falling. Dozily, she looked up at the stars on the tented canopy above her bed and then, as three tinny chimes from the Drapers Yard Clock drifted into the dorm, she slipped back into her quiet, purposeful dream.

In Gothyk Grotto the candles were burning low, but Ariel and Star played on. As was so often the case with Hangman Jack, the game had expanded to include the onlookers—all teens, all dressed in varying shades of black. Thirteen were now gathered around the table: the Grot's favorite number. The atmosphere was buzzing with tension, for the stakes were high: a minimum of five luminous eyeballs was now required to stay in the game. It was shaping up to be a long night—someone had just found a new box of eyeballs in the storeroom.

Across the Moat in the Infirmary, Marissa was awake and sitting at the nurses' desk in the middle of the empty ward. In front of her was the bag of Kraan and on the desk a dark brown scrap of paper that looked as though it had been scorched. On the paper was a spiral of tiny words written in black ink, very precisely lettered. This was the **Engender** and it was, as Marissa would have put it, freaking her out.

Marissa was not the world's best reader and there were some words she had never seen before and was unsure how to say. However, she knew enough about **Darke Magyk** to recognize one particularly terrifying word, written in all its horror, at the very end of the **Engender**. Marissa sat staring at the paper, her mind full of stories gleefully told around late-night campfires about stupid Wizards who had misread **Engenders** and the awful things that had happened to them as a result.

Marissa yawned. She was too tired to concentrate, she told herself, that was the trouble. She'd have a nap and take another look in the morning. She put the **Engender** back into the bag of Kraan and shoved the bag into the desk drawer. Then she went back to her hard hospital bed, wrapped herself up in the thin blanket and fell into a deep, dreamless sleep.

Thousands of miles away, in Hospitable Gard, someone else was also in a deep, dreamless sleep: Oraton-Marr.

The Red Queen's Guards had returned, as they had

promised. They watched impassively as Mitza and the Lady
yelled, shook and pinched the sorcerer in increasingly desperate attempts to wake him. But Oraton-Marr was deep in
the dark pit of his green lozenge slumber, and nothing could
reach him.

At last, in desperation, Mitza and the Lady picked up the
sorcerer's bed, bumped it down the stairs, and then, escorted
by the guards, they carried him, snoring, through the silent
streets to the Palace.

In a chamber deep within the Palace, the Red Queen
surveyed her catch: one useless sorcerer and two terrified
and equally useless women. She had them all thrown into a
dungeon and then she turned to the Captain of the Guard.
"The girl—that little witch—you said she had a key to a
castle?"

The Captain waited five long seconds then replied, "Yes,
Your Majesty. I questioned the guard to whom she spoke.
She told him it was the key to a castle, Your Majesty. She
said it was something you wanted to get your hands on, Your
Majesty."

The Red Queen smiled. All was not yet lost. "Go," she told
the Captain. "Bring me that little witch. *Now.*"

Tracking

After a fruitless visit to Hospitable Gard, the Captain went home to his wife and bade her a tearful farewell. There was no way, he said, he would survive this mission. The witch was gone and he had no idea where. His wife waited out his tears and then, as the sun rose, she took the Captain to the sorcerer her family had used for years. In a tiny room at the top of a turret, in return for a whole year of the Captain's salary plus the use of their firstborn as a runner, an ancient sorcerer, bald as an egg, handed the Captain a small green ball covered in finely stitched leather. It was a new, untried Tracker ball.

"I won it in a bet," the sorcerer told them. "It was a wild night down in the Port of the Singing Sands and I gambled my head of hair against his Tracker ball over the turn of the cards." The sorcerer looked up at the bemused expression on the Captain's face. His wife, who had heard the joke many times before, wore a fixed smile as the sorcerer grinned and rubbed his hand over his smooth, bald head. "I won that night. But not the next. Always stop while you are ahead," he said. "Or at least, while you have a head of hair."

The wife of the Captain of the Guard laughed politely and she nudged her husband to do the same—it was wise to humor sorcerers. When the laughter died away, she asked, "Could you tell us how to use this **Magykal** thing, O Wise One?"

"You touch it to the person and then it will **Track** them," the sorcerer replied.

The Captain's wife was aghast; she had forgotten what an idiot their family sorcerer was. But she must make the best of it. Sorcerers were a close-knit bunch and she could not now change her mind and go to another. "What a charming idea," she said, trying her best to smile. "And if the person one wishes to **Track** is not actually there at the time, what does one do?"

The sorcerer frowned and rubbed his head in thought. "An interesting question," he said. "Yes, indeed . . . most thought-provoking."

The Captain and his wife waited for an answer. At last they got it. "I believe it is possible to wrap the **Tracker** ball in an article of the person's clothing and leave it for . . . hmm . . . let me see now . . . yes . . . thirteen minutes."

"Thirteen," the Captain's wife said sharply. "So do I under-stand this to be a **Darke** device?"

The sorcerer looked at her with irritation. He didn't like clients who were too clever. "It contains an element of the **Darke**, madam," he replied frostily. "As do all **Tracker** balls. Indeed, how else would they operate? After all, they rarely **Track** people with their informed consent, ha-ha. And to operate without consent requires a touch of **Darke Magyk**. As you are no doubt aware. You may go now."

The Captain's wife knew that when a sorcerer told you to go, you went. And you did not say: *Suppose we don't have any clothing, you stupid old man. What do we do then?* However much you wanted to.

The dejected couple wandered back home in silence. At last the Captain's wife spoke. "Cecil, I have been thinking. We must go to that Hospitable Gard place and get a piece of the witch's clothing."

The Captain looked gloomy. "She will have packed it all up and taken it with her."

"She sounds a scatty young thing," his wife said. "She's bound to have left something behind."

"But how do I know what clothes belong to *her*?" the Captain asked plaintively.

His wife sighed out loud. "From your description of the other women living there I should have thought it would be obvious." She looked at her husband and decided that he was in such a state that he wouldn't even recognize a little frilly nightdress with *I Belong to a Witch* embroidered across its front. "I'll come with you as part of the Queen's Guard," she said. "You can say you've got a warrant to search the place. It'll be easy. I'll know a piece of witch stuff when I see one."

The Captain looked at his wife with an expression of relief. Everything would be fine if she was with him. And then he remembered something. "But Celia, you can't be part of the Queen's Guard," he said. "You're not a man."

"Oh, do shut up, Cecil," said his wife.

The housekeeper at Hospitable Gard was cleaning at the very top of the tower when she heard pounding on the front door six floors down. She was not in a good mood when she at last flung it open. "What," she demanded, "do you want?" She saw the full dress uniform of the Captain of the Queen's Guard and nearly fainted. "Oh, sir," she said, "oh, I am so sorry. I was not expecting . . ."

"I have a search warrant," said the Captain. "Let us in. At once."

The housekeeper stood aside for the Captain and his young soldier. The housekeeper waited for more to troop in but she was surprised to see that there were no others. She waited respectfully for the Captain to speak. He said nothing. The housekeeper began to feel nervous. She thought she saw the young soldier nudge the Captain in the ribs but she told herself that was not possible. And then at last the Captain spoke.

"I have reason to believe there is a witch here," he said.

The housekeeper was shocked. She did not like witches. "There is no one here, sir. They are removed to the Palace. I am cleaning up their mess. Mucky baggages the lot of them."

"Stand aside, woman," said the Captain. "I intend to search the tower."

The housekeeper sank thankfully onto one of the divans and watched the Captain and his oddly feminine soldier hurry away up the stairs. She swung her feet up, lay her head on the soft nest of cushions and fell asleep.

Ten minutes later the Captain and his wife clattered down the stairs. In her hands the wife held a tiny green slip that smelled of patchouli. The Captain agreed that there was no way either of the women could have fit into that. "Although I suppose one of them could have worn it as a scarf," he said, doubts beginning to grow once more.

"Don't be ridiculous, Cecil," his wife told him.

The housekeeper opened her eyes dozily, decided she must be dreaming and went back to sleep.

The **Tracker** ball spent its thirteen minutes wrapped in the piece of patchouli-scented silk. The Captain of the Queen's Guard spent the thirteen minutes sharpening his sword, and his wife spent it wondering if the Captain was worth all the trouble. Half an hour later, the Captain's wife waved her husband good-bye. She watched him follow the **Tracker** ball as it bounced away down the alley. She hoped he would come back, but she thought it unlikely.

The Captain followed the ball as it rolled and tumbled along. It moved fast and at times he struggled to keep sight of it. Hot and flustered, carrying his sword and a knapsack, he attracted many amused glances: the Captain of the Queen's Guard chasing after a ball was not something often seen.

The **Tracker** ball moved fast, and the Captain was soon

out of breath in the afternoon heat. He just about managed to keep it in sight until suddenly, with an enormous bounce, it flew over a high wall and disappeared. The Captain ran to the only door in the wall and found it was locked. In desperation he threw himself against it, but it did not move. He pummeled the door with his fists, shouted, screamed, and then, as people began leaning out of nearby windows to see what the fuss was about, he sank to the ground in tears.

That night the Captain left a note for his wife under the pot by their front door and then he walked out of the city. At first light he hired a camel. He didn't know where it was going. All he knew was that he would never return.

PART
~ III ~

THE ORMLET

It *was a beautiful morning* in the Castle—too good, Marwick told his self-defense class, to stay inside. And so, on the wide sweep of Palace lawns that led down to the river, the class was out in the sunshine, practicing blocking with staves. The class was a mixed bunch, chosen because each had once been in mortal danger. Among them were Tod, Oskar and Ferdie. There were an assortment of scribes from the Manuscriptorium and a few Apprentices from the Wizard Tower including, much to Tod's discomfort, a certain Drammer Makken. There was also, at her own insistence, the Castle Queen, Jenna. Watching them from a grassy bank was a pale, convalescing Sam Heap and his brother Septimus, looking rather hot in his heavy purple ExtraOrdinary Wizard robes.

The class instructor, Marwick, was a skinny, wild-looking

young man with his hair worn in dreadlocks. Marwick had
clearly used his skills for real in the past and many of the
younger ones were a little in awe of him. But even Marwick
could not compete with the sight of the Ormlet suddenly
appearing over the tall hedge that separated the Dragon Field
from the Palace lawns.

With a flash of blue, a flutter of spiky wings and a flick of
a long, flippy tail, the Ormlet rose into the air like a rocket.
In the field behind the hedge a large green dragon named Spit
Fyre watched his adopted baby with an expression of pride.
The expression worn by everyone else was more wary. Many
were wondering anxiously what the creature was going to do
this time.

Tod was not worried. Like Ferdie and Oskar she loved to
see the Ormlet flying free. At a distance the creature looked
like a tiny electric blue dragon as it soared high into the clear
sky. Oskar followed it closely, trying to commit to memory
the way it moved: quick, unpredictable, erratic—just like an
automaton. Which was, Oskar thought, perfect. For it was
Oskar's dearest wish that one day, when the Ormlet had
become an adult Orm and was nothing more than a huge
hollow tube eating its way through rock, he might be able

to create its mechanical twin so that the joyful flight of the Ormlet would never be forgotten.

The Ormlet threw itself into a succession of complex spins. The creature had grown to appreciate the attention of humans. It loved the gasps of wonder at its acrobatics, but even more it loved the screams of alarm as it swooped down on unsuspecting victims—only to swerve past them at the very last minute. That morning it was thrilled to see so many upturned faces watching it.

In addition to the self-defense class, the Ormlet's audience comprised passengers on a pleasure boat tour around the Castle, a group of farmhands mowing a meadow on the opposite bank and, from an upstairs window at the Palace, a new and highly excitable wolfhound puppy called Millicent. To the background of frantic yapping, the Ormlet now launched into a series of breathtaking loops and spirals, feeling the cool morning air rushing by its shimmering leathery skin and delighting in the moment.

Queen Jenna squinted up into the sky, watching the unpredictable flash of blue. The Ormlet was a responsibility that Jenna felt keenly. She had promised Septimus that she would keep it safe with Spit Fyre until the time came for it to **TransfOrm**. But the task had not been an easy one. For some reason, the presence of the Ormlet had attracted the attentions of the Wendron Witch coven. But at least, Jenna thought as she watched the Ormlet throw itself into a double loop and twist, that threat was gone now. A smile crossed Jenna's face as she remembered the early-morning visit from her faithful witch spies, Ariel and Star. They had looked disheveled and weary with dark rings under their eyes. They had obviously had a difficult journey through the nighttime Forest, but even so they had struggled through to give her the message that the Wendron Witches were no longer intending to steal the Ormlet. That, thought Jenna, was true loyalty. And so, after Ariel and Star had gone to their Palace rooms for a well-deserved rest, Jenna had stood down the guard on the Dragon Kennel.

Welcome though the message was, it did not take away the difficulties of playing host to the Ormlet. The snappy little reptile was accused of a series of crimes and misdemeanors.

The charge sheet was as follows:

*For the Prosecution: Biting the boot of Barney Pot, the
dragon keeper, and eating three of his toes.*

For the Defense: This was a mistake. And the toes did not taste good.

For the Prosecution: Escaping into the Palace garden and eating the entire afternoon tea for the Garden Party of Port Officials.

For the Defense: The officials were very boring.

For the Prosecution: The disappearance of all the Palace cats.

For the Defense: What cats?

For the Prosecution: Overturning two small boats in the river.

For the Defense: The Ormlet cannot be held responsible for spectators all choosing to stand on the same side of a boat.

There were also a few crimes as yet to be recorded: biting off the left little finger of witch novice Selina Simpkins (on which she wore her favorite silver ring) and the theft of assorted small, shiny objects. Like a giant magpie, the Ormlet with its delicate, prehensile lips would lift a sparkling piece of jewelry left near an open window, but if the shiny thing happened to be a ring on the finger of an annoying witch poking the Ormlet with a long stick, so much the better.

However, that morning the Ormlet looked so joyful and innocent that even Jenna forgot its wrongdoings and watched in delight.

The Ormlet flew for the sheer joy of the sensation of air rushing beneath its wings and the warmth of the sun on its shimmering, leathery skin. Recently a feeling of impending doom had taken root in the Ormlet's brain. It didn't know why, but it had a presentiment that things were about to change—and not for the better. On that bright and beautiful morning, the Ormlet was trying to outfly the dark fate that it felt creeping up behind it.

At the zenith of its arc the Ormlet stopped and hovered far above the river, flapping its wings so rapidly that they were a barely visible blur. It looked down and far below saw the upturned faces of its admirers. It watched the shimmer of the reflections on the surface of the river, the gleam of the polished brass on the river boat and then, on the Palace lawns, it saw something irresistible—a deliciously bright sparkle of gold shining on the head of a young woman in red.

A thrill of joy went through the Ormlet's thin, sharp nerves. It folded its wings and tipped downward so it looked like a sleek, blue arrow pointing to earth. A gasp drifted up from below as it spiraled down in a spectacular nosedive. The Ormlet waited just long enough to garner a satisfying tally of screams from the riverboat passengers before it pulled out of the dive no more than three feet above their heads. To the background of applause from the relieved passengers, the Ormlet proceeded to zigzag like a delinquent firecracker just above the water. It then took a sudden right turn, shot up the Palace lawns and—locking onto its target—flew straight for Queen Jenna, its brilliant blue eyes focused on the twinkling gold of the circlet that she wore around her hair. The self-defense class scattered like a bow wave before the onrushing missile.

Jenna grabbed Marwick's stave and stood ready for the attack. Oskar leaped into the air, waving his hands as though trying to catch a ball. "Ormie!" he yelled. "Ormie!"

"Oskar!" screamed Tod, tackling his knees and throwing him to the ground out of the path of the sharp snout, danger-ous as a spear. The Ormlet whizzed by so close that Tod could feel the rush of air and hear the buzz of its wings. She sat up and saw the flash of blue make a sharp right turn and zoom to the back of Jenna's head. Tod was impressed with Jenna's lightning reaction. The Queen wheeled around, swung her stave whistling through the air, but she was a fraction of a second too late. The Ormlet's dexterous lips had already lifted the golden circlet from her head. Jenna succeeded in landing a glancing blow on the barb of its tail but all that did was speed the creature upon its way, a ring of gold hanging from its mouth like a huge, misplaced earring. The Ormlet soared into the sky wearing its earring with pride, along with what looked like a very smug smile.

LAST CHANCE

Two shouts went up simultaneously, both from young men but from opposite directions. Tod watched the two men race toward the scattered self-defense class. One was her tutor, Septimus Heap; the other, who came hurtling through a hole in the hedge that separated the Dragon Field from the Palace gardens, wore a scuffed leather jerkin and trousers covered in bite marks. He was, Tod guessed, Barney Pot, the Palace dragon keeper. Despite his limp Barney reached them first. Hastily brushing strands of straw from his jerkin, he said, "I am so, so sorry, Queen Jenna."

"It's not your fault, Barney," Jenna replied, wiping the Orm spit from her hair. "Anyway, I've come off much more lightly than you did."

Breathless, Septimus joined them. "Only by luck, Jen," he said. "It could have bitten your head off."

Barney looked horrified.

Tod could see that Jenna was more shaken than she cared to admit. Which explained why the Queen rounded on Septimus and said, "No, Sep, it could *not* have bitten my head off. I was ready for it. And this is exactly why I asked Marwick to teach us self-defense. So that wherever the attack comes from—Orm, witch or . . . or *whatever*, we are ready."

Septimus backpedaled fast. "Okay, Jen. I do see the point of the class. Really I do." He grinned at his old friend Marwick. "And you have the best teacher possible."

Marwick put his arm around Septimus's shoulder. "Always the diplomat, eh, Sep?"

Septimus grinned ruefully. "I have to be," he said.

Marwick addressed the class. He praised everyone for taking what he called "successful avoidance action" and declared that practice was over for the day. Then he took Sam off for a reviving drink at Wizard Sandwiches.

As the class trooped back to the Palace to collect their things, Oskar saw Septimus go over to Lucy Heap. Lucy was supervising the construction of the Orm Pit—the secure place beneath the Wizard Tower where the Ormlet was destined to spend its time as a cocoon and embark upon its new life as a mature Orm. Alarm bells rang for Oskar. He dropped back from Ferdie and Tod and changed course with a rather comical sideways shuffle, trying to hear what Septimus was saying. He need not have taken the trouble. Lucy's reply rang out loud and clear.

"Are you totally crazy? Do two weeks' work in twenty-four hours?"

A placating murmur came from Septimus.

"I don't care how 'essential to safety' it is, Septimus," Lucy told him. "Unlike you, I cannot just snap my fingers and make things happen. And neither can my builders."

More murmuring followed and Lucy seemed conciliatory. "Well . . . I suppose it might be just possible. But I'll need extra help. And I can't promise anything. Understand?"

"Thank you, Lucy," Septimus said. "I'm sorry to ask this. I know you have enough to worry about already. How is Simon?"

Lucy looked like she might burst into tears. She bit her lip and said tersely, "Just the same."

"Lucy," said Septimus, "I was thinking that maybe he should be in the Sick Bay, where we can look after him."

Lucy shook her head. "Si wants to be at home." She lowered her voice. "He has nightmares. Shouts in his sleep. It wouldn't be good for the others in Sick Bay."

Septimus gave Lucy a hug. "Well, you know best. Just tell me if there is anything I can do."

Lucy nodded and strode off, the ribbons on her cuffs flowing behind her as she went. She didn't want anyone to see the tears running down her face.

"Hey, Oskar." The voice behind Oskar made him jump. It was Jenna. She smiled and said, "It's a lovely day. Too sunny for sighing."

Oskar smiled shyly. He liked Jenna, but he still felt a little overawed by the Castle Queen. He was trying to think of a suitable reply when Septimus appeared.

Septimus nodded to Oskar and then turned to Jenna. "The Ormlet is out of control; we can't risk it being at large a moment longer. It will be going into the Orm Pit tomorrow afternoon."

Jenna laughed. "If you can catch it."

Oskar knew it was rude to interrupt a conversation between

the Queen and the ExtraOrdinary Wizard, but he couldn't stop himself. "Please don't lock Ormie up," he begged. "*Please. Let her have her last days of freedom. She won't be able to fly for much longer.*"

Septimus looked cross at being interrupted, but Jenna was more understanding. "It's true, Sep. This stage won't last long. And after that the poor creature's going to spend the rest of its life like a blind mole beneath the ground, eating rock."

Septimus was not to be convinced. "The Ormlet is a pest, Jen—and besides, there are other considerations. We must be careful not to lose it at the very last minute. Its behavior has become so erratic that I would not be surprised if it suddenly flew away and we never saw it again."

"Spit Fyre would soon be after it," Jenna said. "He's besotted with the creature; you know he is."

Septimus sighed. "Yes. And then we'd lose Spit Fyre again." He turned to Oskar. "I'm sorry, Oskar. My mind is made up. For the good of the Castle, it is time for the Ormlet to enter the Orm Pit."

Oskar bit his lip and stared at the ground.

Tod and Ferdie had joined them and heard the last few exchanges. "Please, Septimus," Tod said, "would you consider giving the Ormlet one more chance?"

"*Please?*" Ferdie and Oskar added for good measure.

Under the combined onslaught Septimus weakened. "What kind of chance?" he asked warily.

"Suppose it gave the circlet back?" Tod said.

Septimus laughed. "And apologized and said it would never do it again?" he asked. "Well, that might do, I suppose."

"I could talk to Ormie and tell her she has to be good from now on," Oskar offered. "And then tomorrow when you come to take her to the Orm Pit, if she lets you take the circlet, would that be okay? That would really prove she was behaving better, wouldn't it?"

Jenna weighed in. "I *would* like to get my circlet back, Sep. And Oskar does seem to have a way with the Ormlet. So how about it—one last chance?"

Septimus could never say no to Jenna for long. "All right," he said. "One last chance." He looked at Oskar. "That Ormlet has to give the circlet back. And it has to be very well behaved from now on. No more dive-bombing, no more zigzagging down Wizard Way at knee height, no more pooping on people's heads, okay?"

"Okay," Oskar said.

Tod and Ferdie exchanged worried glances. There was no way Oskar could fix all that. No way at all.

Drammer Makken

Oskar knew Drammer Makken was trouble. And he knew from the way Drammer was staring that he wanted to talk. But Oskar did not want to talk to Drammer. The boy scared him. In the last month or so Drammer Makken had broadened out and grown a good few inches taller. He was now bigger than his older brother, Newt, and a whole lot nastier, too. So as Tod hurried away with Septimus, Oskar hung back with Ferdie. He watched Drammer walk away with his distinctive rolling gait, like a sailor looking for trouble on a night ashore. Oskar wanted to give him plenty of time to get ahead.

Once Drammer was safely out of sight, Oskar and Ferdie headed up Wizard Way. They stopped outside a small shop with the sign above reading: *Number Thirteen,* **Magykal** *Manuscriptorium and Spell Checkers Incorporated.*

"Have a nice day, Oskie," Ferdie said. And then she added, "I'm sorry."

"What for?" asked Oskar.

"Um. Well. I promised Lucy I'd help her today. With the Orm Pit. And I know how you feel about that place."

"Hey, Ferd, that's okay," Oskar said. "I know it has to be done. But the Ormlet's not going in there just yet."

Ferdie smiled. She hoped Oskar was right.

Acting more confident than he felt, Oskar gave Ferdie a cheery wave and pushed open the Manuscriptorium door with its distinctive *ping*. He walked jauntily through the front office, giving Foxy, who was on the desk, the PathFinder sign for "hello." Foxy returned the sign—a flat outward palm with splayed fingers held at a 45-degree tilt away from the body. Foxy smiled. He liked Oskar and his weird signs.

Oskar headed through the door in the screen that divided the front office from the actual Manuscriptorium and stepped into a high-ceilinged room where twenty-one desks were arranged in rows, each with a long, dangling light above it. This was where the scribes worked, copying spells, **Charms** and any other documents that were too **Magykal** or complicated to be printed. Oskar padded quietly around the edge, gathering murmured hellos as he went. Although he did not work upstairs with the scribes but helped out in the basement in the Conservation and Preservation department, Oskar was a popular member of the Manuscriptorium. He had made the Conservation department much more accessible by happily explaining what they did there and persuading its incumbent, the reclusive Ephaniah Grebe, to set up a course in making automata.

As Oskar headed around the dimly lit edge of the Manuscriptorium, someone laid a heavy hand on his arm. "Hey." Drammer Makken's voice came out of the gloom.

Oskar jumped. "What are *you* doing here?"

Drammer contrived to look hurt. "I hoped we might have walked back together, Oskie."

Oskar bridled. "Only my friends call me that."

Drammer steadfastly maintained his expression. "Well, I hope we are friends. Seeing as we're *workmates* for the next month."

Oskar's face fell. In a scheme set up to foster understanding between both institutions, Apprentices from the Wizard Tower now did a month's rotation in the Manuscriptorium, while every scribe did a month at the Wizard Tower.

Drammer looked pleased with the effect he was having. "Yeah, a whole *month* away from the Wizzer." "The Wizzer" was a new slang for the Wizard Tower, favored by the more senior Apprentices. Drammer, who hung out with many of his older brother's friends, used it whenever he could. He grinned at Oskar. "Of course I won't be spending much time with you backroom boys down in the basement."

"Ah." Oskar tried not to sound relieved.

"My skills are more suitable for the complexities of the Hermetic Chamber."

"Right." Oskar did not sound convinced. Beetle, the Chief Hermetic Scribe, was very picky about who he allowed into the innermost sanctum of the Manuscriptorium. "Gotta go," Oskar said, edging toward the basement stairs. "I'm a bit busy."

Drammer stepped in front of him. "Shame about the Ormlet," he said.

"Oh. Yes," Oskar muttered. He didn't want to talk about something he cared for so much with Drammer Makken.

"It's not going to like being put in prison," Drammer said.

"No."

Drammer pushed the point home. "It's so sad. Losing its last precious moments of freedom."

Oskar looked at Drammer closely. Was he mocking him?

Or was he genuine? "Yes, it is," Oskar agreed. "But it might not happen. I'm going to ask for the afternoon off and then I'll try to explain to Ormie—I mean the Ormlet—how important it is for her to behave."

"Think that will work?" asked Drammer in a voice that skirted the edges of scathing.

Oskar didn't, but he was not going to admit it. He shrugged. "It's worth a try."

"Yeah. But I've got a better idea. I can get you"—Drammer looked around and dropped his voice to a whisper—"some stuff."

"What stuff?" Oskar asked suspiciously.

"I was in the Wild Book Store yesterday. There are some **Charms** there that would do the trick. You know. Calm it down a bit." Drammer leaned close to Oskar in a confidential manner. "You know it's never going to give that circlet back, don't you?"

Oskar feared as much. But he was not going to give Drammer the satisfaction of agreeing.

Drammer continued in a low murmur. "We all know that the EOW only made a fuss to impress the Queen. But if *you* get the circlet back, you can give it to him, then he can give it to the Queen and she'll think he's wonderful and all the Ormlet trouble will be forgotten. Am I right or am I right?"

Oskar looked blank. He was trying to work out what an EOW was.

Drammer gave a heavy sigh to indicate that he was a paragon of patience dealing with a fool. "EOW? ExtraOrdinary Wizard? Septimus Heap? Got it now? Give him the circlet and all will be fine. Am I right or am I *right*?" Drammer folded his arms and looked very pleased with himself. "So, *Oskie*, I have the perfect solution: Languid Lizard **Charms**."

"What do you mean?" Oskar asked, despite himself.

"I can get you some if you want," Drammer said. "I've still got my pass. See?" Drammer showed Oskar his Wild Book Store pass—a clawed animal foot on a blue rope. Only one pass was available at any time, but it was not exactly sought after. No one chose to go into the Wild Book Store more than once. Except, it seemed, Drammer Makken.

Oskar did not trust Drammer, but the offer of the **Charms** was too tempting. Deep down he knew that merely talking to the Ormlet would do nothing. "All right, then," he said reluctantly. And then, because it felt rude not to, he added, "Thanks."

"Any time, kiddo. Any time at all," Drammer said with a smirk.

Drammer headed back to the front office with Oskar in tow. As they came in, Foxy looked up. He smiled at Oskar. "Back again?" he said.

"I've got the pass for the Wilds," Drammer said, using the Manuscriptorium slang, much to Foxy's obvious annoyance. "And Oskar wants something in there. Can I take him in?"

"No, you can't," Foxy told him curtly. "You've not done your safety certificate yet." Foxy would have offered to take Oskar in himself, but that would have meant leaving Drammer Makken in charge of the front office. And, after what Beetle had called "serious office protocol malfunctions," the Chief was insistent that only senior scribes staffed the desk. Besides, Foxy thought, he didn't trust the Makken kid as far as he could throw him—and that was not far at all: Drammer was a heavy, square-set boy and Foxy a thin, somewhat weedy young man.

Drammer gave Oskar a sharp nudge in the ribs. "Um," said Oskar. "Please, Foxy. Drammer promised to . . . um . . . look something up for me."

"Look up what, exactly?" Foxy asked suspiciously.

"Lizards," Drammer said. "Something about how their tails drop off. For the Ormlet project. Eh, Oskie?"

Oskar nodded. He felt really bad about lying, especially to Foxy. But then he thought of the Ormlet bound for its prison and he knew he had to do it.

Foxy knew about Oskar's fascination with lizards and that he was building an automaton Orm with Ephaniah Grebe. "Okay, I'll take you in," he said, a little reluctantly. "Wait there and I'll get someone to take over the desk." With that Foxy hurried into the Manuscriptorium to find a senior scribe.

To Oskar's dismay, Drammer sprang into action. He pressed the key into a claw-shaped depression in the door. It swung open, and from inside the Wild Book Store came a musty smell and a feral rustle that put Oskar in mind of creatures fighting in undergrowth. And then Drammer was inside and the door shut. Oskar watched both the door to the Manuscriptorium and that to the Wild Book Store nervously. He wasn't sure who he wanted to appear first—Drammer or Foxy.

It was Drammer. No more than thirty seconds later, Drammer was back in the front office, hastily brushing off some small black feathers stuck in his hair. "Blasted

Pteragon," he muttered. "It was guarding the Lizard Section. But I got the stuff. Want to see?" With that Drammer was out of the front door and into the open, with Oskar following on his heels.

Ten seconds later Foxy returned. "Oh!" he said to his companion, a senior scribe named Romilly. "They've gone. That's most unlike Oskar. He's usually so considerate."

Romilly picked a small black feather off the desk. "Hmm," she said. "He is. Unlike that Drammer boy . . ."

"Who is bad news," Foxy finished.

Romilly regarded the feather quizzically. "If I were you, Foxy, I'd put a second lock on the Wild Book Store."

"Yeah, so would I," Foxy said. He grinned at Romilly. "So, seeing as I *am* me, I will do just that. Right now."

LANGUID LIZARDS

At five o'clock the next morning, in the Junior Girls' Apprentice Dorm of the Wizard Tower, a small, highly irritable **Alarm** bug jumped off its perch and landed with a soft thump on Tod's pillow. The bug proceeded to emit a loud

buzz while jumping up and down and flashing a bright blue
light that lit up the tented curtains surrounding Tod's bed.
Blearily, Tod opened her eyes and found herself staring into
the unblinking pinpoint brilliance of the bug's single eye. She
shot out a hand and trapped the bug beneath her fingers. As
soon at it was safely enclosed, it switched off its light and lay
in Tod's hand, pulsing just enough to let Tod know that it was
still on duty. Tod yawned and sat up. She felt along the shelf
at the back of her bed for the **Alarm** box, shoved the bug into
it and snapped the lid closed.

Five minutes later, dressed in her green Apprentice tunic
and leggings, Tod was heading out of the Junior Apprentice
Dormitory along the corridor to the silver spiral stairs, which
were turning slowly on nighttime mode. They took her down
through the gently shimmering ceiling showing the constel-
lations of the night sky to the Great Hall below, which Tod
was relieved to find was empty. She stepped off the spiral stairs
and glanced down at the floor. GOOD MORNING, APPRENTICE, it
said. YOU'RE UP EARLY. Tod always felt slightly unsettled by the
floor, which made comments that seemed kind of nosy. She
hurried over its soft, sandlike surface hoping that it wouldn't
make any remarks later to Septimus about her being up so

early—Tod was pretty sure that Septimus would not approve of her mission that morning. In fact, Tod was not sure that she herself approved. But she had been unable to resist Oskar's plea for help. And besides, she saw no harm in what they were about to do. No harm at all. She just didn't want anyone to know about it.

With these uneasy thoughts in her mind, Tod headed for the tall silver doors, the tops of which disappeared into the misty blue nighttime light of the Great Hall. Tod loved the predawn atmosphere of the Wizard Tower, its purposeful soft hum of sleeping **Magyk**, the lingering scent of the previous day's spells combined with the musty scent of dead-of-night forays into the **Darke** that Septimus occasionally allowed the Senior Apprentices.

Tod murmured the password and the doors swung slowly open. The crisp early-morning air blew in and swept the guilty feelings right out of her head. It was, she could tell, going to be another beautiful day. Stuffing her hands into the pockets of her thick wool jacket, Tod hurried down the wide, white marble steps and headed into the courtyard. She took the long way around the base of the Wizard Tower to look at progress on the Orm Pit. This was the place where the Ormlet would, if Septimus had his way, be taken this very afternoon, never to fly free in the summer sky again.

Tod stopped in front of a sheet of wood nailed over the Orm Pit entrance on which was painted *Keep Out*. Beside it was a pile of rubble, on top of which lay an upturned wheelbarrow, an empty milk bottle and a pair of boots. On the other side of the notice was a large stack of bricks and the locked shed that contained the builders' tools and, more important, their tea-making equipment. It did not look to her as though Oskar had anything to be concerned about. It seemed impossible that the Orm Pit was going to be finished any time soon. But Tod had promised to help Oskar, and help him she would.

Tod completed her circle of the broad base of the Wizard Tower and hurried across the courtyard to the Great Arch. When she reached the cool lapis interior of the arch she turned, as she always did, to look up at the Wizard Tower. It still gave her a strange mixture of awe and happiness. This morning the Wizard Tower looked particularly striking. The great buttresses that supported the building glowed deep silver as they reared up to the crowning golden pyramid. The shape of the tower reminded Tod of the ancient PathFinder drawings of ships that had flown to the stars, which she had once glimpsed in a secret drawer in her father's room. She wondered if that was why she loved the Wizard Tower so much—because it felt like shared history.

Tod gazed up at the pattern of tiny purple windows with shifting **Magykal** screens. A few lazy loops of blue and green **Magykal** lights—known as **Sprites**—came slowly dropping down; she felt the popping of **Magyk** on her upturned face and watched as a green **Sprite** landed at her feet. Mesmerized, she picked it up. She watched it slowly fade until there was nothing left but the warm prickly buzz of **Magyk** on her palm. Tod smiled. This morning she really felt the power of the Wizard Tower, a repository of so many thousands of years of **Magyk**. She thought of the huge block of lapis lazuli on which it stood, concentrating the **Magyk**, increasing it, driving it, and she shivered. Sometimes the place almost overwhelmed her. She shook herself out of her daze and hurried away—she mustn't be late for Oskar.

Tod strode purposefully out through the Great Arch and into the deserted wide avenue of Wizard Way, which stretched away in front of her. Lit by matching pairs of silver torch posts, Wizard Way was quietly beautiful in the morning twilight. As the tinny chimes of the Drapers Yard Clock drifted over the rooftops, Tod counted five and broke into a jog. She could already see a small figure leaning against the doorway of the Manuscriptorium.

"You're late," hissed Oskar, stepping from the shadows. "I was about to go without you."

"Sorry, Oskie," Tod whispered. "It always takes longer to get out of the Wizard Tower than I expect."

Oskar could never be cross with Tod for long. "It's okay. I'm glad you're here."

They walked rapidly down the Way, hurrying from one pool of torchlight to the next. "So what's this stuff you've got, Oskie?" Tod asked.

Oskar took a brown paper bag from his pocket and gave it to Tod. She stopped beneath a torch post, gingerly opened the bag and peered in. It was full of delicate blue balls like little sparkling sugar sweets. "They're Languid Lizard **Charms**," Oskar said proudly. "From the Wild Book Store."

"The Wild Book Store?" Tod said. "I didn't know you were allowed in there."

Oskar looked shifty. "Er, well, it wasn't me who went in, actually."

Tod caught Oskar's expression. "So who did?" she asked.

"Um," said Oskar. "Well. It was Drammer Makken."

Tod nearly dropped the bag. *"Drammer?"*

"He was very helpful," Oskar said defensively. "He seemed to really care about the Ormlet."

"Seemed," Tod said scornfully.

"No, I think he did. He mentioned Ormie first, not me. And the Wild Book Store is a scary place. There were horrible growls when he went in, and a Pteragon tried to bite him. Drammer's not so bad, you know."

"You be careful of him, Oskie. I don't trust him."

"Oh, he's over all that *Wiz* stuff," Oskar said, referring to the sled race that Drammer had lost his chance to run. "He said seeing as you never finished anyway, it didn't bother him."

"Huh," was Tod's response.

"I know," Oskar said sympathetically. "It bugs me that I didn't finish either. But there's always next year."

Tod grinned. "Yeah, we're going to win next year, Oskie." She peered again into the little paper bag. "These are lovely. They feel kind of . . . calm. Gentle."

"Yeah. They were in a book called *Draxx*."

"Septimus has a *Draxx* too," Tod said. "But there aren't any **Charms** in it."

"There weren't any in ours either," Oskar said, "until this one was discovered. Apparently one of the dinosaur books had eaten it ages ago. And then the dinosaur book died and fell apart and the *Draxx* dropped out—complete with **Charms**."

"That is so weird," Tod said.

Oskar smiled. "It is. That's why I like it at the Manu-scriptorium."

Tod and Oskar walked companionably down Wizard Way, chatting about the Castle. They were both still new to the place and enjoyed swapping notes, but Oskar's conversation always came back to the Ormlet. "I so hope this works," he said. "I just want to get it right for Ormie."

"Its name is *not* Ormie, Oskie," Tod said.

"It's Ormie to me, whatever anyone says. So there."

At the end of Wizard Way, they crossed over to a tall fence of iron railings that enclosed some woods. Tod opened a gate and led the way into a dark footpath that ran through the narrow strip of woodland bordering the Palace gardens. The path was overhung by trees and had an uneasy atmosphere due to the fact that it was a regular haunt for members of the Wendron Witch coven, who were keeping watch on the Palace. Tod could feel remnants of the witchy presence and it made her nervous.

The path took them down to the riverbank and then along to the Palace Landing Stage where blazing torches lit the stone quay. They stopped and looked out at the mist hovering over the sluggish waters of the river and listened to the quiet peeping of the river birds searching the mud for worms.

"It's going to be a beautiful day," Oskar whispered. "You can tell by the mist. It's already evaporating off the surface. And I so want Ormie to enjoy it. She's not got long now before . . . well, *you know.*"

You know referred to the next stage of the Ormlet's development: Stasis. According to *Orm Fancier's Factoids*—a short version of which had recently been printed for the public and was generally referred to as the *OFF*—Stasis was a state of coma. It would occur toward the end of the first six months of the Ormlet's life, which the *OFF* called the larval stage. Once in Stasis, a cocoon would form around the young Orm. About one hundred hours later the cocoon would explode, and a small, fragile, hollow tube with a ferocious cutting tool at one end would emerge and immediately burrow down into the earth. From that moment on, it would eat its way through rock, turning it to lapis lazuli. Why it did this, the *OFF* had no idea.

Tod and Oskar walked on toward a very tall hedge, dark and dense. Beyond this lay the Dragon Field, where the Ormlet resided with its Imprinted Orm-Mother, Septimus's dragon, Spit Fyre. They opened the gate and followed the path to what was known as the Dragon Kennel—a long, tall, stone building with a line of windows just below the roofline, set high enough for a dragon to look out of. Nervously they approached a ramp leading up to a set of battered double doors, secured with a broad iron bar. Above was a sign painted in green and outlined in gold: *Dragon Kennel*, beneath which *Orm Nursery* had been added. From within came the unmistakable sound of a sleeping dragon: long, slow breaths like the wind sighing in the treetops.

Tod and Oskar skirted the ramp and headed for a small door in the side of the Dragon Kennel. Oskar took off his rucksack. "I've got her a chicken," he said. "She loves chicken."

Tod was touched by Oskar's devotion to the Ormlet, but she didn't share it. The Ormlet's very existence had nearly led to the loss of her home village and the death of her father. And now its presence in the Castle had caused a rift between two people of whom Tod was extremely fond: Septimus and the previous ExtraOrdinary Wizard, Marcia Overstrand.

Septimus had been diplomatic about their differences, but Tod knew he and Marcia had fallen out over the consequences of putting the Ormlet beneath the Wizard Tower. After a particularly angry exchange with Septimus ten days ago, Marcia had walked out and had not been seen since—and the cause of all the strife and unhappiness was the snappy, spiteful little Ormlet that Oskar unaccountably loved. Tod's thoughts were rudely interrupted by a cold roast chicken hurtling toward her. She caught it, protesting. "Oh, *yuck*, Oskie."

"Hang on to it while I get the **Charms** out," Oskar said. "I'm going to put them into the chicken like stuffing. Ormie's going to *love* it."

Tod held the chicken and felt the crackle of **Magyk** as Oskar poured a stream of sparkling blue balls into it. "That's a lot of **Charms**," she said. "Are you sure you need so many? Oops, that one missed."

Tod picked up the tiny **Charm** and held it between her finger and thumb, feeling the buzz of **Magyk** zipping through her hand. "Can I keep it?" she asked.

Oskar peered into the chicken. It was almost overflowing with the **Charms**. He nodded. "I reckon we've got plenty here. Drammer says you need one for each pound of weight and there were fifty-five. Fifty-four is easily okay."

Tod bit back a comment about Drammer saying whatever suited him and put the **Charm** into the pocket of her Apprentice belt.

"Time for Ormie's breakfast," Oskar said jauntily. "Do you suppose she's awake yet?"

As if in answer a tremendous thud came from inside the Dragon Kennel.

"Well, someone is," Tod said.

"All set?" Oskar said a little anxiously.

"Yep," Tod replied. "In we go."

THE DRAGON KENNEL

Tod switched her **FlashLight** to red—a color considered soothing for reptiles. Oskar pushed open the door and he and Tod slipped inside. The Dragon Kennel was dark, musty and full of dragon. Tod and Oskar stood knee-deep in straw, staring at the serrated shape of Spit Fyre's back, a glowing black in the red light. Spit Fyre's mouth watered; he adored roast chicken. He raised his head and his brilliant green eye ringed with a circle of red regarded the bringers of the feast. Spit Fyre took in the familiar forms of the two young humans who had been with him at the hatching of the Ormlet and had helped to save it from the clutches of a particularly nasty sorcerer. They were always welcome. Especially when they brought roast chicken.

"Hello, Spit Fyre," Tod whispered.

Spit Fyre practiced a recently acquired skill—he winked.

"We've come to see Ormie," Oskar added. "I've got a chicken for her."

Spit Fyre suppressed a sigh. His baby must come first, even with chicken. Resigned, he laid his head back down on the straw and closed his eyes.

Tod peered into the gloom, looking for the Ormlet. Suddenly her FlashLight caught a glimpse of gold. She crept forward and saw the blue of the Ormlet curled up against the pale whiteness of Spit Fyre's stomach. Wedged at a jauntily crooked angle upon its flat head was Jenna's golden circlet. "Oskie," she whispered. "It's here."

Oskar remembered Barney Pot's toes and felt suddenly nervous. The Ormlet had a tendency to snap. And when it snapped it did damage, for the Orm had a line of sharp, curved bone in its mouth like a solid row of teeth, which acted like a guillotine. Holding the roast chicken out in front of him like a shield, Oskar crept around the bulge of Spit Fyre's belly and, taking care to hold the chicken upright so that the Languid Lizard **Charms** stayed inside, he nervously waved the bird beneath the flared nostrils of the sleeping Ormlet. It opened one brilliant blue eye and looked at him. "Hello, Ormie," Oskar whispered.

The Ormlet had mixed feelings associated with Oskar Sarn. Oskar had been present at its hatching but so had a lot of humans, and one of them had pulled its tail off. The Ormlet was pretty sure that wasn't Oskar, but an Orm always knows where its tail is, and the Ormlet knew that Oskar had it. That did not please the Ormlet at all, despite the fact it had grown a perfect new tail. However, the Ormlet also knew that its Orm-Mother (Spit Fyre) had saved Oskar from a fatal fall, and it suspected that if it tried to eat Oskar, its mother would be angry. And the Ormlet did not want that.

Oskar looked into the clear blue eye of the Ormlet. He was aware that something was going on inside its flat little brain, but luckily he was unaware that he was treading a narrow line between friend and food.

It was the roast chicken that decided the Ormlet. Food did not bring more food. Therefore Oskar was friend. And so very delicately, the Ormlet took the chicken between its prehensile lips, threw it up into the air, opened its mouth so it gaped like a snake's, and the chicken—along with its cargo of fifty-four Languid Lizard **Charms**—disappeared into oblivion.

The Ormlet licked its lips and awaited chicken number two: Barney Pot always fed it three. The Ormlet had reached its counting-to-three milestone only a few days ago and it was enjoying its newfound skill. It opened its mouth for Oskar to pop the next chicken in.

Oskar gazed back at the Orm happily. It looked so sweet, he thought. Like a little baby bird.

Tod thought otherwise. In her opinion the Orm looked dangerously hungry. "Oskar," she hissed urgently, "*we need to get out of here.*"

"Okay," Oskar said. "I'll just get the circlet." He reached out to lift it from the Ormlet's head only for Tod to grab his arm—hard.

"Ouch," Oskar protested. "What are you doing?"

"Oskie, *don't*. It'll bite."

"No, it won't. It's eaten all the **Charms** now."

"Eaten them, yes, but not digested them."

Oskar turned around. "It needs to *digest* them? Don't they work at once? You know, like **Magyk**?"

"No, Oskie, they don't," Tod said. "Edible **Charms** have to be digested. Didn't Drammer tell you that?"

"No," Oskar replied grumpily. "He didn't mention that. At all." He broke off as something wet and rasping touched his hand. "Oh look, Ormie's trying to lick me . . . Oh! Hey! *Get off!*"

The Ormlet had grown tired of waiting for chicken number two and had decided to eat Oskar's hand, which smelled quite chickeny. Oskar managed to snatch his hand away but the Ormlet snapped at his sleeve, pulling Oskar toward it, then it put a clawed foot on Oskar's stomach and began to shake Oskar's arm violently.

"Tod!" Oskar cried in dismay.

Tod seized Oskar's jacket and pulled him back. In reply, the Ormlet tugged him forward. Spit Fyre, used to the Ormlet's wrigglings, paid no attention. The Ormlet had come to the conclusion that Oskar was food—he was the chicken-number-two substitute and the other human was the chicken-number-three substitute. The Ormlet licked its lips, opened its mouth, and a spurt of saliva shot into the air.

Oskar, who had read everything possible about Orms, knew exactly what that meant. "Help!" he yelled. *"Help!"*

In one deft movement, Tod spun Oskar around, pulling him out of his jacket, and propelled him toward the side door. As a disappointed Ormlet munched on the jacket and the packet of FrootLumps left in the pocket, Tod pushed Oskar out into the fresh air and slammed the door behind them.

"Thanks, Tod," Oskar said, pale and trembling.

"I don't know what you see in that creature," Tod said. "It would be much better for everyone if it was locked up safely beneath the Wizard Tower."

But Oskar loved the Ormlet no matter what. "Better for everyone," he said, "except Ormie."

PART
~ IV ~

PART

IV

A LETTER

Tod *slipped back into the* Wizard Tower and was relieved to see that no one was around. She went off to the canteen to find some breakfast.

Some twenty floors above, Septimus Heap was sitting at his writing desk in his study. Septimus was not a great letter writer, but there was one letter he could put off no longer. He selected his favorite pen—one that Marcia had given him on his induction as ExtraOrdinary Wizard—and, with a twinge of regret about his last irritable words to the giver of the pen, he began the final copy of many attempts. It read:

The Wizard Tower
The Castle
From the desk of the ExtraOrdinary Wizard, Septimus Heap
By the hand of Benhira-Benhara Grula-Grula

Dear Princess Driffa,

I hope you are well.

I had hoped to be able to bring you your precious Orm Egg as I promised to do, but unfortunately, due to circumstances beyond my control, the Egg has hatched. However, all is not lost. We managed to get to the Egg for the very moment of hatching and my dragon, Spit Fyre, Imprinted it. We now have the baby Orm residing at the Castle, and I hope soon to place it beneath the Wizard Tower for the benefit of us all.

I sincerely hope that in the fullness of time, this Orm will lay another Egg, which I will be able to bring you and once more your beautiful Chamber of the Great Orm will be complete.

Septimus paused and reread the letter. It seemed rather stilted, but he was unused to writing to princesses, especially attractive yet haughty ones. He sat for some minutes staring out of the window, and then picked up his pen and added:

I wonder if you would like to visit the former occupant of your Egg? It is healthy and growing fast and I am sure would prove interesting for you to see. I would be happy to escort you through the Ways to our Wizard Tower, where we do have some very pleasant guest accommodations.

Septimus broke off and thought of the ratty little guest room at the end of the Apprentice corridor. That would not do for a princess. He must do something about that at once. He picked up the pen again.

You would be most welcome. Please send your reply by the hand of the deliverer of this letter, and I will meet you at your convenience.

With very best wishes,

Septimus Heap, EOW

Septimus reread the letter and sighed. It wasn't witty, it wasn't amusing and it didn't even sound like he had written it, but it was the best he could do. He folded it into three, sealed it with the ExtraOrdinary Wizard Seal and took it down to the Great Hall.

A bowl of oatmeal in one hand and a mug of hot cinnamon milk in the other, Tod was heading across the canteen toward Rose, who was sitting at a corner table near a noisy group of Senior Apprentices, members of the notorious Knights of Knee gang.

Rose tucked her long brown plait over her shoulder and

smiled up at Tod. "Hey, Tod," she said. "Come and join me."

"Hey." Tod faltered, aware of being stared at.

"Hay?" one of the Knights of Knee mimicked in a high voice.

"Neigh . . . neigh . . ." another whinnied, to the great amusement of the rest of the gang.

Rose wheeled around and eyeballed them. "Stop that right now," she said.

One of the gang snorted like a horse.

"Newt Makken," Rose said. "I *Name* you."

Tod felt very awkward. If a Wizard Named an Apprentice they had to make themselves available for cleanup duties in the evening—and that evening Tod knew there was a party at the old Infirmary. She guessed the Knights of Knee had been planning to go.

"Oh, come *on*," Newt protested. "What did I do?"

"You know what you did," Rose said. "You were intimidating someone younger than yourself."

"That is *not* fair," Newt whined.

"Most definitely *unfair* . . . *unfairly* unfair, in fact," his friends joined in.

"Oh, I'm so sorry," Rose said. Tod saw a triumphant smirk

pass between Newt and his friends—until Rose proceeded to Name the rest of the gang sitting at the table. "There," Rose said, "now that is perfectly fair."

Aware of the angry silence from the neighboring table, Tod ate her oatmeal with little pleasure. She gulped down her drink and then she and Rose got up and left, Tod uncomfortably aware of the gimlet stares from the Knights of Knee following them. Outside the canteen she said, "Rose, can I ask you something, please?"

Rose smiled. "Of course you can. What do you want to know?"

"It's about some **Charms**. From *Draxx*."

Rose looked puzzled. "But there aren't any **Charms** in *Draxx*."

"There were some in the Manuscriptorium's copy," Tod said, hoping that she wasn't giving away Oskar's secret.

Rose frowned. "Are you sure? It's not on our shared inventory."

"I think they just found them," Tod said.

"The Manuscriptorium should have told me," Rose said. "We are meant to share our **Charm** inventories. I shall be having a word with their Chief about this."

"Oh, but I'm sure they *will* tell you," Tod said, feeling bad.

"Hmm." Rose seemed unconvinced. "So, what did you want to know about these **Charms**? They're old reptile ones, I imagine?"

"I've got one . . . look . . ." Tod began to open the pocket in her Apprentice belt but Rose stopped her.

"Not here." Rose glanced back to see the Knights of Knee wandering gloomily out of the canteen. "Why don't you come up to the **Charm** Chamber? It's more private."

Halfway up the spiral stairs the priority signal—an insistent beep—sounded. This alert was for a change in direction—the ExtraOrdinary Wizard was on his way down. Tod and Rose stepped off and waited. A few minutes later they saw the distinctive purple hem of robes of the ExtraOrdinary Wizard. Rose looked awkward, Tod thought, as Septimus revolved down toward them. He caught sight of his Apprentice and smiled. "Good Morning, Tod," he said, his voice changing as the stairs took him around, and then as he revolved back, a more strained "Hello, Rose."

"Hello, Septimus," Rose replied.

"Sorry to override the stairs," Septimus said. "I was happy to wait, but you know the stairs have a mind of their own."

"That's okay," Rose said.

"Oh . . . good," Septimus said. "I'm just, um, posting a letter."

"Fine," Rose said.

Septimus glanced down a little guiltily at the letter he was carrying. "Tod, I was hoping you might be free, actually."

"Oh!" Tod said.

Septimus had now traveled past them and was disappearing down to the floor below. Rose gave Tod a little push. "You should go," she said. "The ExtraOrdinary Wizard takes priority."

"Not always, Rose," Septimus's voice drifted up toward them. "As you well know."

Rose sighed. She gave Tod a rueful smile and said, "Come and see me when you can. I'm in the **Charm** Chamber all day."

And so Tod found herself heading back down to the Great Hall, with an uncomfortable feeling that there was more to the Languid Lizard **Charms** than Oskar realized. And a good deal more to Rose and Septimus, too.

GRULA GAMES

Septimus was waiting at the foot of the stairs. "I'd like you to help Lucy Heap today," he told Tod. "It's a tight schedule to get the Orm Pit ready for this afternoon and Lucy needs a runner."

Tod did not look enthusiastic and Septimus mistook her expression.

"Tod," he said, "you must not pay too much attention to what Marcia says about the risks of having the Ormlet here. She worries too much. And I believe she is, on this occasion, wrong."

"But the Ormlet might not have to come here yet. It might give the circlet back," Tod said.

"And pigs might fly," Septimus said, laughing. "And loop the loop with the Ormlet."

Tod resigned herself to a day of being bossed around by Lucy Heap. "But can I see the Grula first? *Please?*" she asked. Benhira-Benhara Grula-Grula was a skilled **ShapeShifter**. He had a fine repertoire of guises and enjoyed playing to his audience. Most mornings the Grula-Grula appeared in a different **Shape**, and Tod loved to see him.

Septimus smiled. "All right, stay and see what Ben's doing today. But after that it's straight off to Lucy."

On the other side of the hall was a newly painted, shiny orange door. This had until recently been the entrance to the Stranger Chamber—a holding pen for undesirables who had found their way into the Wizard Tower. It now sported a large brass knocker and a sign declaring it to be: *The Residence of Benhira-Benhara Grula-Grula.* Suddenly three Senior Apprentices—Newt and two friends—came hurtling toward it. Newt slammed the doorknocker and another yelled through the keyhole, "Wakey wakey, Fuzzball!" then fell laughing against the door.

Septimus was across the Great Hall like a missile. "*What,*" he demanded, "do you think you are doing?"

Tod was pleased to see Newt go white with shock. "Ner-nothing," he stammered. "I . . . er . . ."

"I will not have this kind of—" The orange door began to open; Septimus stopped midsentence and turned as pale as Newt. Newt shrieked and fell into a faint. His two accomplices turned and ran. Someone behind Tod screamed. Septimus swore. Tod put her hands over her face.

Dripping with slime, a ten-foot-tall, matte black human skeleton with a tusked head of a beast stood in the doorway, surveying those trembling before it. Tod peered through her fingers with a mixture of horror and fascination. It looked terrifying, but oddly it didn't feel **Darke**. Tod lowered her hands and looked at Septimus, wondering what he was going to do.

Like Tod, Septimus could feel no **Darkenesse** in the manifestation of what he knew to be a Kraan: something extremely dangerous for Wizards, particularly young ones. Despite being almost certain that the Kraan was actually Benhira-Benhara Grula-Grula performing an angry **ShapeShift**, Septimus had learned not to take things at face value. The Wizard Tower was a strange place, and it was not unknown for truly **Darke** beings to manifest themselves within its walls. Somewhat anxiously, Septimus recalled the subject of another of his disagreements with Marcia—the **Darke Magyk** tutorials for final year Apprentices that he held on floor eighteen. The thought crossed his mind that maybe Marcia was right about the perils of "inviting the **Darke**," as she put it. But whether this was real or not, Septimus knew he must show no weakness. If this was a real Kraan, it would be fatal. And if it wasn't, which he sincerely hoped was the case, it would do his reputation no good. Taking care not to be within arm's length of the beast—he knew that one touch of a Kraan would kill—Septimus stepped forward and looked up at its face. He breathed a sigh of relief. Not only did the creature have merely two eyes—rather than the standard Kraan complement of six—but they were undoubtedly Grula-Grula pink rather than Kraan red.

"Benhira-Benhara, I request that you **Shift** your **Shape** immediately," Septimus said, trying to keep the annoyance from his voice. He did not succeed and the Grula-Grula became distressed. Its **Shape** began to drip copious amounts of black slime, to which the floor responded with the words, FOUL! FOUL! FOUL! spreading out from the slime like shrieks of disgust and encircling Septimus's feet. The floor then added: GET IT OUT OF HERE, EXTRAORDINARY WIZARD. THE SLIME IS SOAK-ING INTO MY BITS.

Septimus took a deep breath and said in the most pleas-ant tone he could muster, "Dear Benhira-Benhara, I pray you become your beautiful Grula self once more."

This was more acceptable. A tint of orange began to creep across the darkness of the Kraan skeleton and its outlines became fuzzy. Within thirty seconds the comforting sight of a ten-foot-tall triangle of orange fur stood in its place. From within the fur two little arms emerged; they reached up to the Grula-Grula's head and two slender hands parted the fur to reveal a shiny, pink, flat face. The little mouth smiled at Septimus. "Good morning, ExtraOrdinary Wizard," came a surprisingly high-pitched voice.

"Good morning, Benhira-Benhara Grula-Grula," Septimus replied, a little snappily. "I would be grateful if you would keep the **Darke ShapeShifts** for outside this place. Perhaps for Hallowseeth in the Port. But not here, please."

"I apologize." The Grula-Grula sounded crestfallen. "I was alarmed by the assault upon my door. It is our default **Shape**, you know. When we are distressed."

"I understand," Septimus said. "And I in turn apologize for the rude behavior of our Apprentices. I am so sorry you have been distressed by their actions."

The Grula-Grula bowed. "And I am desolated to have distressed *you*, ExtraOrdinary Wizard. Pray, how may I make amends?"

Septimus fished the precious letter out of his pocket. "Well, seeing as you have asked, Benhira-Benhara, I would be most grateful if you would take a letter to the Eastern SnowPlains for me."

Tod—who was enjoying watching Newt Makken's friends unceremoniously dragging him away by his feet—suddenly paid attention. Why was Septimus sending a letter to the Eastern SnowPlains? She soon found out.

"It is for Princess Driffa," Septimus said. "Would you be able to deliver it to the Snow Palace? I realize that is a little out of your way."

The Grula-Grula was anxious to get back into Septimus's good books. He loved being at the Wizard Tower. After years of drifting around the Ancient Ways, trying to find somewhere he belonged, he had—after a false start in a shop selling cloaks—found in the Castle a place where people liked him and sought his company. The Grula-Grula loved being invited to parties and asked out to lunch; he basked in the smiles and friendly greetings that came his way when he sat in the Great Hall of the Wizard Tower and watched the world go by. He had at last found a home, and he dreaded being asked to leave. And so he said, "It will be my pleasure to deliver this personally to Snow Princess Driffa, the Most High and Bountiful."

Dismayed, Septimus looked down at the plain *Princess Driffa* that he had written on the front of the sealed letter. He had totally forgotten about Driffa's numerous honorifics—and her insistence upon their use. But there was no way he could face rewriting the letter. It would have to go as it was. Septimus placed the letter on the Grula-Grula's delicate pink upturned palm with a heavy heart. He no longer expected a reply.

The Grula-Grula stuffed the letter deep into his fur and then he turned to Tod and bowed. "Miss Alice," he said. "Greetings, PathFinder."

Tod smiled. The Grula-Grula was—apart from her guardian, Dr. Dandra Draa—the only person who called her Alice without annoying her. "Good morning, Benhira-Benhara," she replied, and bowed in return.

"Miss Alice, I would be most honored if you would accompany me upon my journey," Benhira-Benhara said. "It is always a delight to travel the Ways with a PathFinder."

But Tod's hopes of avoiding a day as Lucy Heap's runner were soon dashed.

"Benhira-Benhara, I thank you," Septimus quickly replied. "You honor my Apprentice with your generous offer, but I regret that I must decline on her behalf. She has essential **Magykal** work to do today and I cannot possibly spare her. Perhaps another time?"

The Grula-Grula bowed. "Indeed, ExtraOrdinary, another time. I shall look forward to it immensely. But I trust you will spare Miss Alice to accompany me to the arch and wish me well?"

"With pleasure, Benhira-Benhara," Septimus replied. As

Tod and the Grula-Grula walked out of the Wizard Tower, Septimus called out, "Homework tonight, Tod—read up about Kraan."

"Kraan?" asked Tod.

Septimus smiled. "You'll see why," he said, and then added, "Have a nice day."

Tod thought that was unlikely. Together she and the Grula-Grula went down the wide white marble steps. They made a strange couple, a ten-foot-tall triangle of orange fur accompanying a small human in green, half its size. At the foot of the steps, they took a sharp left turn and walked back to the base of the Wizard Tower. Here, where most people would have a cupboard under the stairs, the Wizard Tower had a Hidden arch—its very own entrance to the Ancient Ways. This one connected directly with the Keep, where Marcia Overstrand, ex–ExtraOrdinary Wizard, now lived. Unlike most people, both Tod and the Grula-Grula could see within the white marble the shadowy shape of the arch, with the number *VII* inscribed upon its keystone. The Grula-Grula stretched out his arm, and at the touch of his little pink palm the arch began to glow. Tod looked at it wistfully. With the choke of dust in the air and the sound of hammering from behind the Tower, she imagined traveling the Ways home and spending the day out at sea, fishing with her father. The thought was almost too much to bear, but Tod told herself sternly that she was an Apprentice now, and her job was to be at the Wizard Tower and learn **Magyk**. Besides, soon enough she would be going home for her birthday and the MidSummer Circle.

The Grula-Grula gave a farewell bow. Tod returned it and stepped back. She watched the triangle of orange fur step into the arch and move smoothly toward an enticing white mist. With a sense of awe Tod saw the Grula-Grula blend into the mist, and then he was gone. The glow faded from the arch beneath the steps, and it resumed its shadowy form.

Tod walked slowly around to the back of the Wizard Tower, where she was greeted by Lucy Heap with a clipboard directing operations. "Ah, Tod!" Lucy said. "You're just in time. We need essential supplies." She handed Tod a list:

10 packets of Squashed Fly biscuits
10 Nut Bomb bars
2 boxes of tea
1 bottle of milk
4 bags of sugar

"Thanks, Tod," Lucy said. "That should keep them going for the morning. And when you come back you can help with mixing the mortar."

Great, thought Tod gloomily, as she went out through the back gate and headed off to the Castle General Stores. *Mixing mortar. Just great.*

SERPENT'S SNOOK

Kicking a pebble as she went, Tod walked slowly along Serpent's Snook, the winding alley that led to the Castle Stores. The alley did not raise her spirits. It was dark and smelled of cat pee. Thoughts of the sun, boats and fresh sea breezes began to torment Tod yet again, and she was very nearly tempted to turn around, run through Arch VII and go home. If she hadn't found a small, green ball made of scuffed leather bouncing along the alley in an oddly purposeful manner, she might well have done so.

It was the sound that Tod had first noticed: a gentle *bing-bing-bing*, as the sound of its bounces echoed off the alleyway's high brick walls. Tod fell into step beside the ball, fascinated by its slow but determined onward motion. She put her hand out to touch the ball as it came up from a bounce, and a twinge of **Darke Magyk** sent a tingle through her fingers. She dropped back a little, but was not deterred. She had never found anything obviously **Magykal** outside the Wizard Tower—and she had never seen anything like the green ball inside the Wizard Tower either. This was something special.

Some five minutes later the ball and Tod rounded the last bend of Serpent's Snook. The alley opened out into Snook's Nook, a square bounded by small workshops on three sides and on the fourth the high walls of the most populated area of the Castle: the Ramblings. Set into the base of the walls was a line of five vaulted caverns from which the Castle Stores traded. Above the vaults, the walls of the Ramblings rose up, dotted with myriad windows, balconies and lines of washing stuck precariously out on sticks. Tod had spent a whole day on a tour of the Ramblings and had only seen a small part of it. It was a massive warren of a place, full of winding corridors, tiny courtyards, wells, shops, theaters, a hospital, workshops and schools. Thousands of people lived there in a variety of rooms, apartments and rooftop houses—and most of them did their grocery shopping at the Castle Stores.

As the ball bounced merrily into Snook's Nook, Tod considered what to do. She could keep following the ball, or she could get Lucy's shopping. Lucy's shopping lost: it did not stand a chance against the mystery of the little green ball. Tod focused all her attention on the ball. It had now sped up and was moving in short, quick bounces so she had to break into a trot to keep up. It bounced rapidly across the front of the Castle Stores, past the store backboard, the vegetable display, the bread stall, and then with a dramatic spin to the left it headed into the stores. Tod was after it in seconds, but she was too late. The ball was nowhere to be seen.

It was dark inside and busy with shoppers. Tod pushed her way through, keeping her eyes to the ground, determined to catch up with what she now thought of as *her* ball. It was so easy to lose a ball in a shop, she thought. It could have bounced into someone's bag, it could be hiding in a dark and dusty corner—there were plenty of those to choose from—or maybe, Tod thought as she checked out a display of limes, it might just be resting somewhere it would not be noticed. She was on the verge of giving up the search and actually getting Lucy's shopping when a piercing scream rang out and she heard a familiar voice yell, "Argh! Get it off! *Get it off me!*"

Tod pushed her way through the shoppers and headed toward the back of the store where the yells were coming from. There she found exactly whom she had expected—Marissa. But she also found something she had not expected—the little green ball.

The ball was bouncing on the spot beside Marissa, seeming to Tod to be excited to have found a long-lost friend. Marissa clearly did not feel the same way. Shrieking, "Get off me! Get *off!*" she was flailing her arms, trying to bat the ball away, but with no success. Nimbly avoiding every swipe and yet bouncing in tight enough circles to prevent Marissa from moving, the ball reminded Tod of a sheepdog she had recently watched in the Farmlands, corralling a lost sheep and keeping it penned in until the farmer came to collect it.

Tod began to hear muttering from nearby customers— "Witch" . . . "Witch" . . . "Witch"—and people began to move away. Soon Marissa was alone in an empty space—apart from Tod, the ball and a bundle of candles that Marissa had dropped, which were now rolling across the floor.

A large woman wearing a brown shopkeeper's coat and a grubby apron pushed her way through the onlookers. She stood, arms folded and angry, taking in the scene: her precious candles scattered across the floor, a known witch causing trouble, along with the ExtraOrdinary Apprentice—who should know better—messing around with a ball. Picking the smaller of the problem customers, she stormed up to Tod and said, "No ball games are allowed inside the stores. Take your ball and leave, Apprentice."

"But it's not my ball," Tod protested.

"Oh, 'it's not my ball,' 'it's not my fault,' 'it's not my dog's poop,'—I've heard it all before," the shopkeeper snapped. And then, to Tod's amazement, she stuck out her brawny arm, and in a catch worthy of the star of the Castle catch team, the shopkeeper plucked the ball out of the air. Her broad fingers closed around it and within her grasp the ball lay still and content at last. It had **Tracked** its quarry and now it had been caught: all was well. All was complete.

"Apprentice, do you want your ball or not?" the shopkeeper demanded.

"Oh! Well, yes. Yes, please. I do want it," Tod stammered.

"And what's the magic word?" the shopkeeper demanded.

Tod tried to think of a **Magykal** word to do with shops that the woman might want to know, but her mind was blank. "Um . . ." she said. "I . . ." And then Tod realized. "Please," she said. "Please could I have the ball?"

The shopkeeper handed it over. Tod took the ball, which

felt surprisingly hot, and held it tightly, afraid that it might decide to jump out of her grip. "Thank you," she said, smiling broadly. "Thank you very much."

"That's all right," the shopkeeper replied, mollified. "You run along now and I'll get rid of the nasty witch who took your ball." But there was no witch to get rid of. Marissa had gone, and so had three bundles of candles from a nearby display.

Tod dutifully bought Lucy's shopping and lugged it all the way back to the building site. The ball sat quietly at the bottom of the Castle Stores bag, weighed down by packets of biscuits and sugar. Tod smiled as she walked. Finding the little green ball had transformed her day. She no longer minded how many cups of tea she had to make or how much mortar she had to mix. She didn't know what the ball was or where it had come from, but she didn't care. Despite its little twinge of **Darke**, it already felt like a friend.

An Ormnap

The sun was setting when at last the Orm Pit was finished. All that could be seen of weeks of laborious tunneling down through the lapis lazuli was a neat iron grille covering a circular hole at the foot of the Wizard Tower. There had been no need for it to be circular, Septimus had pointed out, as the mature Orm would never come up through it. But Lucy had been adamant; a structure must respect those who lived within, she had told Septimus sternly. Also, Lucy had said, the empty circle would act as a reminder of what the mature Orm would be doing deep beneath the ground. This had given Septimus an uneasy feeling.

But now all was done. While Tod swept up the last of the blue dust, Lucy Heap paid the builders. Then she thanked Tod for her help and wearily went home to her Simon, hoping that she might find him a little better. But she did not.

Half an hour later, darkness was falling and Tod and Septimus were walking down Wizard Way, heading for the Dragon Kennel and the nervously awaited Orm test. Tod at last got a chance to show the little green ball to Septimus.

"It's a **Tracker** ball," he said, throwing it from one hand to another. "It's not nearly as **Darke** as most of them, I am pleased to say. And it is **UnNamed** too. Where did you get it from?"

Tod told Septimus about her meeting with Marissa in the Castle Stores.

"The ball stayed with her, you say?"

"Yes," said Tod. "It kept bouncing up and down, like it was keeping her in one place."

"It sounds like a simple **Track**," Septimus said. "Leading its Master—or Mistress—to its quarry. But there was no one following it?"

Tod shook her head. "No. We were there for at least five minutes and no one turned up. Then the shopkeeper took the ball and Marissa ran away."

"So, did it touch Marissa?"

"Yes, it kept bouncing up at her and hitting her. She kept batting it away, but it wouldn't stop."

"Until it was caught. It sounds to me like the shopkeeper unwittingly ended the **Track**," Septimus said.

"So, if I let it go now, would it still go after Marissa?" Tod asked.

"Only if you **Re-Instruct** it."

"*Me?*"

Septimus smiled. "Well, it looks like it belongs to you now. Finders keepers—isn't that what they say about **Tracker** balls?"

"Is it?"

They had reached the entrance to the Palace gardens
when Septimus said, "We've not had any **Tracker** balls in the
Wizard Tower—apart from one Marcia confiscated from my
brother Simon."

"Lucy's Simon?" Tod asked.

"The very same," Septimus said. "Simon has a bit of a
Darke history, believe it or not. The thing with **Tracker** balls
is that they are often used without consent of the person who
is being **Tracked**. They are covert **Magyk**, and that's an area
that tends toward the **Darke**."

"Does that mean I can't keep it in the Wizard Tower?" Tod
asked anxiously.

"Not at all," Septimus said. "We must not be afraid of the
Darke. I believe we should learn to understand it. I'll give you
a **Safe** to keep it in just in case, though."

They walked down to the riverbank and across the Palace
Landing stage, which was lit with torches sending flames high
into the still night air, and headed for the tall dense hedge that
separated the Dragon Field from the Palace gardens. Septimus
pushed open the gate and walked in. He stopped so suddenly
that Tod trod on his cloak.

"Oh . . . *rats!*" Septimus exclaimed.

Tod squeezed past Septimus to see what was wrong. She gasped: something had exploded inside the Dragon Kennel. The roof was gone, and what was left of it was lying strewn across the grass. Oskar and Ferdie were hurtling toward them, and behind them came Barney Pot, running somewhat awkwardly.

"Ormie . . ." Oskar gasped as he reached them. "Ormie's *gone!*"

Barney reached them, breathless. "They took the Ormlet . . ." He puffed. "Put it in a sack . . . massive bang . . . roof went flying . . . so did Mr. Spit Fyre."

"*Who* took the Ormlet?" Septimus asked.

"Witches," Barney said. "They always come at twilight, don't they?" He looked over both shoulders and then spat upon the ground—the old way of keeping away harm when a witch's name is said. "It was Bryony and Madron. I know them."

Tod knew them too. Bryony and Madron were the Wendron Witch Mother's assistants. Only a few months ago they had tried to throw Oskar and Ferdie onto a fire.

"Witches!" Septimus was shocked.

"Yes," said Barney. "I saw them running out of the field

with a sack. And I knew at once what they had in there. You can't mistake a bright blue tail sticking out of a sack. I tried to catch up with them but, well, what with my toes—or rather, *not* with my toes—I'm not very fast at the moment. So before I can do anything, they take off in a boat with some kind of Enchanted *thing* pushing it." Barney Pot shook his head. "I dunno. I never seen anything like *that*."

"Like what?" Septimus asked.

"Some kind of creature stuck to the back of the boat. It made a nasty noise and was pushing the boat along faster than you would have thought possible. They were gone in a flash. Down the river, around Raven's Rock and that was it."

Septimus shook his head. "I don't understand," he said. "Why didn't Spit Fyre stop them?"

"It was awful," Barney said. "He was flat out on the straw. Head lolling, eyes wide-open. Couldn't get a spark out of him . . ." Barney's voice broke and he paused to collect himself. "I thought he was dead. But it was some kind of witchy Enchantment. It lasted just long enough for them to get away. He woke up all of a sudden, sent me flying with his tail, and then that was it. Smashed his head through the roof like a fist through rice paper. Then his wings went up and he was gone, up like a star rocket." Barney pointed up to the sky.

"That's my dragon," Septimus said proudly. "But how witches got the Ormlet into a sack I cannot imagine."

Barney looked embarrassed. "Well, ExtraOrdinary, the thing is, the Ormlet's been very quiet today. To be honest, I was glad of the break after all the trouble yesterday, but this afternoon I began to get a bit concerned, like. So I looked in and it was fast asleep and Mr. Spit Fyre was licking it. He was being quite rough with it, like he was trying to wake it up. Didn't seem right somehow." Barney Pot shook his head.

Tod, Oskar and Ferdie exchanged guilty glances. Tod wondered if she should tell Septimus about their morning expedition, but it felt like tattling on Oskar.

Barney was still in full flow. "What I think is that those witches came in the morning twilight and fed the Ormlet something dodgy. It wouldn't be difficult; it eats anything." Barney sighed. "As I know all too well."

"So why didn't they take it this morning?" Septimus wondered.

Barney had worked it out. "Well, you see, they couldn't do an **Enchantment**; it wouldn't last long enough. No one would want to be stuck with an Ormlet in a boat and find it was suddenly wide awake. So they fed it something in the morning twilight and came back for it in the evening twilight." Barney shook his head. "It was strong stuff they gave it, that's for sure."

Oskar gave a loud sigh of despair.

"I'm so sorry, Oskar," Septimus said kindly. "I know how much you loved the Ormlet."

"It's all my fault, I—" Oskar began, but Septimus stopped him.

"Of course it isn't your fault," he said briskly. "In fact, it isn't *anyone's* fault the Ormlet's fallen asleep. Not even the witches."

"How do you make that out, then?" asked Barney, puzzled.

"Barney," Septimus said, "you remember how I said that you only had to put up with the Ormlet until it went into Stasis?"

"Yes, I do," Barney said. "And I can't say I wasn't looking forward to it going off to Stasis. And hoping it wasn't too near here if I'm honest."

Septimus looked puzzled, but he carried on. "Well, I believe that has happened a little early, that's all."

Barney looked even more puzzled than Septimus.

"Right . . ." he said. "So why, if you don't mind me asking, did you get those witches to take it? I would have happily taken it there for you." Barney sounded hurt.

"Taken it where?" asked Septimus.

"To the Stasis place. Wherever it is."

At last Septimus understood. "Stasis isn't a place, Barney. It's a state of being. It's what happens to the Ormlet when it is about to change into an adult. It spends a few days in Stasis, then it forms a cocoon and then it explodes."

Barney looked shocked. "*Explodes?*"

"Apparently," Septimus said.

"Well, you might have told me," Barney said huffily. "If I'm being asked to look after a reptile that's going to explode, I think it is only fair and reasonable to be told."

Septimus felt he was losing grip of the situation. An apology seemed the quickest way out of it. "I'm really sorry, Barney. I should have told you. I see that now."

Barney was mollified, but not much.

"We have to get the Ormlet back quickly," Septimus said. "It will be spinning its cocoon *right now*. Barney, did you see which direction Spit Fyre went?"

Barney pointed downriver. "Forest," he replied a little curtly.

"The Forest," Septimus muttered. "Of course. Where else would the witches go? We'll get straight back to the Wizard Tower. I hope we can see Spit Fyre from the LookOut. Then I'm going out to find him and get our Orm back. I will *not* have those witches messing us about any more."

"Couldn't my **Tracker** ball find the Ormlet?" Tod asked.

"In theory, yes, but in practice, no. You would need something belonging to the Ormlet to wrap it in it for . . . hmm, I think it's thirteen minutes." Septimus turned to Barney. "Do you have anything belonging to the Ormlet? Or anything it touched?"

"Nothing," Barney said grumpily. "It was a greedy little reptile. It ate most of the stuff it touched."

Suddenly Oskar spoke. "I do! I've got its tail!" Thrilled to be able to do something truly helpful at last, Oskar could hardly contain his excitement. "I'll bring it to the Wizard Tower, shall I?" Then, turning to Ferdie, he said, "Hey, Ferd, come and help me. It's really heavy."

Back at the Wizard Tower, Septimus went straight up to the **LookOut**, leaving Tod sitting outside on the steps to wait for her friends. A few minutes later Tod saw Oskar and Ferdie struggling through the Great Arch carrying a long parcel wrapped in brown paper. She ran to meet them and helped carry the surprisingly heavy tail.

"I put the wrong stuffing in," Oskar said, breathless. "Which is why it weighs a ton."

They plonked the tail down on the visitors' bench. By the time Oskar had unwrapped it, Septimus was back from the LookOut. "Spit Fyre's hovering over the Forest," he said. "About three miles away over one of the densest parts. We're going to need this Tracker ball, so let's get it working." He turned to Tod. "First, you'll need to give it a name so that when it Tracks it will allow you to follow it, and also so that it will come when you call."

"You could call it something nice, like Ormie-Finder," Oskar suggested.

"Don't be daft, Oskie," Tod said. She remembered the sound that had made her first notice the ball. "I'll call it Bing."

"Bing!" Oskar scoffed. "And you call *me* daft."

"Bing it is," Septimus said. He handed her a piece of paper. "This is the Naming Incantation. Take the ball in both hands and say this. Here, I'll hold the paper for you."

And so by the Grula-Grula's orange door, to the great interest of a few passing Wizards, Tod read the words:

Finders: keepers, Losers: weepers.
Tracker *ball: never sleepers,*
Tracker *ball: softly creepers,*
Tracker *ball, I **Name** you "Bing!"*

They curled the tail around Bing and Oskar tied it with the string from the parcel to make sure it stayed put. Then they sat beside Bing and the tail and watched the second hand on the huge clock above the doors sweep slowly around thirteen times. It seemed to take forever.

As the hand began its fourteenth sweep, Septimus stood up. "Good, you can unwrap it now, Tod." He turned to Oskar and Ferdie. "I assume it is no use me trying to stop you coming on the Ormlet **Track**?"

Oskar and Ferdie shook their heads.

"I thought not. Now, as you three know all too well, the Forest is a dangerous place. We will need some protection. Tod, would you go and fetch my brothers Edd and Erik, please?"

Tod hurried away, keeping a tight hold on Bing. She could feel the ball buzzing with excitement, almost as much as she was at the prospect of her very first **Track**.

PART
V

WOLVERINE WAYS

Tod *found Edd and Erik* Heap a little intimidating. A certain feral self-sufficiency—a hangover from the years they had spent as teens living in the Forest and adopting the Forest ways—was always with them. And so it was with a feeling of nervousness that she knocked on the door of their shared rooms on the third floor of the Wizard Tower. After some time, just as Tod was wondering whether it would be rude to knock again, the door was flung open. It was all she could do not to scream. Confronting her was a large wolverine standing on two legs, its eyes flashing a bright yellow.

"Oh!" said the wolverine, sounding surprised. "We thought you were Foxy. What do you want, Tod?"

"Um . . . I'm sorry. It's really important."

Another wolverine joined the first. "What is it?" it growled.

"Dunno," said the first.

Tod took a deep breath and said, "I have a message from Septimus. He needs you to come to the Forest with him. It's urgent. I'm sorry to interrupt the party stuff."

The wolverines looked at each other, and then one of them wrenched off its head to reveal Edd Heap. Edd had long straw-colored hair like Septimus's and his eyes shone a friendly green. Tod found Edd the easier of the twins to talk to. "You look really scary," she ventured.

"Good," Edd said with a smile. "So what's up in the Forest then?"

The words came tumbling out in a rush. "It's the Ormlet. The witches have taken it but Spit Fyre's found it and Septimus wants to go and get it and we can **Track** it with my **Tracker** ball called Bing and we have to go right now!"

"Crumbs," said Edd.

The other wolverine pulled off its head to reveal the short-haired Erik. "We're not getting out of these suits," Erik said. "They took ages to get on."

"No need," Edd said. "They're ideal Forest dress."

Septimus knew better than to react when two giant wolverines joined them in the Great Hall. He always made a point of being unflustered with the twins, particularly Erik. Besides, he reckoned the wolverine costumes might turn out to be an advantage in the Forest at night.

Not wishing to draw attention to themselves, the party set off through the quieter alleyways, heading for the North Gate, the main entrance to the Castle. This was a large gatehouse that guarded the drawbridge and where Gringe, the gatekeeper, and his wife, Mrs. Gringe, lived.

The drawbridge was lowered at sunrise and raised at sunset. By the time the wolverine party arrived, the bridge was up, the Bridge Boy had gone home and Gringe was settling down beside a cheery fire for his nightly supper of stew. He was not pleased to hear insistent knocking on his front door. He was even less pleased when he learned that his callers required him to lower the drawbridge and that one of them was no less than the ExtraOrdinary Wizard, whose requests Gringe was duty-bound to grant. However, this did not stop Gringe from making things difficult.

"The Bridge Boy's gone 'ome," Gringe growled. "I can't be doing this on my own at my age. Come back tomorrow." He began to close the door but Septimus stopped it with his foot.

"You are obliged by your terms of employment to operate the drawbridge whenever I require it," Septimus told Gringe. "And I require it *now*." Septimus fixed Gringe with what he hoped was a steely stare.

Gringe—who still thought of Septimus as the annoying Apprentice kid who used to play chicken on the bridge—was not happy. "It'll cost you," he said.

Septimus was ready: he knew he had to pay for out-of-hours bridge use. He held out a heavy shining silver coin—a crown, no less—and Gringe's eyes widened. He hadn't seen one of those for a long time. Mrs. Gringe would be thrilled. She might even heat up his stew again if he asked nicely.

Fifteen minutes later the drawbridge was down and Gringe was hot, sweaty and out of breath. "You . . . staying out all . . . night?" he asked. "Or are you . . . comin' back?"

"We're coming back," Septimus told him.

Gringe sighed. "An' I suppose you'll want the bridge down again?"

"You suppose correctly," Septimus assured him.

Gringe shook his head. He'd found the last ExtraOrdinary Wizard difficult at times, but she was nothing like this one. This one was crazy. What did he think he was doing, taking three kids and two of his daft brothers dressed like wolverines into the Forest at night?

As soon as they reached the far side of the Moat, Gringe wearily began the work of raising the bridge. At last he staggered into the gatehouse and slumped down in his chair by the fire. He was not impressed by Mrs. Gringe's comment that he'd catch his breath better if he'd only stop swearing for a few minutes. He had, he told her, a lot to swear about. And for once Mrs. Gringe did not disagree.

ILL MET BY TORCHLIGHT

Tod heard the clanking of the drawbridge chains and glanced back. She saw the massive bridge slowly rising into the air, leaving the bare bank of the dark Moat behind. It was an impressive sight, but not a comfortable one. The sight of their way back into the safety of the Castle disappearing gave her a bad feeling.

Sandwiched between the two wolverine Heaps, Tod, Oskar, Ferdie and Septimus walked swiftly along the winding path that led through the outlying trees, heading toward the dense darkness beyond. Tod noticed that the twins had adopted a loping gait that suited their costumes well—possibly a little too well. It seemed to her as though the Heap twins were transforming into actual Forest wolverines. Tod slipped between Oskar and Ferdie and linked arms; it was good to keep your friends close in the Forest.

Soon the moonlight was gone and densely packed, tall trees lined their narrow path. When Tod looked up she saw nothing but a thick canopy of leaves, and when she looked ahead she saw darkness. She felt as though the Forest was engulfing them. The **Tracker** ball began to push impatiently against her grip as if to remind her why she was there. "Shall I let Bing go now?" she asked Septimus.

"Bing is a **Tracker** ball," Septimus hastened to assure his brothers.

"Yeah," said Edd with a grin. "So we heard."

"Won't be easy following that in the nighttime Forest," Erik added.

"I know," Septimus said. "But we can do it. Okay, Tod, time to—"

Edd interrupted him. "Wait a moment, Sep. There is something I want to say to our three young ones here. From now on we must practice what is known as Forest Mindfulness. With every step we take, we will think of ourselves as part of the Forest. We will plant our feet with care, understanding that we tread upon many tiny, living creatures and being aware that we walk through the territory of much larger ones. We will respect the trees and wish them well, but remember that as we go deeper into the Forest, not all trees will wish us well. Do you understand?"

Tod, Ferdie and Oskar nodded solemnly. Edd's words had given them a sense of awe, which took the edge off the fear they had been feeling.

"Thank you, Edd," Septimus whispered. He switched on his Forest FlashLight. A dull red beam lit up their immediate surroundings but did not spread far. It would allow them to see where they were going without alerting the nighttime inhabitants. "Okay, Tod," Septimus said. "It's time to release Bing."

Tod took Bing out of her pocket, cradled it in her hands and whispered, "Track." She let the ball go and, unlike its behavior with the Captain of the Guard, it bounced on the spot, waiting for Tod to follow—because Tod had Named it, the ball considered her to be part of the Track. Bing set off at a low, slow bounce, regulating its pace so that Tod was easily able to keep up with it, keeping to paths that she could follow.

Bing took them slowly up into the less-explored northern plateau of the Forest. They walked silently with Tod and Edd in the lead, then Septimus, Oskar and Ferdie, with Erik at the back. Both of the Forest Heaps were on the alert, their eyes flicking from side to side, forever on guard.

They now began to hear shouting and see glimpses of the red glow of flames through the trees.

"Witch fire," Edd muttered.

They were nearing a blind bend in the path when suddenly, hurtling around it came a cloaked figure carrying a familiar flash of blue.

"Ormie!" Oskar gasped. "Oh! That's Ormie!"

It was also Marissa. Cloak flying, eyes flashing brilliant witch blue, she came thudding toward them with the Ormlet tucked under her arm.

Tod caught Bing on an upward bounce and shoved the **Tracker** ball deep into her pocket. Edd and Erik positioned themselves on the path, arms folded, an impenetrable wolverine barrier through which Marissa was not going to pass.

But there was no need. Marissa skidded to a halt in front of them. "Oh, thank goodness you've come," she said breathlessly. "Here's your Orm thingy. Septimus, take it. Quick!" She pushed past Edd and Erik and thrust the Ormlet into Septimus's arms. "Keep it safe. It needs to go under the Wizard Tower as soon as you can get it there."

Septimus was dumbstruck. He stood holding the limp Ormlet, unable to believe that Marissa had actually *given* it to him. Marissa was in no mood for explaining anything. She grabbed Septimus's arm and hissed, "Come on, Wiz, get a move on. There's a whole swarm of witches after it." She pointed back into the trees. The flames were coming closer and the shouts getting louder.

"I thought they were with *you*," Septimus said.

"No way, dumbo," Marissa said. "They are *chasing* me. So get a move on. Or do some wiz-bang spell or something to stop them. See ya!" Marissa darted into the shadows of the trees and was gone.

Septimus looked anxiously at the rapidly advancing flames. "We must get back to the Castle right now."

"But the drawbridge is up," Tod said.

"I know," Septimus said. "I'll do a **Transport** back and get

Gringe to start lowering it. Edd, Erik, can you find a safe way to get everyone down to the bridge?"

"No worries," said Edd and Erik together.

"Oskar—for you." Septimus thrust the Ormlet into Oskar's arms. Oskar was shocked at how heavy it was.

"Now *go*," Septimus said, looking anxiously back through the trees at the rapidly advancing flames.

Edd and Erik beckoned Tod, Oskar and Ferdie into the trees, leaving Septimus alone on the track. When Tod glanced back she saw Septimus enclosed in a haze of purple mist. She longed to hang back and watch the Transport, but a brusque *"Come on, Tod"* from Erik set her running to catch up. When she next looked around, Septimus was gone.

ON THE RUN

Oskar was struggling to keep up. The Ormlet was a dead weight. Its smooth blue scales were slippery; its wings were spiky yet delicate, and Oskar was afraid of damaging them. Its spiny legs swung awkwardly, hitting his knees as he hurried along.

Edd saw that Oskar was in trouble. "Hey, let me take it," he said.

"No, I can do it," Oskar insisted.

"No, you can't," Ferdie told Oskar sternly.

"I can!"

"Oskie," Ferdie hissed. "Give it to Edd."

"But—"

"Oskie, you are slowing us down. The witches will catch us and then *they'll* have the Ormlet. And it will be all *your fault*."

Sullenly Oskar handed the Ormlet to Edd, who slung the creature around his shoulders with ease. The Ormlet lay there like a shimmering blue stole.

"Whoooooo-*hoo!*" A wild, ululating whoop, high and piercing, shocked them all. The witches had left the path and were plunging into the undergrowth, following their trail, the flames of their torches sending up showers of sparks into the darkness.

Erik glanced back. "Too many to fight," he said, sounding a little regretful. Better do a rabbit run, yeah? There's one down there. By the three stones."

"I know," said Edd. "I found it, remember?" He turned to Tod, Oskar and Ferdie. "Okay, guys, this is how we disappear in the Forest. There are secret paths everywhere. The trick is to get into one without anyone seeing you. Once we're in it, keep dead quiet and follow me, got that?"

They followed Edd. He wove past a couple more trees and then, at three big round stones covered in moss, like a rabbit diving for its burrow, he plunged into the undergrowth.

Tod fought her way in after him. She fended off a barrage of sharp twigs and skidded down a slope to find a low corridor, clear of undergrowth, that ran beneath the bushes. Ferdie and Oskar, then Erik came tumbling after her. They set off silently following Edd, who stooped low as he loped along, carrying the Ormlet easily on his shoulders. Erik was last, watchful as ever.

As they hurried through the rabbit run, the whoops and shouts of the witches became ever louder. Soon it seemed to Tod that the witches were so close she only had to push her arm through the undergrowth and she would touch them. Edd stopped and turned, putting a finger to his lips. They all stood silent, hearts thumping, while, to their relief, the noise of the chase passed by.

They set off once more through the run with Edd keeping a fast pace along the twists and turns that took them around densely packed trees. Oskar felt as though they were traveling through the inside of a giant bracken snake and quite forgot his disappointment in not holding the Ormlet. He loved every moment of the rabbit run, and as he padded along he became determined to make one in his home forest, the Far.

The run finished on top of a small hill overlooking the Castle. They stumbled into the night air with burrs on their clothes and twigs in their hair, and stopped to take stock. Below, the lights of the Castle shone clear, but it was too dark to see whether the drawbridge had been lowered. They decided to take the track down and hope for the best. As they descended toward the flat grassy area beside the Moat, a movement above made them all look up.

"Spit Fyre!" Edd and Erik said together.

"He wants Ormie," Oskar said.

Edd shifted the dead weight that lay across his shoulders. "He's welcome to it," he growled. "It's like carrying a sack of dead fish."

Oskar didn't like the sound of that. "Ormie's not . . . *dead*, is she?" he whispered.

"The dog breath in my ear tells me not, Oskar," Edd replied.

Spit Fyre began to descend, but at the sounds of a

high-pitched whistle from Septimus in the Castle the dragon stopped. He hovered for some seconds, considering what to do—the Ormlet won. Spit Fyre dropped through the air and landed on the grass in front of them.

"Great," said Edd, "he can get us out of here. Come on, you guys."

They headed off fast toward Spit Fyre, loud whoops from the Forest spurring them on. Edd thrust the Ormlet at Spit Fyre, who reached out his great head and gently took the Ormlet in his mouth. Then, before anyone had a chance to clamber aboard, Spit Fyre raised his wings and brought them down with a great rush of air that knocked Oskar, hovering anxiously beside the Ormlet, off his feet. And then the dragon was gone, rising up and flying swiftly across the Moat. They watched his dark shape disappear over the North Gate.

"Maybe he's going to come back with Sep and get us?" Edd asked hopefully.

"And maybe he's not," Erik suggested. Loud shouts from the North Gate and a rumble of falling masonry stopped the discussion.

"Doesn't sound good," Edd said. "We'd better shift for ourselves."

As they hurried across the grass toward the Moat they
heard the welcome clanking of the drawbridge chains. They
ran fast, watching the massive shape of the drawbridge slowly
descending. They were halfway across the open grass when
there was a loud clang and the drawbridge juddered to a halt.

"It's stuck," Tod said.

Erik swore. From across the Moat the unmistakable voice
of Gringe echoed his sentiments.

"Bother," said the more restrained Edd. "What say, Erik?
Go for the bridge and hope it gets free?"

An ululating cry came from the Forest. "Yeah," said Erik
said. "Go for it."

All eyes upon the drawbridge, they raced across the open
space. They reached the resting plate—the long, flat stone on
which the end of the drawbridge should sit—and looked up.
As they stared at the dark underbelly of the bridge looming
high above, willing it to move, a great scream of triumph came
from the outskirts of the forest. All five wheeled around to
see the witches, torches ablaze, breaking out from the cover
of the trees.

"Sep! We need help!" Edd yelled across the Moat.

Septimus appeared in a gatehouse window. "Spit Fyre won't

leave the blasted Ormlet!" he yelled. "I'm getting a boat!"

"Too late for that," Erik muttered, watching witches advancing toward them.

The witches were silent now. They had formed a semicircle and were walking slowly and deliberately toward them. The flames of their torches burned bright in the still night air, and as they came nearer, Tod, Oskar and Ferdie heard something they never wanted to hear again—the Witch Hum.

There was a splash from the other side of the Moat and the sound of oars being hastily pushed into rowlocks along with some muttered curses. Tod glanced around to see Septimus struggling with a large rowboat, and she longed to show him how to do it properly. To the background of splashing and the sound of clanking and shouting from within the gatehouse, the witch semicircle advanced in step, their low, menacing Hum growing louder.

Edd, Erik, Tod, Oskar and Ferdie turned to face the advance, standing shoulder to shoulder. "Stare them out," Edd whispered.

"It spooks them," added Erik.

The witches stopped a few feet away, close enough for them to feel the heat of the flames. Bryony and Madron stepped forward. "Hand over the creature and we will do you no harm," said Bryony.

"We don't have it," Erik said steadily.

"As you see," Edd added.

"We see nothing," Bryony told him.

"Because you are hiding it," Madron said.

"If you do not hand it over," Bryony said icily, "we will take it from you."

"I am sure you would rather we did not do that," Madron added. "Because your dinky little suits of fur . . ." She giggled and Edd flushed. He realized he and Erik looked somewhat silly, and with an audience of young witches, he wished they didn't. But what Madron went on to say made looking silly seem a minor problem. ". . . will burn *beautifully*."

Edd and Erik exchanged anxious glances.

"We will count to seven," Bryony said.

"And then we will set fire to a whole *Heap* of fur," Madron finished.

Slowly, the witches began to count, "One . . . two . . . three . . . four . . . five . . . six . . . sev—"

Suddenly there was a flash of purple and Septimus was there, standing between his brothers and the flames, brandishing a long, shimmering sword with a rain of sparks flying from its tip. "You want to play with fire?" he yelled. "Then play with this!"

There were no takers. The witches threw down their torches in disgust. "That's not fair, Septimus Heap," Bryony told him. "We don't have any swords."

"You don't have any *conscience*," Septimus reposted. "Now shove off, the lot of you."

The witches shoved off.

Enclosed in a semicircle of abandoned burning torches like the footlights of a stage, the three Heap brothers and the Tribe of Three watched their audience straggle away into the night, throwing curses into the wind.

A sudden yell from the gatehouse brought them back to reality. "'Ware bridge, 'ware bridge!" And then, when they didn't leap out of the way fast enough, "Get out of the blasted way, you nurdles! The bloomin' bridge is comin' down! Fast!"

A rapid rattling of chains ensued, there was a loud splash, and Edd slipped and fell into the Moat.

PATCHOULI

Spit Fyre was waiting for them in the Wizard Tower courtyard. The dragon was unusually subdued. He sat, head bowed,
with the Ormlet lying limp across his two front feet. Septimus
stopped a respectful distance away. "Hey, Spit Fyre," he said
gently.

Spit Fyre put his head on one side and snorted like an
uncertain horse. Septimus took a step back. He resented how
the Ormlet had come between him and his dragon, but he told
himself that it was ridiculous to be jealous of a small reptile
that was going to explode in a few days time. He also told
himself that had it not been for the Ormlet, Spit Fyre would
probably still be away on his search for a mate; it was the
Ormlet that had brought Spit Fyre home. And so, with a more
generous feeling he said, "Spit Fyre, your Ormlet is about to
TransfOrm. It's time for you to say good-bye."

Spit Fyre would not meet Septimus's eye. Septimus sighed—
he knew that meant trouble. He decided to try to explain.
"Spit Fyre, your Ormlet has gone into Stasis and—"

Suddenly Oskar was at his side. "But Ormie *hasn't* gone into Stasis," Oskar burst out. "I *know* she hasn't. Please, please don't put her away. She'll be better soon."

"Oskar," Septimus said gently, "you mustn't grieve. This is the Ormlet's natural way of being."

Tod put her arm around Oskar. "Hey, Oskie," she said. "It's okay."

"It's not okay!" Oskar shouted. "And it's not Stasis. *It's not!*"

Septimus looked Oskar in the eye. "Oskar, why are you so sure? Do you know something we don't?"

Tod said nothing. It was for Oskar to say—or not.

Oskar could not bring himself to tell Septimus what he'd done. It sounded so wrong. And stupid. And nasty. And besides, he told himself, the Charms were part of the Manuscriptorium's stock and so he would be breaking the Manuscriptorium Promise. Oskar stared at his feet and said nothing.

Septimus knew Oskar was hiding something and he did not like being lied to. "Oskar, the Ormlet is going into the Orm Pit, and that is final," he said. "If it upsets you I suggest you go home now. I'm sure they'll wonder where you are at the Manuscriptorium."

Oskar stared at Septimus in dismay. The Manuscriptorium

was not home—home was his PathFinder village. And right now that was the only place he wanted to be. He'd failed the Ormlet, he'd lied to Septimus and he'd helped Drammer Makken do something bad. He's messed up all his chances. It was time to go.

"Okay," Oskar said quietly. "I'll go home." He shook away Tod's comforting arm and then, to Septimus's surprise—but not Tod's or Ferdie's—Oskar did not turn around to walk back to the Manuscriptorium. Instead he ran past Spit Fyre to the base of the Wizard Tower where it joined the white marble steps, took a sharp left and disappeared into the white marble.

"Oskie!" Ferdie yelled, and raced after her twin.

Tod listened to the sound of her friends' retreating footsteps and then the silence as they stepped into the **Vanishing Point** and were gone. It was so strange, Tod thought, that right now they were both already hundreds of miles away, in Marcia's Hub—the first of many on their way back home. Tod turned around to look at the courtyard; she saw a shower of brilliant blue **Sprites** drifting down and smiled. She was sad that Oskar and Ferdie had gone, but there was no way she wanted to run after them. She was in a **Magykal** place—and there was an Ormlet to attend to.

*   *   *

"Hey! Sep!" A shout came from beneath the Great Arch and suddenly there was Marissa, running across the courtyard, her green cloak flying behind her. She looked, Septimus thought, wild in a rather interesting way. As she scooted to a halt in front of him, trying to catch her breath, Septimus sternly told himself that Marissa was trouble. "What do you want?" he snapped.

Marissa looked surprised. "What's got your goat?" she said.

"It's more a question of what got his Orm," said Edd.

Marissa bestowed a smiley giggle upon Edd. She turned back to Septimus and her expression darkened. "Septimus Heap. I risked my *life* to get that Orm away from Bryony's crew and bring the revolting little creature to you. Do I get any thanks? No. Not one little *Oh, thank you, Marissa, for saving our Orm and bringing it back to us.* Not one. Well, Septimus, that is the last time I ever do anything to help you out. *Ever.*" With that she spun around and began to stalk out of the courtyard. But not too fast, because she wanted to be within earshot when Septimus called her back, as she knew he would.

"Marissa!" Septimus yelled. "Wait a minute!"

Marissa walked five more steps just to keep him guessing and then turned around. "*What?*" she demanded. She folded her arms and did not move. If Septimus wanted to apologize, he could come to her. Which he did.

Septimus was pretty sure now that Marissa would soon be Witch Mother of the Wendron Witches and he had no wish to fall out with her. Life was so much easier if the Wendrons were, if not actively on the Castle's side, then at least not plotting against it. So Septimus hurried over and said, "Marissa, I'm sorry. This Orm has been nothing but trouble right from the start. And we have to get it under the Wizard Tower fast—now, before it explodes."

"Explodes?" Marissa sounded horrified.

"Well, first it makes a cocoon, then it explodes and out comes an Orm. Well, that's the idea, anyway."

"A proper Orm? One that makes lapis lazuli?" Marissa asked just to make sure.

"So we hope," Septimus said. "Which is why I have to get it safely into its reinforced pit beneath the Wizard Tower. Out of harm's way."

"I know you do," Marissa told him soothingly. "And this is where it must go. The Orm belongs here. I really feel that."

Marissa paused and placed her hand over her heart. "I *feel* it. Which is why, Septimus, I brought it back to you."

Septimus had a distinct feeling that, like Oskar, Marissa was not being entirely straight with him. He had noticed since becoming ExtraOrdinary Wizard that people did not always tell him the whole truth, but he had learned that there was little he could do about it. So he merely smiled and said, "Thank you, Marissa. Thank you very much indeed."

"You're welcome," Marissa said. "Just get that Ormlet of yours settled in its little nest under the dear old WT before anyone else tries to grab it, and then lock it in and keep it there."

"I intend to," Septimus assured her.

"Great. I hope it all goes well." Marissa gave Septimus a hug and nearly drowned him in the scent of patchouli. Then she hurried away through the lapis-blue shadows of the Great Arch, leaving Septimus feeling quite bemused. It was only after Marissa had disappeared that Septimus realized that he had never asked her if she had seen Jenna's circlet. He felt cross with himself for forgetting all about it, but the scent of patchouli had quite driven the circlet from his mind. Septimus comforted himself with the thought that even if Marissa did know anything about it, she wouldn't have told him.

Marissa ran across the brightly lit, almost-white limestone paving of Wizard Way and slipped into the welcome darkness of Sled Alley, where she stopped and looked furtively about her. When she was satisfied there was no one around, she fumbled deep into her secret pocket, which hung inside the lining of her cloak. She drew out a gleaming golden circlet and, holding it in two hands, she placed it almost reverently upon her head, as though crowning herself.

Then she walked slowly, regally even, down Sled Alley to the Manuscriptorium boathouse. Tied to the mooring post were four rowboats bobbing gently, waiting patiently to ferry partygoers across to the Infirmary. A few minutes later Marissa was rowing across the Moat, heading for the Infirmary bank.

In the East Gate Lookout Tower two rats were taking the night air. One—a tubby rat of advanced years named Stanley—was seated in a wheeled basket chair. The other, his adopted son, Morris, was perched on the battlements beside him. They had come to watch for shooting stars, one of Stanley's favorite pastimes.

While Stanley leaned back in his chair, gazing up at the sky, Morris's attention was on more earthly matters. "Look, Da, Queen Jenna's going off to that party," he said.

Stanley peered into the night. He saw the rowboat, the rower wearing a witch's cloak and the glint of gold around dark hair. He shook his head sorrowfully. Royalty was not what it used to be, that was for sure.

INTO THE ORM PIT

Septimus walked slowly back to Spit Fyre, steeling himself for what he had to do. He approached carefully, while Spit Fyre kept an oblique, suspicious eye upon him, watching his every step. A few feet away from his dragon, Septimus stopped. He felt that any closer would intrude into Spit Fyre's personal space. The last thing he needed was to spook Spit Fyre and send him rocketing away into the night with the Ormlet.

Septimus and Spit Fyre looked studiedly past each other, each waiting for the other to make the next move. This might have continued for some time had it not been for a brilliant blue **Magykal Sprite** that drifted down and landed softly upon the Ormlet. It sat on the Ormlet's pointy snout for some seconds, infusing the creature with a soft, **Magykal** light, and then it slowly faded away.

Spit Fyre looked up and at last, he allowed Septimus to meet his gaze. A flash of **Synchronicity** passed between them and Septimus knew that Spit Fyre understood what must happen to his Ormlet.

Septimus kneeled down beside his dragon and took the Ormlet from its bed on Spit Fyre's scaly feet. Then with the Ormlet lying heavy in his arms, he walked over to his Apprentice. "Tod," he said, "would you come with me into the Orm Pit?"

It was a solemn procession that made its way around the base of the Wizard Tower—Tod, Septimus with the unconscious Ormlet, and behind them a slow, sad dragon. Behind the dragon came two giant wolverines: Edd and Erik, still on guard.

At the dark circle of the gaping mouth that was soon to swallow Spit Fyre's baby, Septimus stopped. He turned to his dragon and held the Ormlet out for a last good-bye. Spit Fyre nuzzled the Ormlet and then shuffled back, his head bowed.

It was time to go.

Tod opened the grille and stepped inside. She took out her FlashLight and its cool blue light showed how beautifully the tunnel was made—smooth bricks laid to create an almost perfect circle, apart from a narrow strip of limestone for the floor shining white like a backbone.

Septimus squeezed in and the tunnel was suddenly full. He was too tall to stand upright and was forced to hunch down over the Ormlet. "Okay," he said, "let's go."

The tunnel dropped steeply downward and wound around in a very tight curve, its coils reflecting what the Ormlet would soon become—an empty rock-transforming worm. After seven turns the brick walls gave way to lapis lazuli and Tod knew that they were now burrowing through the bedrock of the Wizard Tower. Down, down, down she went, her boots throwing a tinny echo as she walked ever deeper into the chill of the rock. Tod had lost count of the turns when the tunnel leveled out and showed a smaller dark circle ahead.

"This is it," Septimus said, his voice hissing along the tunnel like a snake. "The entrance to the Orm Pit."

The Orm Pit was tiny—an egg-shaped chamber carved to

fit what was still, when curled up, an egg-shaped reptile.

"Do you mind going in?" Septimus asked. "I don't think I'll fit."

Tod wasn't at all keen, but she didn't think that Septimus would fit either. And even if he did squeeze in, she doubted he would be able to get out again. So she rolled her FlashLight into the Orm Pit and crawled in after it. Then she shuffled around to face Septimus and he passed her the Ormlet. Tod took its dead weight in her arms and very carefully she laid it upon the bare lapis lazuli. The FlashLight threw misshapen shadows of the Ormlet up to the curving roof, turning it into a spiny, spiked demon. Tod shivered. She wanted to get out as soon as possible.

Septimus stuck his head through the entrance, his face made eerie by the shadows cast by the FlashLight.

"Tod," he whispered, "I didn't want to say this in front of Spit Fyre, but I think the Ormlet has died."

"No!" Tod was horrified.

"It's not breathing. But it's best to put it here, just in case."

Tod was speechless. *She and Oskar had killed the Ormlet.*

"Anyway, I'll just say good-bye . . . for Spit Fyre," Septimus whispered. He reached in and laid his hand on the chubby shape of the reptile, smooth and ice-cold to his touch. "Rest in peace," he murmured, then he looked at Tod and smiled. "Thank you," he said. "I couldn't have done this without you."

Tears in her eyes, Tod shook her head. *You wouldn't have had to do this at all without me*, she thought.

They emerged into the chill of a cloudless night. Tod watched miserably while Septimus walked over to his waiting dragon and patted him gently on his velvety snout. Then she accompanied Septimus around the base of the Wizard Tower, unable to stop thinking of the little blue body of the Ormlet, once so vibrant, now lying cold and dulled in the darkness deep below. She sniffed and rubbed the tears from her eyes and Septimus silently passed her his handkerchief.

As they headed toward the **Hidden** arch beneath the steps, Septimus said, "I thought you might have wanted to go after Oskar and Ferdie."

"No," Tod said. "I want to stay here. I'm your Apprentice now." *But not a good one*, she thought.

"And I'm very glad you are," Septimus said. He saw Tod's troubled expression. "I know it's sad about the Ormlet, but what really matters is that Oraton-Marr doesn't have it."

Tod said nothing. She thought that if Oraton-Marr had

kept the Ormlet at least it would still be alive.

As they drew level with the Hidden arch it began to glow with a bright purple light. Tod and Septimus exchanged glances. Someone was Coming Through. But who?

PART
VI

PART

V

SNOWSTORM

Snow Princess Driffa, *the Most* High and Bountiful—and the most exceedingly furious—came storming out of the arch in a flurry of snow. From within the swirling whiteness of the snowflakes, Tod could see the distinctive form of the Snow Princess, encased in her **Emotoclime** (a personal weather bubble manifested when a person becomes highly emotional, the use of snow being particular to the inhabitants of the Eastern SnowPlains). The **Blizzard** swirled off across the courtyard, with Septimus in pursuit.

The rush of freezing air in Driffa's wake brought another traveler through the Way, someone Tod was very pleased to see: Marcia Overstrand. Marcia smiled at Tod, took in the scene in the courtyard and hurried after Septimus.

"Septimus. Listen—" she said, grabbing his arm.

"Marcia, let *go*," Septimus said.

Marcia faltered as she saw the lack of welcome in Septimus's eyes. "Septimus. Please. Driffa has something very important to tell you. Please listen to her."

Septimus did not reply. He turned on his heel and strode away after Driffa.

Meanwhile, another figure emerged from the arch: a swarthy man sporting a cluster of gold earrings and wearing a red silk padded jacket with a large knife sheathed in a scabbard hanging from his belt. He was Milo Banda, Marcia's husband of just over a year. After giving a conspiratorial wink to Tod, Milo hurried over to Marcia, who was walking dejectedly back from her brush-off by Septimus.

"I tried to explain," she said miserably. "But he won't listen."

"You stay right here," Milo said. "I'm having a word with that young Heap."

Septimus was hovering anxiously on the edge of the snowstorm. It was a dramatic sight. The swirling snowflakes sparkled and glistened, shining with the blues, greens and occasional pinks and oranges of the **Magykal** lights of the Wizard Tower.

"Septimus, a word, please." Without waiting for a reply, Milo said what he had come to say. "There are times in one's life when you look back and wish someone had given you some fatherly advice. And this, Septimus, is one of those times

you will look back on. And now I'm giving you that advice. So
listen, if you don't mind."

Septimus frowned. He didn't like Milo's tone at all.

Milo continued. "I know I'm not your father—"

"No, you're not," Septimus agreed curtly.

"However, I am the father of your adoptive sister and as
such I hope you will take this as well-meant."

"Take *what* as well-meant?" Septimus asked snappily.

"Advice," Milo snapped back. "Listen to Marcia. Don't shut
her out. I know you've disagreed on all this wretched Orm
stuff, but it seems to me she might actually have a point. I suspect you might think so too, once you've heard what Princess
Driffa has to say."

"If I ever get to hear it," Septimus said, staring at the
Blizzard and irritably brushing the snowflakes from his cloak.

"Oh, I wouldn't worry about that," Milo said with a wry
smile. "You'll get to hear it, all right."

A ROUND TABLE

At the top of the Wizard Tower in Septimus's rooms was a
new, round table. Septimus had installed it in order to make

discussions flow better, but that evening the table didn't seem to be working.

It had taken all of Milo's persuasive powers to get Driffa to consent to even sit down, and now the Snow Princess sat silently simmering with rage. Her face was so pale as to be almost translucent and her hair hung in snow-white braids. The only color about her was blue: ice-blue eyes, thin blue ribbons threaded through her braids and bright blue fingernails.

Beside Driffa sat Marcia, a colorful contrast with her dark wavy hair, deep green eyes and multicolored cloak. Marcia too was quiet: subdued and deadly serious. Next to her was Milo, tipping back in his chair, trying to look nonchalant but succeeding only in looking like he was about to fall backward. Tod was sitting next to the empty chair that should have held Septimus. She excused herself to go and help him.

Insisting on making hot chocolate for them all, Septimus had taken refuge in the kitchen. As Tod came in he looked up anxiously. "All right?" he whispered.

"No one's saying anything," Tod whispered in return. "They're waiting for you. Can I help?"

Septimus gave Tod the mugs to carry in and followed her with the steaming jug of hot chocolate. Aware of Driffa's gimlet gaze upon him, Septimus carefully poured her the first drink and placed the mug in front of her. "You must be cold," he said, "after being in all that snow."

"Snow! Huh!" Driffa snorted with derision. She sounded, Septimus thought, not unlike her rather haughty horse.

The mugs were soon full and Septimus knew he could delay no longer. He sat down, took a deep breath and said, "Princess Driffa, welcome to the Wizard Tower. It is good to see you. I trust you received my letter?"

Driffa raised her fist and for a moment Septimus thought she was going to punch him. He did not move a muscle. In a sudden movement, Driffa flung open her fingers and threw a balled-up piece of paper high over everyone's head. With deadly accuracy, it hit the middle of the fire. The flames flared up around it, momentarily bright green, then died away.

"*That*, Septimus Heap, is what I think of your letter!" Driffa said.

Septimus knew his letter wasn't great, but he didn't think it was that bad. "Driffa . . . I mean, Princess Driffa. I apologize if my letter offended you. I—"

Driffa's blue eyes seemed to darken. "It is not your letter that offended me, ExtraOrdinary Wizard. It is your *treachery*."

Septimus shook his head in bewilderment. "Treachery? What treachery?"

"Ha!" Driffa snorted. "You promise me that you will return our sacred Orm Egg to us. You even tell me not to send our own sorcerers after it, for you will do that yourself. And then you betray us. You find the Egg but you do not bring it back. Instead, you hatch it. *How could you?*"

Tod longed to tell Driffa that this was not what happened, that the hatching of the Egg had nothing to do with Septimus at all, but Tod knew the argument was not hers to interrupt. She must let Septimus speak for himself.

But Septimus was dumbstruck.

It was Marcia who spoke. "Princess Driffa. As I tried to explain before, it was not Septimus who hatched your Egg. It was Oraton-Marr—the sorcerer who enslaved your people and destroyed your sacred places. It was in fact Septimus's dragon, Spit Fyre, who snatched the hatchling from the sorcerer's grasp. All Septimus did was bring the creature here and keep it safe."

Driffa glared at Septimus. "I do not listen to excuses," she said. "The fact is you gave me your promise, upon your own **Magyk**, that you would bring back our sacred Egg of the Orm. And I hear nothing from you—*not a word*—until your letter inviting me to see the hatchling—the very results of you breaking your promise!"

"But—" Septimus just managed to slip in before Driffa continued.

"And now we, in the Eastern SnowPlains, are condemned to live with the results of your broken promise. This." In a sudden movement, Driffa jabbed her hands outward like two fans, splaying her fingers.

Tod gasped. The silver bands of her rings glinted, but what Tod remembered as brilliant blue lapis stones within them were now dull, powdery gray.

Septimus looked blank. "What?" he asked.

"Your Apprentice understands what you do not," Driffa snapped.

Septimus threw Tod a questioning glance.

"The lapis in Princess Driffa's rings isn't blue anymore," Tod explained. Septimus still looked puzzled, so Tod continued. "Princess Driffa lent me the big ring so I could find the Heart of the Ways. It's the same ring. But the lapis has changed. It's turned gray."

A chill ran through Septimus and the color drained from his face. He stared at Driffa's rings in horror, while in his mind he saw once again the ball of sticky gray dust in Simon's eye socket.

Driffa was pleased to at last get a reaction from Septimus.

She managed a doleful smile for Tod. She felt sorry for her, being Apprenticed to such a useless Wizard.

"Septimus," Marcia said quietly. "*All* of the lapis in Driffa's home has undergone this change."

"*All*," said Driffa. "All of our beautiful lapis. The blue Pinnacle is a pile of gray dust. Our sacred Orm Chamber collapsed a few days ago. The Heart of the Ways is crumbling as I speak."

"No!" Septimus said. "This can't be possible. It . . . it can't be." But even as he spoke, he knew that it was.

"This, Septimus Heap," Driffa said, "is what happens to our **Enchantment** without the Orm Egg." She looked at Marcia. "I do not wish to speak to him. Please, tell him what you told me. Tell him the reason for this."

Marcia did not want to undermine Septimus's position as ExtraOrdinary Wizard by instructing him like a student. "I am sure the ExtraOrdinary Wizard knows the reason," she demurred.

Septimus was not sure that he did know the reason. He looked at Marcia. "Please, tell us all," he said. "My Apprentice would like to hear."

"Very well," Marcia said. "Septimus, as you know, there

are consequences of the kind of massive Earth **Enchantment** that Driffa's people have in the SnowPlains. The bigger the **Enchantment**, the more delicate and finely balanced it becomes. The most complex of these ancient **Magyks**—and the one of the Eastern SnowPlains is probably the most complex there has ever been, for it spreads across the whole world—are often held in equilibrium by a **KeyStone**, just like any archway. These Earth **Enchantments** are remarkably stable—until the **KeyStone** goes, then they tumble like nine-pins. It is called an **UnRaveling**."

Septimus nodded. He knew now what was coming.

"It seems," Marcia said, "that the Orm Egg was such a **KeyStone**."

"How, er, how fast is it collapsing?" Septimus asked.

"Driffa?" asked Marcia.

Driffa addressed her answer to Marcia alone. "It began slowly. One day a few weeks after our Sacred Egg was stolen, I was looking at our beautiful blue Pinnacle from the battlement walk and I noticed that its tip was no longer sharp. When I looked through my **Enlarging Glass** I saw why. It had crumbled to dust. I asked our sorcerers what was happening and they went away to think about it. When they returned they told me that it was because we had lost the Egg." Driffa looked angrily at Septimus. "The sorcerers we have left are not very good ones, but even they are better than you, Septimus Heap. Our sorcerers begged to be allowed to search for the Egg, but I told them that you would soon bring it back and I did not want them to hinder your search in any way. The Pinnacle continued to crumble. Our people were frightened, afraid that soon their homes would be nothing more than dust."

Driffa gave a bitter laugh. "I told them not to worry. I told them you were a powerful sorcerer and you would find the Egg and bring it back to us. But you didn't bring it back. Instead you kept it for yourself, while we watched our Enchanted snows turn to slush and our beautiful lapis crumble to dust. You lied to me. And because of that I have lied to my people."

Septimus looked stunned. "Driffa, please believe me. I did *not* take the Egg. It was already hatched when I found it."

Driffa glared at him. "You betrayed us."

"I have an idea." Milo's voice made everybody jump. All eyes turned toward him. "How about letting the Princess here have the Ormlet?"

Tod and Septimus exchanged glances. This was not a good

time to mention that the Ormlet was dead. They were saved by Driffa herself.

"The hatchling is no good to us," Driffa told Milo. "The **Enchantment** was within the *Egg*. It was released with the hatching of the creature."

Milo looked at Marcia. "Would it be possible to restore the **Enchantment** with another egg?"

"Yes, it would," Marcia replied. "It needs to be placed exactly where it was before. And then there must be a reenactment of the original **Incantation**."

"So if you have a new Orm, then surely, one day, it will create a new egg?" asked Milo.

"Ha!" Driffa said scathingly. "One little egg. Buried deep in thousands of miles of rock. How do you suggest we find *that*?"

Milo was not to be deterred. "But surely, Princess, there are other Orm Eggs from ancient Orms still to be found?"

"There are none," Driffa told him. "They were plundered thousands of years ago by a pack of thieving shamans." Driffa looked down at her ring. Very deliberately, she stuck her long blue fingernail into the soft gray rock and flicked it. Gray grit skittered onto the table. "So much for your **Magyk**, Septimus

Heap. You are not as powerful as you think you are." Driffa
was silent for a moment. "Or as I thought you were either,"
she said a little sadly.

Driffa pushed back her chair and stood up. A few snowflakes began to fall. "Septimus Heap," she said. "I came here
only to tell you about your future destruction, so that you
will be as miserable as we are. Because, like a slow fire inside
a wall, the crumbling of our **Enchantment** will spread through
the Ancient Ways. And because you are joined to our Heart
of the Ways it will reach you eventually. One day the rock on
which your tower is built will turn to dust. Your lapis will
be gone, your **Magyk**—such as it is—will be gone, and your
precious Tower will be gone. All will be dust. And there is
nothing you can do about it. *Nothing at all.*"

Trailing snowflakes, Driffa strode to the door. It threw
itself open with a flourish—the large purple door had a fine
sense of drama—and the Snow Princess was gone, leaving a
cloud of snow and her last angry words hanging in the air.

Septimus looked stricken. He jumped to his feet.

"Let her go, Septimus," Marcia said.

"I can't let her go without hope," he said. "I can't . . ." He
rushed off to his study. There was the loud hiss of a **Safe**

being **UnSealed**, and in seconds Septimus reappeared holding a shard of lapis. "It's from the Heart of the Ways, one of the pieces that Simon picked up. I kept it in my **Safe**. To remind me. Oh, it must go in a box. A **Sealed** box. To protect its **Enchantment**."

Septimus turned to run back to the study, but Tod stopped him. "Please," she said, hurrying over to him. "Please, have my StarChaser box. It's from the **Charm** chamber."

Septimus took it gratefully. "Perfect," he said. Hurriedly, he flipped the lid open, put in the lapis shard and handed it to Marcia. "Please, will *you* **Seal** it? To keep the lapis free of the **UnRaveling**? I'm not thinking straight right now."

Marcia took the little silver, star-strewn box and enclosed it in her hands. Murmuring words that Tod could not quite hear, Marcia focused her brilliant green eyes upon her hands. When a purple mist began to flow up from between her fingers Marcia gently placed the box on the table. It lay there, a few wisps of purple floating across its soft silver sheen. "All done," she said.

"Thank you!" Septimus snatched up the box and raced out of the room. They heard the emergency siren sound on the stairs, and then all was silent.

Marcia sighed and walked over to the fire. "Well," she said. "It's a bad business."

"But it's not true, what Driffa said," Tod said.

"Unfortunately, I suspect it might be," Marcia replied.

"I meant what she said about there being nothing at all that we could do," Tod explained. "*That's* not true. There is always something you can do. *Always.*"

Marcia looked at Tod with approval. Here was an Apprentice after her own heart.

Septimus caught up with Driffa just as she was about to **Go Through** the **Hidden** arch. He pushed the starry box into her unwilling hand.

"I want nothing from you," Driffa said.

"Please," Septimus said. "Take it. Nothing here is from me. The box is from my Apprentice, the **Enchantment** is from Marcia, and inside is something that belongs to you anyway: a shard of lapis from the Heart of the Ways. Keep the box closed and the **Enchantment** will stay safe within."

Driffa took the box. "A *shard*," she said scornfully. "That is all you have left me." She turned and walked into the **Hidden** arch, leaving Septimus staring at a blank, cold wall.

A WALK UPON THE WALLS

It was past midnight. Tod was asleep in her starry tent in the dorm, dreaming of her home village. Her **Alarm** was set and her backpack ready. Inside were the presents she had collected over the past weeks for her father and the Sarn family and her Ancient Ways travel kit. To her delight Septimus had told her that she could go home early for her birthday. Tod had Marcia to thank for that, for she had told Septimus that he should allow Tod to use the Ways while they were still there to be traveled.

Upstairs, in Septimus's rooms, Milo was also asleep. He lay stretched out on Marcia's old sofa. Marcia looked at both Milo and her old sofa affectionately. "Milo can sleep anywhere," she whispered to Septimus. "It comes of all those years of seafaring, I suppose."

"I don't think I'll be sleeping much tonight," Septimus said.

"Me neither," Marcia agreed. She thought back to when the rooms had belonged to her, and Septimus had been her young Apprentice. Things had been so much simpler then.

"It all seems so complicated now," Septimus said.

Marcia flashed him a quizzical look. "I could almost believe you were doing a MindRead there, Septimus."

"I wouldn't dream of intruding," Septimus protested. "But I am allowed to read your expression, I hope?"

"Of course you are." Marcia smiled. "Shall we go for a walk to clear our heads?"

They left Milo snoring and took the slow, dimly lit stairs down through the Wizard Tower. Ten minutes later Marcia and Septimus were wandering along the top of the Castle walls, heading toward the East Gate Lookout Tower. It was a cloudy night, the air was still, and as they walked they heard the sounds of a party coming from the old Infirmary on the other side of the Moat.

Marcia made no comment. Feeling a little uncomfortable, Septimus risked a few glances over to the Infirmary. There were candles burning in all the windows, and beneath the shouts, squeals and laughter came the sound of Forest pipes— a strange, unearthly wailing noise—and the insistent beat of tambours and drums.

After some minutes, Marcia said, "Septimus, I hope you will excuse me, but there is something I must say."

"Go ahead," Septimus said, and waited for Marcia's opinion on parties. He got something rather different.

"The Ormlet."

"Ah, *that*," said Septimus.

"Yes, *that*. Septimus, I know you disagree with me about the danger of putting it under the Tower. But please, listen."

"Marcia, there's no point in discussing this—"

Marcia cut Septimus off. "Please, let me explain. Our **Magyk**, just like Driffa's **Enchantment**, is a matter of a fine balance. However much lapis is under the Wizard Tower, it is the perfect amount for us. It works with the people we have in the Tower, it works with the **Magyk** we—or now you—do. But if we change that balance by adding new lapis, who knows what might happen? Maybe anyone with a few spells at hand could walk into the Wizard Tower and have tremendous power."

"I think that's unlikely," Septimus said. "Anyway, they'd have to get in first, wouldn't they?"

"It might be someone you already know, someone you would happily allow into the Wizard Tower. What about that awful witch you went out with once—oh, what was her name?"

"Marissa," Septimus mumbled. "And I didn't 'go out' with

her, as you put it. And anyway, I was only seventeen."

"Whatever," Marcia replied, using a word that had infuriated her when Septimus used it, but which she now found rather useful—and had a certain satisfaction in returning the favor. "So just imagine for a moment that Marissa decides she'd like to become ExtraOrdinary Wizard—"

A snort of derision burst from Septimus. "*Marissa!*"

"Shh," Marcia hissed. "Sound travels over the water. Anyway, suppose Marissa walks into the Wizard Tower one day and starts spinning all kinds of spells to enable her to take over. And by then, courtesy of your Orm, you've got tons of nice fresh lapis underneath. New lapis is unpredictable. It has no loyalty: it will soak up anyone's **Magyk**. Marissa's spells might even *work*."

"Marcia," Septimus said, "trust me, you have nothing to worry about on that score. There won't be any new lapis. I think the Ormlet is dead."

"*What?*"

"Dead. I don't know why. Oskar Sarn knows something, but he's not telling. I suspect it might have been poisoned."

"*Poisoned?*" Marcia exclaimed. "Well, that is a shock. And a great shame. Because I was going to suggest keeping the

Ormlet in the Castle, although not under the Wizard Tower, of course. Maybe under the Palace. You know, just in case this is indeed the beginning of an UnRaveling."

"Which I think," Septimus said, "it very well might be."

Marcia looked at her ex-Apprentice. "There's something you haven't told me yet," she said.

"Simon's eye has turned to dust," Septimus said.

"*What?*" Marcia looked at Septimus as though he had gone crazy.

"You remember that the iris of his right eye turned to lapis. In the Heart of the Ways."

"Are you going to tell me what I think you are?" Marcia asked.

"I am. I went to see him. His eye is a ball of gray dust."

Marcia looked horrified. "The *whole* eye? Oh, how terrible. Poor Simon. And Lucy."

"He's afraid the dust will spread into his head."

"I suppose," Marcia said, "that depends on whether he has lapis fragments in there too."

"I suppose it does," Septimus agreed.

Marcia sighed. "I think Simon has given us our answer. This must indeed be an UnRaveling. Everything connected to the **Enchantment** disintegrates, however far away it may be." She turned to look at the Wizard Tower. "I suspect Simon's brush with the **Darke** has sped up the effect for him personally, but we will have to face it. The **UnRaveling** *will* reach the Wizard Tower. And very possibly sooner rather than later."

Septimus felt sick. He too turned and looked back at the Wizard Tower. It rose up into the night, topped with its golden pyramid, shining with silvery, **Magykal** light and clothed with indigo, nighttime **Sprites** lazily floating around it. Its beauty and power took his breath away. He struggled to speak. "We . . . we can't lose this. We *can't.*"

Marcia sighed. "One day, maybe sooner than we think, we will lose it. And, even though your superb Apprentice thinks otherwise, there is actually nothing we can do to stop it."

"Except put back the **KeyStone**."

"Indeed. With an Orm Egg," Marcia said.

"Which is utterly impossible," Septimus said, "because there aren't any. Anywhere."

"And we don't even have an Orm anymore."

Septimus said nothing. Marcia linked her arm through his and they walked on in silence for a while, looking across to the lights in the old Infirmary, which now seemed threatening to Septimus, as if they too were encroaching upon all he loved and held dear.

On the roof of the East Gate Lookout Tower, headquarters of the Castle Message Rat Service, the two rats were still sitting out under the stars. "Hey, Da," Morris said, "there's the new EOW down there, walking along the walls with the old one."

"That's nice, Morris," Stanley murmured dozily. "I always thought she left him to take over too young. I'm glad she's come back to lend a hand."

Unwittingly, Marcia was at that moment echoing Stanley's thoughts. "I sometimes feel I burdened you with all this far too young," she was saying.

Sometimes Septimus felt that too. But what was done was done. "You went when you needed to," he said.

"But not when *you* needed me to," Marcia replied. "Septimus, I am sorry. I was so caught up in my own plans. But now, if you will allow me, we can fight this threat—this **UnRaveling**—shoulder to shoulder. I won't leave you to face this alone." She faltered. "Unless, of course, you would rather

I did . . . I mean . . . I don't want to intrude."

Septimus felt as though a great weight had been lifted from him. "Thank you," he said. "I would like that very much indeed . . . if we could do this together." Septimus reached inside his tunic and from around his neck he lifted off a lapis amulet with the shape of a dragon incised into it. This was the Akhu Amulet, the symbol and source of much of his power as ExtraOrdinary Wizard. He cradled the amulet in his palm, gazing at the blue stone bound with gold, lying heavy with the weight of his **Magyk**. "We can't lose our **Magyk**," he said. "I couldn't bear it if one day this crumbled to dust like Driffa's ring."

"We will not let that happen," Marcia said. "I promise you, we will *not*. Now put that amulet back on, Septimus." Septimus did as he was told. "Let's go back now," said Marcia. "We have work to do. Plans to make. **Magyk** to mend. *Together*."

Septimus blinked a sudden blurriness from his eyes. "I've missed you," he said.

"Well, I'm sure you'll soon get fed up with me," Marcia retorted, finding that her eyes had gone a little fuzzy too.

Morris watched the pair walk away arm in arm: one resplendent in the purple robes of the office of the ExtraOrdinary

Wizard, the other equally impressive in a long, flowing, multicolored cloak and purple pointy shoes that caught the light as she walked. Then the rat looked across to the other side of the Moat at what really interested him—the party in the Infirmary.

"What is that awful noise?" the old rat in the basket chair grumbled.

"It's the party, Da," Morris said.

"Ghastly things, parties," said the old rat. "My tummy's cold."

Morris, remarkably adroit with only one arm, tucked the rug around Stanley's large stomach and looked longingly across the water. He watched the rowboats heading across the Moat, packed with people. He saw the steady stream of dark figures making their way to the Infirmary from both the Castle and the Forest. He heard the music and laughter grow loud every time the Infirmary door was opened, he saw the blazing lights of the candles, and he sighed. Morris didn't often wish he were human, but tonight was one of those nights when he did. Humans knew how to have fun.

PART
VII

A WORM TURNS

Marissa *was looking good and* she knew it. She wore a long purple cloak—just to get used to the idea of running the Wizzer, she told herself—and around her brown curly hair was Jenna's gold circlet, which made her feel surprisingly regal. Tonight was going to be a blast; she knew it. There was good music, plenty of party potions and a great crowd of people. She was going to forget all about the bag of Kraan for the night. *Anyway, who needed bodyguards when you had so many friends?* Marissa thought, smiling at two handsome young fishermen who had just arrived on the night barge from the Port.

Marissa took her duties as hostess seriously. She stood in the entrance lobby, greeting the waves of new arrivals as they poured in—scribes, apprentices of all descriptions, the entire staff of the Grot and, best of all, the Knights of Knee, who always made a party go with a bang.

"Hey, Drammer," Marissa said as Newt Makken and his younger brother arrived, "It's way past your bedtime."

Drammer grinned sheepishly and sloped off to find something more interesting than FizzFroot to drink. Newt encircled Marissa in a bad-breath bear hug. "Get *off*, Newt," Marissa said, pushing him away.

Newt looked hurt. "Hey, I broke out of the Wizzer just for you. I'm not meant to be here, you know."

"No one's *meant* to be here, Newt," Marissa drawled. "That's the whole point. Now run away and play, why don't you?"

Newt sulked off into the shadows.

The flow of guests had slowed to a few stragglers, and Marissa was casting her eyes over the throng, considering who looked the most interesting, when the door opened and Jo-Jo Heap walked in. Jo-Jo looked good. He wore his Gothyk Grotto black cloak with a certain swagger and had on a new, but artfully scuffed, leather jerkin. Apart from the usual party offering of a bottle, Jo-Jo was also carrying a tiny box wrapped in red paper tied with purple string, which he put into Marissa's hand.

"Ooh, Jo-Jo, how sweet," Marissa trilled. "I'll open it later." She turned to put it on a similar pile of offerings, but Jo-Jo grabbed her wrist.

"No. *Now*," he told her. Jo-Jo had decided to try a new approach with Marissa and stop being so nice. To his surprise it seemed to work—obediently, Marissa unwrapped the gift to find a little box covered in green snakeskin.

Marissa had been expecting a love **Charm** of some description and was gleefully readying herself to hurl it straight out of the door. But when she opened the box she saw a tiny strip of what looked like thin black leather, forked at one end. She knew at once that was no love **Charm**. "What is it?" she asked.

"Snake tongue," Jo-Jo said in his new terse mode. He grinned. "Reminded me of you."

Marissa stared at Jo-Jo in shock. "Oh!" she said lamely.

What Jo-Jo didn't say was that he had indeed been intending to give Marissa a love **Charm**. But in the **Charm** Library he had come across something that had suddenly felt absolutely right for Marissa. Jo-Jo had enough **Magykal** schooling to know that where **Charms** were concerned you listened to your heart, not your head. And so while Rose and Tod were closeted in the **Charm** Chamber, Jo-Jo had used the automatic checkout service and borrowed the snake tongue. He knew no one would check up on the loan until it became overdue in two weeks' time. And by then, Jo-Jo thought, who knew what might have happened? For Jo-Jo, who was probably the most intuitive of all the Heap brothers, had a feeling that something big and possibly nasty was brewing in the Wizard Tower.

Marissa tentatively touched the snake tongue with the tip of a finger. "What does it do?" she whispered.

Jo-Jo shrugged. "Makes people believe whatever you say."

"Wow!" Marissa breathed.

Jo-Jo grinned. "As long as you have it in your mouth."

"Oh, *gross*," said Marissa.

Sticking to his resolution, Jo-Jo said no more. He threw his cloak over his shoulder, showing its new deep blue—and rather expensive—silk lining, walked haughtily past Marissa and disappeared in search of the piper. Jo-Jo had made a flute and he wanted to mark where the holes went.

Marissa stared after Jo-Jo in stunned amazement. The evening was not turning out quite how she had expected.

But that was only the start of it.

SKITTLES

Marcia and Septimus had retreated to the Pyramid Library—the only place in Septimus's rooms where Milo's snores did not reach. They were sitting together at the main desk. In front of them, illuminated by a trio of brightly burning candles, lay a small, tatty book titled *Orm Fancier's Factoids* by Francis Fa Oom. The book was handwritten, the paper was fragile, and the writing looped untidily across the page. It was not an easy read. Marcia peered at it through her spectacles, Septimus through his **Enlarging Glass**. They were looking at the very last chapter, called "Orm Egg Distribution and Frequency."

"So . . ." murmured Marcia, running her finger along the closely written lines, "basically, Oom says that Orm eggs were always as rare as hens' teeth and virtually impossible to find as they were trapped deep within the bedrock. Apparently a group of sorcerers—of whom he does not approve—spent hundreds of years harvesting them. He reckons there is not even one left." Marcia took off her spectacles and rubbed her eyes wearily. "Driffa was right."

Septimus nodded. "According to Fa Oom."

Marcia smiled. "What a silly name. Can you imagine what his Apprentices called him?"

Septimus chuckled. Marcia made even the worst of situations feel better. He leaned back in his chair and allowed his gaze to travel around the Pyramid Library. He loved its atmosphere at this time of night. In his last year as Marcia's Apprentice, Septimus had often worked through the night at this very desk. He would breathe in the smell of the old books, secret papers and pamphlets, and emerge in the early hours of the morning heady with Ancient **Magyk**. Septimus hoped that in a few years time Tod would be doing the same, exploring the most **Magykal** Library in the world. But if what Driffa had said was true, there would be no library left for Tod to explore, because there would be no Wizard Tower. There would be nothing left but a cloud of dust. Wearily, Septimus closed *Orm Fancier's Factoids* and blew out the candles. Then he and Marcia went quietly down the stone steps to their beds.

Neither slept well. Marcia, sleeping in Septimus's old room, had a recurring dream that she was dropping giant blue eggs out of Septimus's window and knocking down Wizard-shaped skittles in the courtyard far below. Septimus fared no better. He dreamed he was rowing across the Moat to the Infirmary party. The water had turned to treacle and there were shark-finned Kraan swimming in it, trying to saw his boat in half. The sawing noise sounding remarkably like Milo's snores.

PARTY BAG

Marissa was losing control of the party. It had begun with a rampage led by Drammer, which had quickly degenerated into a food fight in the corridor. Now there was a full-blown brawl going on in the middle of the ward and already Marissa had heard the sound of breaking glass. To the accompaniment of the ever-increasing beat of the tambours and the wailing of Forest pipes by three excited musicians who were stirring it up, Marissa pushed her way through the throng, her passage helped by well-placed kicks and vicious elbow jabs. "Hey, guys!" she yelled at the top of her voice. "Break it up! Break it up!"

Her answer was the crash of the nurses' desk being overturned and the shriek of one of the Knights of Knee, upon whose foot it had landed. Marissa waded in. She pulled Newt Makken off a small Port apprentice, whom he appeared to be strangling, and threw the brawlers apart, yelling, "Stoppit, will you?" But the brawl was acting like a magnet. Anyone with a score to settle was throwing themselves into the fight with enthusiasm, landing their blows at first where they intended and then wherever else they could. Marissa was trying to separate Drammer and a chef from Wizard Sandwiches—both trading wide, swinging punches—when she became aware that someone had taken charge and things were calming down; people were helping others to their feet and slinking sheepishly away. Marissa sent Drammer off with a shove and turned to see who the referee was.

"Jo-Jo!" she gasped.

Jo-Jo was pulling a pile of crestfallen Port apprentices to their feet. "You come to a Castle party," he was telling them, "and you stick to Castle rules. If you want to stay, you behave. Got that?"

A mixture of nods and groans was the reply.

"I knew there was going to be trouble as soon as I saw the Portsmen come in," he growled.

"Port who?" asked Marissa faintly. She felt quite overwhelmed, although she wasn't sure why.

"Portsmen. A gang of apprentices from the Port. The Knights of Knee went down there last summer and trashed their boat. I suppose this was a return match."

"The cheek of it!" Marissa said indignantly. She was feeling back on form now that order had returned. Marissa was not good with chaos; she liked to be in control.

"Could have told you this would happen," Jo-Jo said gruffly. "Should have had security on the door."

"Security?"

"Yeah. Security." True to his new persona, Jo-Jo did not elaborate. Thinking it was best to walk away while he was winning, he turned to go. Jo-Jo had spent the whole afternoon rehearsing how to walk away from Marissa, but as he performed his nonchalant turn, the floor moved from under his feet and the next moment he was lying on his back staring up at Marissa's shocked face. He waited for her to break into a cascade of giggles, but to his surprise she didn't.

"Jo-Jo!" Marissa dropped to her knees beside him—then screamed and leaped to her feet. "Ouch-ouch-ouch! That *hurt*."

Jo-Jo got up carefully. "Some idiot's put ball bearings on the floor," he said. "That's fighting dirty." He picked up one of the offending objects and held it out to Marissa. "Nasty thing. It's got a lot of **Darke** on it."

"Oh dear," Marissa said with studied innocence. "Can I see?"

Jo-Jo held out his hand. In the dip of his palm was what Marissa feared: a red Kraan bead. She swore under her breath.

"Yeah," Jo-Jo agreed. "Not nice. I'll chuck it in the Moat.

Are they all like that? I'll chuck them in too."

Very slowly, all the while trying to think how she was going to get the beads back without raising Jo-Jo's suspicions, Marissa helped gather the Kraan beads together. It was not difficult. Although they had rolled far and wide across the floor, they shone like little red eyes in the candlelight and were easy to spot. Soon other party guests joined in, and to Marissa's discomfort, it rapidly turned into a game they had all played as children: Hunt the Bug.

Minutes later both Jo-Jo and Marissa had a handful of nasty little red eyes staring up at them. Drammer, who was trying to get back into favor, helped to right the nurses' desk and found beneath it the little black leather bag with three beads still inside. Looking very pleased with himself, he handed it to Marissa, saying, "There's your necklace bag."

"Thanks." Marissa snatched the bag and began to shovel in her stash of Kraan beads. As soon as she finished, Jo-Jo—without saying a word—reached over and took the bag. He was intending merely to add his own haul of beads but as he opened the drawstring to its full extent he saw a rolled up piece of paper tied with a black silk thread. Jo-Jo knew an **Incantation** when he saw one. Holding the offending scrap of paper between finger and thumb, he held it up, frowning at Marissa. "Where did you get this?" he asked coldly.

Marissa faltered, shocked by the disapproval in Jo-Jo's voice. In that brief moment of hesitation, Newt Makken—who for lack of anything better to do had come to harass his little brother—snatched the Incantation from Jo-Jo's grasp.

"Makken! Give that back!" Jo-Jo yelled, swinging around to grab it.

Newt ducked under Jo-Jo's arm and in a lightning-quick movement he grabbed the bag of Kraan beads too.

"Give it back!" Marissa screamed.

"Scumbag!" Jo-Jo added for good measure.

"Come and get it, Heap boy!" Newt yelled, taking off down the ward, swinging the little bag of beads around his head.

Marissa grabbed Jo-Jo. "Please. *Get them back.*" The alarm in Marissa's eyes sent Jo-Jo after Newt like a rocket. Whatever these beads were, Jo-Jo suspected that Newt was the very worst person to have them.

The partygoers decided to treat the chase as entertainment. The Forest pipes stopped wailing as the piper began to shout for his man: Jo-Jo Heap. However, the tambour players were all for Newt and began a chant to that effect. Soon rival chants filled the Infirmary: "Newt! Newt!" "Heap! Heap!" as the chase hurtled through the two long wards, leaving a trail of overturned chairs, tables and the occasional bed in its wake.

Jo-Jo cornered Newt at the end of the ward. Newt leaped onto a bed and jumped up and down like a demented three-year-old, waving the bag of Kraan above his head. "Come and get them, Heap boy! Come and get them!" he yelled.

Jo-Jo Heap accepted the invitation.

Running Away

Septimus woke just after dawn with the sudden certainty that it was too dangerous for Tod to use the Ways. He leaped out of bed, threw a cloak over his pajamas and hurried down the stone steps to the big room with the purple sofa. He found Milo quietly tending the fire, feeding it small twigs as though it were a hungry pet. Milo looked up. "The boss is still asleep," he said.

Septimus nodded. They both knew that Marcia was still the boss.

"Cup of coffee?" Milo asked.

"When I get back. Won't be long." With that Septimus hurried out.

Two minutes later, Boris Catchpole, doorkeeper, was won-dering what was wrong. It wasn't every day you saw the EOW in his pajamas.

"Catchpole!" Septimus said.

"Yes?" Catchpole tried not to bristle. It rankled that some-one over whom he once had power of life and death was now able to address him by his surname with impunity.

"My Apprentice will be leaving soon. Will you tell her I wish to see her before she goes, please?" And then, remem-bering that Tod did not always take notice of Catchpole's door instructions, he began to scribble a note.

"She's already gone," Catchpole said. "Shall I tell her when she gets back?"

"She's *gone*?"

Catchpole made a point of getting back at Septimus in little ways. Tod had actually only left a few minutes beforehand, but Catchpole saw no reason to be entirely accurate. "She left ages ago. With her backpack." With some satisfaction, he saw Septimus's expression of dismay. "Running away, was she?" Catchpole asked. "I always thought she was trouble, that one. No manners at all."

"Of course she wasn't running away," Septimus snapped back. "And you will keep your opinions to yourself, Catchpole, thank you very much." He turned on his heel and strode away to the stairs.

Tod however, was still in the courtyard. She was enjoying watching the early-morning **Sprites** dropping slowly to the ground and trying to catch one for luck. They all eluded her and after some minutes she gave up, stepped into the **Hidden** arch and began her journey.

On the other side of the silver doors, Catchpole watched the swirl of purple as it ascended. He could not resist a smirk. Of course the kid was running away. And good riddance too, he thought.

But on the far side of the Moat, Jo-Jo Heap was running away for real.

RAT'S-EYE VIEW

On the East Gate Lookout Tower, Morris was sitting on the battlements, contentedly swinging his little legs, while he listened to the clanking of the drawbridge being lowered, telling him that his night shift was over.

After Stanley had retired to bed, Morris had stayed up all night on emergency message duty and had enjoyed every minute of it. He had jigged and twirled to the wild music of the Forest pipes wailing across the water and stamped his little rat feet in perfect time to the drumming of the tambours. No one had rung the night bell with a message—or, to be more accurate, Morris hadn't actually *heard* anyone ring the night bell.

Now, the night was over, the party had gone very quiet, and the sky above the Forest was pale yellow. Morris began to think about breakfast. Suddenly there was an enormous *BANG* from inside the Infirmary. It was such a shock that Morris very nearly lost his balance and fell. He grabbed on to the battlements with his one remaining arm and rolled safely backward, onto the roof. When he got to his feet he could not believe what he saw. The entire end wall of the Infirmary had been blown into splinters, and lurching out through the gaping hole was a line of huge, black, beast-headed skeletons, each with six glittering red eyes. Morris instinctively ducked down. And then, unable to resist, he peered back up again, his eyes wide with alarm.

Morris was a well-read rat. While delivering a message to

the ExtraOrdinary Wizard he had lost his arm in an attack
by a Garmin. During his time recovering as an honored guest
in the Wizard Tower Sick Bay, Morris had made it his business to read about every **Darke** creature possible. Should he
ever come face-to-face with one in the future, Morris wanted
to know exactly what he was dealing with. And so, as the rat
stared in dismay out over the battlements, he knew exactly
what he was looking at: Kraan. He remembered them well
because they had, the book had gleefully informed its readers, a
predilection for tearing rats to pieces. Morris also remembered
that the Kraan had a particular dislike for the Wizards—the
younger ones particularly annoyed them—and homed in on
their green eyes. One touch of a Kraan was lethal; it sent a
powerful shock through the body and killed instantly.

His little mouth agape with horror, Morris stared at the
stream of Kraan emerging from the Infirmary. It seemed endless, flowing out like a tide of treacle. Morris knew what that
was too. He remembered the instructions in the book: *One
Kraan may be **Engendered** from six red beads, which become the
eyes. Please Note: Care must be taken to keep these beads in separate
groups of six to avoid a **Chain Reaction**.*

The Kraan walked with an awkward gait, swinging to and

fro like pendulums, kicking each leg out in front as though they were aiming for an invisible football. They would have been funny had it not been for their frightening, beastlike skulls and the glittering stare of their tiny red eyes—all six of them, lined up three on either side of the snout.

As the Kraan kept on coming, Morris saw people pouring out from the Infirmary. Like ants running from a destroyed nest they came scrambling from the windows, throwing themselves out of the doors and then scattering in all directions. Some went racing for the Forest, others tore along the bank toward the safety of the heights of Raven's Rock, or in the opposite direction to the One Way Bridge and the safety of the Farmlands beyond—anywhere but where the Kraan were now clearly headed: the North Gate drawbridge and, beyond it, the Castle.

Suddenly Morris saw a lone figure in a short black cloak come running from the newly lowered drawbridge and head back *toward* the Kraan. Morris stared, aghast. It was Jo-Jo Heap, but what was he doing? If he carried on like that, Morris thought, very soon there were going to be only six Heap brothers. Morris began to chew his little rat claws. This was scary. And sad. Morris liked Jo-Jo Heap.

Down and Up Again

As Jo-Jo fled from the mayhem that Newt Makken had let loose, the first rays of the rising sun were breaking through the treetops and the Bridge Boy was lowering the Castle drawbridge. As the edge of the bridge touched its resting plate, Jo-Jo leaped onto it and hurtled across.

The thudding of boots echoing on the planks drew Gringe out of his cubbyhole to take the first toll of the day, only to be confronted by a wild-eyed, terrified Heap. Gringe wasn't sure which one it was; they all looked the same to him. The Heap wasn't wearing purple so that narrowed it down a bit, but not much. Suddenly the Heap grabbed hold of him.

"Hey, get off!" Gringe growled.

"Gringe!" Jo-Jo gasped. "You have to raise the bridge. Now!"

Gringe was feeling rather sensitive about Heaps telling him what to do with his bridge. "Not until sunset, I don't," he snarled. "Now push off, will you?"

"Look, Gringe! *Look!*" Jo-Jo wheeled around and pointed

back the way he had come. "You *have* to raise the bridge!"

Gringe sighed. *Nothing changes,* he thought. *Heaps were always trouble and they always will be.* Wearily he put on the long-distance spectacles that Mrs. Gringe had forced him to buy after he had begun to raise the bridge while Sarah Heap was still standing on it. The spectacles settled onto his broad, red nose, and the rest of Gringe's face turned ashen. "*What the . . .*" he gasped.

Gringe's spectacles revealed that a whole wall of the old Infirmary was missing. And marching toward Gringe's precious bridge was a dark stream of terror with a myriad of beady red eyes all, it seemed, focused on *him.*

"Raise the bridge, Gringe," Jo-Jo was gabbling. "Protect the Castle! Now!"

Gringe found himself unable to speak: his tongue had stuck itself to the roof of his mouth. He gave an inappropriate thumbs-up and watched Jo-Jo run back across the bridge, jump off and turn around, yelling, "Up! Up!"

Gringe ran to the lifting gear, yelling all the while for the Bridge Boy, who had just gone inside for his breakfast. In the absence of any response, Gringe began to raise the bridge. The noise brought Mrs. Gringe out to see what was happening. Seconds later there were three people turning the huge wheels that raised the bridge. It had never gone up so fast.

On the other side of the bank, Jo-Jo resolutely turned his back to the Castle and stood watching the advancing Kraan. He knew what he had to do—if he was brave enough to do it. *Come on, Jo-Jo*, he told himself. *Compared to Marissa, these Kraan are a piece of cake.*

OUT OF THE BAG

Septimus, Marcia and Milo were drinking coffee beside the fire and eating Septimus's special eggy-toast when the door to his rooms sprang open with a crash. In the doorway stood Jo-Jo Heap: wild-eyed, shaking, soaked and covered with mud. Marcia and Septimus jumped from their seats and rushed over to Jo-Jo. Milo continued to eat his toast—he'd seen worse at sea.

Ten minutes later, fortified with coffee, his shivering slowed by the fire and three blankets, Jo-Jo began his story. He spoke slowly, as though he did not quite understand what had happened—or how.

"It was Newt's fault . . . he took Marissa's bag of beads . . . there was an **Incantation** in them . . . **Darke** stuff . . . I chased him and he swung himself up onto one of the ceiling beams . . . sat there like a ship's monkey in the rigging grinning at us . . . jiggling the bag up and down . . . Marissa was screaming for him to give it back . . . I was trying to get up there after him and . . . everyone was laughing and making monkey noises." Jo-Jo paused and took a gulp of coffee. "Marissa was begging me to be careful . . . telling everyone to be quiet. Though she didn't put it quite as politely as that."

"No, she wouldn't," Septimus said.

"She was terrified because . . ." Jo-Jo hesitated for a few seconds, took a deep breath and said, "Because the bag was full of Kraan beads."

Septimus and Marcia looked horrified. "*Kraan?*" they repeated.

Jo-Jo nodded. "Kraan. And Newt Makken **Engendered** them."

Once again Septimus and Marcia both spoke together. "Newt Makken did *what?*"

"Um. He **Engendered** a bag of Kraan."

"A *bag* of Kraan," Marcia whispered.

Milo was finally paying attention. "What," he whispered to Marcia, "are Kraan?"

Marcia shook her head, unable to speak.

"I take it they are not fluffy little kittens?" Milo commented to Jo-Jo.

"No, not really," Jo-Jo said.

"So . . . how many were in this bag?" Septimus asked slowly.

"Tons," said Jo-Jo.

"So how many Kraan?" asked Marcia.

Jo-Jo shuddered. "Dunno. I lost count."

Septimus began to pace the room, muttering under his breath. "Where did that wretched witch get a whole bag of Kraan from?" he demanded angrily.

Jo-Jo looked warily at Septimus. He had never seen him like this. Septimus's eyes flashed with anger; even the purple on his robes seem to glow with energy. For the first time ever, Jo-Jo Heap understood the power his younger brother possessed.

"I don't know where she got them," Jo-Jo said. "I didn't even know what they were. I did my best to stop this. Really I did."

Septimus sat down beside Jo-Jo. "I apologize, Jo-Jo. I realize that you are not responsible for this and that you didn't have to come and tell us. But I do need to know a few things."

"Anything. Ask me *anything*."

"Did Newt say one **Engender** for each Kraan?" Septimus asked.

"No. He read it once. He was laughing, like he was reading a joke out of a cracker. And the more Marissa begged him to stop, the louder he said it."

"So he said it to the *whole bag?*"

"Yep." Jo-Jo nodded.

"A **Chain Reaction**," Marcia muttered.

"Explosion, more like," Jo-Jo said. "It just went kind of . . . *wherrr-ooomph!* Very loud but soft too. Weird." He shuddered. "Everything went black and filled up with choking **Darke** stuff. People were screaming and panicking . . . It was awful. I couldn't breathe. I pulled Marissa out with me. But then she ran off. Into the Forest. I don't know what happened to Newt . . ."

Marcia and Septimus exchanged somber glances. "It all depends," Marcia said, "on whether Newt let go of the bag in time."

"And closed his eyes," added Septimus. "Green is not a good eye color to have when you're standing next to a Kraan."

"Jeez," Jo-Jo said. "Newt's a pain, but even so . . ."

"We'll go over later and check," Septimus said. "But first things first. Where are the Kraan now?"

"In the Moat," Jo-Jo replied.

"In the *Moat?*"

Relieved at having got the bad news over with, Jo-Jo was beginning to feel a little better. Now he could begin on the slightly less bad news. Maybe, he thought, it was even good news. And so Jo-Jo told how he had made Gringe raise the bridge to protect the Castle and then lured the Kraan into the Moat. He had hoped that maybe they might drown, but anything was better than letting them loose to wander the Forest or Castle. Jo-Jo told how he had hidden under the water, using his unpierced flute as a breathing tube, and by the time he came to the end of his story, Jo-Jo was aware that Milo, Marcia and Septimus were looking at him with a new respect. Jo-Jo felt relieved. For once in his life he seemed to have done something right.

Septimus broke into a smile. "I don't know what impresses me more," he said. "Luring a **Chain** of Kraan into the Moat or getting Gringe to raise that drawbridge."

THE RAT'S TALE

Leaving Jo-Jo to sleep off his ordeal, Septimus and Marcia set off in search of the Kraan. They talked to Gringe, but he was still too shaken to make any sense, so they decided to walk the walls of the Castle, peering down into the murky depths of the water as they went.

"Do you really think they drowned?" Septimus said.

"It was a brave thing for Jo-Jo to do," Marcia said, "but unfortunately it won't have drowned them. Kraan can exist quite happily underwater. However, it has probably got them far away from the Castle." Marcia sighed. "But not in a way I would have chosen."

"How do you mean?" Septimus asked.

"Septimus, as custodian of an Ancient Way Hub, I've made it my business to discover all I possibly can about the Ancient Ways. They were once infested with Kraan until some enterprising sorcerer made it his life's work to rid the Ways of them. But being a sorcerer he was loath to lose such powerful beasts . . ."

"So he kept them," Septimus finished for her.

"Indeed he did. He **Enchanted** their eyes and put them in a bag."

"What an idiot," Septimus muttered.

"I would agree with you on that," Marcia said. "And the problem is that Kraan have an affinity for the Ancient Ways, and I fear that is where they will be heading. And that is the last thing we want in the Ways right now; their **Darke** presence will speed up the **UnRaveling** tremendously. Let's hope they haven't gotten in."

"Tod's in the Ways. Right now," Septimus said quietly. "She's going home."

Marcia remembered how she had persuaded Septimus to let Tod go and felt awful. "Oh, Septimus . . ."

They walked on in silence until they came to the East Gate Lookout Tower. "The rats might have seen something," Septimus suggested.

They rang the bell and waited. A young rat called Florence opened the door. She stared up at the impressive visitors towering over her. Florence was a sensitive rat and she could tell that something was wrong. "Good morning, ExtraOrdinaries," she said. "How may I help you?"

"We are looking for witnesses to the, er, explosion at the

old Infirmary," Marcia said. "We wondered if anyone here saw anything?"

"Morris," Florence said. "He saw it. Shall I go and fetch him?"

"That would be most kind," Marcia said.

Morris was very relieved to talk. Stanley had been dismissive. "Night terrors," he had told Morris over his breakfast egg. "You've had them ever since that Garmin trouble. Pass the salt, will you?" Morris had felt foolish and said nothing more. But now here he was up on the roof, with *two* top Castle dignitaries hanging on his every word, while Stanley, who was a nosy rat, gaped open-mouthed. It should have been a good feeling—but it wasn't. Morris had something awful to tell one of them. "It was your brother, ExtraOrdinary. It was Jo-Jo, I'm sure it was," Morris said.

"It was," Septimus said.

"He was so brave," Morris said. "There was a line of Kraan heading toward the Castle and he came dancing out in front of them trying to make them follow him. He was like the Pied Piper—he even had a flute in his hand—and he waved his arms and they *all* followed him to the Moat, and then Jo-Jo jumped into the water and . . ." Morris looked up at Septimus sadly. "And, that was it. I watched for ages but he didn't come back up. I'm so sorry," he said, his thin, high rat voice trying not to wobble.

"Morris, please don't be upset. Jo-Jo is alive and well," Septimus said.

"Oh, that is wonderful news!" Morris said. "I was so sure he had . . ."

"Could you please tell us what happened next?" Marcia prompted gently.

"Oh, yes . . . sorry. Well, after I stopped watching for Jo-Jo I felt really sad and I leaned over the battlements and just stared down at the Moat. And then I noticed lots of little whirlpools going along the surface, all in a line and heading that way . . ." Morris pointed to the left, down toward Snake Slipway. "I just *knew* they were from the Kraan walking along the bottom of the Moat," he said.

"I am sure you were right," said Septimus.

"You didn't see them leave the Moat?" Marcia asked.

Morris shook his head. "No. I watched the whirlpools all the way around the bend until I couldn't see them anymore."

"Thank you, Morris," Septimus said. "We really are very grateful. You've been extremely helpful."

Morris showed his visitors out. As they went he could not help but ask, "Um, do you think they might come up here at all? I know that Kraan like killing us rats. And we are right by the Moat . . ."

"I think you are perfectly safe," Septimus said. "But if you are at all worried, you have my permission to ring the emergency button for the Wizard Tower. Someone will be with you straightaway."

Relief flooded Morris's features. "Oh, thank you so much," he said.

Septimus and Marcia hurried away. "That is one intelligent and thoughtful rat," Marcia said.

"And a brave one too," Septimus said. "We have some very good rats in this Castle."

"So let's keep it that way," said Marcia.

As they made their way to Snake Slipway, Marcia and Septimus breathlessly discussed strategy, finishing each other's sentences like a long-married couple.

"They'll be making for the **Hidden** arch on the Outside Path, I reckon . . ."

"Definitely . . ."

"We might be in time . . ."

"With any luck. It's slow going through the mud on the bottom of the Moat."

"If we get there before the last one, we'll need a . . ."

"Strategy."

"A good one."

"A single entity from a **Chain** carries the power of the whole **Chain** . . ."

"Well remembered. We act together . . ."

"**Synchrony** . . ."

"Exactly. Remember how?"

Septimus grinned. "It was our very last tutorial. How could I forget?"

Marcia held out her hands as though accepting a gift. "**Synchronized Transport?**"

In reply, Septimus placed his hands in Marcia's. "And if we get a Kraan?"

"**Chain Break** first. Can't deal with more than one."

"Quite. Then **Fast Freeze?**"

"**Fast Freeze** and **Safe Shield** combo . . ."

"You've got it. Okay, let's go."

Morris was the only one in the Castle to see the rare sight of a **Synchronized Transport**. Being a nosy rat, just like his father, Morris had rather sheepishly followed the two ExtraOrdinaries. He watched as Septimus and Marcia became encased in a haze of purple mist and when the **Synchronicity** kicked in with a burst of blindingly bright light, Morris squealed with shock and hid his eyes. When he opened his eyes he thought Septimus and Marcia were still there, although they were now a shimmering green color. But when Morris blinked and looked up at the sky he saw them there, too. And when he looked down at his feet there they were as well. The afterimage took hours to fade, and when it finally went, Morris rather missed seeing the two green Wizards hanging around the Rat Office.

SYNCHRONIZED SWIMMING

The **Synchronized Transport** took Marcia and Septimus to exactly where they had planned—the **Hidden** arch. It was to be found in the Castle wall, along the Outside Path, some twenty feet above the Moat. They arrived to find the path slippery with Moat mud and strands of wet weed dripping on the wall. There was no doubt that the Kraan had recently passed that way, but of them there was no sign.

"We're too late," Septimus said.

The path was little more than a ledge. Marcia shuffled around carefully and stared at the wall, trying to see the **Hidden** arch within, but all she saw was the remains of a chalk mark drawn by Lucy Heap some months earlier. Tentatively, Marcia pushed her hand against the stone and felt a softness to it. "It's still open," she said. "We'll have to go after them, Septimus. For Tod's sake."

"We'll go **Synchronized**," Septimus said. He stretched out his hand to take Marcia's once more, and as he did there was a soft splash from the Moat below. They both gingerly leaned out and looked down to see a black, bony skull breaking the surface.

"We've got one . . ." breathed Marcia.

Never had the advent of a Kraan been greeted with such pleasure. Utterly still, Marcia and Septimus watched the beast claw its way up the wall, like a giant spider climbing out of the bath.

Synchronicity is a **Magykal** state where two Wizards with equal power and knowledge act together as one. This can, if used well, increase the combined strength of their **Magyk** by up to seven times.

The Kraan looked up and saw two green-eyed humans staring down at it. Its six red eyes lit up with delight at the prospect of a double Wizard kill so early in its existence. It leaped forward for the lethal blow and found itself suddenly surrounded by a purple mist. An overpowering weakness enveloped the Kraan and it fell, limbs flailing, a spider out of control. There was a splash and it began to sink.

"Bother," said Marcia. "We'll have to . . ."

"Jump," Septimus finished.

They landed beside the Kraan, which was sinking, slowed by its encasing purple bubble. Marcia grabbed an arm, feeling only a slight tingle as she touched the slimy bone, and Septimus found a leg. Stupefied by the **Magyk**, the Kraan did nothing, but Marcia and Septimus were struggling. Their heavy, waterlogged cloaks were pulling them down, the fight to stay afloat was using up much of their power, and direct contact with the Kraan was leaching their **Magyk** away fast.

Rupert Gringe, Lucy Heap's brother, was the proprietor of Rupert's Paddleboat Hire at the end of Snake Slipway. He was embarking on his annual clear-out of junk when he heard splashing from just around the bend in the Moat. Rupert knew the sound of someone in trouble; he grabbed the nearest boat and set off. The sight of Rupert's pink paddleboat tearing

toward them, paddles whirling furiously, was all Septimus
and Marcia needed to give them the energy to keep their
Synchronicity going.

Rupert drew up beside them. "Bit cold for a swim, isn't it?"
he said, regarding Marcia and Septimus with amusement.

"Very funny, Rupert . . . give us a hand to get this . . . into
the boat, will you?" Septimus said, breathless with the effort
of keeping afloat.

"Get what in?" Suddenly Rupert's grin vanished. "What
the . . . what is *that*?" he whispered, pointing to the purple-
shrouded Kraan bobbing just beneath the surface.

"It won't hurt you," Marcia said. "It's **Shielded**."

"I'm not having that thing in my boat," Rupert told them.
"No way. I just painted it for the season."

"Then . . . tow it," Septimus puffed. "Please, Rupert. It's
important."

"All right," Rupert agreed reluctantly. "Now, do you two
want to get in or are you still enjoying your swim?"

There was only one answer to that. Rupert put the ladder
down and soon his pink paddleboat was full of two dripping
Wizards and the strangeness of **Magyk**.

Under instructions, Rupert took them to the Manuscriptorium landing stage at the end of Sled Alley. As they paddled along the Moat towing the Kraan encased in its purple bubble, they passed the wreckage of the old Infirmary. "That was some party last night," Rupert commented. He received no reply. Both Septimus and Marcia were tiring fast and they needed all their concentration to keep hold of the Kraan and remain in **Synchronicity**.

At the landing stage Septimus managed two words to Rupert: *"Don't touch."* Rupert needed no telling. He stood back while Marcia and Septimus heaved the Kraan from the water and the enormity of the thing revealed itself. Then he watched the two Wizards carry it up the alley, enfolded in its purple caul. Rupert paddled slowly home in the sunshine, feeling unsettled. What, he wondered, was going on?

At the Wizard Tower a terrified Catchpole barricaded him-self into the porter's lodge. Septimus put the Tower into **LockDown** to protect the more sensitive areas and then he and Marcia embarked upon the tricky task of maneuvering the Kraan up the spiral stairs. At last they reached the **Darke** eighteenth floor. They staggered along the corridor, hauling the unwieldy creature toward the **Safe Chamber**: a small

Darke-proofed room with a highly effective Lock.

With one hand, Septimus managed to UnLock the Chamber. He pushed the door ajar and then stopped. "There's someone in here," he whispered.

"Who on earth would want to—" Marcia's comment was cut off by a quavering voice.

"Don't come in. Please don't. I'm contaminated. Keep clear."

"Newt?" Septimus said. "Is that you?"

"Yes . . . it's me. I'm so sorry, ExtraOrdinary. I've done a terrible thing."

"We know what you've done, Newt," Septimus told him curtly. "Come out of there and keep away from us. You'll see why."

Newt's pale, scared face appeared from the gloom. His eyes widened with shock at the sight of the shadowy form of the Kraan within a purple haze. He flattened himself against the doorframe and squeezed by. Then he stood, chewing his fingernails, watching Marcia and Septimus deposit the Kraan in the Safe Chamber.

At last, with the door Locked, Marcia and Septimus let go of their Synchronicity. Newt now saw clearly the bedraggled state the two Wizards were in. He was shocked.

"Newt Makken," Septimus said, "I suggest you stop gawking like a stranded fish and start to do something useful."

"Yes. Anything. I'll do anything you want," Newt said.

Septimus left Newt in the Darke book room with a pen and paper. "You can write out the Incantation you so cleverly managed to say right the first time," Septimus told him.

Septimus released the Wizard Tower from its LockDown and he and Marcia went up to his rooms. While they changed into dry clothes Milo made them coffee. He knew better than to ask what had happened; Marcia would tell him when she was ready.

Milo saw no more of Marcia that day or for much of the next. She and Septimus, along with the chastened Newt, worked tirelessly to find the Reverse of the Kraan Incantation. They had custody of one Link from the Chain Reaction, and whatever happened to that Link would happen to the entire Chain. Now all they had to do was to find the Reverse of the Incantation and apply it to their captive.

But first they had to find it.

PART
~VIII~

A Near Miss

Tod's *PathFinder was a beautiful* thing. It consisted of two parts: a smooth onyx sphere attached to a leather triangle that she held between finger and thumb and a hollow lapis lazuli dome attached to a beautiful pointer of filigreed silver shaped like a long triangle. On the opposite side of the lapis dome was a thick curl of silver through which Tod threaded a leather cord so that when she was not using it, the **PathFinder** hung around her neck like a pendant. The two parts fit together beautifully: the lapis dome sat snugly on the onyx sphere and moved fluidly to point in the right direction. All Tod had to do was to touch the tip of the pointer to a piece of rock from the place she wanted to go, then the **PathFinder** would guide her through the Hubs, showing the archways she needed to take.

The Ancient Ways consisted of a network of strange and **Magykal** tunnels linked to a worldwide system of Hubs. Each Hub had twelve tunnels leading from it, marked with the old PathFinder numbering system from I to XII. Tod had to negotiate nine Hubs in order to get home because two on her way home were unusable. One was full of lava from a volcanic eruption and the other, the nearest to her village, was now beneath the sea. And so she had to travel great distances across the world in order to arrive at a place not so very far from where she had started. But this was no hardship; Tod loved the Ways and even going through nine Hubs would only take about an hour—if all went well.

All did go well to begin with.

Marcia's Keep was the first Hub. Tod hurried across and headed into Arch II. She walked toward the white mist of the **Vanishing Point**—and then she was gone.

A few minutes later, Tod was stepping into one of her favorite Hubs. It felt like a tiny, wild wood. Its twelve arches were set into an enclosing wall built from mellow brick festooned with ivy. The Hub was suffused with a soft green light; it was calm and peaceful. Birds sang brightly and this time Tod was entranced to see a sea of wild roses tumbling over the walls.

Had she not been so excited about going home she would have been tempted to sit among the roses for a while and listen to the birdsong. But with the happy thought of surprising her father when he came back from his day's fishing, Tod followed the direction her PathFinder was pointing and walked into the next arch.

Tod ticked the subsequent Hubs off as they appeared in their usual sequence.

Hub three: an ancient, bare arena of white marble, glaring in the heat of the sun.

Hub four: a muddy pool, ankle-deep, writhing with tadpoles.

Hub five: a slate quarry, glittering with frost, with the arches hewn into the rock.

Hub six: inside a house, with swinging wooden doors on the arches. There was a baby crying in the room above.

Hub seven: a hushed temple and its priest. Tod had a coin ready in her pocket in case the priest noticed her as she ran across the bright mosaic floor. But the old man was asleep and Tod's footfall was so light he did not wake up.

Hub eight, the last one before her home Hub in the Far Fortress, was a nasty, oppressive maze and Tod dreaded it. This was where Tod really needed her PathFinder. She stepped out of the archway and was confronted by a blank wall of blackened bricks, burned long ago in an ancient kiln. The wall rose up a little more than an arm's length away and ran parallel to the Hub wall so that it formed a narrow, dark corridor. Its height—almost ten feet—meant that there was no way Tod could see what lay beyond. She had the choice to turn either right or left, but although the wall formed a concentric circle within the Hub, it was not possible to reach the other arches by following the corridor. The passage was blocked just before each neighboring arch, forcing the traveler deep into the maze.

Tod hated the maze. It made her feel trapped, like a rat in a run. To take her mind off the sensation of stepping into a prison cell, she looked up at the sky. It was not a heartening sight. A heavy blanket of gray cloud hung low, and a fine mist of chilly drizzle was descending. Tod had no idea where in the world this Hub was—it was not on Marwick's map—but judging by the low level of light it lay much farther north than her village.

Tod turned her attention to the immediate task in front of her. The PathFinder was indicating that she must go left, and so she did. The narrow corridor curved gently around to the right, and before it had reached the next arch the way was blocked, so Tod was forced to take a sharp turn to the right. Ten steps later, Tod was presented with a choice of two turnings. The **PathFinder** indicated left once again, and so left she went.

Tod trod quietly, taking care not to betray her presence. It bothered her that she could not see more than a few feet ahead—who knew what might be lurking? The corridor was so narrow that if she did meet anyone there would scarcely be room to squeeze past. The thought of suddenly meeting a stranger in such a confined space was not good, but what really spooked Tod were the random patches of **Darke Magyk** that had been left by travelers over the millennia. The sharp twists and turns of the maze and its immensely high walls meant that these gloomy miasmas never shifted. They lurked in the dead ends and unnerved Tod as she passed by.

The only good thing about the maze Hub was the navigating. This was actually fun with the **PathFinder**, which happily adjusted to every change of direction and was always very definite when faced with a choice of turnings. How anyone without a **PathFinder** managed to find their path through to the right arch, Tod had no idea. She and Oskar had done a trial run with the PathFinder some months ago, and Oskar had written down every turn. He had made a copy for Ferdie and offered one to Tod in case she ever lost the PathFinder. But Tod had refused to take it—she was never going to lose her precious PathFinder.

The Hub was huge. Even with the PathFinder the maze took about twenty minutes to navigate; how long it might take without one, Tod could not imagine. Somewhere deep in the center of the maze there was said to be a skeleton lying sprawled in despair across a three-way junction. Luckily Tod's route did not take her past any skeletons, but it did go by some nasty swirls of Darke Magyk.

After about fifteen minutes, Tod felt she was making progress. The PathFinder had just taken her through a rapid series of left-right-left-right turnings that she remembered as being near the end, and now she was on the long straight run that led to the very last convolutions before her destination.

As Tod neared the final series of twists and turns, she saw something out of the corner of her eye that sent a stab of fear shooting through her. A black, round shape like the dome of a huge, bald head was moving rather jerkily just above the top

of the wall. She stopped and stared, her heart beating so fast
that her hand holding the PathFinder shook. Something ten
feet tall was in the maze with her. And right then it was only
one wall away.

A deep sense of fear seeped into Tod's bones as she watched
the lurching up-and-down movement of the skull-top traveling
along the neighboring run, no more than a few feet away. Now
Tod was grateful for the high, obscuring walls and wished
they were even higher. The PathFinder, after adjusting itself
to her trembling hand, pointed steadily on. Tod walked
quickly along the long straight corridor, relieved to see it was
taking her in the opposite direction from the skull-top, which
had turned suddenly and was now moving away.

Tod hurried through the rapid series of turns and could
not resist breaking into a run down a long, curving corridor.
At the end of the corridor was a fork. Tod was pretty sure she
should take the left turn, but for once the PathFinder had no
opinion. It sat trembling on its sphere, pointing accusingly at
Tod herself as if to say, *You know how running upsets me.*

"Please," Tod whispered, "please show me the way." As
she stood at the fork waiting for the PathFinder to settle, she
felt a pricking sensation in the back of her neck. Very slowly,

she turned around and saw something coming around the bend that would haunt her nightmares for years to come. A ten-foot-tall shining black skeleton: the body had a human configuration, but the head was that of a beast. Domed, long in the snout with two short yellow tusks on either side of the jaw like a warthog. Tod froze. She knew at once what it was and, thanks to her homework, she knew how lethal it was. Just as Septimus had done with Benhira-Benhara, Tod counted the eyes. But unlike Septimus she counted six: ranged down either side of the snout were three shining points of red. And each one was focused on *her*. This was the real thing

Tod didn't intend to, but she screamed. The PathFinder pointer fell off its onyx sphere and tumbled to the sandy floor. She scooped it up, fumbled and dropped the sphere, which rolled into the shadows. Clutching the PathFinder in one hand, Tod looked desperately for its sphere, but it seemed to have vanished. She glanced up to see the Kraan advancing toward her with a mechanical, shuddering gait. Behind her, divided only by a skin of bricks, Tod knew, lay the arch she needed to get home, but it may as well have been in another country, for she had no idea how to get to it. All she did know was that she had to escape the monstrosity pitching rapidly toward her. And so Tod did the only thing possible—she turned and ran.

THE FAR HUB

"It's Tod!" Ferdie said to Oskar excitedly.

Oskar and Ferdie were in the Far Hub. It was the nearest one to their village, but was half a day's walk away, situated deep in a forest called the Far. The Far Hub followed the configuration of all Hubs with twelve arches leading off from a central circular space. When, as prisoners of the Lady, Ferdie and Oskar had first seen the Hub, it had seemed like a dungeon, but the villagers had made some changes over the past few months and it now looked and felt quite different. The Far Hub was almost cozy. It had a selection of rugs laid upon the flagstones, along with some comfortable chairs and blankets for when the chill of the night air seeped through the thick stone walls. It also had twelve stout doors covering the arches, each door secured by two long bolts.

Mindful of previous incursions of malicious intruders like Garmin, the Lady and Mitza, the PathFinder villagers had decided they were not prepared to leave the arches open. They knew that this went against the spirit of the Ancient Ways—which was to allow free passage—and so they kept a permanent Watch in the Hub in order to open the doors to any well-intentioned travelers. Behind each door they had set a lantern and a sign reading: *Welcome, Friend, to the Far Hub. Please knock and we will open the door.*

Oskar and Ferdie's elder brother, Jerra, had been on Watch when they had Come Through the previous day. Jerra had listened to Oskar's story, calmed him down, and made Oskar feel a whole lot better about the Ormlet and pretty much everything. Ferdie and Oskar had decided to keep Jerra company on his Watch and had spent a happy time catching up on village news.

Jerra, who was dozing on a chair, opened one eye. "Someone coming?" he inquired.

Oskar no longer doubted Ferdie's gift of **Feeling** the nearby presence of people they were connected to. "Tod's coming!" Oskar told Jerra. "Can you help us with the bolt?" The top bolt was just out of their reach.

"Wait," Ferdie said. "I can't **Feel** her anymore. She's gone away . . ."

"Gone away?" Oskar said. "Why would she do that?"

"It can't have been her after all, Ferd," Jerra said. Jerra was fairly skeptical of his little sister's abilities. Unlike Oskar, he had not seen her in action.

Ferdie swung around to Jerra. "It *was* Tod," she said crossly.

"Well, it can't have been, can it?" Jerra said in his annoying trying-to-be-patient voice. "She would have Come Through by now."

"But it *was* Tod. I *know* it was!" Ferdie very nearly stamped her foot, but remembered just in time that she was meant to have grown out of that.

Oskar was concerned. If Ferdie was so sure, then he believed her. "Let's go and see," he said. "She might be in trouble."

Jerra leaped up from his chair. "Hey, not on my Watch!"

"Jerra," Oskar said. "If Tod's in trouble we have to help her."

"Of course Tod's not in trouble," Jerra said irritably.

Ferdie went up to Jerra and looked him in the eye. "Jerra," she said. "Remember that night the Garmin took me away?"

Jerra went pale.

"Well," Ferdie continued, "Mum told me later that you thought you heard something in my room. But you decided you were imagining it."

Jerra swallowed hard. He hated being reminded of the fact that maybe he could have stopped Ferdie being abducted by the Garmin.

"Well, even if I *am* imagining **Feeling** that Tod was near," Ferdie said, "isn't it better to check just in case?"

Jerra nodded. "Yeah, Ferd. 'Course it is."

Each door had a spyhole to check on the traveler—no one wanted to inadvertently open the door to a Garmin, however politely it might knock. Jerra went over to the door where Ferdie had **Felt** something, flipped open the covering to the spyhole and checked the Way. "No one there," he said.

"We still want to check it out," Oskar said.

Jerra pulled back the bolts and opened the door. The musty, damp-earth smell of the Way poured into the Hub. "I'm keeping the door open. I'll give you five minutes. Don't go into the maze, okay? Just yell out. She'll hear you if she's there."

Oskar and Ferdie walked into the **Vanishing Point**, and then a thousand miles north of the Far, they crept out into the maze. "It **Feels** bad," Ferdie whispered.

Even Oskar could feel a sense of dread hanging in the air. "I'll call out, shall I?" he whispered.

Ferdie nodded. It went against both their instincts to draw attention to themselves, but if Tod was in trouble she needed to know they were there.

"We'll do it together," Ferdie whispered. "One . . . two . . . three . . ."

"*Tod!*" they both yelled as loud as they could. "Tod! Are you there? *Tod!*"

The reply that came was not what they hoped for.

Oskar saw the movement first. He began to run toward it, thinking it was Tod, but in a split second he had skidded to a halt. Behind him Ferdie screamed out, "Oskie! Come back!"

With a giant, black, beast-headed skeleton at his heels, Oskar needed no telling. As soon as he was near, Ferdie grabbed her brother's hand and pulled him through the arch. They hurtled through the **Vanishing Point** without a backward glance. In a moment they were rushing through the open door to the Far Hub.

"Shut the door, Jerra!" Ferdie yelled. "Quick! Bolt it. Hurry, hurry!"

Jerra slammed the door, shot the bolts and turned to the twins. "What was it?" he asked anxiously.

Oskar shook his head. "Horrible . . ."

"Jerra. Look through the spyhole," Ferdie whispered. "See if it's followed us."

Jerra flipped the spyhole cover across. Then he turned around to Ferdie and Oskar. One look at Jerra's face told them the answer.

"Will it break the door down?" Ferdie whispered.

"We're not waiting around to see," Jerra told them. "Come on, we're out of here."

"But what about Tod?" Oskar said.

"You don't know that Tod was there," Jerra said. "But we do know there's a Kraan outside. *Come on*." Jerra went to grab hold of his little brother and sister, but they resisted. They were not leaving without Tod.

"Jeez, you two," Jerra said impatiently. "Come *on*, will you?"

And then Ferdie **Felt** the Kraan leave. "It's gone," she said.

Jerra sighed. "You can't possibly know that, Ferd."

Ferdie reached up and flipped open the spyhole cover. She was too short to see through. "Then have a look, Jerra."

Rather nervously, Jerra peered through the lens of the spyhole. The tunnel was empty. He let the cover drop back and turned to Ferdie. "You're right. It's gone," he said. He shook his head. "Weird."

"That's our Ferdie," Oskar said.

Ferdie stuck her tongue out at Oskar and then felt bad. They were safe—but what about Tod?

FRIGHT AND FLIGHT

Tod was racing along the rat runs of the maze with the sole aim of putting as much space between her and the Kraan as possible. But the maze played tricks with her, just as it had done with the unfortunate possessor of the skeleton at the three-way junction. Tod ran blindly this way and that until, coming around a sharp bend, she saw the bony back of the Kraan no more than four feet ahead of her. It turned at the sound of her footstep and for a moment, Tod and the monster regarded each other with what appeared to be polite interest.

The manners did not last. Tod's green eyes were like a magnet to the Kraan. Suddenly the beast was after her, running with long, loping strides, its bony arms outstretched, ready to grab. Tod took off like a rocket. The skeleton was fast, but Tod had agility on her side. She scooted around the bends, ducking into narrow corridors and when at last she dared to look back, the path behind her was clear. She slowed to catch her breath, randomly took the next turn to the right and saw an archway ahead. It was not the one she wanted, but right then anything that would get her out of the maze would do. As Tod ran into the arch she was sure she heard Oskar calling her name. She hesitated, turned—and saw the Kraan heading fast toward her. She raced into the Vanishing Point and was gone.

Tod emerged into a small Hub covered in snow. Its low enclosing wall was topped by stunted trees, their branches swaying in the brisk, cold wind that moaned through the Hub. She glanced back down the tunnel and saw a telltale disturbance in the white mist of the Vanishing Point; a second later she saw a tall, dark shape within. In a moment Tod was racing into the neighboring arch, hurtling toward another Vanishing Point.

She came out into another Hub, this one knee-deep in dried grass like a collapsed haystack. She kicked her way through the grass and, trying to cover her tracks, she dove into the nearest arch. And so she continued: racing through countless Hubs, taking random arches, not caring where they led as long as it was away from the Kraan.

After many Hubs, Tod emerged into a large, peaceful one.

Covered in short, rough grass dotted with yellow flowers, it looked like an overgrown garden. In the center was a copper bowl with water trickling into it. Tod stopped her flight and mustered the courage to look back at the **Vanishing Point** she had just Come Through. The white mist lay undisturbed, with no trace of an emerging shadow.

After five long minutes staring at the **Vanishing Point**, Tod decided she was safe—or as safe as it is possible to be when lost in the Ways infested with Kraan. She drank from the spring bubbling into the copper bowl and sat on the grass beside it. In the distance she was sure she could hear the pounding of the surf, and a pang of homesickness swept over her. This was a strange, wild ocean. She longed for the quieter *swish-swash* of waves creeping up the beach at home.

The Hub was heavy with heat and Tod sat for a while, letting it disperse the bone-chilling cold of the maze, all the while keeping watch on the arches and trying to forget how far away from home she felt. Now she understood that it was indeed possible to be lost in the Ways, and that tales of people wandering the world forever were probably true.

As she began to feel warm again, Tod turned her thoughts toward what to do. She unclenched her fist and looked at her

PathFinder: it lay warm and heavy in her hand. But without its onyx sphere to turn on, it was nothing more than a beautiful, useless object. After a few minutes it crossed her mind that she might be able to find a stone that would do the same job. She hunted through the grass and slowly walked the flagstone paths, but not one of the stones she found was the right size or shape.

Tod sat down beside the copper bowl, still keeping watch on the arches. She took out the paint-splashed stone that came from beneath her house in the PathFinder village. She stroked it gently and watched its little legs unfold. Her stone had been given a Pet Rock spell when she had first become an Apprentice, but it had since spent most of its time in her pocket. Tod knew she neglected it and she put her Pet Rock down on the ground to have a run around. Then she turned her attention back to the PathFinder. "Please," she whispered to it. "Please, show me the Ways home."

The PathFinder lay unresponsive in her palm, and so Tod, with an idea of looking it in the eye, put her thumb into its hollow dome and raised the PathFinder up so she was looking straight at it. "Show me the Ways home," she said. "Please, PathFinder."

The silver pointer wobbled a little. Then, as though it was trying to get comfortable, it shifted its position on her thumb and settled so that it was pointing down slightly. Something told Tod that maybe, just maybe, the PathFinder would work like this. Very carefully, she put her hand down to pick up the Pet Rock.

It wasn't there.

Tod looked at the ground, sure she would easily spot the green-splashed pebble, but she couldn't see it.

Pet Rocks move fast in the heat, and even faster when they have been cooped up in a pocket for weeks with nothing to eat but half an old toffee covered in fluff. Tod's Pet Rock was now happily having lunch and was oblivious to her despair. It had found some dried crumbs of bread and was eating quietly, sitting beneath a similar pile of gray stones, its green paint obscured by the green shadows of the grass above.

Tod could not believe how stupid she had been. Why hadn't she watched the rock properly? Even if the PathFinder did work sitting on her thumb, it was no use without something from home to touch its pointer to.

Tod got to her feet and began to walk slowly and methodically in circles, staring at the ground, sure that any moment she would see the bright green splashes of paint that Dan Moon had dropped while he had painted the windows of their house. The thought of her home gave Tod a pang of fear: how many years would it be before she found her Way home? If she ever did . . . She pushed down the fear and carried on with her search. Her arm ached with the effort of keeping the PathFinder balanced on the top of her thumb, and her eyes ached with staring at grass and shadows. Once or twice she dropped to her knees to check on a likely-looking pebble but not one was splashed with green paint.

Tod looked up to rest her eyes, and as she gazed at the clear blue sky something Rose had said came into her head: *the StarChaser* **Charm** *was from the PathFinder archive.*

A whisper of hope came to Tod. She lifted the StarChaser from around her neck and held it in the palm of her left hand. It lay heavy and cool, its mysterious oily-blue hue showing swirls of green and purple in the sunlight. Scarcely daring to breathe, Tod touched the smooth silver point of the PathFinder to it and then held the PathFinder up high, its lapis dome sitting snug on the tip of her thumb, the thin streaks of gold shimmering in the sunlight.

The PathFinder tipped its nose up as if sniffing the air

and then—*it moved*. Slowly but surely, it swiveled around and stopped, pointing to an arch. Tod felt like jumping with excitement, but she restrained herself: she was not going to upset the PathFinder. She cast a last glance around the Hub, hoping to catch a flash of green paint from her Pet Rock, but she saw no sign of it. She felt sad to be leaving it behind, but she hoped it would be happy; it seemed a nice place to live. Then she walked into the shadows of the arch thinking that when she got home she would look underneath the house for another green-splashed pebble. There were lots to choose from. Dan Moon was a messy painter.

WAY SURFING

This was the first time that Tod had traveled through the Ways with no idea how long her journey would be, and she found it hard to pace herself. Would the next Vanishing Point lead her to the welcome sign on one of the doors of the Far Hub, or would it be days, weeks or even months until she finally got there? Tod pushed away the fear that maybe she never would—that she would wander the Ways forever.

Four more Hubs went by. There was another temple, this time small, dark and damp. There was a circle of huts inside a palisade, each hut with a Way inside. There was a Hub in the basement of a castle, where hundreds of rats emerged from their burrows in the walls and watched silently as she waited for the PathFinder to make its decision.

As Tod walked into the arch the PathFinder had selected, the rats listened to the tinny sound of her footsteps, and when the sound suddenly stopped as she stepped into the Vanishing Point, they went back to their burrows and waited to greet the next traveler. It was unfortunate for the rats, who were an amiable tribe and merely curious to see who passed through their Hub, that the next travelers they scampered out to greet would be their doom.

As the rats scuttled back to their burrows for their last time, Tod was already in the next Hub—a lake of milky green water. The sky was a deep blue, air warm and scented with blossom, noisy with the sound of cicadas. The Hub was bordered by a low wall of crumbling sandstone into which the arches were set, and from each arch a line of stepping-stones led to a large flat rock in the middle of the lake.

Tod picked her way across the stepping-stones and stood

on the central rock, holding her PathFinder up in the air. It teetered lightly on the very tip of her thumbnail and slowly turned and pointed to an arch. "Thank you," Tod whispered. She took the PathFinder off her thumb and put it into her safe pocket—it was, she thought, time to take a break.

The warmth of the sun and the cool of the water was a delight. Tod sat on the central rock, eating a WizzBar and watching the flickering of water snakes across the surface of the water. A small frog hopped out at her feet, regarded her with wide, froggy eyes, and then leaped back into the lake with a delicate *plip*.

It was with some difficulty that Tod tore herself away to continue her journey. She set off across the stepping-stones and headed into the coolness of the next arch. She stopped for a moment to allow her eyes to adjust to the dim light and then walked into the tunnel. As soon as Tod had taken a few steps she knew something was wrong—there was no welcoming glow of the Vanishing Point. She switched on her FlashLight and walked slowly forward and then stopped, puzzled. The beam showed a change from brick to bright blue lapis lazuli; this was the line where the Magykal Vanishing Point began and it was always hidden by white mist. But there was no sign of any mist at all. Tod crept forward with a feeling of trepidation. The tunnels of the Ways always had an energy within that had made them feel like active, living things. But this one was like an ordinary, underground tunnel: damp, cold and pitch-dark. She walked on, her FlashLight showing nothing but bare lapis and a dusty stone floor. On the edge of the beam darkness lurked, deep and dense, and Tod pushed away thoughts of what creatures might be hidden within. She forced herself on, hoping that soon she would see the welcome sign of a hovering white mist.

Tod had walked for ten long minutes, going ever deeper into the tunnel, when she noticed an unpleasant smell of sulphur in the air. Fearful of poisonous gas, she stopped, considering whether to turn back. It was then she saw that the lapis walls looked different. Gone were its glints of gold, and the brilliant blue had become dull. Tod put out her hand to touch it. The surface felt rough and powdery, just like the stone in Driffa's ring. She took her hand away and looked at it: her palm was covered in fine gray dust. Driffa's words came back to her: *Like a slow fire inside a wall, the crumbling of our* **Enchantment** *will spread through the Ancient Ways . . . it will reach you eventually. . . . there is nothing you can do about it.* Tod stared at the gray dust in horror, then she turned and ran, hurtling back through the lapis tunnel, knowing that soon it would all be dust.

Tod emerged into the sunlight and calm of the dappled green water. She leaned against the warm stone, breathing in the sweet, fresh air. It took her some time to get the courage to take the PathFinder from her pocket, and when she did, she laughed with relief. The lapis shone deep blue and gold in the sunlight. She ran her finger over it to check the stone: it still felt hard and smooth to the touch. The PathFinder was healthy.

The disintegration of the Way forced a decision upon Tod: she would go back to the Far Hub through the Ways she had just traveled. It would mean braving the maze, but she had no choice. She set off across the stepping-stones toward the rock at the center of the lake. As she reached it, a movement ahead caught her eye. Tod's heart leaped with fear: a tall, dark shape was emerging from the very arch she was heading for. As Tod stared in horror, six red eyes locked onto her pair of green eyes.

Tod turned and ran, hopping from one stepping-stone to another, racing for another arch—she didn't care which one, any arch would do. But as she reached it she saw another ten-foot-tall shadow emerging from its **Vanishing Point**.

Tod stopped dead, teetered on the stepping-stone, then turned and headed back to the central rock. The first Kraan was now also advancing toward the center, and Tod knew that she and the Kraan were going to arrive on it at the same time. Tod stopped and turned around. Behind her came the second Kraan; less coordinated than the first, it was having trouble with the stepping-stones, but unless it actually fell off, she knew she was trapped.

Tod hovered on her stepping-stone; her trembling fingers found her Apprentice belt and ran over the contents of its pocket. She had a basic **UnSeen Charm**, but that was no use when in a few seconds she would be sharing her stepping-stone with a Kraan. Thanks to her homework, Tod knew that **UnSeen** or not, the touch of a Kraan killed. The only other thing of use she had was a **SmokeBom** that she had made in her Conjuring Class. It would have to do. She took out the green glass tube, shook it to **Activate** it and snapped it in half. A great cloud of thick green smoke billowed out and engulfed her. Tod seized her chance and under its cover she slipped noiselessly into the water.

BREATHE

Even though Tod was one of the ten percent of PathFinders who had gills, even though she had used her gills before and knew she could breathe underwater, her first intake of water went against all her natural instincts. She spluttered and gagged as the lake water hit the back of her palate and the sensitive skin flap that had automatically closed off the top of her windpipe. She felt the gills deep in her sinuses open up and fill with water. Her head became heavy and a muddy, fishy smell filled her senses. Tod forced herself to keep on breathing in until she no longer felt the need for oxygen, and then very slowly she breathed out and began to sink down through the bright sun-slanted green water into the cooler, darker depths. By the time her boots hit the bottom of the lake she was used to the blurry vision and the strange feeling of being both outside and inside the water.

Very slowly, so that she did not disturb the surface of the water, Tod walked across the pebbly lake bed slippery with, she guessed, snake poop. As she moved steadily forward in

slow motion, she felt the flickering of water snakes, and saw
the occasional glancing beam of sunlight catch them darting
like flashes of lightning. Tod had read somewhere that all
water snakes were poisonous, but she tried not to think about
that. She remembered how Oskar, who knew all about land
snakes, had told her that all a snake wants to do is to get out of
your way. As long as you did not corner it, he said, the snake
would just slink away.

Doing her very best not to corner any snake, or upset its
snake sensitivities in any way whatsoever, Tod moved slowly
onward. She soon came to a line of pillars that rose up and
broke the surface of the water—these were the stepping-
stones. Like a water snake herself, she threaded through
them, and found that she was almost enjoying being under
the water. She negotiated three more lines of stepping-stone
pillars, and at the fourth she stopped; these were the stepping-
stones leading to the arch that would take her home.

The tall dark pillars of granite rose up like trees and broke
the silver skin of the surface. Brilliant with sunlight, it shone
like a mirror, and Tod could see nothing above it. She walked
along the pillars until she reached the slimy green wall of the
Hub. The arch leading to the Ways home was now directly

above, but was it safe to come out yet? Were the Kraan gone or had they seen what she did and were waiting for her to surface? There was only one way to find out.

Hand over hand, Tod pulled herself up the slippery wall of the Hub, keeping her eyes on the surface, watching for any Kraan-shaped shadows. She broke the surface with scarcely a ripple and stayed in the shadow of the wall, watching the Hub.

It was empty.

With a long whoop of relief Tod breathed out a spout of water that would not have disgraced a small whale, then she hauled herself up onto the threshold of the arch. Tod sat on the warm stone and let the sun melt the chill that had lodged in her bones. She blew the water from her nose, coughed it from her throat. She sat, a little dizzy, while her sinuses once more filled with warm air and her ears popped and crackled. When at last her nose had stopped running, Tod got to her feet, waited for the dizziness to settle and turned to face the arch.

It was time to go home.

Welcome

The saddest Hub Tod walked through was the first one after the lake: silent as the grave, strewn with broken, bloodied bodies of rats. Tod squelched across to her archway, trying not to think about the blood and rat fur sticking to the soles of her boots.

But each and every Hub was frightening. With the fear that any moment another Kraan would appear—for if there were two, how many more would she find?—Tod took them all at a run and was at the maze Hub sooner than she expected. The PathFinder took her through, and when she was not checking the direction, Tod was watching the tops of the walls for bald, black skeleton heads. She saw none and could hardly believe it when she reached the arch that led to the Far Hub. She thanked her PathFinder, put it into her safe pocket and ran into the Vanishing Point.

Two minutes later, she walked out of the mist and broke into a huge grin. In front of her was a lantern beside a door with a shining knocker and the sign saying: *Welcome, Friend, to the Far Hub. Please knock and we will open the door.* As she went to lift the knocker, the door was flung open.

"Tod!"

"Hey, Tod!"

Two redheaded bullets hurled themselves at her, laughing and hugging her so hard that water squeezed from her jacket and puddled onto the floor.

"You smell of snake," Oskar said.

"And mud," added Ferdie, pulling her into the cozy warmth of the Far Hub.

Tod heard the bolt being shot across the door and Jerra saying, "Give her a break, you two." And then, "Hey, Tod, come and sit by the fire. You're soaked."

Tod allowed Ferdie and Oskar to lead her to the cushions beside the charcoal brazier. Jerra looked down at Tod anxiously. "You've got blood on your boots," he said.

"It's rat blood," Tod told Jerra sadly. She shuddered, ice-cold at the thought of the Kraan—she suddenly realized what a narrow escape she had had.

Wrapped in a huge towel, her clothes drying by the brazier, Tod slowly sipped a large mug of Jerra's hot chocolate. After a while she stopped shivering and began to tell about the terrifying journey through the Ways. Jerra, Oskar and Ferdie listened in shocked silence until she had finished, and then Jerra spoke.

"This is serious," he said. "Kraan in the Ways. It makes them almost unusable."

"It makes no difference," Tod said flatly. "Soon all the Ways will be unusable anyway."

Three pairs of bright blue Sarn eyes looked at Tod. "Why?" asked Oskar.

And so Tod added the last part to her tale—Driffa's visit to the Castle and the UnRaveling of the Ways.

"Jeez . . ." Jerra said when Tod was finished. Like many of the younger ones from the village, Jerra had been enjoying the freedom that the Ways had given him to travel the world. Their isolated lives had been transformed. Jerra sighed. "And we'd only just discovered them."

"But Tod, you won't be able to go back to the Castle," Ferdie said.

"None of us will," Oskar said sadly.

"Yes, we will. We'll go by boat," Tod said. "But the thing is . . . oh, I can hardly believe it, but it's true . . ."

"What is it?" Oskar asked anxiously.

"There might not be a Castle to go back to. It's built on a bedrock of lapis; there is tons of the stuff beneath it. If that turns to dust then everything's going to collapse."

"*Collapse?*" Oskar and Ferdie gasped.

"But the Wizard Tower is **Magykal**," Ferdie said. "It *can't* collapse."

"It is **Magykal** because of the lapis," Tod explained. "If the lapis goes, it won't be **Magykal** anymore. It won't even *be* there anymore." Even though she knew this was true, Tod couldn't imagine the Wizard Tower, with its golden pyramid, its hazy purple windows and its beautiful, lazy **Sprites** disappearing in a pile of dust.

However, Oskar was not worried. "But it's okay," he said. "Ormie will make some more."

Tod was silent. She couldn't bring herself to tell Oskar what Septimus had said: that the Ormlet was dead.

PART
IX

A PROPOSAL

Mitza Draddenmora Draa *had a* score to settle. Her step-sister was Tod's mother, Cassi TodHunter Draa. Cassi had committed the crime of marrying Dan Moon, the only man—indeed the only human being—whom Mitza had ever loved. Cassi had destroyed Mitza's dreams, and she had paid the price when she had opened a letter from Mitza containing a flurry of sand within which lurked lethal sand flies. After a long illness, Cassi had died. But Cassi's death was no longer enough for Mitza. The older Cassi's daughter grew, the more she looked like her mother, and Mitza now felt mocked by Tod's very existence.

In the depths of the Red Queen's dungeons, to the background of the Lady lamenting her lot in life and Oraton-Marr groaning with pain, Mitza seethed with frustration. She was sick of waiting: it was time for Tod to pay the price of being her mother's daughter, and time for Dan to have nothing left of his foolish marriage. Mitza knew what she must do, but how was she to do it, imprisoned as she was?

However, nothing stopped Mitza on her path of revenge for long and soon she had hatched a plan. She sent a note to the Red Queen by a guard who was too scared to refuse. The note said:

> *Dear Your Majesty,*
>
> *I write to inform Your Royal Graciousness that I am able to obtain for You the key to the Castle that the Sorcerer promised You.*
>
> *Your most humble and incredibly obedient servant,*
> *Mitza Draddenmora Draa*

Calmly, Mitza awaited a reply; she knew the Red Queen would not be able to resist. She was right. Late next morning Mitza was taken from the dungeon and marched blindfolded for two long hours through the cold corridors of the Red Palace. Just as Mitza was beginning to fear that she had misjudged the Red Queen and was on her way to have her head chopped off, the guards came to a halt and pulled off her blindfold. Mitza recognized the gold doors at once: she was outside the audience chamber again. She pushed down a smug smile and composed herself. Now was her big chance.

Eyes downcast, she entered the chamber and curtseyed.

"I want that key," the Red Queen said. "Get it."

Five seconds later Mitza said, "Your wish is my command, Majesty."

"You're not a bloody jinnee, woman," the Queen retorted. "I'll tell you what my command is. I don't want a key from that little witch trollop; I want the real thing from the Castle Queen herself. You will arrange for the Queen to meet me and hand over her keys. She will then escort me to her palace. Do you understand?"

Mitza went pale. This was not what she had offered the Red Queen, but she dared not protest. Grateful for the five-second pause, Mitza did some rapid thinking. "I will need a bag of gold for a Hawk, Majesty," she said.

"A *hawk?*" the Red Queen spluttered.

There was a seven-second silence. Mitza decided to keep the queen waiting just a little bit longer than she was used to. "A Hawk," she repeated impassively. "And another bag of gold for a HoodWink."

The Queen stared at Mitza through narrowed eyes. The

woman was impressive. "Give her what she needs," the Queen instructed the guards. She coolly returned Mitza's dead-eyed stare. "You will return in three hours. You will then conduct me to my new Palace."

Mitza did not react. She had long ago learned that when something scared her witless it was best not to show it.

The Red Queen got to her feet. "Three hours from now. Or I shall have your head on a spike. Now, go!"

TO HIRE A HAWK

Mitza walked out of the Palace, shocked. *Three hours*—how could she do everything in three short hours? She considered fleeing the Red City, but she knew it would be useless; the Queen's outriders would track her down. Clutching her bags of gold, Mitza hurried along the narrow alleyways of the Red City, her thoughts whirling rapidly into panic. She stopped, took a few deep breaths and told herself to calm down; all she had to do was to find a couple of sorcerers. And that, she thought, would be easy in a city reputed to be infested with them.

However, it was anything but easy. Despite the saying in the Red City that there was one rat for every sorcerer, although it was sometimes hard to tell the difference—sorcerers did not generally advertise their whereabouts. They relied on a system of young runners—wannabe Apprentices—to guide clients whom they liked the look of to them. Unfortunately for Mitza, not one runner liked the look of her at all.

At first Mitza was not concerned. She hurried along the maze of alleyways, preoccupied with rehearsing her plan. It was, she told herself, a good one. The important thing was to get the Red Queen to the Castle, where she would be away from her Palace Guards. Once the Queen was in the Castle she would be in no position to be fussy about anything at all. Mitza would get the key from Marissa, show the Red Queen to the Palace, escort her over the threshold, and then lock her in and run for it. The two Queens could fight it out between them and she, Mitza Draddenmora Draa, would have the key to the Castle. She would be free to go wherever she wanted and—more important—free to track down young Alice TodHunter Moon. It was, Mitza thought, a very good plan indeed.

But first she had to find a sorcerer.

Watched from the shadows by cautious runners, Mitza plodded the hot and dusty byways with no luck. After an increasingly anxious hour, she found herself in a dead end and was faced with the long walk back. Panic was rising, when she suddenly spotted a tiny sign above a sun-bleached door. Written in faint gold letters was the word *Sorcery*.

Mitza pushed open the door and was faced with a curl of fiendishly steep stairs up one of the tallest towers in the city. Slowly, she began to climb. Ten minutes later, breathless and red-faced, Mitza was standing in front of a black velvet-covered door at the top of the tower. She wiped the sweat from her brow, wrung out her handkerchief and then swung a brass toad on a rope against a silver plate beside the door. A faint tinkling came from deep within.

After some long minutes a hominid with pink scales and black button eyes let her in. "Follow," it whispered. Mitza went duck-footed behind the creature along a dark and thankfully cold corridor that smelled of burned pumpkin. She was shown into a tiny room lined with distorting mirrors. "Show me your money," whispered the hominid.

Mitza held out one bag of gold.

"Show inside bag," said the hominid.

Taking care to keep it out of snatching distance, Mitza undid the drawstring to reveal yellow gold coins as thick as butter pats. The hominid licked its lips and scuttled away, leaving Mitza surrounded by a myriad of shining versions of herself. She closed her eyes. Some things were best left unseen.

The gold got Mitza admitted to the sorcerer's room at once. The room was taller than it was wide and lit by a small slit window so high that all it showed was a strip of bright blue sky. A bar of light shone down onto a strikingly beautiful gray-haired woman who wore the typical Red City sorcerer's scarlet robes heavy with gold embroidery. As Mitza entered, the sorcerer looked up and two beams of **Darke** light shone from her eyes. Mitza gasped and jumped backward. The beams stung.

"What is it that you lack?" asked the sorcerer in a soft voice.

Mitza decided to go for the difficult one first. "A **Hawk** to find a witch and take her to a place of my choosing. At a time of my choosing," Mitza replied, careful to say all that she needed.

"Gold first. **Hawk** second."

Mitza handed over the bag and the sorcerer poured the

coins onto the floor. She looked down at them disdainfully. "New minted."

"From the *Royal* Mint," Mitza said.

The sorcerer picked one up and sniffed it. "Hmm . . . they smell right. You will need an article from the witch to give the Hawk."

That was no problem for Mitza; she kept what she called "tabs" on everyone she could. She had a button from one of Tod's tunics, a handkerchief from Dan Moon, a sliver of blue silk surreptitiously cut from inside the hem of the Lady's dress and a silver star pried from Oraton-Marr's cloak. She even had a long white hair from the Red Queen that she had found lying in the dust outside her audience chamber. And from Marissa she had one of the grubby green ribbons that she threaded through her hair. "Yes," said Mitza.

The sorcerer eyed her client appreciatively. Here was someone who knew what she was doing. "You're not looking for a job, I suppose?" she asked. "I have a position vacant here. My last assistant was not entirely . . . *suitable*."

"Few are," Mitza commented.

The sorcerer gave a thin smile. "Indeed. My creature will give you the Hawk. If you choose to return it I shall refund half your gold. If you choose to stay as my assistant I shall return all your gold, bar one coin for my trouble." She handed Mitza a tiny scroll, sealed with a blob of fat black wax. "The Incantation. Make eye contact with the bird at all times. Say it slow and clear. Make no mistakes. You will not get a second chance. I wish you good hunting."

"I thank you," Mitza replied in what she thought of as sorcerer-speak.

The sorcerer laughed. "You are sorely pressed for time," she observed. "And still you lack two things."

"I am," Mitza agreed. "And I do."

"What is it that you lack?" the sorcerer asked once again.

Mitza decided to go for business first, pleasure second. "A pair of HoodWinks," she replied.

The sorcerer chuckled. "You are hatching a fine plan, I can see. I am sorry to say I sold my last HoodWink only this morning—and for less gold than you would have paid. Yes, I know you have another bag. So, I will do a deal. For half of that bag I will give you a pass to the Gremelzin in the caverns. It will provide you with a fine pair of HoodWinks, I guarantee. But stand well back. It bites. Be sure to wear a shawl, for the cavern is infested with Maunds."

Mitza accepted the offer. She handed over half of the second bag of coins in return for a metal token in the shape of an eye. "Thank you," Mitza said, looking at the cheap piece of tin for which she had just exchanged a queen's ransom. "You have been most helpful," she said, hoping that this was true.

"What is your third lack?" the sorcerer inquired.

Mitza named the lethal sand flies that she had used so successfully with Cassi.

The sorcerer regarded her with a new wariness. "They kill at a touch," she said.

"Yes," Mitza agreed. "They do."

"You are familiar with their use?" the sorcerer asked.

"I am," Mitza said placidly.

The sorcerer began to regret her offer of a job. Acquiring a murderous assistant was a sure way of shortening one's professional career. She gave Mitza a cool smile. "I fear I am out of sand flies at present. But from the goodness of my heart I will give you another token for the Gremelzin. It will have the sand flies in stock."

Mitza took the token: a small, black, seven-pointed star.

"A Death token," said the sorcerer. "It will give you what you lack." The sorcerer got to her feet and fixed Mitza in her gaze. "At the end of this alley you will find a small girl wearing black. She is my runner. At the sight of the tokens she will conduct you to the Gremelzin. I give you farewell."

The hominid was waiting for Mitza by the velvet-covered door. He was holding a wooden box with an open grille for a top. Huddled in the dusty corner of the box was a tiny sparrow, trembling with fear. The hominid handed the box to Mitza with a respectful bow. It was impressed—it wasn't every day the sorcerer agreed to hire out a **Hawk**.

To Find a Pair of **HoodWinks**

It was Ayla's first week as a sorcerer's runner and she was learning fast. Ayla had watched Mitza go down the alley and had guessed that she was looking for a sorcerer, but after Mitza had roughly elbowed her out of the way, Ayla had not been inclined to help the hatchet-faced woman. But now the woman was back. She had a bird-in-the-box and two tokens for the Gremelzin's cavern, which was the most dangerous place in the Red City, and where she wanted Ayla to take her. Ayla gulped. She saw the seven-pointed black star lying in the woman's palm and goose bumps ran down her neck. It was the first Death token she had ever seen. This was not, she thought, turning out to be a good day.

Some runners would have turned the job down, but not Ayla. Ayla was from a poor family who lived in a tiny tent in the City of the Free. She longed to become a sorcerer, and the only way for an outsider to become accepted into the Guild of Sorcerers was to spend many years as a faithful runner, until at last a sorcerer trusted her enough to take her on as Apprentice. Feeling rather nervous, Ayla conducted Hatchet-Face through a maze of alleyways until they arrived at the entrance to the underground cavern of the Gremelzin.

To Ayla's surprise, the woman showed her a gold coin and said it would be hers if she guarded the bird-in-the-box with her life while Mitza went into the cavern. Ayla nodded. But she had learned a lot in her first week and she did not expect to receive the coin. One look at the woman's hard eyes told her all she needed to know.

The network of caverns where the Gremelzin lurked was formed by an ancient underground river that fed the wells of the Red City. Few people ventured there unless they were desperate, for it was known to be inhabited by infant Maunds. Mitza had taken the sorcerer's advice and had placed her shawl around her shoulders.

After wobbling down a series of ladders, Mitza found

herself in a tunnel, which was just a little too tight and a little too low for comfort. At the end of it glowed the dim red light of the cavern where the Gremelzin lived.

The Gremelzin was not a creature anyone would visit unless desperate. Covered in yellow scales, six-legged, with two sets of lizardlike hands and a long, pointed snout, it lay curled on an abundance of ragged cushions piled on a huge gilt chair. The Gremelzin was an intelligent creature. It had been found in a cave by the most powerful sorcerer the Red City had ever had, who captured it while it slept and set it to work in his storeroom. The creature took to the work at once and became obsessed by storage systems. Unfortunately, during a heated argument—the Gremelzin favored screw-top jars and the sorcerer preferred old-fashioned corks—the creature had bitten the sorcerer. The bite was venomous, and despite frantically trying every antidote possible, the sorcerer had died a lingering death. Unaware that its master had died, the Gremelzin faithfully continued dispensing the contents of the storeroom on production of one of the sorcerer's tokens. It lived on the bats and spiders that inhabited the cave and drank the cool fresh water from the underground river. It never wondered why the sorcerer no longer visited and was perfectly content with its lot.

Mitza entered the red-lit storeroom and put the tokens on the nail: a tall metal pillar with a flattened top. The Gremelzin scuttled over to it and inspected the tokens. Its flat, reptilian eyes regarded Mitza. "Gold," it hissed. "Gold for Death."

Mitza counted out the gold from her bag, keeping one coin back for the runner. "That's all I have," she said.

The Gremelzin pushed the gold around disdainfully with its tiny pointed digits. It stared at Mitza. "Lie," it said in a nasal, high-pitched voice.

And so Mitza handed over her last gold coin. "That *is* all I have," she said.

"Truth," the Gremelzin said. It slithered away and Mitza watched its suckered feet carry it effortlessly over the wall of screw-top jars, searching for the sand flies and the HoodWinks.

As Mitza stood in the gloom, one, then two, then three infant Maunds climbed rapidly up her dress and settled upon the broad space her shoulders provided. A Maund was an invisible, parasitic creature. An infant Maund would search for trailing hems, and then using its long, curved claws, it would climb the clothing until it reached the shoulders of its host. There it would squat, growing heavier at such a slow rate that all the unwitting host knew was a gradual sense of being weighted down, accompanied by a growing feeling of doom. In its adult stages a Maund's claws would grow into the skin and curve around the collarbone until it roosted like an invisible vulture. Its host would become reclusive, depleted of energy, and fade into an early death. Mitza knew very well what a Maund would do, and thanks to the sorcerer's warning, she was prepared.

At last the Gremelzin scuttled back, Mitza's requests clutched in its top set of hands. First it gave her the HoodWinks: two matched necklaces of cut crystals the size of walnuts. Mitza took them and, surprised at their weight, she carefully put them into her pocket, which she wore in the old-fashioned way, as a soft leather bag tied around her waist.

The Gremelzin now showed Mitza a tiny gold vial with a silver top sealed with black wax lying in its lined, white palm. "Here is Death," it said. "Take."

Terrified of breaking the seal, Mitza took the vial between finger and thumb and placed it extremely carefully in her pocket. She thanked the Gremelzin, bowed and squeezed back down the tunnel. As she stepped into the courtyard, Mitza pulled her shawl from her shoulders in a rapid, deft movement and threw it to the ground. Taken by surprise, the infant Maunds tumbled down with the shawl. Mitza stamped on the shawl with her heavy boots, squashing two of the Maunds. The third, in a panic, clutched the hem of her skirts and did not let go.

Mitza was so jubilant at her success that she was oblivious to the third Maund, which was now climbing back up her skirt. She snatched the bird box from Ayla, who asked for her gold coin. Mitza gave Ayla a brass penny and told her to be grateful. And Ayla was grateful—she had expected nothing more than a sharp kick, and a brass penny bought a lot in the City of the Free. However, she was not going to show it. Ayla gave Mitza a rude sign and ran off to find her next job, thinking that it was turning out to be not such a bad day after all.

Five minutes later, with a key she had stolen from Marissa, copied and returned, Mitza was opening a door into a hot, enclosed courtyard with just a single palm in its center and a channel of cool water running around its perimeter. She walked into the shadow of the palm tree and closed her eyes. She felt the air grow cool and her next breath tasted of damp leaves and mold. She opened her eyes to see dark green gloom and the outline of an ill-fitting door in front of her. Clutching the bird box, she pushed it open and stepped out into a quiet forest glade surrounded by trees hundreds of feet tall.

Mitza turned around to see the place she had just come out of, so that she would know it again. She was shocked—it was nothing more than a ramshackle pile of logs and leaves that had once, before it became an entrance to a Forest Way, been a charcoal-burner's hut.

Mitza was amazed that the Forest Way had actually worked. Marissa had told her about it many times, but Mitza had not expected the witch to be telling the truth. But here she was: thousands of miles away from the Red City, and as free as a bird. Why would she want to go back to the Red Queen and place herself in danger when she could just walk away and begin a completely new life?

The answer lay in one word: revenge. Revenge on Dan Moon, revenge on that two-faced witch Marissa and revenge on the Castle, which had given the wretched Alice safe harbor. Let the Red Queen come and lop off a few Castle heads—it would do them all good.

At that comforting thought, Mitza Draddenmora Draa allowed herself a small, tight smile.

HAWK-EYED

Mitza had heard that the Castle Forest was dense and she had been concerned that the Hawk might not easily fly away.

But she was pleased with what she found in the glade. High above her was a gap in the tree canopy showing a clear patch of blue sky, which was quite big enough for a bird to fly through unimpeded. Mitza knew that the fewer obstacles put in front of a **Hawk** on a mission, the better.

Mitza put the sparrow's box on the ground. Kneeling beside it, she took out the Incantation, broke the seal and began to memorize the words, while the surrounding trees looked down with an air of disapproval. Ten minutes later, Mitza was ready. She lifted off the grille, reached into the box, grabbed the sparrow and held it up to her eye level. Two frightened black eyes stared at her. Slowly, clearly, not breaking the stare, Mitza said the Incantation:

Bird you are, bird you be.
No longer wild, no longer free,
You will now serve only me.
Of you now I do require,
To find someone within the hour.
Bring her to a place I tell,
Do my bidding wise and well,
And I will free you from this spell,

But until then you work for me.
*Bird you are, now **Hawk** you be!*

The sparrow did not take its eyes off her for one second. Mitza said the **Darke** words at the end of the **Incantation**— words that may be written only by the hand of a **Darke** sorcerer.

The sparrow began to change. Its feathers sprouted, its beak grew large and curved, and its frightened eyes changed to an angry, suspicious yellow. Quickly, Mitza pushed Marissa's green ribbon into the **Hawk's** ready beak. It held it fast and Mitza caught a glance from its eye. It understood.

"You **Seek** Marissa Janice Lane. A witch," Mitza told the **Hawk**. "Bring her to Snake Slipway beside the Moat at sun-down."

Mitza stepped back and the **Hawk** jumped out of the box. It ran a few steps, and then with a powerful thrust of its wings, it lifted up into the air. Mitza watched it go, shooting up through the gap in the trees, its silhouette dark against the brilliant sky, the scrap of ribbon hanging from its beak. And then it was gone; Mitza was alone in the Forest and all was silent.

A sensation that she was being watched came over Mitza. She hurried back into the ramshackle entrance to the Forest Way, and then she was gone. Behind her the trees of the glade relaxed, glad to see an ill-wisher gone.

On the top of the hill in the Wendron Witches' Summer Circle, Marissa was sitting in the afternoon sun with what she thought of as "her" group of witches, known to other Wendrons as "the Toadies." They were discussing the party and in particular what Newt had done with the Kraan. Marissa had last seen Jo-Jo being pursued by the Kraan and she feared the worst. However, Marissa considered worrying about someone to be a weakness, and she was determined not to be weak. She was lying on the grass, staring up at the sky and trying— unsuccessfully—not to think about Jo-Jo when she saw the black shape of a bird hovering above the summer circle.

"Ooh, look, it's a hawk," said Byrony.

"Anyone got a spare mouse, ha-ha?" asked Madron.

"Yeah, I've got one." Ariel, determined to tamp down recent suspicions about her loyalty, took her pet mouse from her pocket and held it, wriggling, by its tail. "Come on, hawky, hawky! Come and get your supper!" Ariel trilled.

Star looked horrified. "Ariel, you can't do that to Pinkie," she protested.

"Why not?" Marissa said. "It's *her* mouse. And it's fun. Look, the hawk's diving. Oh, look it's— Argh!"

The Hawk's dive ended not with Pinkie in its claws but with Marissa. It landed on her stomach, its talons digging into her flesh. Marissa screamed in pain and leaped to her feet. "Aaargh!" she yelled, jumping around, swatting at the Hawk, which let go and rose up, fluttering in front of her, at head height. The swish of air from the beating of its wings and the glint of its yellow eye besieged her. "Go away, you stupid bird! Go *away!*" she shrieked, flailing her arms, batting at its wings. But the Hawk was immovable and its yellow eyes did not leave Marissa's face for a moment.

"Do something!" Marissa yelled to the other witches. Bryony made a tentative swipe but the Hawk lashed out with its beak and made a deep cut across the top of her hand. Bryony added her yells to Marissa's and retreated fast.

A circle of onlookers had gathered to enjoy Marissa's discomfort, for it was now clear to all that this was no ordinary hawk. "Marissa," Ariel said. "It's an Enchanted Hawk. It's got your ribbon and it won't leave you alone until you go with it."

"But I . . . I don't want to go with it," said Marissa, unsuccessfully trying to look away from the Hawk's piercing gaze.

"Well, it's not going to go away," Star said. "So you may as well go with it and see what it wants."

Marissa knew Star was right. "Someone come with me," she said. "Please. I don't want to go on my own."

The witches made faces at one another.

"Sorry, I'm on supper duty tonight," said Madron. "Otherwise I'd love to. Obviously."

"I can't leave the Witch Mother," said Bryony, clutching her hand. "I'm her gofer this afternoon."

"*Someone* come," Marissa said desperately. "Please!"

Ariel and Star looked at each other. This was something Queen Jenna would want to know about: a **Hawk** was serious **Darke Magyk.**

"All right," said Star, taking care to sound very reluctant.

"We'll go with you," said Ariel.

"Oh thank you, thank you," Marissa said gratefully. She tried to look at Ariel but she could not take her gaze from the **Hawk.** "I can't stop looking at it," she said in a small, scared voice. "What . . . what shall I *do*?"

"I think you have to promise to follow it," Ariel said.

"But you'll have to keep your promise," Star said.

"Because if you don't," said Ariel, "it will . . ."

"It will *what?*" Marissa asked tetchily, already reverting to her old self.

Ariel and Star spoke gleefully in unison. "It will peck your eyes out!"

JERRA'S DUTY

Tod, Ferdie, Oskar and Jerra settled down for the night in the Far Hub. They demolished Jerra's supper of cheesy bean soup and sat around the fire toasting the supply of sweet crumpets that his girlfriend, Annar, had sent him off with.

Oskar and Ferdie were still catching up with all the news of the village, and Jerra had much to tell them about the rebuilding of the houses, the new village meeting place and the latest gossip. At first, Tod listened, happy to hear what had been happening and smiling at any mention of her father, Dan. But as conversation drifted to the Sarn family itself, Tod found her thoughts straying to the Castle, and she could not get an image of the Wizard Tower crashing to the ground out of her head. She thought of Septimus and how he had no idea that it might actually happen very soon indeed. She worried too that neither he nor Marcia knew about the Kraan loose in the Ways. She imagined the creatures creeping out of the Hidden arch in the Wizard Tower courtyard, just as the Garmin had done not so very long ago. To the background of Oskar and Ferdie giggling at a family joke, Tod came to a decision. As Septimus's Apprentice it was her job to warn him. And she must do that as soon as possible—even if it did mean going back into the Ways. The sooner she went, the better: she must go that very night.

There was a lull in the conversation while Jerra hung the kettle on its tripod over the fire. "Hot chocolate," he said. "Then sleep."

"Aw . . ." Ferdie and Oskar protested.

Jerra noticed that Tod was silent. "Hey, Tod, you look wiped out. Here," he said, wrapping a blanket around her shoulders. "You're still cold."

Jerra's gesture brought tears to Tod's eyes, which she blinked away quickly. She longed to stay in the warmth with her friends but she knew what she must do. She stood up and handed the blanket back to Jerra with a wistful smile.

"Thanks," she said. "But I've got to go now."

"Huh?" Jerra looked nonplussed.

Oskar and Ferdie were on their feet.

"Go?" asked Oskar.

"Where?" demanded Ferdie.

"Back to the Castle," Tod said. "I have to tell Septimus what's happening to the Ways."

"No, you don't!" Oskar and Ferdie said together.

"That's crazy," Oskar added. "You were lucky to get here at all, Tod. There's no way you're going back in there again. Suppose you meet the Kraan again?"

Tod had thought of that. "I'm going to go **UnSeen**," she said. "I'll be fine."

Jerra was adamant. "Tod, no. You mustn't do this. If you go back now I don't think we will ever see you again. Seriously. I mean it." Jerra's tone took Tod aback. She opened her mouth to protest, but Jerra hadn't finished. "And how," he demanded, "am I going to explain to Dan that we had you here safe—by the skin of your teeth—and let you go straight back into danger? And that is why he will never see his daughter again? Huh, Tod? Tell me that, please." By the time he had finished Jerra sounded almost angry.

There was an awkward silence in the Hub while Tod tried to choose between the impossible: Septimus or Dan. She felt annoyed with Jerra for making her feel guilty about Dan. "It will be fine," she said brusquely. She pointed to the door to Arch VII. "I'm going to go the quick way. I'll be on the Outside Path in seconds."

"Not necessarily," Jerra told her. "You may think it's a direct route to the Castle but I can tell you that is one weird Way through there. It has Hidden branches. I know because I thought I'd go and see Oskie and Ferd and it took me three days to get back here. It's a horrible journey if you get it wrong."

"I won't get it wrong," Tod told him tersely.

"Tod, listen to me," Jerra said, a quiet desperation in his voice. "There's some kind of current in that Way. It's terrifying. It pulls you in. You feel like you're falling for miles and miles. You're taken wherever it wants you to go. You are utterly helpless. Please, believe me."

Tod was silent. She remembered something Marwick had called the Wild Way Wind and how it lurked in Hidden Ways. "Lucy was always fine when she used it," she said stubbornly.

"That was last year," Jerra said. "This is now. The Ways change. As you know, Tod."

Tod stood irresolute as the three Sarns glared at her, daring her to move. She knew that none of them understood how much she had come to love the Castle, and how responsible her Apprenticeship had made her feel. "I'm sorry," she said. "I have to go."

Jerra strode across the Hub and stood in front of the door to Arch VII. "No," he said. "I will not be party to this. I will not let you through."

"You have to," Tod told him crossly. "It's the rule of the Ways. You agreed to let all pass through here freely."

Jerra shook his head. "I don't care what I agreed, Tod. This door stays closed and that is that."

Tod was furious—how dare Jerra do this? She was considering her next move—an **UnSeen** . . . slip the bolt . . . she could just about reach . . . and then run like crazy—when there was a knock on the door of Arch II.

Rap—rappity—rap.

The standoff in the Far Hub evaporated. All eyes turned to the door across Arch II.

Who—or what—was behind it?

HoodWinked

Jerra turned to his three guests. "I'll have to open the door," he said. "You three go upstairs. Just in case it's . . ."

Jerra got a taste of his own medicine from Tod. "No, Jerra. We're staying here with you."

"Too right," said Ferdie.

"You bet," added Oskar.

Rap—rappity—rap came again from the door of Arch II.

"Okay," Jerra said. "But stay by the stairs. So you can run if—"

A louder, more insistent *rap—rappity, rappity—rap* came from the door. Someone was getting impatient.

"Open the door, Jerra," Oskar said. "We'll be fine."

They retreated to the shadows by the stairs and watched Jerra draw back the bolts and pull the door open. Two figures, one tall and thin, the other short and wide, both wrapped in long, hooded traveling cloaks, hurried into the Hub, bringing with them a mixture of musty air and annoyance. On the outside of their cloaks each wore, rather incongruously, an identical necklace of large cut crystal beads. It was odd, Jerra thought, that two such mismatched figures should have such similar taste in jewelry. The facets of the beads flashed like fire, throwing the wearers' faces beneath their hoods into deep shadow and giving Jerra a strange feeling of not quite understanding what he saw.

"That is not, young man, what *I* call a prompt answer," the short traveler said.

"I apologize," Jerra said. "Which Way do you wish to exit by?"

"Four," was the curt reply.

The three watchers in the shadows exchanged glances— *they were going to the Castle.*

It had been agreed that those letting travelers through the Ways would never comment upon their destination, but Jerra could not resist. "You are traveling to the Castle?" he asked as he walked them politely across to Way VII.

"To *my* Castle," the tall one corrected him.

"*If* we ever get there," the short one added grumpily.

Tod, Ferdie and Oskar stared at the figures, trying to make out their features. They had a strange fuzziness to them that seemed to repel detailed inspection. It was even hard to tell if they were male or female; the voices were oddly indistinct. They watched as Jerra held the door open and the figures stepped into the darkness of the Way, their fuzziness blending into the gloom. With the swish of cloaks upon the stone floor they were gone.

Jerra closed the door and shot home the bolts. "Well," he said, walking back to the fire, "that was a strange pair. I looked straight at them, but it was odd, I couldn't quite *see* them."

"There was some kind of **Enchantment** on them," Tod said.

Jerra shivered. "Spooky. Being so close to something like that. They did feel kind of . . . weird."

"They did," Tod said, "and the *really* weird thing is I felt I had seen them before." She turned to Oskar and Ferdie. "Did you feel that too?"

"A bit," Oskar said, unsure. "Maybe."

"I know what you mean," Ferdie said. "It was like a word that you can't quite remember."

"Well, I can't say I recognized either of them," Jerra said as he took the kettle off the fire. "And I don't think I'd want to either. Miserable dingbats, both of them. They couldn't even manage one little thank-you."

Tod said nothing more about her decision to go back to

the Castle and the three Sarns assumed that she had seen sense. She sat quietly with her friends beside the fire and helped Jerra shave curls of chocolate into a mixture of water and milk heating over the fire. But all was not as it seemed. Tod had decided to wait until everyone was asleep and then creep away. She did not want to make Jerra feel bad for allowing her to leave, and she also wanted to give the two unsettling strangers time to get out of the Way. The short one gave Tod the creeps.

Feeling a little guilty about her plans, Tod helped make up three beds from cushions and blankets and then, for appearances' sake, she settled down. Oskar and Ferdie fell asleep at once, but annoyingly, Jerra sat reading by the fire while Tod lay fighting to keep her eyes open. Tod longed for Jerra to go to sleep, but Jerra was restless. He prowled the Hub, he checked the doors, he made another hot chocolate, he wrote a letter—anything, it seemed to Tod, to avoid going to sleep. From beneath half-closed eyes, she watched and waited, until sleep crept up on her, and she could fight it no longer.

At the sound of Tod's regular breathing, Jerra whispered, "Tod . . ."

He got no response. *At last*, he thought, *she's gone to sleep.*

Wearily, Jerra put down his book, leaned back in his chair and closed his eyes. Within seconds he, too, was asleep.

SNAKE ON THE SLIPWAY

The **Hawk** drove Marissa across the drawbridge and into the Castle. It was early evening by now, and a summer squall was blowing in. The wind was cold and rain was beginning to fall.

Marissa was scratched, bruised and exhausted. The **Hawk** had dogged her every step, the relentless beat of its wings above sounding like the heartbeat of a determined, deadly pursuer. It had taken no trouble over such niceties as footpaths and had dragged her through brambles, over rocks and fallen trees. The **Hawk** had allowed her not a second's rest; whenever she had slowed down it had dived and pecked the top of her head. As the **Hawk** hurried her along a deserted Wizard Way, Marissa was thankful that all the shops were closed and the place was quiet. She did not want anyone to see her in such a powerless state. At the end of the Way, the **Hawk** forced Marissa to take the turn into Snake Slipway, and she grew seriously frightened. In front of her lay the Moat: deep and dark. *The Hawk was going to drown her.*

At the foot of Snake Slipway Marissa, terrified of the water, refused to take another step. She threw her hands over her head and waited for the Hawk to dive-bomb her. Nothing happened. She risked a quick upward glance and saw the Hawk was merely hovering, marking the spot where she stood. Marissa understood that she had reached her destination. She sank gratefully to the ground and sat with her arms folded over her head, feeling the gold circlet for comfort. The rain beat down and the wind blew straight across the Moat and set her shivering as the damp seeped through her clothes. Her head hurt from where the Hawk had pecked her, and she felt wretched. She was grateful that she had not been forced into the Moat, but now she began to be afraid of the reason she had been brought here. Whatever it was, it was not going to be good.

At the other end of Snake Slipway, lurking in the shadows, Ariel and Star watched with interest. It was cold and wet and what they really wanted to do was have a coffee in Wizard Sandwiches and get warm, but they knew the wait would be worth it. Queen Jenna would be very pleased to know what Marissa was up to.

It was a long half an hour later when Ariel and Star saw two cloaked figures step down from the Outside Path.

"They're wearing **HoodWinks**," Ariel whispered.

"Nice," Star said. "I always wanted one of those. I wonder who they are?"

As if in answer to her question, the tall figure threw back her hood, pulled the heavy crystal necklace over her head and hurled it into the Moat. The two watching witches now saw her to be a thin, severe-looking woman with white hair in very long plaits that were dark at the ends. Beneath her cloak she wore a pale red robe, and placed firmly on her head was a simple crown set with rubies that glistened in the rain.

"Wow. She looks like a Queen," whispered Ariel.

"Jenna won't like that," Star whispered back. "Two Queens in one castle is bad news."

"Maybe we could work for her, too." Ariel giggled.

"No way," Star said. "She'd chop your head off as soon as look at you."

They watched with interest as the second, short figure copied the Queen's actions, pulling off her **HoodWink** and sending it flying into the water.

"What a waste," muttered Star.

"Shh," hissed Ariel. "Look, it's *her* **Hawk**."

They watched the woman hold up her hand to the **Hawk**. The bird fluttered down to her wrist and accepted a morsel of food. There was a flash of yellow light, and a small, terrified brown bird sat in its place. With a practiced flick of the wrist, the woman snapped the little bird's neck and threw it to the ground.

"Oh!" Star gasped.

"Oh, that's horrible," Ariel said. "How could she do that to a poor forest creature?"

"Come on," Star said, "Let's get out of here before she does that to us."

"I'd like to see her try," Ariel scoffed. But she hurried after Star. She wasn't going to hang around. Just in case.

Marissa felt much better now that the **Hawk** was gone. She was also extremely relieved to see that the person controlling it was only stupid old Mitza. Marissa was less happy to see the Red Queen, however. There were quite enough Queens cluttering up the Castle as it was. If she was going to have any chance of realizing her ambitions, she needed the Castle to be Queen-free. She was going to have to put the Red Queen somewhere and keep her quiet while she decided what to do with her. But where did one hide a Queen? And then it came to her—in a palace, of course.

Marissa thought fast. If Jo-Jo's rather unpleasant gift actually worked, she could talk anyone into anything, the Red Queen included. She slipped her hand into her pocket, flipped open the lid of the little green box, and her fingers found the dried snake tongue. Feigning a polite cough, Marissa raised her hand to her mouth and popped the dried snake tongue in. She gagged. It tasted vile.

Marissa took a deep breath and addressed the Red Queen. "Sister. I, the Castle Queen, bid you welcome."

Mitza's mouth fell open in amazement.

The Red Queen stared at Marissa. She took in her gold circlet, which she could tell was the real thing. She noted Marissa's haughty bearing and queenly way of speaking and thought how strange that she had once considered her to be a mere witch. "Sister," she replied, "I thank you."

Marissa was jubilant—Jo-Jo's snake tongue worked!

The Red Queen gave an embarrassed simper. "I must confess, sister Queen, that in the past I mistook you for a witch. I cannot imagine how I made such a mistake."

Marissa laughed. "It is a little hobby of mine, to go among my people dressed as a witch." Buzzing with her success, Marissa continued. "Sister, I am so pleased that you have come to my Castle at last, after all my pleas to you. It gives me great pleasure to consign my Castle to your tender care."

The Red Queen felt puzzled. Her memory was not what it was, she thought. She had no recollection of Queen Marissa pleading with her to take over her Castle. "The pleasure is all mine," she said, not entirely truthfully. A feeling of disappointment was beginning to steal over the Red Queen. She cast a glance at the results of Rupert Gringe's clear-out spilling out over the slipway and pursed her lips. The place was a mess. It was also windy, and the rain was freezing cold. The Red Queen loved rain, but in the Red City it was always warm and gentle, not icy and sharp as dagger points. No wonder Queen Marissa was leaving.

It had not escaped Marissa's notice that the Red Queen was shivering. "Sister, allow me to conduct you to your Palace. The fires are lit and your welcome banquet awaits," Marissa lied with increasing delight. She held out her left hand, palm upward, at shoulder height. The Red Queen placed her own hand upon it and then, at a sedate and queenly pace, they set

off through the rain, progressing past Rupert Gringe's pile of
boat junk, with Mitza hurrying beside them.

Mitza was not at all happy with the turn of events. "But
Your Majesty," she began, "she really *is* just a witch. She's
bewitched you and—"

Marissa cut Mitza short with a loud laugh. "I see you
brought your fool," she said to the Queen.

The Red Queen laughed a conspiratorial, just-between-us-
Queens kind of laugh. Marissa savored it. "How perceptive
you are, sister Queen," the Red Queen said. "You open my
eyes to so many things. You are right, I have indeed brought
my fool."

This was a step too far for Mitza. "I am not a fool," she
protested.

Marissa took note. It seemed that the snake tongue worked
best when addressed to the person to whom the lies were
directed. She turned to Mitza, making sure to look her in the
eye. "Well said, fool. It is what any fool would say. But you
have been in the service of her Majesty as her fool for many
years. Your fame has spread far and wide."

Mitza looked mortified. How could she have forgotten such
a thing? It was true—she was indeed a fool. Embarrassed

at her own presumption at walking beside the two queens, Mitza dropped back into a suitably respectful position some five paces behind. She followed them, head bowed against the rain, feeling foolish in so many ways.

A SURFEIT OF QUEENS

The Palace was not an imposing building. It was built of weatherworn stone and sat long and low. Its windows were small and numerous, each with a single candle burning. It looked pretty, but was nothing like the immense, gold-strewn, closely guarded fortress that the Red Queen was used to. The rain was now coming down in slanting sheets, and the wind was blowing up the drive, which wound artistically through Queen Jenna's new wildflower meadow. The Red Queen was seriously unimpressed—this palace was no better than a hut in a field.

They walked over the simple plank bridge across the ornamental moat—which the Red Queen took for a ditch—and approached the battered old wooden doors. Marissa was about to use her Universal Castle Key when, to her surprise, the doors swung open. She led the Red Queen over the threshold only to very nearly collide with the reason for the doors' opening—Queen Jenna herself.

Jenna stopped dead. "My circlet!" she gasped.

Marissa knew she must speak—and fast. She fixed Jenna in her gaze and put the snake tongue into action.

"Sister, I—" she gabbled.

Jenna was so cross about her circlet she did not give Marissa the chance to continue. However, the snake tongue had done its work: Jenna now saw Marissa as her sister. And her sister had clearly stolen her circlet. "*What* are you doing with my circlet, Marissa?" she demanded. "Give it back at once!"

Desperately, Marissa plowed on. "It is *my* circlet, sister. You know it is *mine*." Afraid that the Red Queen would become suspicious, Marissa turned to her and said, "My little sister is somewhat . . . *different*. You know how it is in families."

The Red Queen gave an awkward smile: she had disposed of her own annoying little sister years ago.

Jenna stared at Marissa, her bemusement deepening. Why, she wondered, had she thought that her sister's circlet belonged to her?

Marissa continued, determined to cover all bases. "Just as you know, little sister, that this is *my* Palace, ha-ha!"

Jenna felt utterly bewildered by now. It was so odd that she had been thinking of the Palace as her own, but of course it belonged to her sister. It was all most unsettling.

Marissa did not let up. "And you are leaving *my* Palace now, sister. To go home to . . ." Marissa paused to decide what to say. Jenna had not always been very nice to her and she decided to have some fun. "To your little hut at the back of Gothyk Grotto."

Jenna looked puzzled. Try as she might, she just couldn't picture her hut.

"You know, the one with the leaky roof," Marissa explained. "Beside the toilets."

"Oh . . . yes . . . of course," Jenna said. "Silly me, forgetting."

"Well, you know how dippy you are, little sis," Marissa said cheerfully. "Off you go now."

And so Jenna hurried away into the rain, feeling extremely disconcerted. If she had not bumped into Septimus coming up the drive, she would have spent a very uncomfortable night indeed.

While Septimus was trying to work out why Jenna was being so odd, Marissa was leading the Red Queen and Mitza up the sweeping Palace staircase. Marissa had once been to a party there and thought she remembered where the Throne Room was. She led the two bewildered women along a galleried corridor at the end of which she was relieved to see the ornate double doors of the Throne Room. With a confident flourish, Marissa unlocked them with her Universal Castle Key and showed the Red Queen and Mitza inside. And there she left them, the Red Queen ensconced upon the throne, Mitza sitting glumly at her feet.

Five minutes later, snake tongue still in place, Marissa was back with another, even crazier plan. "Sister Queen," she said, "I am sure you would wish to start your new reign with a clean crown. My Palace has an overnight crown-cleaning service, which you *will* want to use."

The Red Queen thought that there was nothing she would like better. She handed her crown to Marissa, then she leaned back in the throne with a sigh and closed her eyes. It had been a long and rather trying day. With her fool curled up at her feet, the Red Queen fell into a sleep full of strange dreams. The fool at her feet, however, did not sleep a wink. The Red Queen had the most outrageous snore.

Marissa retreated to one of the guest rooms. She put the snake tongue back in its little green box and swapped Jenna's circlet for the Red Queen's crown. It fit perfectly. It is not easy to sleep wearing a crown, but Marissa managed it with no trouble at all.

As soon as Jenna told Septimus about her "sister" Marissa returning to "her" Palace Septimus realized that Jenna had been BeWitched—and it was obvious by whom. Gently but firmly, he led her to the Wizard Tower, then he sent for Jo-Jo. Jo-Jo had been enjoying his hero status and was mortified to find he was once again the no-good Heap brother. Almost tearfully, he confessed to giving Marissa the snake tongue.

Armed with a Mongoose Reverse, Septimus released Jenna from her BeWitchment. Jenna was furious when she understood what had happened and it was all Septimus could do to dissuade her from setting off for the Palace right away.

"Jen," he said, "you need to sleep this off. Being BeWitched messes with your head. Leave Marissa and her weird friends there for tonight; they can't do any harm. I'll come back with you tomorrow and we'll sort them out together."

Jenna discovered that Septimus was right. She felt edgy and anxious and could not sleep. She stayed up all night playing cards with Milo and slept most of the next day, leaving Marissa the run of the Palace.

✳   ✳   ✳

The next morning, while Jenna at last drifted off to sleep in the spare room at the top of the Wizard Tower, the occupants of the Throne Room were wide-awake and furious: their **BeWitchment** had worn off. Mitza now knew she was nobody's fool and the Red Queen knew that the Castle was a dismal place unworthy of her talents. They both wanted out. But when they tried to open the Throne Room doors they found they were prisoners in what the Red Queen called "this ratty little dump."

With the Red Queen's crown stowed safely inside her secret cloak pocket, Marissa walked past the shouts and the reverberating thuds upon the door with her head held high and proceeded down the stairs. Let them see what it's like to be helpless, she thought. It served them both right.

As Marissa reached the Palace doors, a ghostly ancient knight with one arm and a serious dent in his head stepped forward and barred her way with his sword.

"Halt!" barked the knight, whose name was Sir Hereward.

Marissa let out a loud shriek.

"I shall raise the alarm," Sir Hereward said in a low, threatening voice. "Unless you leave Queen Jenna's circlet here, in my custody."

"Huh, you daft old ghost," Marissa said, recovering fast, "I was going to do that anyway. See?" With that she hung the circlet on the doorknob. From it dangled a note saying, *Jenna: All yours, I've got a better one now. Have fun! Marissa x*

Sir Hereward gave a disapproving sniff and watched Marissa flounce out and head off down the drive. Then he **Caused** the door to slam shut and stood guarding the circlet until its rightful owner returned.

Marissa set off to look for Jo-Jo. She found him in Gothyk Grotto in a very gloomy state, and took him to Wizard Sandwiches. There, over a Palace Special (a long hot dog covered in red ketchup and yellow mustard—red and gold being the colors of the Castle Queen), Marissa told Jo-Jo her latest, most daring plan. Jo-Jo listened, his eyes growing ever wider with amazement. Sometimes Marissa's sheer nerve astounded him.

"Well?" Marissa asked. "What do you think? Are you up for it?"

Jo-Jo stared at Marissa. "I think it's a crazy idea," he said.

Marissa's face fell. She wanted to do this so much, but only—she suddenly realized—if Jo-Jo was with her.

But Jo-Jo hadn't finished. "And yeah," he said, "I'm up for it."

Marissa broke into a huge smile. "You *are*?"

"Yeah. I am. *Queen* Marissa."

"King Jo-Jo?" asked Marissa.

Jo-Jo laughed. "No, thanks. Not for me. But I'll enjoy hanging out in the Palace."

"And the Red City too," said Marissa. "You'll love it. There are tons of sorcerers. You can have your own sorcerer tower and everything. Because when I'm Queen of the Red City, you can have anything you want."

And so Marissa and Jo-Jo sat planning their future over the Palace Special. When they were finished, Marissa paid the bill—to the surprise of the staff—and then she and Jo-Jo walked out and headed for the Hidden arch that the Red Queen and Mitza had Come Through the night before.

It was late morning when the senior Palace housekeeper heard some very rude language coming from the Throne Room. She opened the doors to find not a couple of drunken sailors—as she had expected—but two very peculiar women who she assumed had wandered off from the Castle Home for Confused and Deluded Persons. The housekeeper's suspicions were confirmed when the tall, scary-looking one stormed out, declaring she was returning to her Queendom *at once* and anyone who tried to stop her would soon find they had mislaid their head. The housekeeper watched her go, shaking her own still firmly attached head, thinking how sad it was, the state that some people ended up in. When the housekeeper turned around, the weird one with a mouth like a hatchet had gone. The housekeeper was on edge all day, hoping she wasn't going to bump into her around some dark corner. That night she armed herself with a saucepan and bolted her bedroom door.

In the gloom of the eighteenth floor of the Wizard Tower, Septimus, Marcia and Newt were closeted in the **Darke Archives**, a circular room clad with ancient slate that glimmered in the candlelight like the surface of a deep, black lake. This was where Septimus had placed all the **Darke** documents from the Pyramid Library. It also contained the contents of Sorcerer's Secret, an ancient and surprisingly **Darke** bookshop that had recently closed in the Port.

Septimus had rescued the entire stock just as it was being thrown on a large bonfire. Much of it was still packed in boxes and all of it smelled of smoke. It was these boxes that they were now examining, for Septimus and Marcia knew that there was no **Kraan Reverse** to be found in the Wizard Tower.

"So we can do the **Reverse** on that Kraan you've got in the **Sealed Cell**, and then all the others get **Reversed** too?" asked Newt. "At the same time. All at once?"

"Yes. That's what happens with a **Chain Reaction**," Marcia said.

"They go back to being beads, right?" asked Newt. "Six for each Kraan?"

"Right," Marcia said curtly. "Now get on with those boxes."

"Yes. Sorry." Newt got back to work unpacking the boxes and sorting the books and pamphlets into possibilities.

Septimus and Marcia carried on methodically going through each page of every book, trawling through endless permutations of nasty, vindictive and vicious spells, **Enchantments** and **Incantations**. It made for dismal reading.

"The things people want to do to others," Marcia said, exasperated at one particularly gruesome **Hex**. "It makes you despair."

"Horrible," Septimus agreed, as he reached the end of a small pamphlet called *A Fear a Day the Easy Way*.

They worked steadily on through the mire of nastiness, desperate to find the **Kraan Reverse**. Newt made them coffee, brought them sandwiches, stacked away used books and did anything he could to speed their search, but they dared not go too fast for fear of missing a vital clue. And they dared not go too slow either, for they knew that every hour that passed was another hour that Tod, whom Septimus feared was still deep in the Ways, was in mortal danger.

PART X

THE NEXT WATCH

Tod *awoke in the Far* Hub to find that everyone was up and getting ready to leave.

"Morning, Tod," Jerra said cheerily. "I left you to sleep. You looked like you needed it." He grinned. "It's five hours after dawn now; the next Watch should be here pretty soon."

"Oh." Tod felt wretched. What kind of Apprentice fell asleep when there was something so important to do?

"Fancy any breakfast?" Jerra asked.

The bacon smelled wonderful. "Yes, please," Tod said, telling herself that there was no point traveling the Ways faint with hunger.

Jerra's bacon sandwiches were even better than his cheesy bean soup. As Tod ate, a feeling of dread crept over her at the thought of going back into the Ways. But it was her duty, she told herself, and she must do it.

Breakfast over, Tod helped put the Hub to rights, leaving it tidy for the next Watch. She tried her best to look relaxed, but inside she felt like a coiled spring wound up tight—ready to run as soon as she got the opportunity. At last it came, with the thud of purposeful footsteps crossing the room above. The next Watch had arrived.

Jerra grinned. "Bang on time," he said. "I would expect no less." Jerra picked up the Way Book—where all travelers through the Hub were logged—in order to hand it over. Ferdie asked to see it and Oskar, always curious, peered over his twin's shoulder as she leafed through, looking at the descriptions of the occasional traveler wandering the Ways.

Tod took her chance. She slipped over to Way IV, drew back the bolts, and as Jerra turned around she was through the door and running. Far behind her, unheard by Tod, came Dan Moon's cheery voice as he hurried down the steps into the Far Hub.

As soon as Tod ran into the **Vanishing Point**, the acrid, eerie smell of sulfur invaded her nostrils. She hesitated for a moment, then forced herself to go on. This was her last chance to get to the Castle. If she did not take it, Septimus would know nothing of the danger until the Wizard Tower collapsed. At least if she managed to get to him he could evacuate the Tower and save the lives of hundreds of people.

Despite the weird smell, the **Vanishing Point** appeared to be still working. The mist closed behind her and as ever, Tod felt as though she was moving forward at breathtaking speed. All was as it should be, she told herself. Any minute now she would walk out of the mist and see the shape of the **Hidden** arch in the Castle Wall before her. And then her direction of travel shifted, and instead of going forward, she was falling. Down, down, down she fell, slowly like a leaf, twisting as she went, supported by the Wild Way Wind—until suddenly it disappeared and she dropped like a stone. Seconds later, the ground seemed to come up and hit her.

In the Far Hub, Dan Moon found three Sarns staring at the open door to Way VII. They looked shocked.

"Morning, all," said Dan cheerily. "Typical. I've just missed the only excitement for the next three days. Well, rather them than me down that unstable Way."

"Jeez," Jerra said, still staring at the door. "I can't believe she did that."

"Who? Did what?" Dan asked.

"Tod. **Went Through** Way VII," Jerra said.

"Tod?" Dan looked blank.

"Your Alice, Dan. She just took off."

"Tod was *here*?"

"Until a few seconds ago, yes."

"So why did she go?" Dan asked, staring at the open door.

"There's bad stuff happening in the Ways, Dan," Jerra said. "And she wanted to go and tell Septimus at the Castle."

"Go back to Septimus? Even though I was coming?" Dan sounded hurt.

"I didn't tell her you were doing the next Watch," Jerra said. "I wanted it to be a fun surprise. Stupid idea, obviously."

Dan went over to the open door to Way VII. He turned to Jerra with a worried look. "This Way smells weird to me. I don't like it. I'm going after her."

Jerra expected no less from Dan. "Hurry, Dan," he said. "If there's a Way Wind blowing through, then with any luck you can catch the same one as Tod."

"Let's hope so," Dan said, already through the door.

Silently, Jerra, Ferdie and Oskar watched the tall, wiry figure of Dan Moon run along the Way and disappear into the white mist of the **Vanishing Point**.

✳   ✳   ✳

Winded, Tod lay in pitch darkness, coughing and spluttering. She had landed heavily in what felt like a deep pile of soft sand. As her breath returned, she gingerly tried out each arm and leg in turn. They seemed to work, so she found her FlashLight in her pocket and switched it on, to reveal nothing but a thick cloud of gray dust.

Tod had just got to her feet when there was a loud thud behind her. She spun around and to her amazement saw Dan Moon lying facedown in the dust. "Dad!" she gasped. "Dad, Dad!" She threw herself down beside Dan, coughing as clouds of dust swirled up into the air.

Dan Moon did not bounce as well as he used to, he woozily told Tod as he struggled to sit up. Tod told him that she didn't care about how well he bounced; she was just so pleased he was here.

"Well, Alice," Dan began, but stopped as he was overcome by a fit of coughing. Tod's smile faded. Dan only called her Alice when he was cross with her. Dan fought down his cough and continued. "I can't say that *I* am pleased to be here. Whatever were you thinking of, running into an unstable Way?"

"Dad, the Ways are crumbling fast and I had to warn Septimus. I didn't want to go, but it's my job now. You know that."

"Of course I know that." Dan paused for another coughing fit. "But you mustn't go putting yourself in danger. Septimus would never expect that, not *ever*."

Tod knew Dan did not understand. "But *Dad*," she said, "this is really, *really* bad. The whole Wizard Tower could collapse at any moment. And kill everyone in it."

Dan shook his head. "A few unstable Ways aren't going to make that happen," he said. But Tod knew better. She scooped up a handful of the fine gray dust they had landed in and held it out to Dan. "Dad, this is lapis lazuli."

Dan frowned. "What do you mean?" he asked.

But Tod had no time to reply. A violent eddy threw her toward Dan. He caught her and, clutching each other, Dan Moon and his daughter were dragged into a vortex of dust. Like butterflies in a hurricane, they were sucked up into the very center of a Wild Way Wind.

WINDED

Inside Way VII, as close to the **Vanishing Point** as he dared go, Jerra waited, lantern in hand.

Watching him anxiously from the doorway were Ferdie and Oskar, who were under strict instructions not to take even one step into the Way. "Can you see anything?" Oskar asked, his voice echoing along the tunnel.

"*Shh*, Oskie," Jerra hissed. "I'm trying to listen, okay?" In the distance somewhere deep inside the Way came an eerie sound like someone blowing across the top of a bottle, and Jerra thought he could see a few eddies inside the white mist of the Vanishing Point. As he held his lantern higher to get a better look, Tod and Dan came barreling out of the mist and knocked him flying. Jerra hit his head on the tunnel wall and Tod and Dan fell in a heap on top of him.

Oskar and Ferdie raced toward the pile of bodies. They pulled Dan and Tod to their feet, but Jerra did not move. Taking one limb apiece, they carried him out of the tunnel and lowered him gently onto the cushions in the Hub.

"Jerra! Jerra!" Ferdie said, patting her brother's face none too gently.

"Werrr?" Jerra moaned. He blinked and tried to focus. Two people were speaking at once, and they both looked like Ferdie.

"Jerra!" Ferdie said. "It's okay, Jerra. Tod and Dan are safe and you hit your head." She could see a large egg-shaped bump coming up on Jerra's forehead.

While Jerra lay woozily on the cushions, Tod explained to Dan about the crumbing of the lapis lazuli. She told him everything that had happened, except, for Oskar's sake, the fact that Septimus thought the Ormlet had died.

Dan listened quietly and calmly. When at last Tod stopped speaking, he said, "It's bad for the Castle; I can see that. But the Ways have brought nothing but trouble to our village. I think it will be a good thing for us."

Tod was aghast. "But we're PathFinders," she said. "The Ways are part of our history. We can't let them fall to pieces as if they don't matter anymore. Because they do matter—to all kinds of people, all over the world."

"Perhaps," Dan said. "But there is nothing we can do, is there?"

"We're PathFinders," Tod repeated stubbornly. "There must be something we can do. There *must* be."

"I can't think what," Dan said.

Jerra opened his eyes. He blinked hard to get rid of the second Tod, sat up and said, "*The Path*. We found it when we were rebuilding the village. Hidden under the bell.

There might be something there."

"Lie down, Jerra," Oskar said gently. His brother seemed worryingly confused with his talk of a path hidden under the bell.

"I won't lie down, Oskie," Jerra said indignantly. "Dan knows all about *The Path*, don't you, Dan?"

"Not really," Dan said somewhat grumpily. "Your mother has custody of it."

"Well, Tod, you should ask Mum to show you," Jerra said.

"Show me a path?" asked Tod.

"What *path*?" Oskar and Ferdie demanded.

"Where does it go?" asked Tod.

Jerra closed his eyes. It seemed way too complicated to explain.

"You're tiring Jerra," Dan said.

"No, she's not," Jerra said. "Dan, I'm serious. Take Tod to Mum. Let her see *The Path*. I can easily do your Watch for you."

"Jerra, you can't," Ferdie said. "You banged your head really hard. You need to rest. Me and Oskie will do your Watch."

Jerra looked up at Ferdie and then had to do his best not

to seem dizzy. "You will not," he told her. "You are way too young."

"Oskie and I are very nearly grown up," Ferdie said. "We'll be going to the MidSummer Circle soon."

This was a MidSummer meeting where all PathFinders between the ages of twelve and sixteen learned the secrets of their history. The first attendance at the MidSummer Circle was the moment when a PathFinder was considered to come of age.

"But you've not been *yet*," Jerra pointed out. He looked up at Dan. "I shall be fine here, despite my annoying little sister."

Ferdie stuck her tongue out at Jerra.

Jerra laughed. "Not so grown-up now, Ferd," he said. He turned to Tod. "*The Path* would make sense to you; go and have a look. Dan, take her. I'll be fine."

Tod caught a hint of urgency in Jerra's words, which contrasted with the distinct lack of urgency on Dan's part. "I'll go right now," she said. "You stay with Jerra, Dad."

But Dan was not prepared to let his daughter go through the Far on her own. And Jerra, although very pale—apart from an angry red bruise on his forehead—was clearly well enough to joke with Ferdie. So Dan accepted Jerra's offer to

take his Watch, told Ferdie and Oskar to look after their
brother and set off with Tod on the long walk home.

HOMEWARD BOUND

Dan and Tod followed the well-worn track that took them
through the Far forest. The Far felt much less threatening
than the Castle Forest; there were no lurking witches, and
the only animals Tod saw were two elusive wood voles. But
the light was dim, the trees clustered close, and Tod looked
forward to being out in the sunlight and seeing the sand dunes
of her home village and the sparkling sea beyond.

They set a fast pace, and as they went Tod told Dan all
the things she had done since she last saw him. Dan listened
happily, thinking how much she reminded him of his dear
Cassi. Tod was careful not to mention the dangers of the last
few months, but there was one thing that was playing on
her mind, and it was not until they reached the outskirts of
the forest where the shadows were lifting that Tod felt brave
enough to mention it.

"I saw Aunt Mitza," she said.

Dan stopped dead. "Mitza? Where?"

"Um. When I was in the desert, getting the Orm Egg."

Dan frowned. "I hope you kept out of her way."

"I did." Tod twisted her gold-and-silver snake ring that had once belonged to her mother. "But she said something. About Mum."

"Mum?" Dan was taken aback. "Mum" was not a word he and Tod often used. Cassi had been gone so long now.

"Mum," Tod said again, claiming the word for her own. She told Dan how Aunt Mitza had implied that she had sent the sand fly that had killed Cassi TodHunter Draa. Dan stopped dead. He looked shaken. "She . . . she did that? To my Cassi? To your mother? She sent a lethal sand fly?"

Tod nodded. "In an envelope of sand."

Dan felt sick. He remembered Mitza's letter to Cassi—which had puzzled them both, for Mitza was no great writer of letters—and its envelope full of sand. How he and Cassi had laughed at it. *Silly, clumsy Mitza*, they had said, *always so messy*. The thought that if Cassi hadn't opened the letter she might have been here with him and her daughter almost overwhelmed Dan.

"And then," Tod said, "Aunt Mitza told me to be careful.

As though . . . as though she . . . she was planning something. For *me*."

Dan looked horrified.

"And the thing is, Dad, yesterday two travelers came through the Hub. They looked kind of weird, as though there was some **Darke Magyk** on them. One of them was Aunt Mitza. I'm sure of it. And she went through Way Seven. To the Castle."

Now Dan understood. "To find you. Like she threatened. Thank goodness you are not there, Tod." Dan shook his head. "I will not allow that woman to blight our lives any longer. I'm going to the Castle. I'm going to track her down and make sure she never tries to hurt you again. *Ever*."

"But Dad," Tod said. "We can't get to the Castle, can we? Not anymore. Well, not through the Ways."

"I'll go by sea," Dan said.

"By the time you get there, there might not be a Castle left," Tod said sadly. As they neared the last trees of the Far, Tod said, "I don't think Mitza can do me any harm while I'm an Apprentice and have the power of the Wizard Tower behind me. But if that all goes, Mitza has to find me eventually. I don't think she will give up."

Dan was silent. He suspected his daughter was right.

"Dad, I so wish . . ." Tod stopped. What she wished seemed impossible.

"What do you wish, Alice?" Dan asked, using his serious name for her.

"I wish I could help protect the Castle. And the Ancient Ways. And all those beautiful places like the SnowPlains that are crumbling to dust . . . I so wish I could stop it from happening."

Dan and Tod walked out of the Far into the afternoon sun. They took the boarded track that wound through the sand dunes and headed toward the outlying houses of the village, standing tall on their four stilts, looking as though they were striding across the dunes. Tod smiled. Houses on stilts meant she was home.

They headed toward the center of the village where the houses, which still smelled of fresh timber and tar, were newly built after having been set on fire by Oraton-Marr's men. People were still adding the final touches, hammering up shutters, finishing the thatch. As they walked toward the new central space, where the old PathFinder bell now hung, Tod said, "I'll just stop by and see Rosie like Jerra said."

"Ah, yes. *The Path*," Dan said, still sounding unenthusiastic, Tod thought.

The path puzzled Tod. Why did it make her father so grumpy? And why was Rosie looking after it? Rosie was not someone you would ask to keep a path swept clean and tidy. She was one of the village's cleverer, more bookish people. In fact, the old Sarn house had had a whole room full of Rosie's books—before it burned down.

The Sarns' house was a surprise to Tod. In her mind it was still the raggedy thatched, scruffy old house. This one was so new that the wood was pale and not yet painted with tar, the thatch was bright yellow and the windows sparkling clean. But some things did not change. At the top of the ladder, through the open door, Tod saw the familiar figure of Rosie Sarn sitting at the long kitchen table, reading.

The next moment, in response to Tod's call, Rosie was at the doorway. She saw Dan and her hands went to her mouth in fear. "Dan, what's happened? Why aren't you on Watch? Where's Jerra?"

"Jerra's fine, Rosie. He's resting, he had a bit of a bump to his head."

"Oh no!"

"Really, Rosie, Jerra is absolutely okay, I would not have left him otherwise. And besides, Ferdie and Oskar have Come Through and they're with him."

Rosie broke into a smile. "Ferdie and Oskar! Oh, how wonderful." Rosie now spotted Tod standing a little behind Dan. "And Tod too!" she said. "Goodness, you've grown. How lovely to see you. Come on up, both of you."

And so Tod and Dan climbed the ladder up to the Sarns' welcoming kitchen. At the top, Tod turned and gazed at the village spread out before her. The Castle felt a long, long way away.

SECRETS

Ten minutes later Tod was sitting at Rosie's kitchen table looking at one of the most beautiful books she had ever seen. Bound in green leather with swirling silver patterns enclosing its gold-blocked title: *The Path*.

"Jerra found it when he was digging new foundations for the bell tower," Rosie told her. "About six feet down one of the spades hit a metal box. You can imagine how excited he was. All those legends about buried treasure under the bell—they were true."

"I wish I'd been there," Tod said wistfully.

"You'd not have seen much, Tod. Word got around and

soon the whole village was there, trying to get a glimpse. Anyway, Jerra pulled up the box, got some bolt cutters and we opened it. There were a few sighs of 'Oh dear, it's only a book,' but I thought it was the best treasure we could wish for." Rosie's eyes were shining with excitement. "Because Jerra had found it, he was given the choice of where it should go for now. So he said I was good with books and should look after it for the village. Everyone agreed and we took it home. But late that night, three of the Inner Circle came knocking on the door demanding we hand it over to them. They got very unpleasant when we refused."

"We wanted to keep it safe," Dan said. "That was all."

"Dad, were you one of those three people?" Tod asked, shocked.

"I was," Dan admitted. "I was only doing my best for our village. But Rosie thought she knew better."

"Our history belongs to us all, Dan. Despite what some people think," Rosie retorted, looking accusingly at Dan.

Dan sighed. "Rosie, some things are too dangerous for us all to know."

Rosie gave a snort of derision. "We are not children, Dan Moon," she said.

Dan said nothing and there was an awkward silence.

Eventually Tod ventured, "Er. Can I have a look at it? Please?"

"Tod, of course you may," Rosie said. "I've been so looking forward to showing you."

Tod was touched by Rosie's words and she wanted to share something in return. She took the StarChaser from around her neck and held it out to show Rosie. "This is something to do with our village too," she said. "What do you think it might be?"

But it wasn't Rosie who answered; it was Dan. "Goodness," he exclaimed. "A pod key! Where did you get that?"

"A *pod key?*" asked Tod. "It's called a StarChaser. It's a **Charm**. I got it from the **Charm** Library."

"Ah, well, that's what it is. Of course it is," Dan said hurriedly. "A **Charm**."

"So why did you call it a pod key?" Tod asked, puzzled.

"I, um, I shouldn't have said that," Dan said.

"Another of those Inner Circle enigmas, I suppose," Rosie said scathingly.

Dan sighed. He had had this conversation with Rosie Sarn many times.

Tod didn't understand. "But I thought we heard all the secrets at the Summer Circle," she said.

"Well, you don't," Rosie said tersely. "The Inner Circle keeps some for itself."

"What *is* the Inner Circle?" Tod asked.

"That is a question for your father," Rosie said.

Dan looked uncomfortable. "It's just some PathFinders, Tod, who are trusted to know all our secrets."

"So do *you* know our secrets, Dad?" Tod persisted.

"Yes," Dan admitted. "I do."

"Does that mean you can read *The Path*?"

Dan shook his head. "No. No one understands the ancient texts anymore."

"But I am sure you could make a pretty good guess about what is in it," Rosie said.

"Could you, Dad?" asked Tod.

Dan shrugged. "I truly don't know what is in *The Path*, Tod. What Rosie calls 'our secrets' are just myths and legends, no more than that. I really don't know why Rosie makes such a fuss about it."

Rosie let out an exasperated splutter. "Because they are *secret*. And secrets destroy a society, Dan. Secrets create two tribes of people: those who know and those who don't. And eventually, two tribes living side by side will fight."

"Rosie, I don't want to fight," Dan said wearily, "really, I don't. Let's go and sit in the garden and let Tod look at *The Path*. I'll tell you all about Jerra. And Oskar and Ferdie too."

That was a peace offering that Rosie could not refuse. She made a jug of Barley Cup and then she and Dan took it down to the newly planted garden and sat in the sun.

Meanwhile, at Rosie's kitchen table, Tod embarked upon her solitary journey along *The Path*.

A DASH AND A SICKLE

One of Tod's courses at the Wizard Tower was Palaeography and Ciphers—known by all who were required to attend as "Pale and Sick" due to the deathly pallor of the teacher, a pedantic elderly Wizard who spoke in a low, flat drone that made everything, however interesting, seem tedious. But now Tod saw the point of all those boring afternoons—to her delight, she recognized the script *The Path* was written in. It was EAV:B or, to give it its full name, Eastern Arcane Vernacular, version B. With its typical thick black script, its use only of symbols with double dots after each symbol, it was one of the easier scripts to identify.

Tod knew about twenty symbols from EAV:B. She knew colors, including lapis lazuli—a dash enclosed by a sickle curve—some numbers, and a few other random words. At once she set about trying to find the symbol for lapis. Methodically, Tod ran her index finger along each line, checking every symbol, but she could not find it. She had reached the very last block of text in the book and was feeling quite despondent when her finger stopped at a dash enclosed by a sickle curve. But it was the symbol right next to it that made her heart race. It was an ovoid with a large dot in the center: *Egg.*

Tod's finger trembled as it traced its way through the dark forest of letters until, like a lantern shining in the shadows, she saw the two symbols side by side once more—and then again and *again.* Now Tod knew she was onto something. This was about a lapis egg, there was no doubt about it. Tod also noted the plus symbol that was combined with the ovoid, which she remembered made the symbol plural. This was about *more than one egg.*

With memories of the Pale and Sick Wizard droning: "Method, method, *method,* Apprentice," Tod decided to write down in sequence every symbol she recognized. She went back to the top of the page and examined the title. It looked like a fish with big, solid fins and it put her in mind of something Oskar would make: a metal fish. She decided to name the symbol exactly that. And so, headed by Metal Fish, Tod began to write a list of words. By the time she got to the end of the block of text, this is what she had: Metal Fish. Lapis Eggs. Yellow. Three. Metal Fish. Lapis Eggs. Wurm. Zero. Sorrow. Metal Fish. Home. Sea. Sorrow.

Tod looked at her list and she knew she had found something very important. She jumped up, raced down to the garden and thrust the list at Dan. "Dad, look! There's lapis here. And *eggs*. It must be Orm Eggs, it *must* be!"

Reluctantly, Dan took the list. He frowned.

"Dad," Tod said, "if this looks like one of those secret legends, please tell us what it is. Because if there are Orm Eggs in the secret, then it might show us a way to save the Wizard Tower. And the Ancient Ways."

Dan's face remained studiedly blank; it seemed to Tod that he was shutting her out. For comfort—for it was very uncomfortable to see this unknown side of her father—Tod put her hand in her pocket and closed it around the PathFinder. A moment later she snatched her hand from her pocket. "No!" she yelled. "*No!*"

"Tod?" Dan asked anxiously.

Wordlessly, Tod held out her hand. Lying on her palm was her precious PathFinder. Its gold-and-silver filigree shone in the sunlight. But at its very center was an empty socket: the dome of lapis lazuli was gone, leaving only its enclosing silver ring.

Tod handed the blind PathFinder to Dan, then she put her hand back in her pocket, drew it out and sprinkled a fine stream of gray dust onto her list. "Dad," Tod said. "This is the lapis from my PathFinder—*our* PathFinder, the one that belongs to our family. If you know something that might stop this from happening, you have to tell me. You *have* to."

Dan traced his finger through the dust and looked up at Tod and Rosie. There was a story he had to tell and he would tell it. But it frightened him. Not the telling of the story, but what he knew Tod would insist on doing once she had heard it.

And so, with a feeling of dread, Dan began to speak.

THE METAL FISH

"Tod, the symbol you call the metal fish must be the symbol for the *PathFinder*. I don't mean your guide to the Ancient

Ways, but the *PathFinder* you heard about in MidSummer Circle last year: the starship that once took our people to the stars and back. Part of the mission was to find a new planet where we could create powerful **Magyk**. People then had the crazy idea that an abundance of lapis lazuli would give great **Magykal** powers."

"But that's not crazy, Dad, that's true!" Tod said.

"Yes, so it seems. Anyway, the idea was to turn an entire planet into lapis lazuli and then set up a colony on it. There were a few people on board with **Magykal** power—you are descended from them, Tod. It is where your gift is from. These people, who were called shamans, would do great things on this planet. It would be, I suppose, a **Magykal** laboratory. So an important part of the *PathFinder*'s cargo was Orm Eggs."

Tod listened, rapt.

"It took many generations to gather them, but at last the *PathFinder* left with twelve Orm Eggs on board. After countless measures of time, they found what seemed to be a suitable planet. It was the right size and consisted of a soft yellow rock, perfect for burrowing Orms. All three shamans decided to go down to check it out. They came back with good reports and so, one by one, they began to take the Orm Eggs down to the planet. Because a human hatching of an Orm is difficult, they tried it with one Egg first. It was successful. The larval Orm developed as it should and began to eat its way through the rock. One by one, the Orm Eggs were sent down, hatched and set to work. On board the orbiting ship the PathFinders watched enthralled while below the yellow planet turned slowly blue and the shamans began to build a tower—as shamans will.

"The days and nights were long on this planet, each lasting seven of our days. The very last Egg was due to be flown down when, as the band of twilight moved across the planet and day began at last to dawn, the watchers on the *PathFinder* ship were horrified. The shamans' tower was gone and in its place was a great pit, and curled at the bottom of the pit was a giant yellow wurm. They sent a pod down to see what had happened but it never returned. And so, in great sorrow, the PathFinders decided to come home.

"As you know from the MidSummer Circle, our homecoming was not a happy one. This is true. But what is not true is that the *PathFinder* landed on the spot where the village bell now is. It actually crashed into the sea."

"So the people from the Trading Post didn't take the

PathFinders prisoner after all?" Tod asked, thinking that all on board must have been killed.

"Oh, they did that, all right," Dan said. "The *PathFinder* landed on the seabed intact and many managed to escape. They walked home, following the rising seabed."

"Wow, that's amazing," Tod said.

"It was," Dan agreed. "Legend has it that you can still see the path they made along the seabed. It didn't do them much good, sadly. When at last the PathFinders struggled up the beach, weighed down by their space suits, they were attacked by the Trading Post people who had taken over our village. Many were killed and the survivors taken prisoner. Terrible."

Rosie was still in a combative mood. "Well, Dan, you can understand it. They see a fireball coming down from the sky and then strange creatures walking out of the sea. They must have been terrified."

Dan did not agree. "What I don't understand is why they kept our people imprisoned in the Far Fortress for so many generations. So cruel."

Rosie could not disagree with that. But there were still things Rosie had to say. "And what *I* don't understand, Dan Moon, is why this amazing story is a secret. We should be proud of what our ancestors did."

"Rosie, think about it," Dan said. "First you tell a bunch of young teens that one in ten of them have gills and can walk underwater, and then you tell them there is a path under the sea that leads to our old *PathFinder* starship. Who, at the age of twelve, could resist the temptation to walk into the sea to explore that ship? It is easy to find; the old white post on the Circle beach marks the spot. Every year there would be some who would walk straight into the sea and never come home. We would lose virtually all our children."

Rosie sighed. "You are right, Dan. The bravest and best would go."

Tod felt the anger between Rosie and Dan melt away. "And that, Rosie," Dan said, "is exactly what happened. The bravest and best *did* go. This story was not always a secret. In the days when many more of us had gills, there used to be guided expeditions to the ship on MidSummer's Eve. One year they did not return. Worried villagers set out to see what was wrong and found the sea above the starship red with blood."

Rosie and Tod gasped.

"A brave villager went down, only to discover a nightmare. A great hole had been punched in the side of the ship and a horrendous beast was devouring what was left of our beautiful children. The generation was decimated. Our ancestors swore never again to visit the *PathFinder*, but to leave it as a sacred place. They decided to keep it secret to avoid any danger of others being devoured by the beasts that now lived there."

Dan stared down at the dusty list still in his hands, waiting for what he knew would come.

"Dad," Tod said. "That story means there is still an Orm Egg on board the *PathFinder*."

"Yes. It does," Dan agreed with a heavy heart.

Tod held up her silver star. "And you said this was a . . . a *pod key?*"

"I did," Dan said.

"A pod on the starship?"

Dan nodded.

"*An Orm Egg pod?*" Tod asked.

"I have no idea," Dan said. "I am not proposing to find out. And neither, Alice, are you."

Tod was silent.

"Promise me," Dan said, looking Tod in the eye, "that you will *not* go—"

But a sudden sound of pounding feet and the appearance

of Oskar stopped Dan midsentence. Rosie leaped up. "Oskar! Sweetheart, what's wrong?"

"Jerra . . ." Oskar puffed. "Jerra went to sleep and he won't wake up."

Dan was on his feet at once. "I knew I shouldn't have left him. I'll go straightaway."

"You're not going alone," Rosie said. "Jonas will go with you. And Annar. I'll go and find them." Dan did not object. He had had enough of arguing with Rosie.

Rosie, Tod and Oskar spent an anxious afternoon. Rosie planted endless rows of winter kale. Oskar did what he always did when he was upset: he went out snake tracking. And Tod tracked Orm Eggs.

To the rhythmic sound of Rosie's digging, Tod went over every detail of *The Path*. Her persistence paid off, for tucked inside the back cover she found a folded diagram. As Tod smoothed it out on the kitchen table, a thrill of excitement ran through her. It was the Metal Fish—the *PathFinder* starship. She ran her finger over the lines, looking for something that she knew no one else would have searched for: an ovoid with a dot in the middle. Tod made a bargain with herself: if she didn't find the symbol, she would do as Dan had told her. She was still looking when from the garden below she heard Rosie greeting Oskar and Oskar offering to help make supper. Tod knew that once Oskar was in the kitchen she would not be able to think straight. He would be chatting to her and wanting her to explain things. If she didn't find what she was looking for now, she never would. In a last burst of concentration, Tod scanned the diagram looking for shapes rather than meaning. As she heard Rosie telling Oskar to wash his hands in the outside sink, something caught her eye: distorted and made faint by a crease of the fold there were two circles, one within the other, and in the middle was a central dot. Tod felt a shiver of excitement run through her—could this be an Orm Egg inside a pod? The more she looked, the more she was convinced it was. There was the last pod, deep in the tail section of the starship, *just waiting for her to go and get it.*

TRIBE OF THREE

There was a preoccupied atmosphere in Rosie Sarn's kitchen as supper was prepared. Rosie's and Oskar's thoughts were with Jerra, and Tod could not get the image of the Orm Egg out of her head. While Oskar filleted the fish and Rosie put together a pot of vegetables, Tod laid the table—all the while casting glances at the wooden box on top of the shelf where *The Path* now lay with its secrets locked within.

They were sitting down at the table and Rosie was pouring out a jug of her smashed-fruit juice—which Tod loved—when they heard a voice call up from below, "Mum!"

Rosie went pale. She leaped to her feet and ran to the door. "Ferdie! Oh, Ferdie, what is it?"

Ferdie came running up the ladder and threw herself into the room. "It's all right, Mum!" she said, trying to catch her breath. "Dan told me to come home so you didn't worry. Jerra's okay. Annar gave him some stuff . . . don't know what . . . but he woke up."

Rosie sank down onto the nearest chair. "Oh, Ferdie. Oh, thank goodness. And you came all that way on your own."

"Mum," Ferdie said, "I am perfectly capable of walking through the Far."

Tod suppressed a smile. Ferdie sounded just like Lucy Heap.

Rosie caught the new confidence in her daughter. "I

suppose you are, dear," she said.

Oskar heard the weariness in his mother's voice. "Mum," he said, "after supper you are going to bed and we are doing the clearing-up."

Rosie smiled at her twins, amused but touched at the role reversal. "All right," she said meekly. "I think I might just do that."

Tod helped the twins wash up and lay everything out for breakfast, then they took a lantern and went to sit out in the warm summer evening. It was everything Tod had dreamed of during the long winter in the Castle and the tedious hours spent in lectures in the Wizard Tower: the smell of warm sand, the whisper of the breeze through the dune grasses and the distant sound of the waves falling upon the beach like a regular heartbeat.

But Tod's thoughts were distracted. There was something she wanted to talk to Ferdie and Oskar about, but she knew how voices traveled upward, and Rosie's bedroom window was right above them, wide-open to catch the evening breeze. Tod stood up and casually said, "I haven't seen the sea yet. Shall we go to the beach?"

It was a beautiful night. The moon was rising and the sea

glittered darkly through the gap in the dunes. The tide was low, and as they walked out of the dunes a wide swathe of perfectly smooth sand was stretched before them, the strip beside the dark water shining like a satin ribbon. As they made their way down the soft sand at the foot of the dunes, Tod was surprised to hear Ferdie say, "So, what's up, Tod?"

Tod smiled. "How can you tell, Ferd?" she asked.

"You've been scratchy all evening," Ferdie said as they wandered slowly toward the sea. "And when Dan arrived at the Hub he seemed kind of scratchy too. And he kept calling you Alice. Have you two had an argument?"

Tod sighed. "Kind of," she said. "There's something I want to do and Dad doesn't want me to do it."

"They get like that sometimes," Oskar said. "It's really annoying. When I wanted to go to the Manuscriptorium, Dad said no for days before Mum made him say yes."

"But this is different," Tod said. "This is . . ." She stopped. She was going to say *really important*, but she knew that Oskar would not take that well. "This is really *weird*," she said. She looked at them. "Tribe of Three?" she said.

Ferdie and Oskar knew at once what Tod meant: that whatever Tod was going to say was between the three of them only.

"Tribe of Three," Ferdie and Oskar replied.

They wandered along the shoreline and Tod told them about the Orm Egg that lay not so very far away beneath the sea. But she did not tell them everything—she did not mention the beasts in the starship. She was afraid that if she did, Ferdie and Oskar would beg her not to go. And Tod realized that she had already made up her mind—she was going to get that Orm Egg, whatever her friends said. But she would rather go with their support than without it.

When she finished there was silence, unbroken but for the *swish-swash* of the wavelets lapping at their feet, while they looked out over the moonlit ocean, thinking about its secrets below. Tod was determined not to speak first. She knew what she wanted her friends to say, but it had to come from them.

"You have to do it," Ferdie said. "You have to go and get the Egg."

A wave of relief washed over Tod. "Yes," she said, "I do."

"We'll help you," Ferdie said.

"We'll do anything we can," Oskar said. He looked at Tod. "I'd love to come too," he said. "Swimming down under the water to see our starship. Wow . . . what a thing."

"Oskie," Tod said. "You know you can't find out whether you have gills without risking being drowned. There is no way you can come down with me. *No way at all.*"

"So you say," Oskar said.

"Oskar Sarn, do not even *think* about it," Tod told him sternly.

"Yes, miss," Oskar said, and stuck his tongue out at Tod.

They retreated to the dunes to watch the tide come in and discuss their plans. As the water crept up the beach, clouds drifted across the moon, and the air grew colder, the frightening reality of what she had decided to do began to dawn upon Tod.

Late that night in Ferdie's room while the house was quiet with the sounds of sleeping, Tod asked Ferdie to show her how to unpick the stitches in a soft leather ball and then sew it back up again so that it would still bounce. Bing was to go on a mission. If she found the Orm Egg—which Tod hardly dared hope for—then they would need a way of getting it to the Eastern SnowPlains. And she had an idea how to do it.

While Ferdie opened a small gap in Bing's tiny, tight stitching, Tod explained that she wanted to send a message inside the ball. Ferdie grinned and produced from her pocket a length of white string. "Message string," she said, and handed it to Tod.

"Huh?" asked Tod.

"It's William's favorite game," Ferdie explained. "We send secret messages in string. Here, I'll show you."

Instructed by Ferdie, Tod untwisted the string and on one of the strands wrote a short message to Septimus and then allowed the string to twist back into shape. Ferdie threaded the string inside the ball, and while Tod held the edges together, Ferdie stitched them, leaving a tiny bit of string poking out. "To show there is a message there," Ferdie said.

At last they went to bed. Tod wrapped Bing in the handkerchief Septimus had given her after they had laid the Ormlet to rest. Then she put the **Tracker** ball under her pillow and fell quickly asleep. She slept fitfully, dreaming that she had an Orm Egg under her pillow.

GONE FISHING

Early the next morning they left Rosie a note to say they were going fishing, and set off to the beach. They pulled Dan's small, open boat named *Vega* down to the waterline and began to load up.

Tod put in a lightweight fishing net, a long rope, Dan's fishing weights and her FlashLight. In her pocket was Bing, primed and ready to go. Oskar added his own bag of "stuff," as he called it, and Ferdie a picnic basket.

"Okay," Tod said. "Let's go."

Because *Vega* had to follow a precise path, Tod had decided to row rather than sail. They took *Vega* along the shoreline, over the sand spit to the beach where the MidSummer Circle took place. It was here an old white painted post stood, battered and unremarked, its lower part now underwater. Tod looked at the post with new eyes. "There it is!" she said, pointing it out to Ferdie and Oskar. "That's where they came ashore."

"And I thought it was just a boring old post," Oskar said. "Although I did wonder why every now and then someone bothered to paint it."

"So did I," Tod said.

"But you must have found all that out last year in MidSummer Circle?" asked Ferdie.

"No," Tod replied. "They didn't tell us. Or rather, *Dad* didn't tell us," she added crossly. "Like he didn't tell us lots of things."

The MidSummer Circle beach could not be seen from the village, and because of the nearby shallows it was not used for fishing boats. It was empty and, that morning, felt a little desolate. As Ferdie and Oskar rowed closer, Tod began to feel nervous. What was she thinking of, walking into the sea to find an Orm Egg in a sunken starship? Was she totally crazy?

"All right, Tod?" Oskar interrupted her thoughts and then grunted as he struggled to pull his oar from too deep a plunge into the water—Oskar was not a natural rower.

Tod nodded. Her mouth felt too dry to speak.

They tied *Vega* up to the white post and the boat sat rocking gently in the morning sun. Ferdie opened the picnic basket and offered Tod a sandwich. Tod shook her head. She felt sick with nerves. Ferdie closed the basket. "We'll have the picnic when you get back," she said. "To celebrate."

"We can use the Orm Egg as a table," Oskar joked.

Tod tried to smile but did not succeed.

Ferdie hugged her. "We'll be right here, all the time," she said. "As near as we can possibly be."

"Just look up and you'll see us," Oskar added. He rummaged in his bag of *stuff* and took out a pair of goggles. "For you," he said, offering them to Tod. "You'll be able to see so much clearer under the water."

Tod broke into a smile. "Wow, thank you, Oskie," she said. "They're just perfect. They'll make such a difference."

Oskar grinned delightedly. "They're Manuscriptorium goggles. I found them last night. I must have put them in my pocket and forgotten about them."

"Well, I'm glad you did," Tod said, putting the goggles on her head.

Tod began to get ready. She took Rose's **Charm** bracelets out of her pocket and slipped them on. Helped by Ferdie and Oskar, she got into her waterproof all-in-one, which was tight over her three layers of fishing jumpers and woolen leggings. Then she put on a safety belt (normally worn in bad weather in order to fasten the occupant to the boat) and tied one end of the rope to it, giving the other end to Ferdie. Ferdie solemnly took the rope and wrapped it around her hand to show Tod that there was no way she was going to let go.

Tod clambered out of the boat and suddenly remembered her message to Septimus. She retrieved the **Tracker** ball from her pocket. "**Find** Septimus. Go alone," she told it. Then she threw Bing into the water.

"Will it go underwater?" Ferdie asked doubtfully.

"If I can, then I reckon a **Tracker** ball can too," Tod said.

Ferdie peered over the side of the boat. "It's doing it!" she said. "Running along the sand . . . going deeper . . . I hope a fish doesn't eat it."

Oskar hoped a fish didn't eat *Tod*, but he knew better than to say so.

Tod was back on her mission. She checked her Charm bracelets were in place—these would help keep her warm in the chill of the water—then she put on her fishing vest and said tersely, "Weights, Oskie."

One by one, Oskar handed over the lead weights. And Tod slipped them into various pockets, taking care to distribute them evenly. Then, with her feet sinking into the sand, she took out her FlashLight and switched the beam to its underwater setting. It shone pale green—almost invisible in the daylight, but perfect for beneath the sea. "Time to go," she said.

"We'll be with you every step of the way," Oskar promised.

"I've got your rope," Ferdie told her. "We can pull you up in seconds, can't we, Oskie?"

"Yep, we can," said Oskar.

They went over the code of rope tugs they had agreed on and then it was time to go. Tod managed a brief smile and gave the PathFinder sign for "okay": an O formed by placing the tip of her index finger to the tip of her thumb. Oskar and Ferdie returned it. Then solemnly they watched their friend as she walked into the sea. They saw the water close over her dark hair, her elf-lock float briefly upon the surface, and then all trace of her was gone.

PART
~ XI ~

TREADING THE PATH

As if in a dream, Tod walked along the gently sloping seabed, the weights keeping her feet easily on the sand. Rays of sunlight shone down through the water showing flashes of silver as small fish darted away. Tod moved slowly, looking out for the markers that would tell her she was on the right path. Visibility was not good: every step sent up fine clouds of sand that swirled about her. After negotiating her way around a small colony of rocks, Tod saw something that looked like an underwater tree. She headed toward it, and as she approached she realized with a thrill of excitement that it was the first of the marker posts, made not of wood like the one on the beach, but a smooth, dull, copper-colored metal, just like her StarChaser. The post was completely clear of barnacles and weeds, apart from a large frond attached to its top, which waved gently as if beckoning her onward.

Tod was jubilant: she had found the path! The path along which many hundreds of years ago her ancestors had trekked to safety, or so they had thought—and the path along which so many young PathFinders had once taken their last journey.

Resolutely, Tod pushed that last thought from her mind. She stopped beside the post and looked up at the thin snake of the rope glistening with air bubbles, rising to meet the dark underbelly of *Vega* some thirty feet above. The boat looked like a small whale, broad and tubby, and Tod felt a rush of affection for its plump solidity and for her friends within it, watching out for her. She gave a tug on the rope to let Ferdie know she had found a marker post, and in reply she saw the little pink flipper of Ferdie's hand break the surface and do an excited wave. Tod smiled. It was good to know she wasn't alone.

As the seabed sloped ever downward, the light level dropped, but to compensate for this, so did the intervals between the marker posts. Tod was impressed. It seemed to her that her ancestors had intended to make many trips back to their starship. Maybe, she thought, they were planning to repair it, and to continue living in it under the sea. It was, after all, their home and had been their world for many generations.

Tod walked slowly onward, trying to imagine how it must have been to live one's entire life on a starship. At the very moment she was wondering what the *PathFinder* actually looked like, as if in reply to her thoughts, she saw a huge, dark shape ahead. At first sight it looked like a massive rock, but as she drew nearer, a pair of marker posts set together like a gateway told Tod it was much more than that. With a feeling of awe, she stepped between the posts.

Tod found herself standing on the edge of a pit. *This*, she thought, *is the crater that the* PathFinder *made when it crashed.* A swathe of goose bumps washed over her at the thought of what lay ahead. She looked up, hoping to see the underside of *Vega*, but she was too deep; all she saw was the darkness of water and the beam of her **FlashLight** fading before it reached the surface. She gave two tugs of the rope to show she had found the *PathFinder* and received two in reply. Then, with her heart beating fast, she set off, slipping and sliding down a steep drop toward the hull of the *PathFinder*: a massive carapace covered with clouded portholes, topped with battered fins and debris.

At the foot of the slope was an opening: a dark gash reveal- ing layers of metal curling back like delicate fern fronds. On either side of this were the last two marker posts, topped with medusae—plantlike animals with long waving tendrils sporting delicate tufts on the ends. Tod stood for some moments on the threshold of the ship. She touched her **Charm** bracelets for luck—and to remind her of the Wizard Tower and why she was doing this—then she took a step forward. A tug on the rope as it caught on the metal told Tod that it was time to disconnect from her friends. She untied the rope from her belt, gave three tugs to warn Ferdie and fastened it to one of the marker posts.

Feeling utterly alone, she entered the home of her ancestors.

INTO THE METAL FISH

Tod felt as though she were in a sacred space. It reminded her of the Great Chamber of the Orm—the resting place of the last Orm Egg before it was stolen. There was a stillness, a sense of lives lived and lost. Keeping in her head the plan from *The Path*, Tod set off, walking over soft loose sand, which covered all kinds of strange lumps and bumps. Pushing away thoughts of the bones of the massacred PathFinders and the marauding beast that had killed them, Tod slowly wove her way through a forest of lattice uprights, heading toward the stern. The image of the Orm Egg waiting there in its pod drew her steadily onward.

Stepping slowly and carefully, painfully aware that she might well be treading on the remains of her ancestors beneath the sand, Tod traversed the cathedral-like space of the *PathFinder*. At last she came to a sheer face of metal on which swathes of medusae with long trailing fronds hung down and great clumps of goose barnacles popped their long necks out of their shells and eyeballed her. This, Tod was sure, must be the stern bulkhead of the starship.

From the starship plan, Tod knew the only entrance to the tail section was toward the top of the ship. She took out some of the fishing weights from her pockets, laid them on a rock and then pulled herself up on the slippery fronds. As Tod ascended the bulkhead, she realized that she was drifting through the *PathFinder* just as her ancestors had once done on their journey to the stars.

Tod was two-thirds up when her hand disappeared deep into a clump of medusae; she lost her balance, tumbled through the bulkhead and fell out the other side. She somersaulted twice, recovered her equilibrium and caught her water-laden breath in a gasp. Before her was a seemingly **Magykal** space, full of drifting green pinpoints of light wandering like lazy **Sprites**. She floated for some minutes, entranced at the sight until some of the "Sprites" began to float toward her. Tod's delight rapidly faded as the "Sprites" drew near and she saw an army of bony teeth advancing upon her. The teeth belonged to tiny, vicious-looking fish, each of which dangled before its toothy open mouth a glowing green light. In moments, Tod was surrounded.

The fish swam slowly around her, regarding her with wide, unblinking eyes. It occurred to Tod that, with her **FlashLight**, the fish might be thinking that she was one of them. Taking courage from that, Tod dangled the **FlashLight** before her and took a step forward. The forest of teeth parted respectfully to let the Big Fish pass through. Tod began to propel herself down through the tail section, her now devoted followers shadowing her every move. Halfway down, Tod saw a dark space in the hull: a hole cut neatly in the metal. Thinking that this might be an entrance to an Orm pod, she swam up to it and shone her **FlashLight** into the hole. To Tod's astonishment, the light showed something familiar, yet utterly unexpected—a tunnel into the rock ending in a watery, misty **Vanishing Point**. She knew at once that this must be one of the drowned Ancient Ways that Marwick had told her about. She wondered what would happen if one of the Sprite fish swam into it. Would it too travel the Way, maybe to end up floundering in a waterless Hub? She imagined piles of dead Sprite fish blocking up a tunnel and thought how wonderfully weird the Ways were—and how much she wanted them to stay that way. The presence of the Way made Tod feel much happier—if she got trapped, there was an easy exit. She took one more look at the **Vanishing Point**, eerily beautiful in the beam of the **FlashLight**, then continued her downward journey.

Not much farther down Tod reached what seemed to be the floor of the starship. Miserably, she stared down at the sand beneath her feet—where had the Orm pod gone? As if in reply, the beam of her **FlashLight** caught the bright orange section of a circle gleaming through the sand. Excitedly, Tod scuffed the sand away with her foot, which sent clouds up into the water and made it hard to see. Impatiently, she waited for the sand to settle, and as the view cleared she saw at her feet a wonderfully familiar symbol: a huge circle with a dot in the center: *Egg.* Tod did a leap of excitement and sent her acolytes swimming away in panic. *Egg.* She could hardly believe it.

Now all she had to do was get hold of it.

Tod ran her hands through the sand, feeling the outside of the pod. It was made of the same smooth coppery metal of the posts that had marked the underwater path and had repelled all attempts by crustaceans and weeds to attach themselves. Slowly, so as not to cloud her vision, Tod smoothed away the sand and before long found what she was looking for—a circular hatch, in the center of which was, to her delight, a star-shaped indentation with a familiar pattern of points. It was the mirror image of her StarChaser. It seemed that Dan was right: this really was a pod key.

Tod lifted the StarChaser from around her neck. Her hands trembling with excitement, she was about to place it into its lock when she became aware of a movement at the edge of her vision—her guard of Sprite fish had suddenly shot away in all directions. Thoughts of the ancient PathFinder monster flashed into her mind and Tod wheeled around.

At first she merely saw six red pinpoints of light, seemingly swimming in formation, but then her heart leaped in fear. Coming straight for her, guided by her green eyes—which shone big and bright with horror through her goggles—was the ten-foot-tall shape of a Kraan.

A Contraption

On board *Vega*, Ferdie and Oskar were growing concerned.

"She's been in there for *ages*," Ferdie said, giving another tug on the rope and getting no response. She looked at Oskar. "I've got a bad feeling about this, Oskie."

Oskar had a bad feeling too. He picked up some fishing weights from the bottom of the boat and stuffed them into his pockets.

"Oskie, what are you *doing?*" Ferdie asked.

"I'm going down to see what's going on," Oskar said.

Ferdie went ashen. She grabbed hold of her brother with both hands. "No, Oskie, don't," she begged. "*Please don't.*" Not so long ago, Ferdie had watched Tod throw herself into a fifty-foot-deep tube of water not knowing whether her friend would drown or not. She could not bear to watch Oskar doing the same.

Oskar hastened to reassure her. "Hey, Ferd, it's okay. I'm

not brave enough to do that," he said. "Not like Tod." Ferdie
lost her look of terror—but not for long. Oskar was opening
his mysterious bag of *stuff*. With the triumphant air of a magi-
cian pulling a rabbit from a hat, he took out what looked to
Ferdie like a large oilcloth shopping bag with a small oval glass
window and a canister with a crazy tangle of tubes dangling
from it.

"I'm going to use this," Oskar said, holding up the bag
triumphantly.

"Use it to do what?" Ferdie asked.

"To breathe underwater," Oskar told her. "Just like Tod.
Ephaniah and I invented it," he said proudly. "It works really
well. I've made one for you, too. You'll love it, Ferd." With
that Oskar put the bag over his head, put the end of one of
the tubes in his mouth, tucked the canister up inside the bag
and tightened the drawstring around his neck. Loud, rasping
sounds began to come from Oskar's bag-head.

Ferdie was horrified. "Oskar, take it off! You'll suffocate!"
she yelled, grabbing at the bag and trying to yank it off Oskar's
head.

"Nerrr, doppit Ferrrr!" Oskar pulled back from Ferdie,
trying to protect his precious contraption. Desperately, Ferdie

lunged forward; Oskar leaped backward, tripped over the thwart and tumbled out of the boat. There was a loud splash and Oskar sank fast.

Distraught, Ferdie leaned over the side of the boat and yelled, "Oskar! Oskar!" She saw a mass of bubbles coming up to the surface and the dark shape of Oskar dropping down into the depths. She felt the rope tighten as Oskar grabbed hold of it and relief washed over her—now Oskar could pull himself up. But Oskar did no such thing. Ferdie watched his dark, blurry shape with its big, white bag-head very deliberately continue its descent. She stared into the water until she could see him no more and then she sat down among the muddle of baskets and boxes, while the sea lapped against the sides and the boat gently rocked.

Ferdie could not bear it: to be alone in the boat while her twin brother and best friend were far below at the bottom of the sea was just not possible. She picked up Oskar's horrible contraption and stared at it in disgust for a few seconds, breathing in the nauseating smell of the oiled canvas. Then Ferdie took a deep breath of fresh air and pulled the bag over her head. Just as she had seen Oskar do, she shoved the end of one of the tubes in her mouth, pushed the canister up into the bag and pulled the drawstring tight. She stared out through the little piece of glass at the world now shrunk to a green oval and forced herself to take a breath. With a *click* of a valve inside the canister and a metallic *hiss*, Ferdie took in her first gulp of air. It tasted rubbery and stale but it worked—she could actually breathe. Ferdie stood for a moment, gathering her courage, then she too took fishing weights from the basket, dropped them into her pockets, and without giving herself time to think, she held on to to her bag-head and jumped into the sea.

The cold shocked Ferdie, but the act of trying to breathe with her head inside a bag took her mind off it. Unlike Oskar, who had spent time with his head in a fish tank practicing, this was new to Ferdie, and she found that she was breathing in and holding her breath, reluctant to let the precious lungful go. Reminding herself yet again to *breathe out*, Ferdie peered through the thick green glass, looking for the rope. It swam into view, she grabbed it, and then, hand over hand, slowly pulled herself downward, telling herself: *breathe in . . . breathe out . . . breathe in . . . breathe out . . . breathe in . . . breathe out . . .*

The mantra took her safely down to the seabed, where to her surprise she found Oskar with a green glowstick waiting for her. *I knew you'd come,* he signed.

Horrible boy, Ferdie signed. And then, tapping her bag, *These work.*

Of course, Oskar signed, and then, *Shall we go and find Tod?*

Ferdie gave the "okay" sign. She took Oskar's outstretched hand and together they stepped into the belly of the Metal Fish. At once they found themselves surrounded by a cloud of little lights.

Fish! Ferdie signed excitedly.

Teeth, Oskar replied, somewhat less excitedly.

The fish surrounded them. They were less respectful than they had been with Tod: Oskar's light was dimmer, which meant that he was clearly a fish of lesser importance. But the fish were on a mission: their leader was in trouble and they needed a bigger fish to help. Oskar would do nicely. Ferdie, without a light, they did not recognize as a separate being. They assumed, because she was joined to one of Oskar's fins, that she was part of Oskar. And so, nudged and poked, with spiny teeth only inches away from his precious air bag, Oskar had little choice but to go where the Sprite fish wished. And where Oskar went, Ferdie went too. The Sprite fish propelled them across the floor of the starship and then upward and through the hole in the stern bulkhead into the tail section.

On the other side they were met with clouds of swirling sand through which, far below, they glimpsed the dim glow from Tod's discarded FlashLight.

Trouble. Ferdie signed one-handed.

They sank quickly through the water, following the fish, and they very soon saw exactly what trouble Tod was in. She was, in slow motion, fighting off a Kraan using a long pole and the moves that Marwick had shown them only a few days earlier. Oskar and Ferdie moved toward Tod as fast as they could—which was nightmarishly slow—but as they drew near, through the clouds of sand they saw that they were too late. The Kraan had knocked the pole from Tod's hands and was leaning over her, its bony hands about to grab her throat.

"No!" Oskar screamed, the sound almost deafening inside his bag. He rushed forward, tripped and fell headlong. Ferdie came cannoning down after him. When they looked up they saw Tod on her knees staring at something in her hands.

Back at the Wizard Tower Septimus and Marcia hugged each other in relief. On the floor of the Sealed Cell, six evil-looking red beads rolled slowly into a corner.

Newt Makken staggered out, pale with shock. "It worked," he whispered. "The **Reverse** worked."

"It did indeed," Marcia said. "Well done, Newt. It was a brave thing you did, to go into the **Sealed Cell** alone."

"And get the **Reverse** right the first time too," added Septimus. "You kept a cool head."

But Newt's head felt anything but cool—it was spinning and making strange buzzing noises. Very slowly, Newt slid to the floor in a faint. A small, tattered book titled *How to Fix Things You Wish You'd Never Done* dropped from his grasp and fell at Septimus's feet. Septimus picked it up and put it in his pocket. It was one of the most useful books he had come across in a long time—full of all kinds of **Darke Reverses**.

Marcia and Septimus carried Newt back into the **Darke Archives**. They laid him on the floor, covered him with a blanket, and got back to work.

"I hope we were in time," Septimus said somberly as they began to tidy the chaotic mess of books and papers that had been discarded in increasing desperation.

Marcia smiled at him. "You know," she said, "I have the strangest feeling that we were—*just in time.*"

THE SIEVE

Tod was staring in disbelief at six red beads lying in her cupped palms when she became aware of two more figures coming toward her. She leaped up and wheeled around, expecting yet more trouble.

Never in her craziest dreams had Tod expected to meet Ferdie and Oskar on the seabed. But as soon as she saw them, even with their bizarre air bags, running in comical slow motion toward her, Tod knew it was them. She spat out a spurt of water in a huge laugh. *Potato heads*, she signed.

A large, toothy fish positioned itself between them, as though protecting Tod, and Oskar returned the compliment: *Fishface.*

Where's the beast? Ferdie signed anxiously. She did not have a sign for Kraan.

Tod showed her the six red beads. *Here*, she signed.

Oskar and Ferdie were impressed. *Good **Magyk***, they signed.

Yes, Tod signed. *But not mine.* She grabbed their hands and held them tight. *So pleased you are here*, she signed. And then she added, *Egg*.

Egg? Ferdie and Oskar signed in unison.

Egg, Tod confirmed. And then added, *I hope*.

Tod led them to the cleared patch of sand, beneath which the Orm pod lay. Proudly, she shone her **FlashLight** on the orange circle with its central dot and then onto the StarChaser still sitting crooked in the lock. With a sense of awe, wondering who had been the last person to do this, Tod pushed the StarChaser home into its bed. She felt a click and then, beneath her hands, a buzzing began. The sand began to move. Tod stepped back and very slowly a round hatch opened at their feet.

Tod stared down in utter disappointment. Below was an obviously empty chamber. There was no Egg. But she could not bear to give up after coming so far. Maybe, she thought, there was a hidden compartment within, where an Egg might still be lying. *I'm going in to check*, she signed.

Not without us, Ferdie signed.

Right, Oskar agreed.

Tod dropped down through the hatch first, her feet finding solid, smooth metal beneath them; then she moved to one side to allow Oskar and Ferdie to follow. The chamber was easily big enough for three, even with two potato heads. Tod let her **FlashLight** beam roam around the smooth, gray walls of the chamber, but there was nothing to be seen and no hatch leading to anywhere else. It was an empty dead end.

She shook her head desolately and signed, *Nothing. After all this. We find nothing.*

But Ferdie was not so sure. *Move your big feet,* she signed to Oskar.

Move your own, he returned irritably.

I already have, she replied. *But you've just stood there all the time like a lemon. Move.*

Now Oskar understood. He stepped away and beneath his boots was another StarChaser indentation.

Ferdie tapped Tod on the shoulder. *Found it,* she signed.

Tod was out of the chamber and back with the StarChaser in seconds. Ferdie held her **FlashLight** while Tod dropped the StarChaser into the lock. Once more there was a vibration, and a buzzing that sent ripples through the water. And then, to their horror, the hatch above them closed.

They looked at one other, shocked: they had expected an opening, not a closing. Tod dropped to her knees to pull the StarChaser out of its lock, but it fitted so tightly that it seemed to have become part of the metal floor. Tod looked up at Ferdie and Oskar; the air bags over their heads no longer seemed quite so comical. She wondered how much air they had left.

Oskar had just sneaked a look at his timepiece and he knew exactly: four minutes and fifty seconds. He fell to his knees and was trying desperately to pry the StarChaser out with the point of his knife when a vibration began to spread through the metal beneath him and he became aware of a disturbance in the water. Oskar looked up at the hatch, but it was still firmly closed. However, within the pod, something very strange was happening. From the smooth metal encasing them a mass of tiny bubbles were streaming out, turning the water a dense milky white.

Oskar's hand found Ferdie's and Tod's hand found Oskar's. They held tight to one another as all around them bubbles whirled, lifting them off their feet, taking them up into a powerful eddy. Ferdie and Oskar could see nothing out of their glass windows for they were now covered with tiny air bubbles, but Tod had no such trouble. To her amazement she saw a big silver bubble of air forming just above her head in the top of the chamber; she felt warm air touch her hair and then suddenly she was coughing, spluttering, retching as her breathing made the transition from gills to lungs.

Tod took her first breath of ancient air and gagged with the taste of metal. She let go of Ferdie's hand and wiped her friend's visor. *Air*, she signed. *You can breathe!*

By the time Ferdie and Oskar had taken off their air bags the three were standing in an empty chamber full of stale but wonderfully warm air. Like a snake gratefully leaving its old skin, Tod shucked off her waterproofs, and as fast as the water cascaded from their clothes it was sucked into what they could now see were thousands of minute holes covering the chamber wall—they were inside a giant sieve.

"What *is* this?" Oskar whispered.

As if in answer to his question, a zigzag pattern appeared on the side of the sieve like a crack in an eggshell. It rapidly widened, the two sides swinging away from each other in a smooth, spiraling motion so fast that seconds later they were looking into the strangest space any of them had ever seen.

THE POD

"Wow," Oskar murmured. "Look at all those lights! It's just like MidWinter's Eve with lots of tiny candles in the window."

"And there's a seat, too, so you can watch them," said Ferdie.

They were inside a small, spherical space lit by tiny white spots of light, randomly flicking on and off. The lights were ranged along a broad, slightly angled shelf, in front of which was a long bench seat in blue padded leather. The seat was shaped to fit five and had an unusually high back, topped with five shiny black tubes.

But Tod had eyes only for the dull metal ovoid that sat behind the seat. She felt shivery with excitement, for stamped upon it was a large circle with a dot in the middle: *Egg*.

It did not take Tod long to see the telltale StarChaser indentation in the center of the dot. She easily retrieved the StarChaser from the floor of the sieve—with its job done it was already half out of its bed. Then, with her hands trembling with excitement and Ferdie and Oskar breathing down her neck, she pushed the StarChaser into the middle of the dot.

Like the lid of an ancient tomb, the top half of the metal ovoid slid slowly back. Breathless with excitement, they peered into the depths to see, like the egg of a bird cradled in a nest of down, an Orm Egg lying in a cloud of white padding molded to its shape. The Egg's brilliant blue color shot through with fine streaks of gold was a shock after the monochrome of the silvery black that surrounded them. Hardly able to believe it was real, Tod reached out to touch the Egg. She felt its smooth, leathery surface, cool to her touch, and she knew she wasn't dreaming. She turned around to Oskar and Ferdie. "It's an Orm Egg," she whispered. "*It really is.*"

Ferdie and Oskar were just as wide-eyed. "You did it," Oskar said. "You really did it. You found an Orm Egg."

"*We* did it," Tod corrected. She gazed down at the beautiful lapis egg, taking it in. They had an Orm Egg. There was no sorcerer to snatch it from them, no dragon to whisk it away. It was theirs and theirs alone, to do with as they wished.

"But it's sad it will never hatch," Oskar said. "Ormie could have had a little brother or sister."

Tod was saved from replying by Ferdie's brisk, sisterly response. "Oh, don't be so daft, Oskie."

Oskar turned away in a huff.

While Tod and Ferdie leaned over the Orm nest, trying to work out the best way of lifting up the egg, Oskar, intrigued by the lights, went to inspect them more closely. He sat down on the outside seat of the row to get a better look. As his weight settled onto the seat, he heard a faint whirr, and what looked to him like a large, flat snake shot across his lap and bit the other side of the seat. "Argh!" he yelled.

Ferdie and Tod wheeled around. Ferdie raced over to Oskar. "What is it?" she asked.

"Snake!" Oskar whispered, pointing to the offending strip of shiny black that had him imprisoned in the chair.

Ferdie was scathing. "It's only a belt, Oskie."

Oskar looked down at his lap and saw that Ferdie was right. "Yeah. Well, it *looked* like a snake," he muttered. "And it acted like one too—the way it moved. It just shot across and bit that thing." Oskar pointed to the fastening that kept him in his seat. "And now I'm stuck."

"Of course you're not stuck," Ferdie said. She went around the other end of the bench and shuffled along until she was sitting next to Oskar so she could release him. And as soon as Ferdie sat down another black snake shot across her lap and bit the side of *her* seat.

"Argh!" yelled Ferdie.

"See?" Oskar said triumphantly. "I *told* you."

The two lap belts refused to come free. They also utterly resisted the attempts of Oskar's knife to cut through them.

"I think," Tod said, trying to figure out how they worked, "there's a release button where it goes into the holder thingy. See, here . . ." She pressed the button on top of the fixing for Oskar's lap belt. There was yet another whirr and the shiny, fat, black tube at the top of his seat back detached itself and in a fast, smooth motion swung over Oskar's head and came to a halt resting gently on the front of his shoulders. Oskar was now effectively pinned to the seat.

"Thanks, Tod," Oskar said. "That was *really helpful.*" He shoved the heel of his hand under the tube and pushed up with all his strength, trying to lever it up. It would not budge.

"Trust you to get stuck, Oskar," Ferdie said irritably.

"It's not *my* fault," Oskar replied petulantly. "The seat did it. And *Tod.* All I did was sit down, same as you."

"I only sat down because I was trying to help you," Ferdie said snappily. "Can't think why I bothered."

Tod could hardly believe her two friends had been silly enough to get in such a mess. But there was nothing to be done but to get them out of it. She could hardly take the Orm Egg and leave them behind, however tempted she felt right then with them bickering in the background. Somehow, she had to get them free. "There's another space there for the

StarChaser," she said, pointing to a star indentation in the dashboard. "Maybe that will unlock the belts."

Ferdie and Oskar thought it was worth a try.

Tod closed the lid of the Orm locker and took out the StarChaser, then she shuffled along the bench so she was next to Ferdie, but not sitting down. She knew better than to do that. She placed the StarChaser into the indentation and immediately it lit up, pulsing bright red. A whirr came from behind them: the hatch between the sieve and the pod was moving. It was beginning to close.

"Jeez!" said Oskar.

"No!" Ferdie gasped.

Tod's fingers scrabbled at the StarChaser, trying to pull it out, but they all knew that was not going to work. Once more the StarChaser was sitting tight and was not to be moved.

The hatch settled into the entrance with a soft hiss, entombing them in the metal bubble. The pod gave a lurch, as though something had released it, and Tod fell onto the bench. In an instant, the lap belt had shot across and secured her, too. The lights inside grew dim, and Tod's and Ferdie's seat restraints swung over their heads, securing them like Oskar. All three exchanged uneasy glances. Something was about to happen.

A deep, powerful rumbling shook through their bones and made their teeth tingle. They clasped hands, closed their eyes, and were thrown back into their seats by a violent thrust. Moments later they felt as though they were in a giant ball, kicked hard and heading high into the air.

THE WANDERING MOON

It was Tod who opened her eyes first. Her sharp intake of breath made Oskar and Ferdie open theirs in unison. There was silence while all three took in the sight before them. At last, Oskar broke it.

"We're flying," he whispered.

"It's so . . . *beautiful*," Ferdie said.

What, in the darkness beneath the water, had been smooth featureless black was now—but only to those inside it—transparent. It was as if they were inside a bubble tumbling through the sky.

"This is from the Days of Beyond," Tod said, awed. "This is what we used to do."

There was a brief whirr, and they tensed, but it was merely

the shoulder restraints setting them free and swinging back above their seats. They risked tentative smiles; the pod clearly felt that all was well and there was no need to protect its passengers.

"I suppose we had better figure out how to land this thing," Oskar said. He leaned forward and grinned at Tod. "Over to you—you're in the pilot's seat."

Tod studied the panel before them, seeing how the random flickering lights had transformed to reveal a large, lighted glass map directly in front of her, over which a small red circle was very slowly moving. In the center of the map was a rounded silver stub, which Tod had an urge to press but dared not for fear of what it might do. The map was surrounded by displays showing a mix of numbers and red bars, constantly adjusting. Her StarChaser sat in its place above the map, outlined in a red glow. Tod thought of her promise to Rose to tell her if she found out what the StarChaser did. She reckoned she was going to have a hard time getting Rose to believe *this*.

As Tod sat in their bubble, surrounded by blue sky, moving through the white wisps of low-lying clouds, she felt exhilarated, but also a little scared. She was in the pilot's seat, but had no idea how to actually *be* a pilot.

"You know what would be really, *really* good?" Ferdie was saying. "If we could take the Orm Egg directly to the SnowPlains."

"That would be brilliant," Oskar said excitedly. "Just think. We could save everything. *Today!*"

"Yeah, Oskie, it would be great," Tod said. "If I knew how to fly this. Which I don't."

"You could use **Magyk**?" Ferdie suggested hopefully.

Tod shook her head. "This isn't a **Magykal** thing, Ferd."

"Yeah, Ferd, it's a *PathFinder* thing," Oskar said. Tod pointing out that she did not know how to fly the pod had brought him back to reality. Oskar felt scared—and when he got scared, he got picky.

There was a strained silence as the reality of their predicament began to sink in. They stared out the window watching the world move slowly beneath them. The pod had settled into a steady flight, low enough to see the details of the landscape below. Broad expanses of forests, broken by wide clearings with patchworks of fields and clusters of houses passed silently and serenely beneath them. Those on the ground below who looked up—and there were many who did—saw a dark sphere traveling fast and silently across the sky. It was

the beginning of many legends of a wandering moon searching for its lost light.

Oskar's words went round and round in Tod's mind. *A
PathFinder thing . . . A PathFinder thing.* Almost absentmind-
edly, she took her now empty **PathFinder** from around her
neck. She ran her finger around the silver band that had once
enclosed the lapis dome while she thought: *Magyk may not
work for a PathFinder pod, but maybe **Magykal** thinking will.*

Tod had learned from Septimus to hold an object and **Listen**
to what it told her. So, as the land unrolled beneath them and
began to turn into a series of small lakes, Tod slipped the
empty band of the **PathFinder** onto her right thumb so that
it sat neatly above her mother's snake ring. And then she
Listened. But the **PathFinder** was silent.

"Will it show us the way?" Ferdie whispered.

Yes. The word came unbidden into Tod's mind. *Yes. I will
show you the way.* And then came a question. *Where do you
wish to go?*

Tod felt spooked. She glanced at Ferdie and Oskar to see
if they had heard anything. Ferdie caught her glance. "Tell it
where we want to go," she whispered.

"We want to go to the Heart of the Ways," Tod said out

loud. And then added, "Please."

Point me to that place came into Tod's head.

"The map," Tod said out loud. "I have to point it at the map."

They stared at the map, trying to find the Heart of the Ways, but the landscape was meaningless to them, no more than a jumble of unfamiliar coastlines, mountains, plains and rivers.

"I think it should be over there," Oskar said, putting his stubby finger onto the far right of the map, "but it doesn't go that far."

"It moved!" Ferdie gasped. "The map moved."

Oskar was intrigued. He moved his finger across to the right, and the map scrolled with it. Oskar's finger had reached the edge of the map now, but he kept it pressed down and the map continued to scroll, slowly revealing more. On the left side of the map Tod saw the red dot of their pod disappear, and still Oskar kept his finger pressed, and still the map scrolled, and Oskar inspected every feature that revealed itself.

"That's it!" he said suddenly. "There—look!"

Oskar's nail-bitten finger pointed at a brilliant blue dot. It lay in the middle of a white circle that itself was almost surrounded by mountains.

"That's it," Ferdie said. "Clever old Oskie."

Oskar grinned.

Tod touched the tip of the PathFinder to the blue dot. The map did not react.

"Do what you did before, Tod," Ferdie said.

"Do what?" asked Oskar.

"Shh, Oskie," Ferdie told him. "Just wait."

Buoyed by his success with the map, Oskar did not react. He gazed down at the land far below, watching it slowly move by. It was an amazing sight, and Oskar thought that if he weren't so afraid that he would never walk on it again, this would be the best thing that had ever happened to him. Ferdie's fingers found his and they held hands in silence, waiting for Tod to do whatever it was she was doing.

And then, Tod did it. She took the PathFinder off her thumb and placed it onto the silver stub in the center of the map. "That," she said, "is where it wants to be."

The PathFinder settled onto the stub as though it were made for it—which, Tod thought, it probably was—and the map came to life. It was no longer just a diagram: it showed the world beneath them as if they were looking at it through a lens. The map moved, rolling back to where they were now, showing the pod as a small red dot in the middle, blinking steadily.

They sat for some time, enthralled, watching the world slowly scrolling by unfolding mile upon mile as they moved steadily across the sky, heading toward the Eastern SnowPlains and the Heart of the Ways.

After some time they saw a dark strip across the horizon; slowly it engulfed them and they flew into the night. The lights inside the pod dimmed until all they could see was the soft glow of the map, the gentle movement of the **PathFinder** and the stars above. In the warmth of the pod, lulled by its gentle whirring, they fell into a dreamless sleep.

Tod was awoken by a change of key: the whirring had dropped a semitone. Blinking blearily, she sat up. The sky was still dark but on the horizon she saw a line of orange fire—they were flying into the dawn.

Tod sat quietly. She watched the sky slowly lighten, deliberately savoring the moment and not thinking about how the pod was going to land. As the great orange ball of the sun crept above the horizon—reminding her of the MidSummer

Circle—Oskar and Ferdie stretched and untangled them-selves. "It sounds different," Oskar said, immediately on edge. "What's happening?"

Tod looked at the map. While they had slept it had scrolled across so that the blue circle was now approaching the silver tip of the PathFinder. "We're nearly there," she replied, doing her best to sound calm.

"We can't be," Ferdie said. "Look out the window. It's just miles of rock. Where's the snow?"

Driffa's voice describing her world of snow falling apart came back to Tod. "It's gone," she said sadly. "This is what it's like now."

Ferdie shook her head in dismay. "I had no idea it would be like *this*."

Oskar looked at Tod, fear in his eyes. "But how can we pos-sibly land? We're still going really fast."

"But the *pod* will know how to land, won't it, Tod?" Ferdie asked anxiously.

"Of course it will," Tod said. She had no idea if that was true, but she figured it was a pilot's job to keep her crew reas-sured.

The soft whirring of the pod had become loud like the

buzzing of an angry hornet, and it now began rapidly descending the scale, one semitone to the next. The view was divided equally between bright blue sky and deep red rock, with the rock's share rapidly increasing. There was no doubt about it: they were going down.

Tod knew there was nothing she could do to land the pod, but she could still look after her crew. "Lean back in the seat," she told Ferdie and Oskar, doing the same herself. As Tod touched the back of her seat the shoulder restraint swung over once more. Obedient to their pilot, Ferdie and Oskar did the same. Sitting back in the seat they could see only sky, but very soon the bright blue joined a horizon of red rock, which rapidly began to fill their view.

"We're going down into a crater!" Oskar whispered.

Suddenly Tod understood. "It's not a crater," she said. "It's the Heart of the Ways."

A rapid juddering began and once again they held hands, so tightly this time that Ferdie's fingers went numb. A thick gray dust began to blow upward and the windows became enveloped in its swirling cloud. A high-pitched whine kicked in, seeming to drill into their ears, and the pod began to vibrate rapidly.

"We're going to die," Oskar whispered to his twin.

"Shut *up*," Ferdie shot back.

Tod knew she had to do something, but she had no idea what. And so for comfort as much as anything she placed her hand on the PathFinder, which was now rattling on its silver stub. Tod never knew if it was a coincidence or if the pod would have stopped shaking anyway, but at the very moment her hand touched the PathFinder, the vibrations stopped. Seconds later they felt the pod settle onto the ground, tilt forward a little, and come to rest.

All was silent.

Oskar allowed himself to breathe again: at last he was back on solid ground.

DRIFFA IN CHARGE

With a gentle hiss, the shoulder restraints lifted over their heads and settled to their places on the back of the seat. No one moved. Dimly, through the dust cloud, they saw the steep rocky sides of the crater with a zigzag path, down which a lone figure brandishing a sword was running.

The devastation shocked them all. "We're too late," Ferdie said sadly.

"We might not be," Tod said. "I think it depends if there is any **Enchantment** left."

Oskar pulled off his lap belt, stood up and stretched. He was looking forward to getting out of the pod, back into fresh air. "There's only one way to find out," he said.

Tod put the empty **PathFinder** back around her neck, took the StarChaser from its bed on the dashboard and went to open the Orm locker. There lay the Orm Egg in its bed of fleece, serene and untouched by flights across galaxies and hundreds of years beneath the sea. With a great sense of occasion all three lifted the Egg from its bed. It lay shimmering in their arms, lit by the low light pulsing inside the pod.

"It's so beautiful," Ferdie said.

"It is," Oskar agreed. "And just think, inside there is another little Ormie."

"Which is where, Oskar Sarn, it is going to stay," Tod told him.

"You should take it, Tod," Ferdie told her. "You found it."

And so, cradling the Egg, which was surprisingly heavy, Tod walked into the sieve, while Ferdie fussed around with the StarChaser. They stood there, watching the pod hatch close, listening to the chamber balancing its pressures, and then watched the hatch to the outside hiss slowly open. The early-morning chill gave them goose bumps, and the dusty air caught in their throats, but no one cared. It was fresh and it tasted wonderful.

They emerged from the hatch to see Princess Driffa, the Most High and Bountiful, running fast toward them through the dust, her braids flying, blue ribbons streaming behind her and a long, sharp sword in her hand. Driffa skidded to a halt and stared in shock at the sight before her. Stepping out of the fireball that had just descended from the skies was not some terrible monster as Driffa had feared. It was the young Apprentice of that treacherous, and yet so handsome, Wizard. *And in her arms she held an Orm Egg.*

For one of the few times in her life, Driffa was speechless.

"Princess Driffa, this is for you," Tod said, feeling suddenly shy.

"For *me?*" Driffa said, sounding as though Tod had brought her an unexpected birthday present. Driffa reached out her free hand. "May I . . . may I touch it?"

Tod nodded. She was shocked at the change in Driffa. She

was no longer the haughty, pristine princess dressed in pure
white. She was grubby and disheveled: her clothes were thick
and heavy with gray dust, even her hair was dulled to gray.
The only pure white visible on Driffa was in the desperate
glint in her eyes and the bones of her knuckles that showed
through the skin as her hand gripped the hilt of her sword.

"It is indeed the true Egg of the Orm," Driffa said, her voice
soft with wonder. She looked at Tod. "I do not know how your
ExtraOrdinary Wizard has done this, but I thank him from
the bottom of my heart."

"Oh!" said Tod, surprised. She decided not to explain how
she had got the Egg; it was far too complicated. She held out
the Orm Egg, hoping Driffa would take it quickly. It was very
heavy.

But Driffa did not take it. As Tod's arm muscles shook with
the effort of holding the Egg, Driffa stood stroking it as if in a
dream. "I do understand," she said, "that he would not wish to
bring it to me himself. I said many harsh words to him. Some
were, I can see now, a little unfair. But please tell him that I am
in awe of his power to **Engender** a true Egg of an Orm. And
that I, and my people, are indebted to him forevermore. Never
will we be enemies; forever we will be friends." With a dramatic flourish, Driffa threw her sword to the ground—where

it sank deep into the dust—crossed her hands over her heart, and looked dreamily at the Egg.

Tod could stand it no longer. "Princess Driffa," she said. "Just take the—" She bit back a rude word. "Just take the Egg, will you?" Driffa, who now regarded Tod with new respect, did as she was told.

With the Orm Egg in her arms, Driffa's authority returned. She refused to let Tod, Oskar and Ferdie return to what she called "the fireball," telling them she would not stand by and see the Apprentice of such a powerful and heroic Wizard burned to a crisp before her eyes. To humor Driffa, Tod closed the hatch and put the StarChaser safely away in her pocket. As she did, she saw a look of relief cross Oskar's face: his feet were back on the ground and that was where he wanted them to stay.

They climbed the zigzag path up the side of the crater, looking down at the scene below. Sitting in the middle of a sea of dust, the pod seemed tiny. Tod found it hard to believe that they had just flown halfway around the world in what looked, from where she was, like a fishing weight dropped into a bucket of sand.

When they reached the top of the crater Tod realized that

the bumps she had taken to be rocks were actually Grula-Grulas. Their hair stiff with dirt and covered with a film of gray, they sat morosely staring into the pit that held the ruins of what had been the very reason for their existence. Some scratched irritably, some rocked slowly back and forth, and a few were making soft keening sounds. It was one of the saddest sights Tod had ever seen. She scanned the nearby Grula-Grulas to see if she could recognize Benhira-Benhara. There was no sign of his vibrant orange fur, but in that dismal wilderness there was no color anywhere. Every living being was steeped in the dust of **DisEnchanted** lapis lazuli.

Silently, they followed Driffa past the sorrowing clumps of Grulas toward a small encampment, where Driffa and her entourage kept watch over the desolate remains. It was, Driffa said quietly, all they could do. They could not bear to leave. "Because when we go, who will ever know what this crater once was?"

Driffa settled Tod, Oskar and Ferdie in her tent, then left to, as she put it, "place the Egg." They watched her go, treading carefully, cradling the precious Orm Egg in her arms like a baby.

With its rugs and cushions, Driffa's tent reminded them of another in a distant land where, not so very long ago, people had watched over a different Orm Egg. As the weariness from the last twenty-four hours caught up with them, they sat in the doorway, drinking a strange-tasting, hot, sweet drink while they looked out onto the dusty landscape of the plateau that had once been covered with **Enchanted** snow. On the horizon rose a ring of mountains, which were still snow-topped, but all else was barren rock. Tod remembered the quiet beauty that had once existed: the blanket of snow, the lapis caverns below and the brilliant blue pinnacle above. It was hard to imagine how that could possibly be restored. Ferdie clearly thought the same. "Does Driffa *really* believe that the Orm Egg will put everything back to how it was?" she whispered, careful not to upset the followers Driffa had left in the tent to serve them.

"It doesn't seem possible," Oskar said.

"No," Tod agreed. "It doesn't."

THE KEYSTONE

Driffa came back to the tent some hours later to find Tod, Oskar and Ferdie asleep: the cushions and rugs had proved too tempting. However, the Snow Princess was not to be put off.

She kneeled beside Tod and gently shook her awake. "Pardon, Apprentice," she whispered. "All is in place. If you would favor us with your **Magyk** I do believe we will be successful."

Tod sat up and blearily rubbed her eyes. She was so tired she would have given almost anything to go back to sleep— except for the chance to be part of the **Re-Enchantment** of the Ways. She left Ferdie and Oskar still sleeping and followed Driffa out of the tent. She emerged to see a wall of Grula-Grulas standing shoulder to shoulder around the edge of the crater. They were no longer the despondent, dusty creatures they had been some hours ago; now they stood tall, their fur combed and tended, their little arms linked to form an unbroken chain.

Driffa led Tod past the backs of the Grulas to the top of the path that went down into the crater. The Grula-Grula guarding its entrance bowed. "Good afternoon, PathFinder," it said.

"Ben!" said Tod.

"At your service, now and forevermore," said Benhira-Benhara Grula-Grula. "We, the Grula-Grula tribe, can never repay you for what you have brought us today."

"Thank you," said Tod. "But . . . I'm not sure I've brought anything useful."

"You have brought us hope," Benhira-Benhara replied.

Tod was so touched she did not know what to say.

"Come *on*," Driffa said impatiently. "We've got a Re-Enchantment to do."

As they descended the precarious zigzag path, Tod could not take her eyes off the structure that had risen over the StarChaser pod. The dull metal pod that had carried them halfway across the world now sat beneath a flimsy scaffolding of wooden poles. These rose up some twenty feet above it like the nest of a giant, long-legged bird, on the top of which the Orm Egg perched jauntily.

As they picked their way slowly across the soft, dusty floor of the crater, Driffa, anxious not to offend Tod, launched into an explanation. "Apprentice, please do not think we have imprisoned your fireball in a cage. It just happens that it lies directly beneath the point where we must put the Orm Egg for a successful Re-Enchantment. You see, the Egg must be placed exactly where the previous one lay. You may wonder why it is not higher from the ground, for in our Enchanted days it was suspended some fifty feet above the floor of the Heart of the Ways. However, we are now standing on some twenty-three feet of rubble and lapis dust."

Tod was impressed; she had not expected Driffa to be so methodical.

They had now reached the foot of the scaffolding where a long wooden ladder led up to the Orm Egg. Driffa took out a small, dull silver box covered in stars. Tod smiled to see her StarChaser box once again. "I thank you for the loan of your precious box," Driffa said. "We must have one piece of what was here before to set the Re-Enchantment going." She waved her arm at her surroundings. "But as you see, we have nothing. Not one piece of lapis is left, except what is inside your box."

Tod looked at the StarChaser box, searching for a sign that Marcia's Enchantment was still working—but of the purple glimmer that had once flickered around it like lightning, there was no trace. But there was no point worrying about it, she thought; they would know soon enough.

Driffa glanced up at the Egg, which lay still and quiet, awaiting its fate. "When we reach the Egg," Driffa said, "we must lay the lapis on it to begin the Enchantment. But once its box is open your Wizard's powerful protection will be broken, and I fear that the lapis will turn to dust before the Magyk has time to become established. My sorcerers tell me that these Earth Enchantments are slow and ponderous to begin and I believe that they are, for once, right. They offered to protect the lapis but they are not our best sorcerers—we lost those last year to Oraton-Marr—and I do not think them capable." Driffa stopped and looked at Tod. "However, as the Apprentice of such a powerful Wizard, I believe that you *are* capable."

Tod was aghast. If she could not protect the lapis in her own precious PathFinder, how could she protect any lapis here, at the very center of the UnRaveling?

But Driffa had no such qualms. She set off quickly up the ladder and Tod had no choice but to follow. At the top Tod joined Driffa on the narrow plank walkway around the Orm Egg. She looked down at the wasteland of gray dust below and then up at the circle of Grula-Grulas high above, imagining all the anxious little pink eyes staring down at her. Tod gulped. *This has to work*, she thought. *It really, really has to.*

Driffa flipped open the StarChaser box and Tod saw, to her utter relief, a shard of lapis, bright blue, with a thin streak of gold running through it. Driffa was unsurprised—if this Wizard was powerful enough to Engender an Orm Egg and send his Apprentice in a metal ball of fire to deliver it, then keeping a shard of lapis **Enchanted** must be the simplest thing in the world for him to do.

"Quick, take the lapis, Apprentice," Driffa urged. Tod closed her hand around the lapis, wondering how she could protect it. And then she had an idea. If the StarChaser pod could protect an Orm Egg for thousands of years, then maybe her StarChaser could do the same for a piece of lapis lazuli.

It was the work of a few seconds to put the shard of lapis lazuli on top of the Orm Egg and place the StarChaser on top of it. Tod kept her hand on them both, pressing them into the Egg's pliant, leathery surface, flattening the area so they did not fall off. Driffa watched with a respectful air. It looked to her as though Tod were performing some deeply **Magykal** rite.

As Tod pressed down on the StarChaser, she heard the beginnings of a soft buzzing. It grew louder, swimming through the air like a swarm of bees in the summer sunshine, swirling around her and the Orm Egg, enfolding them in a blanket of sound. Tod looked up and saw the circle of Grula-Grulas, suffused with a **Magykal** yellow light. She understood that the buzzing came from them and she also knew that together, she and the Grula-Grulas could protect the whisper of **Enchantment** left in the shard of lapis and let it gather once more around its new **KeyStone**. Secure with that knowledge, Tod closed her eyes to concentrate. She felt her hand grow warm and a tingle ran up her arm. She heard Driffa whisper, "I see it, I see it." Tod opened her eyes and could hardly believe what she saw—a flickering of **Magykal** purple surrounding the Orm Egg.

The **KeyStone** was in place. **Re-Enchantment** had begun.

A CARPET OF GRULAS

It was evening, snow was falling and the Grula-Grulas were singing in high, reedy voices, crooning long, slow and convoluted songs to the complex **Enchantment** unfolding in the crater below.

In Driffa's tent they drew back the sides, lit a fire and watched the thick, fat flakes of snow drift from the sky and settle on the ground. And there Driffa, her friends and family, with Tod, Oskar and Ferdie as their honored guests, sat under a bright, starry sky watching the spreading **Enchantment** to the haunting background of Grula-Grula music.

Offended by the success of foreign **Magyk**, Driffa's three sorcerers had retired early to their own tent. Just past midnight there was a shriek, and one of the sorcerers came running out into the snow. "Which idiot," he demanded, rubbing his posterior, "which total, utter *dingbat* put our tent where the pinnacle was?"

All eyes turned to Driffa. Everyone knew it was the Snow Princess who had ordered the placement of the camp, right down to the last detail. Nervously, they waited for the explosion of temper. But Driffa merely laughed. "I do believe it was me, Sorcerer. Oh dear, what *was* I thinking of?"

Tod, Oskar and Ferdie exchanged smiles. It really was an **Enchanted** evening.

The next morning was bright, sunny and full of snow. Princess Driffa led Tod, Oskar and Ferdie down into the **Re-Enchantment**. They were followed by a long, meandering carpet of Grula-Grulas ("carpet" being the collective noun for the creatures). They progressed through the new Sacred Chamber of the Orm, looking down into the space below where, deep beneath the newly **Enchanted** ice, the Orm Egg now lay.

Driffa then led them out of the Sacred Chamber of the Orm and down a spiraling tunnel, shining bright with new lapis. On the threshold of the Heart of the Ways, Driffa stopped and turned to Tod. "As PathFinder, you must lead the way," she said. Then Snow Princess Driffa, the Most High and Bountiful, bowed her head and stood aside to let Tod pass.

"Thank you," Tod replied, somewhat unnerved by Driffa's new and profound respect. She stepped into the Heart of the Ways and at once twelve torches burst into flames—as they always did when a true PathFinder stepped into the Hub.

They walked into the Heart of the Ways and gasped at the sight before them. It was magnificent. The new lapis lazuli shone a blindingly brilliant blue and gold. The Hub's traditional twelve arches, formed from rare, pale lapis and edged with thick silver bands, stood smooth and perfect, waiting for their first traveler. The arches' inlaid gold numbers gleamed from the light of torches set in solid silver holders between each Way.

"Wow . . ." Oskar breathed. "I forgot how huge it is."

"And beautiful," murmured Ferdie. "The blues and gold . . . so bright."

"Without you and your ExtraOrdinary Wizard, this

would not exist," Driffa said. "From the bottom of our hearts, I and all my people of the Eastern SnowPlains thank you." With that, the Snow Princess led them across the shimmering Heart of the Ways toward Arch VI—the first of many on their journey home.

In the middle of the Hub they paused and looked up at the roof. Enfolded in the center of its lapis lazuli coils was a dark sphere of metal: the StarChaser pod. Its cargo now lay above it, frozen in Enchantment, the KeyStone supporting the most complex Earth Magyk ever known. The pod had, thought Tod, at last delivered its Orm Egg, albeit to a very different place than had been planned. She whispered it a sad farewell.

"But you will see it again when you return with your ExtraOrdinary Wizard," Driffa said. "Which I hope you will do many times."

On the threshold of Arch VI, they stopped to say their good-byes. Driffa took off her lapis ring—the one whose gray dust she had flicked over Septimus—and handed it to Tod. "Please give this to him as a token of my gratitude and respect, and as an invitation to return to our snow Enchantment whenever he so desires."

Tod took the ring, which seemed laden with far too many messages for her liking.

And so, at last Tod, Oskar and Ferdie headed toward the first **Vanishing Point** on their journey home. Behind them followed their guard of honor—a carpet of Grula-Grulas.

A carpet of fifty Grula-Grulas makes for slow traveling, and it was many long hours later when they at last emerged from a **Vanishing Point** to see a lantern, a door with a large knocker and a sign reading: *Welcome, Friend, to the Far Hub. Please knock and we will open the door.*

Oskar knocked. He saw the spyhole flip open, and he pulled a face and waggled his ears. A moment later the door was flung open and Jerra was there, his face a picture of confusion. "Oskie! Tod, Ferdie! What are you doing here—" Jerra suddenly fell silent. There is something about the sudden sight of a carpet of Grula-Grulas closely packed in a small tunnel, giving polite little waves, that leads to a temporary loss of the power of speech.

The carpet flowed into the Far Hub, the Grulas sang a long and haunting song of thanks, then all but Benhira-Benhara waved their farewells and went their separate Ways, requiring Dan and Jerra to open all twelve doors of the Far Hub. When the last Grula-Grula had left, they closed the doors with a sigh of relief.

"Well, Alice," Dan said to Tod. "I have a distinct feeling you have something to tell me."

"I guess I do," Tod admitted.

With help from Ferdie and Oskar—and a long song of happiness from Benhira-Benhara—Tod told their story late into the night. Dan, Jerra and Annar sat listening in rapt silence. Jerra and Annar could scarcely believe what they heard, but Dan had no such trouble. He saw the **Magykal** green flash in Tod's eyes, and he understood that his daughter was capable of doing all that she described—and more.

When Tod finished she looked at Dan to see if he was angry with her for defying him. "I never did promise you not to search for the Orm Egg, Dad," she said.

"I know," Dan said. "And that's been worrying me ever since, I can tell you." He smiled. "I'm so proud of you. And your mother would be too."

Tod twisted the snake ring on her thumb. The mention of her mother immediately made her think of Aunt Mitza, which upset her. Was it always going to be like this, she wondered—would Mitza forever intrude upon her mother's memory?

The next morning, longing to tell Septimus the news, Tod and Benhira-Benhara Grula-Grula set off back to the Castle. Oskar and Ferdie escorted them through the Maze and then they said their good-byes.

"See you MidSummer's Day," Ferdie said to Tod. "At the Circle."

"No, before then," Oskar said. "You're coming back for your birthday, aren't you, Tod?"

"You bet," Tod said.

They gave the Tribe of Three sign, and then, followed by a ten-foot-tall orange rug, Tod walked into the next arch on her journey to her other home in the Castle.

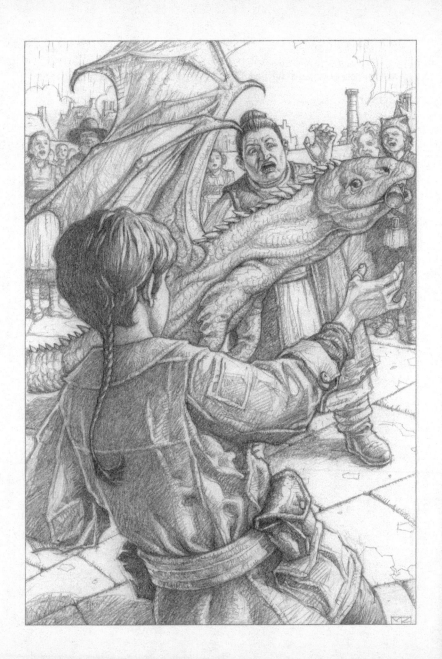

PART
XII

PART

XII

BING'S STRING

Simon Heap sat up in bed with a start.

Lucy was sitting by the window, where there was just enough light to knit by. In a moment she had thrown the knitting to the floor and was at Simon's side. "Si, what is it?"

"It's gone," Simon said. "Lu, it's gone!"

"Gone?" she asked.

"The dust in my eye. *It's gone.* Open the curtains, Lu. I want to see."

The summer sun streamed into the room—from which the dust most certainly had not gone. But that was not the dust Simon Heap meant. He took the hand mirror that Lucy offered him and stared at his reflection. Then he looked up at Lucy, who had already seen all she needed to. Her face was wreathed in a smile. "Oh, Si," she said, throwing her arms around him. "Oh, Si, your eye is blue again. Your lovely lapis has come back!"

Simon Heap laughed, and as he did the beam of sunlight caught the flash of lapis gold in his right eye. He got up from his bed. "I'm going to see Septimus," he said. "I think this might be important." Then he swayed and sat down suddenly.

"Simon Heap, you are not going anywhere," Lucy said firmly. "You've had a head full of dust and you've hardly moved for days. Septimus can come and see *you*. William will go with a message." She hurried downstairs to give their son the good news and send him off at top speed to the Wizard Tower.

Ten minutes later, a breathless and highly excited William Heap returned with his uncle in tow. As they neared the house, hurrying along with the sun glinting on the green water of the Moat at the end of Snake Slipway, Septimus allowed himself a small flicker of hope. Whatever news William Heap wanted him to hear, it was obviously good. He could certainly do with some, Septimus thought.

Suddenly William Heap's excited shout burst into his thoughts. "It's a ball!" Septimus looked up to see a small green object hurling itself out of the water and come bouncing up the slipway toward him.

William had thought his day could not get any better, but now it had. William—already a good fielder for the Castle under-eleven cricket team—lunged at the ball, heading for a catch. He would have easily succeeded with any other ball, but Bing neatly evaded William's expert dives. Suddenly, William stopped and turned to his uncle. "It doesn't want me to catch it," he said sadly. "It wants *you* to."

"It does indeed," Septimus said. He smiled. His nephew was turning out to have a promising feel for **Magyk**. Septimus allowed the **Tracker** ball to lightly touch him on the arm, then he scooped it into his hand. He was amazed at the sodden, soaking weight of it. It must, Septimus thought, have traveled beneath the sea to get to him. "Hello, Bing," he said. "What are you doing here?"

"Is Bing its name?" William asked.

"Yes," Septimus replied. "Bing is a **Tracker** ball. It has come from Tod."

William's eyes widened. He knew all about **Tracker** balls. "Daddy's got one called Sleuth," he said.

"Oh, yes, I know Sleuth well," Septimus said. "Very well indeed." He looked down at the **Tracker** ball sitting quietly in his palm. "Bing," he murmured, trying to **Feel** any distress emanating from it. "Is Tod in trouble?"

"Bing has string!" William shouted excitedly, interrupting Septimus's attempt to read the ball, much to his annoyance. Initial readings were always the best.

"William, please be quiet," Septimus said sternly. "I am trying to concentrate."

"But it *does*," William insisted. "Bing has a string message. Like I play with Ferdie. Look!" He stuck his grubby, nail-bitten finger onto the stub of string sticking out from between Bing's threads. "You have to pull this out and see what Tod says."

Septimus gave up trying to **Feel** anything. To stop William jumping up and down, he pulled, and to his surprise a long piece of string came out. "See!" William said triumphantly. "Untwist the string and there will be a message from Tod!"

Septimus did as William said, and to William's delight the string did indeed have writing on it.

"What does it say, *what does it say?*" William asked, hopping from foot to foot with unbearable excitement.

Feeling somewhat overwhelmed by William's enthusiasm, Septimus gave him the piece of string. "You read it," he said.

William perused it, frowning with concentration. He was a good reader, but he had never had to read anything special like this before. "It says . . . *Mid . . . sum . . . mer Dragon Boat. Please land at Sum . . . mer Cir . . . cle. V. Imp . . . or . . . tant. Tod x.*"

"May I have a look?" Septimus took the string from William and examined it closely. He felt a mixture of relief and anxiety. Tod was clearly fine when she had written it. But something about her writing told Septimus that she was not expecting to be fine for very long—that something frightening was about to happen. "Thank you, William," he said. "You read very well indeed." And then he asked, "What do you think Tod meant when she wrote this?"

William considered the matter. He didn't want to scare his uncle, but he didn't want to tell a lie. "I think she was going to do something very scary," he said.

Septimus put his arm around his nephew's shoulders. "That's what I think too," he said.

"I hope Tod's all right," William said in a small, worried voice.

"So do I," Septimus said. Telling himself there was nothing he could do for Tod right now, he put the **Tracker** ball into his pocket and said to William, "Let's go and see your daddy, shall we?"

William skipped ahead with Septimus following him up
the path to the red front door.

At the far end of Snake Slipway, lurking by the gate that led
to the Palace wood, the square figure of Mitza Draddenmora
Draa watched the ExtraOrdinary Wizard go into his brother's
house.

Mitza had spent the last three days hiding in the Palace
attics, sneaking down to the kitchens at night. She had enjoyed
her solitary time and had made surreptitious forays to the
Wizard Tower in search of her quarry, but had always been
stymied by the interfering doorkeeper, who had insisted that
Alice TodHunter Moon had run away. That was a lie and
Mitza knew it; her step-niece was not the running-away kind.
Twice Mitza had tried to get past the doorman and go in search
of her, but twice she had been discovered and he had called the
ExtraOrdinary Wizard, forcing her to make a run for it.

But now, at the sight of the ExtraOrdinary Wizard safely
out of the way, a smile spread across Mitza's thin lips—this
was the chance she had been waiting for. She would walk right
into the Wizard Tower, and this time there would be no one
the meddling doorman could call. All she needed was a few

minutes with Alice; after that there would be nothing anyone could do—absolutely nothing at all.

Holding the little gold vial tightly in her hand, Mitza set off up Wizard Way as fast as she could. The heaviness she was increasingly feeling on her shoulders made it hard going, but determined to seize her chance, Mitza pushed herself onward. Out of breath and sweating, she hurried beneath the Great Arch and headed toward the dauntingly steep marble steps that led up to the silver doors of the Wizard Tower. Suddenly there was a shout of "Get it, get it!" and a flash of blue shot by, narrowly missing her head. Mitza threw herself to the ground only to be very nearly trampled in a stampede of Wizards and Apprentices in close pursuit of what looked like a tiny blue dragon.

Mitza picked herself up and stared at the object of their chase. For a moment she wondered where she had seen it before, and then she realized what it was—the baby Orm. She watched it wheeling through the air, just out of reach of the grabbing hands, leading the noisy crowd onward in a frantic dance. Mitza checked that Tod was not in the group, then she turned away with an air of disdain. Let them chase the stupid creature, Mitza thought; they would soon find it was nothing but trouble.

REVENGE

As Tod and Benhira-Benhara stepped out of the **Hidden** arch beneath the Wizard Tower steps, a pointy-nosed streak of blue buzzed past them. Tod leaped backward, and it was only after she extricated herself from the soft orange fur that she realized what the pointy-nosed streak of blue actually was— the Ormlet. *Alive.*

As she stared after it, a gang of senior Apprentices came racing by in pursuit, with Newt Makken leading the pack on yet another circuit of the Wizard Tower. Tod was pleased to see the Ormlet had not died as Septimus had thought, but she was less pleased to see that it was, as ever, bringing trouble in its wake.

Ignoring the shouts and whoops of the chase, Tod and Benhira-Benhara set off toward the Wizard Tower steps. The Grula-Grula was looking forward to the quiet comforts of his room and Tod was longing to find Septimus and tell him all that had happened. However, as they reached the foot of the steps, Tod very nearly walked straight into someone she had hoped never to see again: Mitza Draddenmora Draa.

Mitza was as surprised as Tod, but she recovered herself faster. "Alice," she gasped. "Oh, Alice, my lovely niece. Thank goodness, I've found you!"

Benhira-Benhara, ever considerate, bowed to Mitza and set up off the steps, discreetly leaving Tod to talk to her aunt. Not wanting to be anywhere near Mitza, Tod went to go after him, but Mitza said urgently, "Alice! Don't go. *Please.*"

Mitza's desperation to seize her chance lent a genuine urgency to her words, and Tod stopped, uncertain what to do.

Hurriedly, Mitza launched into her spiel. "Alice, I told you I did a bad thing to your mother. But the truth is, I didn't do it. You see, I've been in the power of that awful sorcerer, and he has made me do and say things I now deeply regret. Ever since I got free of him I have tried to find you and set things right between us."

Tod was shocked. This was not what she had expected to hear at all.

Sensing her success, Mitza steamrollered on. "I wish to make amends. To return what I stole."

"Stole?" Tod asked, bewildered.

"I am ashamed to tell you that I took this from your house.

It . . . it belonged to your mother. It's the perfume she used."
Mitza held out the little gold vial. "I am so very sorry. This is
yours by right."

Tod looked at the little gold flask glinting in the sunlight.
She shook her head slowly in disbelief.

Mitza, however, saw the headshake as refusal. She took her
performance up a notch and forced out a couple of crocodile
tears. "I'm so very, very sorry, Alice. But I do understand."
Then she turned away as though she had given up.

The sight of Mitza's dejected stoop, as though she had the
weight of the world resting upon her shoulders, changed Tod's
mind. It seemed that Aunt Mitza's remorse was genuine.
"Wait!" she said.

Wordlessly, Mitza held out the tiny gold vial and Tod took
it. The vial sat lightly in her palm, its gold shining softly. Tod
knew how scents brought back memories, and she longed to
feel that her mother was beside her once again. The vial's silver stopper was sealed with a black film of wax; Tod twisted
it and felt the seal snap. She was about to take out the stopper
when she was aware of two things happening at once. One
was Aunt Mitza stepping backward fast. The other was a
sudden flash of blue, a close-up view of pink, rubbery lips, the

chickeny smell of Ormlet breath and the unopened vial being delicately lifted from her grasp.

There was a scream from Mitza: "No, no! Not my vial! No!"

But the Ormlet was up and away, the gold vial glinting between its lips, with Mitza after it in hot pursuit—and following close on her heels, the Apprentice rabble.

Bemused, Tod sat at the foot of the steps, watching the Ormlet fly over the courtyard wall and the hue and cry chase it out through the Great Arch.

As a welcome silence descended in the courtyard, Mitza's shout echoed in Tod's ears: *my* vial. Tod suddenly understood what had happened—the Ormlet had saved her life.

In the Wizard Tower, Tod discovered that Septimus had been called away by William Heap. She sat down on the visitors' bench outside the shiny orange door to await his return, listening to the sound of loud, regular Grula-Grula snores.

Tod was glad of time to think. There was now no doubt in her mind about what was in the little gold vial. She shuddered to think about what would have happened had the Ormlet not snatched it from her. Tod sat looking at the silver-and-gold double-snake ring that had once been her mother's and felt overcome with anger. Her mother hadn't died of some horrible disease that no one could do anything about. It was cold, cowardly murder. If it hadn't been for Mitza, her mother would still be alive.

Some ten minutes later, a subdued and soaking group of Senior Apprentices trooped into the Wizard Tower. At the sight of Tod they stopped in their tracks and looked away. They stood dripping onto the floor, which went into a panic and flashed the words: FLOOD! FLOOD! FLOOD! in bright red letters across the expanse of the Great Hall. Tod noticed the Apprentices were nudging one another and heard whispers of "You tell her." "No, *you* do it."

At last Newt Makken was pushed forward. He walked slowly up to Tod, twisting the purple beribboned hem of his sodden cloak in supreme awkwardness. "I'm sorry for your loss," he muttered.

Tod, still seething with anger at Aunt Mitza, thought that Newt was playing a joke. "What loss?" she snapped.

Newt looked taken aback. "Um . . . your aunt. We did our best to save her. We really did."

Tod frowned. "What's happened to her?" she asked warily.

"Well . . ." Newt glanced back to his friends for help but received none. "Um, the Ormlet flew off along Sled Alley, down to the Moat. I suppose your aunt didn't see the water . . . She was too busy chasing the Ormlet. I think it had taken something from her. And so she, um, she ran straight into the Moat. And she sank. Totally sank. Never came back up." Newt shook his head. "We jumped in, all of us did, but it's so deep there and muddy too . . . We couldn't see anything and there was no way we could dive to the bottom . . ." He looked up and Tod was shocked to see that Newt had tears in his eyes. "Alice, your aunt has drowned. I'm so sorry."

Stunned, Tod took in the news.

As a final year Apprentice, Newt was not without **Magykal** skills and knowledge. "As she went in," he said in a low voice, "I **Saw** something sitting on her shoulder. It was a Maund. Your aunt didn't have a chance. No one could swim with one of those weighing her down. And a Maund never lets go, you know. I mean, its claws grow into your skin and fasten around your collarbone and . . ." Newt noticed Tod's bemused expression and decided he had said quite enough. "You'd best ask the EOW. He'll tell you. I really am very sorry."

Tod was shocked and just a little bit guilty at how

relieved she felt—*Mitza was dead*. And there was something almost more important: now she could remember her mother untainted by the specter of the murderous Mitza Draddenmora Draa. Slowly, Tod got to her feet. She gave Newt a distant smile. "Thank you for telling me, Newt," she said. "I'm so sorry you all got wet." Then she walked over to the stairs—she had a promise to Rose to make good.

Newt watched her go. "She's got a cool head, that one," he said as he rejoined his friends. "Didn't bat an eyelid."

MidSummer Circle

It was three in the morning on MidSummer's Day, the sky scattered with clouds and sprinkled with stars. Tod, Ferdie and Oskar were making their way along the long, winding track that led through the outlying dunes to the old beach on the sandspit. Each carried a flickering lantern and wore their Circle cloak—long and dark and, for the very first time, embellished with a five-pointed star across which was a scattering of dots: a StarChaser.

Behind them came a straggling line of all the twelve to

sixteen-year-olds in Tod's village, every one carrying a lantern. They walked slowly and quietly, some apart, some together, the older ones savoring their last time at the Circle and the younger ones still a little awed by the occasion.

Tod emerged from the dunes and stopped for a moment. Before her was the wide, pale beach, and beyond lay the darkness of the sea. All she could hear was the gentle *swish-swash* of the wavelets and the soft padding of feet. She turned around to Ferdie and Oskar; they exchanged their three-fingered sign and then together they stepped onto the beach.

Some hundred yards away on the soft sand unwashed by the sea, Tod could see the circle of rugs waiting for them, just like last year. But this time there was the light from three lanterns rather than one, and as they drew nearer, Tod saw that the most distant light came from a lantern set atop the white marker post that only a few days before they had tied *Vega* to. The other lanterns were held by two cloaked figures: one standing in the middle of the circle, the other outside the circle, watching. Tod knew the one inside the Circle was her father—Dan always took the Circle. But who was the other?

Ferdie and Oskar provided the answer. "There's *Mum*," they whispered, not entirely pleased. Ignoring their mother's embarrassing little wave, Ferdie and Oskar took their places on the rugs reserved for first-timers and looked pointedly in the opposite direction. Tod sat next to them, then they put their lanterns on the sand and waited while the circle of rugs filled slowly with cloaked figures.

When the Circle was full, Dan Moon held his lantern high and said quietly, "Douse your lights," and the Circle blew out their candles. Then, just as Tod remembered from last year, Dan began. "Good morning, PathFinders. Welcome to our new people," he said, smiling down at Ferdie and Oskar. "Every year we meet in the early hours of MidSummer morning to hear our history and to understand the secrets that made us who we are, and why we PathFinders are a little different. These secrets are kept between us, and when we leave the Circle we do not speak of them to anyone else. Does everyone here understand?"

Everyone in the circle replied, "I understand."

Dan asked Ferdie and Oskar to stand, and then very formally, he said, "Ferdinanda Sarn, Oskar Sarn, do you promise to faithfully keep the secrets of our PathFinder Circle from all who are not PathFinders and, more important, from all PathFinders who have yet to come of age and join our MidSummer Circle? For all time and in all ways?"

"We promise," Ferdie and Oskar said together.

"Well said," Dan told them. "Circle, let us welcome our new brother and sister."

"Welcome, brother and sister, to the MidSummer Circle," came the response.

Feeling somewhat embarrassed by the lurking presence of their mother—*why was she there?*—Ferdie and Oskar quickly sat down.

Dan began to speak once more. "PathFinders," he said. "Our MidSummer Circle is the time when we tell the secrets of our history when our ancestors went to the stars. But up until now we have not told all. This was wrong. This knowledge belongs to us all. I understand that now, thanks to my daughter, Alice, who was brave enough to use those secrets for the good of us all." Dan stopped and smiled down at Tod. Now it was Tod's turn to be embarrassed. She stared resolutely at her feet and wished Dan would talk about something else.

But Dan had not finished yet. "It is also thanks to our first-timers, Ferdie and Oskar Sarn—who believed in what Alice was doing and helped her to do it—that I now understand that the danger lies not in revealing secrets, but in hiding them. Rosie Sarn has always insisted that there should be no secrets among mature PathFinders, and so it is only right that she is the one to reveal them to you. Which is why I now give the Circle over to Rosie Sarn." With that, Dan stepped out of the Circle and the cloaked figure of Rosie took his place. In her arms she carried a book that Tod knew very well: *The Path*.

And so the Circle listened, rapt, to Rosie Sarn telling the story of the Orm Eggs, the StarChaser, and the old *PathFinder* starship and its part in saving the Ancient Ways. At last, Rosie began to draw to a close. "And so it is true that we PathFinders have traveled to the Great Beyond. And it is true that our starship, our *PathFinder*, lies beneath the sea at the end of an underwater path marked by posts. The first post is over there." All eyes went to the post, shining white in the light of its lantern. Rosie continued. "And here is more truth. If you walk beneath the waves, as Alice did, one in ten of you will reach our starship, our *PathFinder*. Those are the ones who have gills. But nine of you will drown trying to discover if you posses the gills." Rosie stopped to let that sink in. And then she added with a smile, "However, no one now needs to risk this. One of our first-timers, Oskar, has invented a breathing bag that allows anyone to walk beneath the water. You can talk to him about that later."

Rosie allowed a flurry of excited murmurings and then asked for silence. "However, you need to know that there are dangers within the *PathFinder* starship. An Ancient Way leads into the starship and many hundreds of years ago a group of young PathFinders was massacred by creatures who Came Through the Way. Alice TodHunter Moon herself was lucky to escape a similar peril. We hope that now that the Ways are **Re-Enchanted**, the **Darke** has left them and the starship will be safe. We will set up our first expedition, led by Alice, as soon as we can."

Rosie glanced at the lightening sky in the east and knew it was time to bring the Circle to a close. She lowered her voice solemnly. "PathFinders, we have seen many worlds, but we have seen none as beautiful as ours. We have seen many suns, but we have seen none as perfect as this . . ." Rosie turned around and pointed out to the sea. On cue, the sun broke the horizon. "This is our sun. This is our Earth. *This* is where we belong."

The fingernail tip of orange pushed its way up from the sea, setting the thin line of cloud on the horizon on fire. It was beautiful, but no one was watching. All eyes were on a sky-borne golden boat with the head, tail and wings of a dragon, flying low over the sea toward them. Her iridescent scales shone in the sunlight; her head was high; her tail with the golden barb on its end was low, ready for landing. The already overexcited MidSummer Circle broke ranks and raced down the damp sand to the water's edge. And then there was the Dragon Boat, sweeping down to land and plowing through the water, sending rainbows of spume high into the air.

The Dragon Boat coasted to a sedate halt some fifty yards out. Using her wings as sails, she moved slowly forward toward the shore until her bow pushed gently into the sand and she beached herself. With her head quizzically on one side, the dragon regarded her audience while one of her passengers—a young man in purple—put a ladder over the side and the other, a young woman in red wearing a simple gold crown, clambered down the ladder and jumped into the shallows. She was closely followed by the young man, and together, hand in hand, they waded to the beach.

Even the oldest members of the Circle, who made a point of being unimpressed by anything, were dumbstruck. The amazed silence was broken by Tod, who ran splashing through the water to greet Septimus and Jenna, only to find herself lost for words at the meeting of her two worlds.

"Hello, Tod," Septimus said.

"I . . . I can't believe you're here," Tod said.

Septimus grinned. "Well, you did send me a message asking me to come today. And it sounded quite important." He took out the piece of string. "I think you said, 'MidSummer

Dragon Boat. Please land at Summer Circle. Very Important'?"

"Bing found you!" Tod said. "But you never said?"

Septimus handed Tod her **Tracker** ball. "I thought it would be a nice surprise," he said, as Bing settled comfortably back into Tod's hand.

Encouraged by Tod, the others from the Circle came milling around. As Tod accompanied Septimus and Jenna up the beach to greet Dan and Rosie, the Dragon Boat acquired a circle of admirers, all of whom—except Oskar—had a keen interest in boats. But Oskar was equally fascinated by the Dragon Boat, for here was a reptile to rival the Ormlet. As the rest of the circle admired the seaworthy qualities of the boat, Oskar gazed up at the magnificent green-and-gold head of the dragon. And then, to his delight, the dragon leaned down toward him and, in a mannerism caught from Spit Fyre, she slowly and sedately winked one emerald eye.

TWO WORLDS BECOME ONE

The traditional MidSummer Circle breakfast had two honored guests that morning. As they sat at the long table set amid the dunes, Septimus had something to say. "Tod, Ferdie,

Oskar: we can never thank you enough for what you did to save the Ancient Ways. Our Castle and our Wizard Tower are still with us only because of what you did. We can never repay you. Ever."

"What we have is yours," Jenna said simply.

"And what *we* have is *yours*," Dan Moon replied graciously.

There was a smattering of applause and then one of the Circle was heard to mutter, "But what *do* we have?"

"Sand?" someone suggested.

"Fish! We have fish!" came a shout. The cry was taken up and soon the table was chanting, "Fish! Fish! Fish!"

Septimus laughed. "And you have fun," he said.

"And you have courage," Jenna said, more seriously.

"And you have us," Septimus added as he took Jenna's hand. "Forever."

Sitting between her friends, surrounded by all the people she truly cared about, Tod felt completely happy. The two worlds she loved—the village and the Castle—had truly become one.

ENDINGS AND BEGINNINGS

Queen Marissa and Jo-Jo

Marissa and Jo-Jo's journey to the Red City was not uneventful. They were caught up in a Wild Way Wind, Jo-Jo was chased by a Kraan, and many of the Ways they tried to **Go Through** were already **UnRaveling**. But with the **Re-Enchantment** their luck changed, and on MidSimmer's Day Marissa and Jo-Jo arrived at the gates of the Red City. Here, Marissa took the Red Queen's crown from her cloak pocket, placed it on her head and declared herself to be the Queen's successor. No one raised the slightest objection.

The Wife of the Captain of the Queen's Guard

After the Red Queen had left for the Castle, the wife of the Captain of the Queen's Guard arrived at the Palace to beg for more time for his search. She found the Red Queen gone and the Palace in a panic. A strong woman was urgently needed to run the Palace, and the Captain's wife fitted the bill perfectly. She took over the administration and even held audiences, but she did not enjoy it. She was a sensible woman and well aware that she lacked the crazy charisma that the Red City demanded of their Queen. So when Marissa, complete with crown and a large following of excited fans, marched into the Palace, the Captain's wife gave her the Palace keys and wished her the very best of luck. Then she set off to search for her husband. She found him six months later, happily running a seedy bar in the Port of the Singing Sands.

The Red Queen

After Going Through the Hidden arch on the Outside Path, the Red Queen was also caught up in a Wild Way Wind. She became completely disoriented and lost. Without any subjects to terrorize, the Red Queen's life lost all meaning and she wandered wraithlike through the Ways with no sense of purpose. At some point she died, and after a year and a day, her ghost resumed its wanderings. She became one of the most dreaded ghosts in the Ways, for anyone meeting her would be stricken with a fear that their head was about to fly off.

Oraton-Marr and the Lady

It was some weeks after Marissa moved into the Red City Palace that she discovered that the Lady and Oraton-Marr were still languishing there in a dungeon. Queen Marissa was so enjoying her new life that she felt able to be kind to the Lady. She set her free and even took pity on Oraton-Marr, asking Jo-Jo to find an antidote to the **HeadBanger**. The best Jo-Jo could come up with—from the top of his new sorcerer's tower—was a **Muffler**. Oraton-Marr wore it wrapped around his head like a turban; his headache was almost completely **Muffled**, along with any ambitions or desires. Oraton-Marr and the Lady spent the rest of their lives tending the Palace gardens and feeding Marissa's pet sparrows.

The Ormlet

The Ormlet never matured. The Languid Lizard **Charms** had taken away its ability to go into Stasis and so, much to Oskar's delight, it remained in its larval winged state. Many others, including Queen Jenna, Barney Pot and assorted Palace visitors, were less delighted.

Mitza Draddenmora Draa

Like all ghosts, Mitza had to remain in the very place she had entered ghosthood for a year and a day. Her ghost floated beneath the Moat, taking delight in frightening unwary hirers of Rupert's paddleboats. After that Mitza's movements were limited due to the rules of ghosthood, which state: *A ghost may only tread once more where, Living, it has trod before.*

Mitza took to hanging around Sled Alley and one day happened to meet the ghost of Jillie Djinn—an ex–Chief Hermetic Scribe of the Manuscriptorium. They struck up a conversation about Maunds and became inseparable.

Spit Fyre

Occupied with looking after his perpetual-baby Orm, Spit Fyre was not able to leave the Castle to find a mate. However, one morning late that summer, a young blue dragon—all blue dragons are female—was making her way home to her mountains in the Great Continent Across the Ocean. As she flew over the Palace she saw a handsome young green dragon far below. As she swooped down for a closer look, the green dragon caught sight of her and rose up into the air to meet her. Soon most of the Castle was watching a beautiful dragon dance being performed high above them. The dragons stayed in the sky all day. At dusk they descended together, each having at last found their mate.

Spit Fyre was ecstatic—the only worry at the very back of his dragon mind was the prospect of introducing his new mate to the Ormlet. He hoped it wouldn't put her off. But once his mate had recovered from the disappointment that the Ormlet was not to be eaten for supper, she accepted the spiky little creature with good grace. She also encouraged Oskar Sarn to babysit as often as he wanted. Soon, Oskar also found himself engaged in egg-sitting duties too. With three dragon eggs to watch, Oskar called in help. And so, once again the Tribe of Three found that eggs of a large reptile became an important part of their life. But this time, all turned out egg-xactly as it should.

THANK YOU

Writing the TodHunter Moon trilogy has been a wonderful way to explore further afield in the world of Septimus Heap, and it would never have happened without so many lovely, talented people involved in making these books.

My special thanks go to my editor and friend, Katherine Tegen, from whom I continue to learn so much about writing and who has, wonderfully, an identical sense of humor. And lots of thanks, too, to editor Katie Bignell, who makes everything happen just as it should.

Equally special thanks go to my agent and friend, Eunice McMullen, for her unfailing support and from whom I have learned to see the best in everything.

Many, many thanks to the copy editors who have so patiently and expertly gone through my words and offered such subtle and effective suggestions on how to make them better. Big thanks to Bethany Reis, Brenna Franzitta, and Maya Packard for their skillful editing and for all their patience.

But it is not all about words—it's about images, too. I'd like to say a huge thank-you to Amy Ryan and all those in the art department at HarperCollins for putting together such beautiful covers and interiors, and to Joel Tippie for his wonderfully creative and totally perfect typography.

And of course there is one person without whom these books would not be the same: Mark Zug. Thank you so, so much, Mark, for making the whole world come to life. Your drawings are so beautiful, they add another layer of mystery and **Magyk** and always, without exception, capture the very essence of the characters. It is always a special day when I get to see your artwork for the very first time and watch the books coming to life. The covers are standout stunning and have become the quintessence of both Septimus Heap and now TodHunter Moon. Utterly inspired!

Making these books has been an amazing journey, and I know how lucky I have been to have such a wealth of so many talented, interesting and *fun* fellow travelers. Thank you all.

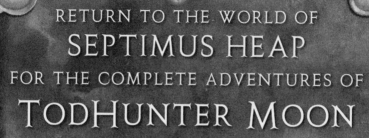